NAKED LOVE

JEWEL E. ANN

This book is a work of fiction. Any resemblances to actual persons, living or dead, events, or locales are purely coincidental.

Copyright © 2019 by Jewel E. Ann

ISBN: 978-1-7359982-7-5

Second Print Edition

Cover Designer: Jennifer Beach

DEDICATION

For Wylie
You are missed like you were loved—beyond words. XO

PLAYLIST

"Bonfire Heart" – James Blunt
"Naked" – James Arthur
"Pony" – Ginuwine
"Build Me Up From Bones" – Sarah Jarosz
"If You Ever Wanna Be In Love" – James Bay
"I Can't Keep From Loving You" – Andrew James
"Awake My Soul" – Mumford & Sons
"Give Me Love" – Ed Sheeran
"Little Things" – One Direction

CHAPTER ONE

"You've ruined my life." The break of the ocean waves outside of my apartment does nothing to soothe my anger.

His head cants to the side like he doesn't understand. Blue-gray eyes make a weak case for his behavior. I used to fall for that puppy dog look. Not anymore.

"That's it? You have nothing to say about ruining my life? You have nothing to say about your completely inexcusable, animalistic behavior?"

He shifts his large frame and scratches behind his ear before returning his focus to me.

Emotion tingles my nose as more tears fill my eyes.

"I worked so hard for this. My life was finally on track, and you've derailed it!"

Satan saunters off to the patio doors, leaving his back to me thinking he can ignore me.

"I hope you're cursed with an eternity of anal itching, and I will make it my life's purpose to ensure you never find anything to hump again. Do you understand me?" I hug my mangled hand to my chest. "Eternal anal itching. NO humping!"

He paws at the door.

"AND STOP SCRATCHING MY DOOR!"

Swarley whines. Why? I don't know. Nobody broke his paw today.

Not all dogs go to Heaven, and when I murder my sister's dog, he will *not* cross over any rainbow bridge. His human-hating soul will burn in Hell, but his body will live forever—with incurable anal itching.

Swarley whines again. Apparently his need to piss his name in the sand is more important than my need to hate him for chasing that stupid cat while the leash tangled around my hand.

I hate cats!

And dogs.

Dogs may be the worst. They disguise themselves as man's best friend, but I know better. The last thing I need is one more *friend* with no self-control.

Pain slices along my hand, shooting up my arm, as a cold sweat breaks out along my brow from the nausea settling into the pit of my stomach. I admit it—if only to myself—I, Avery Montgomery, am a wuss.

I've cancelled clients because of an irritated hangnail. Menstrual cramps leave me bedridden for twenty-four hours. And I'm one of those patients who require nitrous oxide just to get my teeth cleaned. It's genetic. There has to be a low pain tolerance gene.

Inches from the door, I drop to my knees and collapse into a fetal position on my side to keep from fainting. My long, blond hair sticks to my face. My hair—how am I supposed to do my hair with one hand? Bathe? Apply makeup? Latch my Chanel necklace or Tiffany diamond bracelet?

Dear Heavenly Father, I know my relationship with you

has been a bit parasitic—my bad—and I need to get my derrière to church, but if you could find it in your unconditionally loving self to give me the strength to not pass out, I swear to never use your name in the throes of passion again. Okay ... I won't swear because I know you don't like that since I've sworn on the Bible one too many times only to have broken those sacred promises, but you get my point. I'm going to do better. I feel certain this is a coming-to-Jesus moment.

The pain! It's so insufferable. The X-ray showed no broken bones, but I'm certain the extensive ligament damage is just as bad, if not worse. No amount of physical therapy will correct this. I'm ruined. Disabled at twenty-nine. Well, it's been a good run.

Swarley cries. I cry.

The remorseless Weimaraner scratches at the door. I claw at the cold tile with my good hand to get close enough to slide open the door.

"Go!" I grunt. "Go piss on someone else's day."

No leash. No supervision. Just miles of beach for digging holes. *Go dig your grave, buddy. I'm ready to bury your ass.* My sister cannot get upset with me for letting her dog drown or get eaten by a shark. My brutally mangled hand is his fault. I'm her sister. She'll take my side.

I think.

Maybe.

Who am I kidding? It's highly unlikely.

Holding my hand to my chest with the fragility of a newborn baby, I find my feet, wobble a bit, and collapse onto the kitchen stool.

"Hey, Siri, call Anthony."

Siri doesn't respond. Straining my neck, I lean toward my phone on the other side of the counter.

"Call Anthony."

Nothing.

"Dammit, Siri! Call Anthony!"

The screen lights up. "I don't see *Dance with me Anthony* in your contacts. Shall I look for locations by that name?"

"C-ALL AN-THON-Y!"

"Okay, this is what I found on the web for colonoscopy."

Swarley scratches at the door.

"For Pete's sake, have all sharks given up red meat? Why are you still alive?" I slide open the door with my foot, grumbling.

Swarley saunters into the living room and plops down on his designer dog bed that I bought him before we broke up. Yeah, we've broken up. This will be the last time I dog-sit.

I wiggle my toes before using them to slide the door shut. I need a pedicure. The robin's egg blue polish has a few chips in it. And it's been two weeks—*two weeks*—since I've had one. Don't even get me started on the gnarly callous forming on my pinky toe.

As the whirling nausea subsides, I shuffle around the counter to my phone and call Anthony—my everything. He's good at making money—you-could-never-spend-it-all-in-a-lifetime kind of money—and I like the challenge of trying to spend it all in one lifetime. We are a perfect fit.

I went from a lowly massage therapist, barely scraping by each month, to managing L.A.'s newest boutique spa that Anthony funded just for me, his angel. We've traveled the world together via private jet, luxury cars, and fancy yachts. Marriage is next. He's hinted to it so many times, especially when I've suggested moving in together. His parents are devout Catholics, and he wants to please them by "doing things the right way." I can wait.

"Anthony, why aren't you answering your phone? It's almost eight, and I've had the worst day of my life. I need you to send a car for me. I can't drive." I sniffle. "Sw-Swarley ruined my hand!" A sob breaks from my chest because I'm in pain, my sister is gone, Anthony won't answer his phone, and I may never give another massage again.

Swarley cocks his head at me. Maybe it's an apology. I can't forgive him. Not yet. At the moment, he's nothing more than another selfish male in my life, reacting on impulse with no consideration for my feelings.

Except Anthony. He cares.

It took many failed relationships, cheating asshats, and broken hearts to finally find a man who really cares about me. I think it's because he's older and more mature. He comes from a strong family. And I'm young, beautiful, and fertile—his words, not mine. Although, I didn't argue with him.

We're going to have three kids, a Teacup Poodle that doesn't need to be walked on a leash, a tummy tuck and boob job after our last child, and I'm going to be the center of my family's world.

After an hour with no callback and no driver buzzing my door, I kick Swarley out to the sharks again, but he comes back unscathed. I dump some food into his bowl just before heading out to catch an Uber. Maybe my neighbor, Ronnie, will let him out later if I offer a free—No ... Son of a biscuit! I can't offer a chair massage. Swarley robbed every bit of bartering power I have.

A half hour later, I arrive at Anthony's sprawling estate —the castle where one day I will be his queen. The driver pulls forward so I can enter the code to open the security gate. I wonder if I will ever stop having these pinch-me moments that this is my life. Swarley's run-in with the cat probably ruined my chances of ever giving someone a good massage again. I will miss some of my favorite clients, but taking care of the day-to-day tasks around here will be a full-time job.

"Anthony?" My voice echoes across the cathedral ceiling as I shut the front door. The grand marble entry gives way to an even grander split staircase.

"Miss Montgomery." Kim, Anthony's full-time cook, greets me in the foyer, curling a strand of shoulder-length black hair behind her ear. I envy her perfectly straight hair, flawless Asian skin, and shy demeanor.

Her presence calms me. I hope when I move in here, Anthony keeps her here to cook for our family.

She frowns as her gaze affixes to my wrapped hand hugged to my chest. "Oh, dear ..."

"My sister's dog chased a cat on our walk. He didn't seem to care that the leash was wrapped around my hand. Supposedly, it's not broken, but I wonder if they read the X-ray wrong. It's the worst pain imaginable."

Kim grimaces. "I'm so sorry."

"Thank you. Me too. Where's Anthony? I tried calling him."

"He's in his office."

"Thanks." I take a few steps toward his office and turn back to Kim. "You're here late."

"Mr. Bianchi requested I make some meals and freeze them since I will be on vacation next week."

"Oh. Lovely. Where are you going?"

Kim's expression morphs into something between nervous and scared. "Um ..."

I shake my head. "Sorry. It's none of my business. I hope you have a nice trip. We'll probably eat out most of the time." I gesture to my hand. "Clearly I won't be doing any cooking."

A constipated smile settles onto Kim's face as her head dips into a cautious nod.

I knock twice on Anthony's office door.

"Come in."

I ease open the solid cherry door.

"There's my angel." Anthony shuts his laptop and leans back in his leather chair behind the presidential-looking desk.

He's twenty years my senior, but at forty-nine he's the sexiest silver fox I've ever seen. Okay, maybe the second sexiest silver fox I've ever seen. I once dated a guy in his early fifties who looked like the Pretty Woman version of Richard Gere—but with straight teeth and more muscle definition. He died unexpectedly during a routine procedure to repair a hernia. I wasn't in his will. Apparently, three months of deep-throating isn't enough to get as much as a pair of diamond and white gold cufflinks. Lesson learned.

Anthony has an odd-shaped nose, like a three-year-old's first attempt at molding putty, and it's a bit too big for his face. He tastes of thick, molten whisky and the clashing flavor of spicy, full-bodied, hand-rolled Cuban cigars. I used to be more of a minty mouthwash kind of girl, but I've grown accustomed to his particular taste. Money.

Anthony Bianchi Jr. tastes like money, and he treats me like a queen.

I've tried the sweet nice-guy route—the jock, the teacher, the aspiring actor, the musician. I've tried the bad-boy route—the tattoo artist, the wannabe rock star, the guy who always carried a gun but couldn't tell me why. They are all cheaters with no direction and clueless when it comes to knowing how to treat a woman.

"Angel, what happened to your hand?" He stands and closes the distance between us.

"Don't touch it!" I cringe, angling my body away from him.

"I'm not. What happened?"

"Swarley happened. Where have you been?" I shoot him a teary-eyed look. "I called. You never answered. You didn't respond. Ingrid took me to the hospital."

"Ingrid?"

My head juts forward. "Yes. Ingrid."

No light turns on. He has no clue whom I'm talking about. "You hired her as my personal stylist last year."

"Oh ..." He nods.

He still has no clue.

"Why didn't you call your sister?"

"Hello?" I scoff. "Where have you been? My sister is on vacation. I'm dog-sitting Swarley for her. Do you not listen to anything I say?"

He rests his hands on my shoulders and kisses my cheek. "Of course I do, angel. I've just been very busy lately. I'm sorry I missed your call. I thought you were going out with your friends tonight."

Okay, so he kinda listens to me. "I was, but Swarley chased a stupid cat, and my hand may never be the same. I can't go out with friends. I can't see clients. I'm useless at the moment." A lone tear trails down my cheek.

His phone buzzes. He glances at the screen. "I have to take this. It's business. Give me a few minutes, and you'll have my undivided attention."

I nod, wiping the tear I thought he'd wipe away with the

tender pad of his thumb or kiss away with those full ruddy lips. Never mind. I got it. He can catch the next one.

After he slips out of his office to take the call, I collapse into his desk chair, relishing the buttery leather that molds to every curve. I bet it cost more than my first car.

My phone chimes. It's my niece, Ocean, FaceTiming me. In spite of my horrible day, I grin. When I swipe to accept the call, the screen goes black. My battery is dead. Of course it is—par for my day.

Anthony's laptop is a Mac, so I flip up the lid to use his FaceTime to call her back. I click to shut out of the window he has open, but it doesn't close; it plays instead. It's a video.

My body goes rigid for a split second before collapsing in on itself. The weight of utter shock and disbelief drags me to the depths of Hell like an anchor off the side of a boat. That abused organ behind my ribs slows from the sludge of anger crawling through my veins. The only part of me that moves is the cold sweat beading along my skin and the bob of my throat as I try to swallow the truth.

The truth?

Anthony stuck his slightly bent dick into Kim, and he recorded it.

My head eases to one side and then the other. Yep. Any way you look at it, they are going at it in the kitchen. How appropriate. We first had sex on my massage table. He was a client of mine. Not my usual MO. I guess Anthony Crooked Dick Bianchi likes to see how women perform in their element.

He pulls out of her, swipes his finger through a bowl of chocolate mousse, and ... no no no ... he smears it between her legs as she arches her back off the white granite counter top. What a waste of chocolate mousse. Anthony doesn't even like chocolate—

Gasp!

Bile seeps up my throat.

Liar!

Clearly, he likes chocolate mousse. He's eating *it* as if he's starving and it's the last food on earth.

Why am I watching this? I know how it ends, yet I can't look away. Even worse, my finger inches to the volume button. I tap it once, twice, three times until his moans fill the room, accompanied by Kim chanting, "Tony, Tony, Tony..." Wait a damn minute. He told me his name is Anthony like Saint Anthony. Period. Not Tony. No nickname.

"Avery?"

My head snaps up. I don't shut the computer. I don't mute the volume.

Tony's jaw ticks, eyes wide and flitting between me and the computer.

"Spread them wider, my little angel."

He grimaces at his recorded voice full of lust, and my eyebrows shoot up. Well, I *was* raised to believe there is only one God, but many angels. Kim's skin is beautiful, some might say angelic. Moans and the intermittent slurping of Saint Anthony enjoying his mousse keep us both entranced. Who will speak first?

Me. I'll go first.

"So you do like chocolate, *Tony*."

"Avery." Anger purses his lips as he takes three long strides forward, slapping the laptop shut.

I can't even ... Nope. My world is gone. Swarley is off the hook. I can't even feel the pain in my hand at the moment. I can't feel anything. Disbelief is a long-lasting shot of anesthetic.

"Why were you snooping on my computer?"

NAKED LOVE

I choke on a laugh as it attempts to break free. "Why were you sticking your bent dick in Kim? And why is there a video of it?"

He gnashes his teeth some more. "I'm sorry. We can fix this." He tugs at his tie like it's strangling him. If only ...

If disbelief is an anesthetic, then shock is an adhesive that temporarily holds everything together. I can't find a single tear. I can't even find appropriate words to say or muster the energy to scream at him. It's as if I'm on the outside looking in objectively.

"I'll bite. How would we fix this? I mean..." I shake my head and shrug "...had you just asked, I would have let you do that to me."

"Jesus, Avery ..."

"No. Don't say that. I know a lot about Jesus and you should too, *Saint Anthony*. I'm certain he wants nothing to do with this conversation."

I lean back in the chair, cradling my hand. Anthony bends forward, resting his fists on the opposite side of the desk. "My parents like you. I like you. We could be such a great team."

"A *team*?"

"You like the lifestyle, Avery. Don't pretend you don't. You'll get everything you could ever possibly want—kids, mansions, cars, yachts, jets, a closet bigger than your entire apartment filled with the most expensive clothes ..."

"And what do you get?"

"My angel." A satisfied grin slides across his face.

"Which one?" I cock my head to the side.

His lips twist, eyes narrowed. "All of them."

Them. Them! THEM!?!

My jaw plummets to my lap.

"But you will always be my favorite—the chosen one. My wife. Mother of my children. Queen of my empire."

This is the part where I should break something like his computer or his toddler-sculpted nose.

I don't.

As livid as I am with this stranger before me, this man who fooled me for two years, I'm more upset with myself because for a few brief, totally insane seconds I think about his offer. When did I surrender my pride, my sense of self-worth? Who broke me to the point that I don't feel worthy of the one thing he's not offering me?

If I walk out that door, who will I be? What if something better never comes along? I'm knocking on thirty's door while mastering the art of failed relationships. If in ten years I have nothing more than a two-bedroom apartment, arthritic hands, and a measly disability check, will I regret saying no to a family and everything money can buy?

"I just want the spa. We go our separate ways, but you sign over the spa to me."

"Avery." He shakes his head while clucking his tongue. "I haven't acquired this level of wealth and success by handing out million-dollar businesses to every woman who rolls through my bed."

"It's my spa."

The smirk on his face stings. I already know what he's going to say. I let myself become dependent on a man—again. My whole damn life at the moment is a lease.

My job.

My car.

My apartment.

The clothes.

The credit cards he lent me.

Anthony pushes off the desk and slips his hands into the

front pockets of his tailored pants. "I can't give you the spa. I'll shut it down. It's not that profitable. I'll need both credit cards back. Your rent is paid through the end of the month, but then you're on your own. I'll need the car back. Better hope your old one starts. The rest of the stuff is yours. I'd suggest selling it to make ends meet."

I peel myself from the chair. When we're face to face, I let my emotions break freely. "You said you loved me." I sniffle as tears race down my cheeks.

"I do. I love you for you. I love you in spite of your selfish needs. Why can't you love me in spite of mine?"

Unbelievable.

I'm out of here.

I'm done with men.

Done.

Done.

DONE!

CHAPTER TWO

I MISS MY MOM. She died when I was eight. I'm sure a shrink would say I've been trying to fill that void for years. Some voids cannot be filled. Some wounds won't stop bleeding on their own either, but you don't stop applying pressure to them.

Maybe there will come a day when I realize this void is an integral part of who I am, but right now, it just feels like an empty stomach craving something—anything.

My yearning for something leads me home. I call my sister to let her know I'm taking Swarley with me to Illinois to see Dad. There's a little relief when she doesn't answer her phone. I'd rather leave a message so she can't talk me out of making the trip. It also helps that I wait until I'm fourteen hours into my twenty-seven-hour drive before I leave her that message.

And my dad? He has no idea I'm coming for a surprise visit. He's had too many heart issues. I can't stress him out with my impulsive venture halfway across the country in an old Honda Pilot, with an old dog and a gimpy hand.

"Surprise!" I put on my brave face and hope he ignores the bags under my eyes. I turned a three-day trip into two days with the help of coffee, energy drinks, and adrenaline-fueled rage.

"Avery ..." Dad shakes his head. "W-what are you doing here?"

Swarley sniffs his way around the yard, pissing on everything.

I jab my thumb over my shoulder. "Why is there a moving truck in your driveway?"

He gives me an awkward smile then shakes it off. "Did you drive by yourself? From L.A.?"

"Yes. Are you going to let me in the house?"

He steps out of my way.

"But, I'm here now. I'm safe. So there's no need to lecture me about—" I stop three feet inside the front door. There are boxes everywhere. "Are you moving?" I whip back around to face him.

He deflates. "Yes."

"When? Why? Where? Were you going to tell me? Does Sydney know?"

"Calm down. I haven't told Sydney yet either." He frowns. "Sweetheart, what happened to your hand?"

I hold out my bandaged hand like I'm noticing it for the first time. "Nothing ... Swarley..." I shake my head several times "...I don't care about my hand. I want to know what's going on with you. Oh my gosh! Are you moving to California?" The possibility chases away my fatigue and ignites hope in my broken heart. "That's it, isn't it? You were going to surprise Sydney and me? Dad ... gah! You have no idea how happy that makes me. I *need* you right now. My life is a mess and—"

"Avery?" He grabs my face and forces me to focus, which is difficult with so much caffeine still racing through my body. "I'm not moving to California. I'm moving to Milwaukee."

My nose wrinkles. "Milwaukee?"

"Yes." He steps back, clasping his hands behind him and rocking back and forth on his heels. "I met someone."

I lean forward. "Excuse me, what did you say?"

He grins like someone ... No. No, no, no ... he's not in love. He's not standing two feet from me looking all giddy and gaga. It's exhaustion. I'm hallucinating. After a long nap, this will all make sense. The moving truck will disappear. The boxes will vanish. My hand will be healed. And I'll have more than designer handbags and shoes to show for my two years with Anthony.

"Deedy." He sighs while his mouth settles into contentment.

"What's a deedy?"

"Not what, Avery. Who. Deedy is the woman I met online. She lives in Milwaukee. You're going to love her."

Wrong. I hate her already.

"She was in the Peace Corps for a little while, years ago. That's where she met her husband. He died three years ago. We connected through her church's chatroom. Now she organizes mission trips. I'm going to go with her after we get married."

What. The. Actual. Fuck?

"Is it a brain tumor?"

Dad cants his head to the side. "Is what a brain tumor?"

I laugh. "This! The moving truck, the Deedy woman, church chatrooms? Really? Oh, and let's not forget that you just said you're getting *married*. MARRIED!" I bite my lips together, feeling overwhelmed with *everything*. "How long did the doctors give you?"

Massaging his temples, he stares at his feet. "Avery, I know it's a lot to take in. Deedy and I wanted to tell you and Sydney together. But the house sold so quickly, and I didn't want to tell you over the phone. It's just been crazy, but you girls are grown and you have your own lives out in California. I only see you when I make the trip out there. And this relationship with Deedy just sort of happened. I really believe God brought her into my life."

"You've had sex with her?"

"Avery Lynn Montgomery! You are out of line. No. I haven't even met her face to face. I won't have sex with a woman until it's blessed by God."

I stab the fingers of my good hand through my hair and tug at it. "Oh my gosh, oh my gosh, oh my gosh ... this isn't happening! You haven't *met* her? You're planning on marrying a woman you have *never* met? Dad! What is wrong with you? She may not even be a *woman*! You're going to get a dick up your ass on your wedding night. How can you be so irresponsible?"

"Enough! I will not have you disrespect Deedy. I will not have you disrespect me in my own house."

I blink away the tears. This is all too much. What the hell is happening to my life?

"Avery ..." His voice softens. "Come with me to Milwaukee. I know when you meet her you'll see what I see when I video chat with her every day. I'm leaving in the morning. Just ..." He takes my good hand. "Please. I haven't felt this way in many years."

Deedy is a guy with a big dick who likes to wear women's clothes. This won't end well. But he's my dad.

"Fine." I sigh. "But my car is acting up. I fear it won't make it to Milwaukee."

"I'll check it out. At least if you follow me, you won't be traveling alone." He shoots me an accusatory look. We've come full circle.

"No." I roll my eyes. "I'll just be traveling like a snail because you never drive the speed limit."

The five-and-a-half-hour drive takes us eight hours by the time we stop every thirty miles for old-man prostate issues. As luck would have it, my Honda Pilot completely craps out two miles from Deedy's house. Dad calls to have it towed to the nearest garage, and we grab some coffee before arriving at Deedy's.

"I'm nervous." As we walk to her door, he shoots me a stiff smile. He's in love with a stranger, a stranger he wants to marry, and he's nervous about meeting her for the first time.

Sounds about right.

"Does she like dogs?" I glance over my shoulder at Swarley.

"Loves them." He adjusts his tie. When we stopped for coffee, he changed into a suit. It's sweet—but still insane. He has to be drenched with sweat in this eighty-degree weather.

"What if she changes her mind when she sees me?"

My head and my heart are at war. I think this is a mistake, but I have never seen this vulnerability with my dad. I hug his arm, giving it a tight squeeze as I whisper in his ear, "Then she's a fool."

He kisses the side of my head as I release him and let him make the final steps to the door on his own. I pray that he's everything she imagined and more and that she falls short of his expectations. Then he can walk away without feeling dejected—she'll be the dejected one. Insensitive of me? Probably, but he's my dad.

"Tommy!"

Oh precious lord of church chatrooms ... Deedy is ... well, she's *hot*. And young. Wait, maybe that's not Deedy, maybe it's her daughter—oh, shit. They're kissing. Clearly not the daughter.

"Well, praise Jesus we finally made it. You must be Deedy." I walk up the porch steps.

Dear, God, make them stop!

My dad pulls away, breathless, with red lipstick smeared all over his face. "Sorry. Deedy, I'd like you to meet my youngest daughter, Avery."

"Avery, I've heard so much about you. I feel like I know you." She holds out her hand, and I shake it.

"Huh, I'd heard nothing about you until yesterday."

Her jovial expression dies a little.

I revive it with a big, fake smile. "But it's nice to meet you. Clearly, my dad thinks highly of you. I'm sure I will too."

I won't. It seems unlikely that she has the big dick I predicted, but I think I'd prefer it to perky breasts and an ass that could be on the cover of a glorious glutes exercise video.

"This is just like I pictured it," Dad says, dissolving some of the tension as he glances around the outside of the house.

"Come in. Mi casa es su casa." She hugs his arm and

nuzzles his neck like I did just a few moments ago—minus the neck nuzzling.

"Can Swarley come inside?" I ask.

"Of course. I love animals. All life really. Especially this one right here." She bops her finger on my dad's nose then kisses it.

He grins and tips his chin to capture her mouth. It's a quick peck, followed by another, and that leads to a deeper kiss.

"Mmm ..." Dad moans.

I cover my mouth to keep my mini vomit from coming out. Sydney's in Disney World, where dreams come true, and I'm stuck in a nightmare, where my father's engaged to a woman young enough to be his daughter, and they're getting ready to make a porno right here in the entryway.

Clearing my throat, I take a step back toward the door. "Swarley and I are both a little restless after the long car ride. I'm going to take him for a walk before dinner. Then you two can ..." Have strange we-met-on-the-internet sex beneath God's damning eyes, which is better than in front of me.

Deedy rubs the lipstick from my dad's mouth with her thumb while my dad adjusts himself. Wow. As if Anthony licking chocolate mousse off Kim's naked body wasn't enough punishment for some unknown crime I've committed, I now get the pleasure of watching my dad deal with a boner.

"Take the main road two blocks north, and you'll find a strip of shops and waterfront restaurants. I'll get dinner started after I show your dad around his new house. *Our* house."

Aaannnd ... I'm out of here. Even if Swarley tries to rip

my good hand off my arm, I'd prefer that pain to this nauseating nightmare.

We follow Deedy's suggestion and walk two blocks north to the quaint shopping area hugging the water's edge. Swarley tugs on my arm as his tongue drags along the ground, straight toward a water dish among tables in front of a familiar cafe.

Sage Leaf Cafe

We have one in L.A., but I don't go there often. It's a vegan restaurant, and I'm a lean-meat-low-carb kind of girl, but sometimes walking down the street with a green juice in hand will attract the eyes of sexy guys who spend their entire day perfecting their bodies. I never cheated on Anthony, but who doesn't like to get *the look*?

Swarley laps up the rest of the water in the dish.

"Beautiful dog ... and thirsty." A young woman in shorts and a Sage Leaf Cafe tee smiles at us as she wipes down the outdoor tables.

"Thanks. He's not mine."

She collapses the sunshades on the tables, her dark, curly hair escaping the messy bun that looks like it's had a long day. "You steal him?"

"Hardly. He's my sister's dog." I release the leash and let him scrounge for scraps underneath the tables.

"Motorists on this street can be a little crazy." She eyes Swarley on the loose with his leash dragging behind him.

"He won't run into the street." *Unfortunately.* I check my phone for messages. There's a dozen from Sydney. She's pissed off I won't call her back. She knows something catastrophic has happened for me to have packed up her dog for a road trip.

I text her back the standard message.

I'm good. He's good. Have a good time.

"Half off The Kermit if you're interested."

I slip my phone back into my rose Hermes mini bag. "The Kermit?"

"Dandelion greens, romaine, apple, lemon, ginger, turmeric."

"Green juice?"

She nods.

I shake my head. "I don't see any hot guys. No need to accessorize right now."

"Well, there's one inside making half-priced Kermits."

"I'm not in the market for *any* guy. I've had my hand and heart destroyed in the past five days by the male species."

"That sucks."

"Totally." I nod.

She shrugs. "It doesn't hurt to just window-shop." Her head snaps toward the door to the cafe.

I focus on Swarley.

The young woman pulls out a chair and takes a seat. "I'll watch him. Go tell Jake you want The Kermit, half the dandelion, extra apple."

I nod slowly. "Thanks."

Michael Bublé belts out the chorus to "I've Got You Under My Skin" over the high-pitched hum of the blender. It's just like the L.A. location—hippie posters, mismatched tables, everything recycled or reclaimed. I don't fit in here.

"Cute shorts." A tall, very Gwyneth Paltrow looking blonde shoots me a welcoming smile as she pours a dark red smoothie into a mason jar, tops it with fruit and mint garnish, and slides it to an older lady sitting at the bar, reading a book.

"Thanks. They're Paige cuffed denim. And old ... I got them at the beginning of last summer. My boyfriend decided to screw his cook before I could acquire a new wardrobe for this summer."

She laughs. "I don't know anything about Paige cuffed denim, and my wardrobe is from five years ago, and even then I got it from a secondhand store, but I'm sorry to hear about your boyfriend cheating on you."

Five-year-old clothes from a secondhand store. I just want to hug the poor thing or take her shopping. "Yeah, all men are lying, cheating, monkey-spanking dick cheese."

The deep rumble of a man clearing his throat startles me. I didn't see him over in the corner behind the glass display. He's all muscly and tatted up—messy copper and golden blond hair. Challenging, dark eyes pin me to my spot as he glances over his broad shoulder, straining the corded muscles in his neck.

The Gwyneth lookalike chuckles. "Jake, you and your fellow men have a new title. I rather like it, don't you?"

Jake inspects me with wandering eyes. It's nothing new.

"I'm not impressed," he says and turns back to cutting vegetables.

Uh ... wait just a minute. Not impressed with what? Me? What I said? Me?!? Do I care? No. Yes. Hell no.

Okay ... I sort of care.

Gah!

I have—well, had—a client who teaches motivational classes for women. She's a bit unconventional or so I've heard. One of her classes is called Give No Fucks, Take No Shit. She offered me a free class. At the time I was in love with Anthony Bent Dick Bianchi, taking lots of shit and giving lots of fucks, so I declined her offer.

Now, I'm thinking that was a mistake.

"What can we get you?"

My attention snaps back to the *nice* person behind the

counter. "I was told to ask Jake for The Kermit, half the dandelion, extra apples. But ..." My eyes flit to him. He keeps his back to me like I didn't just say his name. "I think I'd prefer you to make it for me."

The knife in his hand *thunks* against the chopping board. Jake turns slowly, a poisonous smile curling his lips. "Bethanne, I've got this."

Gwyneth Bethanne winks at me before grabbing dirty dishes from the counter and disappearing into the back room.

The older lady at the counter slides off the stool. "Bye, Jake." She takes her drink and gives me a polite smile as she breezes to the door. Does he let her just leave with it? Do they not have to-go cups in Milwaukee?

"Have a seat, Paige." Jake nods to the vacated barstool.

"Avery not Paige." I climb up onto the stool. "My shorts are Paige. That's a brand, not my name. What brand are your shorts?"

Jake shoves greens and other things into the juicer, never taking his eyes off me. "Do I look like the kind of guy who knows what brand I'm wearing without looking at the tag?" he yells over the juicer.

I wait for him to finish so I don't have to yell back at him. "I don't know. I'm a preacher's daughter. You know ... thou shalt not judge."

He slides the glass toward me. I catch it on a gasp, eyes wide, jaw slack with disbelief. Had I not stopped it, I would have green juice all down the front of my shirt.

"Yeah, there's nothing about you that feels judgmental." He shrugs. "But what do I know? I'm just monkey-spanking dick cheese."

I take a sip of the green drink. "Not bad."

He shakes his head, tipping his chin down to hide his

smirk. "Something tells me that's the equivalent of a glowing review coming from you."

"Now who's being judgmental?" I set a ten-dollar bill onto the counter as I stand, grabbing my handbag and the green drink.

"I'm not a preacher's daughter. The rules don't apply to me."

I roll my eyes. "Whatever. Keep the change."

"Are you drinking that outside?"

"No." I slide on my sunglasses. "I need to get back to ..." Deedy's? My dad's house? Hell? "Somewhere."

"Then I'll put it in a to-go cup. You can't take off with my glass."

I turn. "Uh ... I just watched that lady walk out of here with a glass."

"She'll be back. Same time. Same order. Everyday."

"I'll bring it back tomorrow."

"I doubt it." He scoffs.

"I will. I promise."

"You better or I'll report it as stolen."

I cough a laugh. "It's a mason jar that probably costs less than a dollar."

"The mason jars we use here were my grandmother's. She used to make jam. So if you walk out the door with that, it's like you're taking part of my grandmother with you. Just..." he lets out a slow breath "...bring her back in one piece."

I don't know what to say. Rarely does a guy's sentimentality surprise me, but that's really sweet. "I'll guard it with my life."

The curly-haired lady rubs Swarley behind his ears. "Thanks for coming, buddy. Stop by again sometime."

"Thanks for watching him." I stir the drink with the straw.

Swarley plants his lazy ass down at my feet, shifting his body just enough to knock me off balance. I stumble back a few feet.

Crash!

The jar of juice splatters and shatters on the ground.

"Swarley! Oh my gosh! No ... I'm so sorry. He bumped me and I couldn't keep ahold of the glass because my other hand is ruined, and—"

"Hey, it's fine. Really. It was an accident. No big deal. Just watch out for the glass." She hunches down, hugging Swarley so he doesn't move. "Jake, come here! Hurry." Kissing the side of Swarley's head, she baby talks to him. "Don't want this handsome guy getting glass in his paws."

His paws? I have green juice splattered all over my Tory Burch Reva Flats.

Jake gives me a hard look as he steps over the glass, picks up Swarley, and carries him away from the dangerous mess.

"I'm sooo sorry."

She waves me off as we bend down to pick up the pieces. "It's *no* big deal."

"It's a huge deal. I broke his grandmother's jar into a million pieces."

"What are you talking about?" She scoots the trash bin closer to us and tosses pieces into it.

"The jar belonged to his grandmother," I grit between my teeth, afraid to talk about it too loudly. I'm sure he's crushed by my carelessness. Swarley's carelessness.

"Oh my god." She laughs. "We get them from a distributor. A dime a dozen. Who said they belonged to Jake's grandmother?"

I lift my gaze to meet his cocky grin as he sweeps the

sidewalk. Standing, I close the distance between us, pointing a finger in his face. "Screw. You."

Wetting his lips, he grins. "Now *that* sounds like something a preacher's daughter would do."

I want to punch out every perfectly aligned white tooth in his mouth. "Let's go, Swarley."

CHAPTER THREE

Please let my dad and Deedy be dressed.

Please let Deedy be older than me by at least a decade.

Please wake me up from this nightmare that's become my life.

No such luck.

The nightmare plays on.

"Hey, Avery, can I get ya some lemonade before we start unloading the moving van? It's fresh squeezed."

Swarley makes friends with the maple tree and half of the shrubs along the front of the house while I force a smile—the one where I pretend it's not at all shocking to see my dad lounging in a wooden rocker on the porch with Deedy on his lap.

Cute. Cozy. Barf!

"Lemonade would be great. Thank you." Get off my dad's lap!

"Coming right up." She kisses my dad on the cheek and flutters into the house, leaving my dad with a twitterpated grin.

He sighs all dreamy and ... just ... no. This is not happening. "So what do you think, Ave?"

I climb the porch steps. "I think you're crazy if you think I'm unloading anything. My hand is injured and my nails were recently manicured."

He pats his knee.

I shake my head. His lap is all Deedied. I'm never sitting on it again. The top step will work just fine. "How old is she, Dad?"

"Does it matter?" He scratches the back of his head. "How old is your boyfriend? What's his name? Tony?"

"We're not exactly together. He had..." I frown because beneath all the anger is this horrific embarrassment laced with a world of insecurities "...honesty issues."

"What did he lie to you about? The balance in his bank account." He winks.

I roll my eyes. "Chocolate. He said he hated chocolate, but I found out he actually likes it *a lot*."

A hearty chuckle rumbles from Dad's chest. "And that's a deal breaker for your relationship?"

I stare at my nails, thankful I got the gel coating since it could be awhile before I get them redone. "Sadly, yes. It was quite the deal breaker. But enough about my latest mistake, stop dodging my question. How old is Deedy?"

"I'm thirty-eight." The screen door creaks as Deedy steps onto the porch, handing me a lemonade garnished with a strawberry and mint leaves.

I love pretty drinks, but this one already tastes sour, and I haven't even taken a sip yet.

"Thank you." My voice breaks with a bit of embarrassment.

"Yes, I'm young enough to be Tommy's daughter, but love doesn't care about age."

Tommy? I shoot my dad a questioning look, but he's too busy helping *the Deedy* get settled onto his lap again. Tommy is a five-year-old boy who wets himself the first day of school or maybe a clothing designer, but not a minister.

Dear Heavenly Father,

If I stop being a hypocrite and vow to never date anyone more than five years older or younger than myself, will you make this woman go away? If I promise to respect the boundaries of my generation, will you remind Tommy that he vowed to serve you and not his dwindling sex drive?

He's running late with his midlife crisis. That's the only logical explanation. Sorry, Dad, you missed that train. Now you have to show maturity or they'll revoke your AARP membership, including your roadside assistance.

Deedy ... it's just disturbing on so many levels. She has my California blond hair, only shorter with an inverted-bob sweeping her chin. Blue eyes resemble mine, just not as light. In this small, aching pit in my stomach, I think of how she looks like my mom might have at thirty-eight had she lived that long.

The Deedy is too pretty, too young, and too .... I don't know ... all over my dad like a horny girl who just figured out how to rub herself off.

Gah! It hits me. They're going to have sex. I cringe. Can he even get it up? My experience with older men is they do best with a pill. Eww ... for the first time in my life, my mind has decided to make the comparison between the older men I've dated and my father.

It's in my head! Make it stop. Will he do his thing missionary style? They have to, right? After all, he's a minister and she's been on mission trips. Will he go down on her? GAH! No. No! NO! Make it stop!

"Avery, are you feeling okay? You have a mortified look

on your face." Dad tears his unholy gaze from Deedy long enough to acknowledge I'm still here.

This trip was an epic mistake. I should have had my car checked at a garage in Illinois and headed straight back to Los Angeles. My days of being the apple of my father's eye are over. He's robbing the cradle, and Anthony likes chocolate. What is happening to the world?

"Yeah, just thinking about something that's a little disturbing. I'm fine."

"How was your walk?" He nuzzles Deedy's neck.

"I stopped by a cafe, but it didn't go so well. Swarley made me spill my green drink all over."

"Oh!" Deedy's back snaps to attention, eyes wide. "You stopped at Sage Leaf Cafe?"

"Yeah, we have one in L.A. I don't go there often, just when I'm trying to impress someone in the hippie crowd."

"It's an all vegan restaurant." She glances back at my dad. "The food is *the best*. Jake Matthews, the owner, is the nicest guy, and he's—"

My brow furrows. "I don't know if I'd agree with that assessment."

"Oh, Avery, he's incredible." She winks. "And single."

He was a dick to me. Of course he's single.

"Then *you* should date him." I shoot them a toothy grin.

Dad frowns. "Avery ..."

"I'm joking." I stand, taking a sip of the lemonade.

Deedy bites back her smile. I give her a little credit for not being offended. The look she shoots me says she knows my game. I know hers too—make the adult daughter look like a selfish, spoiled brat. Make the old man choose between the needy child and the best blowjob he's ever had.

Dammit! Stupid mind.

My phone chimes. I dig it out of my Hermes bag. "Avery Montgomery."

"This is Trace from Wellman's garage. We've inspected your vehicle and found two major problems and several minor ones."

"Okay, how much will it cost to get it road-ready again?"

"Fifty-five hundred."

"What the fu—" I grimace as my dad gives me a disapproving look. "Fudge stripes are you talking about? I don't think the whole vehicle is worth that much."

"I'm afraid I have to agree with you there. It has over 200,000 miles on it, and from what we can see, it doesn't look like you've had regular maintenance on it."

After setting my glass on the railing, I rub my temples, taking a deep breath. "Thanks. Bye."

"Wait, ma'am, what do you want to do?"

"Nothing. Just keep it."

"Wait—"

I press end. "My Honda is dead. I need a car."

"Avery, you can borrow mine." Deedy gives me a sympathy frown that matches the one my dad's wearing.

I shake my head. "No. I don't need to borrow a car. I need a new one, but I don't have a job." I hold up my injured hand. "Or a way to make money."

Or a sugar daddy.

"Since I can't afford one at the moment, I'm going to have to just take a rental car back to L.A. and figure things out from there."

"Avery, I don't want you driving all the way back there by yourself. I'm not at all happy that you drove to Illinois without someone with you. It's not safe for you to travel alone."

I nod toward my nemesis. "I have Swarley."

"An old dog. Not good enough. Maybe we should drive you home."

"No!"

Even Swarley jumps to attention at my adamant refusal to drive *all the way* to Los Angeles with my father and the Deedy.

My apology comes in the form of a stiff smile. "Swarley likes to sprawl out, taking up more than half of the backseat. It would be a miserable trip for the three of us with him and all of my luggage."

"Avery, I'm not letting you go by yourself."

"Let's not worry about this right now. I'll get something figured out."

Hitchhiking.

Leaving Swarley behind and flying home first class.

Slitting my wrists.

Anything that doesn't involve road-tripping with them.

"Deedy, do you need help with dinner?"

"Thanks, but it's all in the Instant Pot. Just twenty more minutes."

"Okay." I smile. "Then let's uh…" I jab my good thumb over my shoulder "…get your things unloaded from the van, Dad."

"Your hand." Deedy removes herself from my father's lap. "You go inside and rest, Avery. I'll call over a few neighbor friends to help out. We'll have this unloaded in no time."

"I have one good hand. I can carry some light stuff."

"Sit." She points to the empty chair that my dad vacated because it's a new law that he and Deedy have to stay within fondling distance of each other at all times.

"Fine." I roll my eyes and take a seat in the chair, having had no real intentions of helping unload the truck. I'm trying to not pop anymore pain pills for my hand, but it aches at the moment.

Ten minutes later, half the neighborhood arrives to unload my dad's stuff. As the worker bees pass in and out of the house, I hug my injured hand to my chest so they know I'm wounded and not simply lazy.

"Hey, handsome dog, fancy seeing you again."

My head snaps up from my phone screen at the sound of Bethanne's voice—one of the *nice* ones from Sage Leaf Cafe. She shoots me a grin while carrying a box up the steps. "Hello again."

"Hi, wow. Small world. You live in the neighborhood?"

She jerks her head to the side. "Two houses over. I love this neighborhood, especially Deedy. She's the bomb."

Before I can add my opinion on Deedy being the bomb, Bethanne continues into the house with the box. When she returns, she wipes her brow and leans against the porch railing. "I'm Bethanne, by the way."

I nod. "Yes, I heard Jake say your name. I'm Avery."

She nods. "How do you know Deedy?"

She's my father's belated midlife crisis.

"My dad met her online."

"Oh my god! You're one of Tom's daughters?"

With a tightlipped smile, I nod.

"Deedy has been talking about him nonstop. She's so in love. I talked her off the ledge of a nervous breakdown the night before she asked him to marry her."

"Wait. *She* asked *him*?"

Bethanne makes a quick glance out to the yard and lowers her voice. "Yes. She said he wouldn't agree to meet her in person because he was lonely and he knew he wouldn't be able to let her go."

I try to hide my flinch. He was lonely. I press my hand

closer to my chest, but not because my hand hurts—this time it's my heart.

Loneliness is the side effect of solitude starving the soul. I know it quite well.

"I didn't know," I whisper.

"Don't feel bad. He found Deedy."

My gaze inches to Bethanne's. "He's not rich."

She chuckles. "Deedy doesn't care about money. It's all about love. I can promise you, she loves him."

My attention shifts from Bethanne to my dad and Deedy unloading the truck with her village of friends. He looks happy.

Really.

Truly.

Happy.

"Thank you." I smile. "I just didn't see it." Probably because I've never had a man look at me like my dad looks at Deedy.

"So how long are you staying in Milwaukee?"

"Just until I figure out how to get back to L.A. with my sister's dog. My car took its last breath. Flying isn't an option. And my dad refuses to let me drive by myself. I already tried closing my eyes and snapping my fingers three times, but it didn't work. I'm still here."

She grins. "Ya know ... I might have just the ticket you need."

"Ticket?"

"Yeah. I bet I can get you a ride if you're willing to wait until next week."

I frown. "I was thinking of sneaking out before my dad swallows his erectile dysfunction pill."

"Ha! I get that. But seriously, if you don't mind waiting, I can get a ride for you and your sister's dog."

"You're not planning on stowing me in the back of a semitrailer filled with cheese are you?"

"I would never." She grins. "Meet me at the cafe around ten tomorrow morning, and we'll get it all planned out."

"Can we meet somewhere else? I think I should avoid that Jake guy at all costs."

"I'm working tomorrow, but I can take a break at ten. And the last thing you should do is avoid Jake."

"Why would you say that?"

Bethanne skips back toward the moving van. "You'll see."

"You going to sleep all day?"

I hide my head under the pillow of the twin bed in Deedy's sewing room. She said the bed belonged to her younger brother who died. Nothing creepy about sleeping in a dead person's bed on sheets that must be the lowest thread count ever.

"Dad, I'm still on West Coast time. Leave me alone."

He tickles my foot peeking out from the veil-thin sheet.

I jerk and draw my knees to my chest. "Stop!"

"It's 9:30. Deedy made breakfast, and yours is cold. I'll warm your coffee up, just come share your beautiful face with us."

I shoot up, batting at the matted hair on my face. "9:30? Shit! I'm going to be late."

"Late for what?"

I stumble toward my suitcase, rifling through its contents. "I'm supposed to meet Bethanne at the cafe at ten."

"Deedy's neighbor?"

After failing to find my Alexis floral romper, I unzip my second suitcase. Of course, it's at the bottom. "Yes. Bethanne works at that Sage Leaf Cafe. She's finding Swarley and me a ride to L.A. so you don't have to stress over me going by myself."

I shove him toward the door. "I have to get ready. My makeup will be hideous at this rate and don't even get me started on my hair."

"But Ave—"

Click.

I jump into my outfit, paint on a terribly hurried layer of makeup, a little antiperspirant, and gather my long hair into a messy bun before flying past my dad and Deedy canoodling on the sofa, straight out the door. "Would someone feed Swarley?" I call just before the door shuts behind me.

CHAPTER FOUR

I MAKE it to the cafe by 10:05. Deedy probably would have loaned me her car, but I haven't decided if I'm ready to ask her for favors. She might misconstrue my desperateness as approval of her engagement to my dad.

My *lonely* dad ... I still can't shake the guilt from Bethanne's revelation.

"I'm so sorry I'm late. I forgot to set my alarm, and my body is on West Coast time, and—"

Bethanne waves off my apologies. "It's fine. I'm running a few minutes late for break anyway. We're pretty chill around here." She slides a pile of chopped mango into a container and snaps the lid on it.

I glance around at the vacant cafe. "Are you open?"

She laughs. "Yes. We survived the morning rush, and in about an hour we'll be filled to capacity with the early lunch crowd."

"Huh ... the one in L.A. is always packed."

"Milwaukee isn't L.A."

I nod. "You can say that again."

"Can I get you a drink? Some breakfast?"

"I'm good. Well ... maybe a cup of coffee?"

"You got it." She gets my coffee as I climb onto a barstool.

"I have coconut sugar, almond or coconut creamer, cinnamon ..."

"Black is great." I take a cautious sip.

"Well, since you're the only customer at the moment, I'll get Jake and we'll get your travel dilemma fixed."

"Jake? Wait ... why do you need him—"

Mr. Tatted Muscle Man saunters through the door from the kitchen, looking all showered and sexy. Not sexy. Gah! Why did I think that?

"Just get out of the shower?" Bethanne flicks at a drop of water hanging from one of the tips of his messy, blond hair.

I stare at his T-shirt—speechless.

He glances down as if he doesn't know what it says. "It's new, Paige. Do you like it?"

My gaze snaps to his. "Avery."

Bethanne giggles. "Jake owns every obnoxious T-shirt ever made."

He rubs his hand over his chest like he's caressing the words.

Eat Pussy Not Meat

"Your boss lets you wear that?"

"Jake's the boss." Bethanne sets a glass of water next to my coffee.

He smirks.

"I know. It was mentioned yesterday." I narrow my eyes. "Hence the mason jars being a precious heirloom from your grandmother."

His smirk blooms into a full-on grin.

I rub my lips together. Dang, I forgot to gloss them.

Retrieving my gloss from my handbag, I bring up my phone's camera to use as a mirror.

"Taking a picture of my shirt?" Jake asks.

I roll my eyes, holding up my phone. "Not a chance. I just need to gloss my lips. I only had a half hour to throw myself together this morning."

"I took a shower and dressed in under ten minutes."

"Good for you." I pucker my lips, giving them one last inspection before capping the gloss and tossing it back in my bag.

Bethanne clears her throat. "You two are so fun together. I love your flirty banter."

I stop the coffee mug an inch from my lips. Jake sets the blender on its base, brow drawn tightly as he shoots Bethanne a WTF look.

"So ..." She slaps her hands on the counter and drums her fingers a few times. "Jake, Avery and her dog need a ride to L.A. Her car died, and it can't be brought back to life. Can you think of some way she could get to L.A.?"

I don't know where this is going, but I have an uneasy feeling slithering across my skin.

He returns his attention to the blender, filling it with fruit, greens, and protein powder. "Buy a new car."

"She can't afford one."

I feel like I'm on trial, and Bethanne is my lawyer.

He purses his lips to the side and hums. "Looks like she better get a job and save up for one."

"She probably has one. In L.A."

That's not an accurate statement, but I keep that to myself.

"Well, sorry. I'm a chef, not a fixer." He dismisses Bethanne by starting the blender.

She plants her hands on her hips, waiting for him to

finish blending. I cup my coffee mug with both my good hand and my gimpy one, attempting to hide behind the steam.

"Jake Matthews..." she pipes up the second he shuts off the blender "...you know exactly what I'm suggesting."

Oh god. I cringe. He has an extra car and she's suggesting he loan it to me. Then what? He flies out to L.A. to drive it home. Well ... that might work. If he owns this cafe, then he must own the one out there. Surely he visits that location. But that doesn't solve the issue of my dad not wanting me to drive home alone.

"I'm not simply driving out to L.A. I'm taking a trip. Taking my time. Enjoying my time alone to recharge just like I do every summer. It's kind of a personal trip I take by myself."

Oh no. No. No. No. She's not suggesting I go *with* him.

"Two years ago you took Mo."

"That was different." He pours the drink into one of those heirloom mason jars and rinses out the blender.

I don't know if I should join in on this conversation, insist that I don't need help, or just stay out of it because I *do* need help. So I do what I do best when I'm nervous—primp.

Fishing out my makeup bag, I powder my nose, even out my eyeliner, apply more mascara, and pluck a few eyebrows.

They continue to bicker like a married couple *and* like I'm not right here, half listening to them, half trying to remember the date of my hair appointment.

"Look ... does she appear to be a camper?"

When the chattering ceases, I glance up. What were they saying? Bethanne looks constipated like I'm doing something wrong and she's disappointed in me. Jake has a smug look like I just proved some point for him.

I think back. *Does she appear to be a camper?*

"Oh..." I shrug "...I've camped before. It's only for what ... two, three nights?"

He rests his palms on the counter in front of me. I untie my hair and work it back into a neater bun.

"As long as I want. That's how long my trip is. No rushing. No schedule. I'll get there when I get there."

Shit. I glance at my thumbnail. It's chipped and rough along the edge, so I look for a file. I know there's one in my bag, but I can't find it. After removing most of the contents onto the counter, I find it.

"Hello?"

Filing the rough edge, I look up.

"Did you hear me?" Jake frowns, glaring at the file in my hand.

"Uh ... yeah." I keep filing. "You like to take your time driving to L.A. That's fine. My job is ... *flexible*." I bite my lips together so he doesn't see my I-don't-have-a-job expression.

Jake chuckles, shaking his head. It's a wicked chuckle. Why is he giving me a wicked chuckle? What did I miss?

"Jake ..." Bethanne says his name like a plea. "Just help her out. You might enjoy the company." She shoots me a look, a cue of sorts.

Okay, I guess I'm up.

"Yes." I give him a toothy grin. "I'll be excellent company."

He shifts his attention to the dumped-out contents of my purse on the counter. Bethanne takes a step back so he can't see her. She holds up her hands in a prayer gesture and mouths, "Say please."

That feels like begging. I'm not good at begging. I'm more of a briber or manipulator.

He sighs. "I don't think it's a good idea—"

"Please!" I said that. Whoa! Where did that come from? My need to get home is more desperate than I thought.

Jake inspects me with nervous apprehension wrinkling his face.

I slowly bring my hands to my chest in prayer position, mirroring Bethanne. "Pretty please." Gah! Another chipped nail. I hold out one hand, inspecting the jagged edge. I'm never going back to that nail salon.

"Two weeks chip-free my ass," I mumble.

"Avery is Tommy's daughter ... Deedy's friend." Bethanne says between clenched teeth.

"Fuck ..." he mumbles, rolling his eyes. "Okay, Princess, I'll take you to L.A., but your crown won't make it there in one piece."

My brows jump up as my breath catches on a gasp. Princess? I will myself to bite my tongue and play nice with my driver, but my poor tongue will be swollen by the time I get back to the Deedy's house.

"Tiara."

"What?" He squints at me.

I put everything back in my purse, avoiding his scrutinizing gaze. "You implied I'm a princess..." I shrug, keeping my head bowed "...which is cool. What woman wouldn't want to be a princess? But then you insinuated I have a crown, which would be incorrect because only kings and queens wear crowns. Princesses wear tiaras."

His hands ball into fists, still propped up on the counter.

I risk a glance up, my lips quivering into a nervous smile. "So either you think I'm actually a queen or you must mean my *tiara* will not make it to L.A. in one piece. Which..." I rub my lips together to hide my nerves "...is not going to be an issue since I left my tiara at home. I usually only take it on girl getaways."

Bethanne snorts a laugh, buckling over and resting her head on Jake's back. "Oh my gosh ..." Her body shakes with laughter.

He's going to strangle me. I swallow hard, feeling grateful for the first time that my dad has Deedy to keep him company when I'm dead.

In an unexpected twist, a tiny grin forms along his mouth. "We leave in two days."

"Two days?" I shoot a teary-eyed Bethanne a questioning look. "You said next week."

Jake clears his throat. "It's two days now. After forty-eight hours, my common sense will catch up to what I've agreed to do and you'll be out of luck again."

I stand, slinging the straps of my bag onto my shoulder. "Two days is perfect. The sooner I get home the better." I offer my hand.

"I said I'm leaving earlier, but I'm still not rushing. You won't hurry me. You won't complain. You won't be a child, nagging me with incessant *Are we there yet's*. Got it?"

How long does he think it takes to drive to California? I withdraw my proffered hand since he shows no interest in sealing the deal with a friendly handshake.

"Got it. Give me your phone and I'll give you my number."

Bethanne grabs his phone from the counter behind them and holds it up to his face to unlock it. He ignores her, giving me a blank stare accented with the occasional blink. I enter my information into his contacts.

"I don't know Deedy's address. Message me and I'll send it to you when I get there. Or ... duh. She's Bethanne's neighbor. Deedy, for some reason, thinks highly of you." My eyes start to roll, but I stop myself.

He nods slowly.

"She's planning on marrying my father. Reason number one why I need to leave as soon as possible. I've hit my limit of shocking, life-changing news."

Jake shoots Bethanne a squinted look.

Her nose wrinkles. "I forgot to mention the new man in Deedy's life is in town. I helped move him into her house yesterday. And ... they are getting married. Sorry ... I should have told you."

"What am I missing?"

They both say, "Nothing," at the same time, which means it's *something*.

Two days later, I say a sad goodbye to my father. A part of me feels like I've lost him. Maybe this is how a father feels when he gives his daughter away at the altar. He gave Sydney away. Will he ever give me away? Or will this be it ... me giving him away?

"What's happened to you?" I sit on my larger suitcase to close it.

My dad leans against the wall by the door, arms crossed over his chest. "I'm not following."

"You're letting your baby girl hitch a ride with a complete stranger. A guy. And you have no misgivings about it?"

"Deedy trusts him implicitly, so I trust her judgment. And I've prayed for your safe return to L.A."

I lug both suitcases to the door of the sewing room.

Hopefully Deedy trusts Jake implicitly to carry my suitcases to his vehicle.

Dad cradles my face, and I rest my hands over his. "Did you call Sydney back yet?"

I nod. "Yesterday."

"Good." He smiles.

I miss his fatherly touch, the comfort only a father can give.

"Have you heard the saying *Love doesn't divide, it multiplies?*"

I blink back the tears.

"My precious daughter, how do you think God can love every single person on this earth? I'm sharing my life with Deedy, but the love I have for you and Sydney can never be shared. Not with each other and not with Deedy."

I set a few tears free.

"And I'm not giving Deedy the love I had and will always have for your mom."

"Bethanne said you were lonely."

He gives me a small smile. "I was but that's life. Peaks and valleys. I thanked God for my life, and I even thanked him for the years I've had by myself to reflect on my life—the love and loss. Then I asked him for ... something."

He rubs his thumbs over my wet cheeks. "I didn't even know what that was until a friend of mine told me about the church chatroom."

"Anthony cheated on me." A sob breaks free. I've been waiting to say those words that have been locked up in a prison of denial for days. "And he's taking away the spa. Now I don't have a job. And my hand may never be the same. A-and ... and I'm almost thirty with no direction, no other skills."

"Oh, Avery, Avery, Avery ..." He pulls me into his arms

and kisses the top of my head. "Have faith. Embrace this time in your life and be open to the lessons life has to teach you."

"I am. I've learned to hate all men except you."

He chuckles. "I fear you're distracted by the little details and therefore missing the bigger picture. Be open to let miracles grace your life."

"Jake's here," Deedy calls from the living room.

I fish a tissue from my purse. "My makeup ..."

"Go do your thing in the bathroom. We'll get your stuff loaded up, and I'll make sure Swarley is ready to go too."

I kiss my dad on the cheek. "Thank you."

After fixing my smeared makeup and using the bathroom one last time, I grab my handbag and meet everyone in the driveway. Jake scratches his head while staring at my luggage, one hand planted on his hip.

"Hi."

He looks up at me with slightly narrowed eyes. My gaze drops to his T-shirt with a duct tape X over the front of it.

Silence is Golden
Duct Tape is Silver

"In case you needed a reminder." He grins.

I frown. "That's a red pickup truck."

"Sorry, did you request a different color?" Jake slips his hands in the front pockets of his jeans.

"Where's the RV?"

"RV?"

"Recreational vehicle."

He shakes his head. "I know what it stands for. I just don't know why you're talking about it."

"Because you said we're going to camp along the way."

"We are." He points to the bed of the truck. "See, there's a tent, two sleeping bags, a cooler, a camping stove, a hand-powered blender, camping chairs, food, and other miscellaneous supplies. But there's no room for two large suitcases, a duffel bag filled with dog supplies, *and* a dog bed."

"You think I'm going to sleep in a tent? In a sleeping bag?"

Jake gives my dad a polite smile. I'm sure behind it he's choking on his words, but why would he offer to give us a ride if he didn't have room?

"Avery, how would you feel about us shipping one of your suitcases to your apartment?" Deedy asks.

"I have stuff I need in both suitcases. I'd have to repack both of them, and I can't guarantee I can get everything I might need for the trip into just one of them."

Jake grumbles as he hops into the bed of the truck, reshuffling everything. After a few minutes, he retrieves ties from under the backseats, heaves my two suitcases onto the pile of camping supplies, and secures everything with the straps.

My dad whistles for Swarley to get in the backseat, then he and Deedy thank Jake for his generosity, which is crazy because how well do any of us know this tattooed, muscle-bound serial killer?

Deedy hugs me and whispers in my ear, "I'll take care of him."

I start to refute her assumption that my dad needs someone to take care of him, but I choke on my stupid emotions that are a culmination of my hand, Anthony, Swarley, my joblessness, the death of my vehicle, and the fact that I'm leaving on a long road trip with a man who feels a bit cold toward me—oh, and we're camping with a tent. A. TENT!

"And this too will pass." My dad gives me an encouraging smile before hugging me. "Be grateful and God will bless you, Avery. I love you."

The lump in my throat feels like it could asphyxiate me, so all I manage to get out is, "You too."

Jake opens my door for me. I'm sure it's just for show. Something tells me by our next stop, I'll be chasing the vehicle so he doesn't leave me—unless I'm dead. He's going to kill me.

Startling me with his close proximity—the warmth of his body and his clean, woodsy scent—he helps me fasten my seat belt so I don't fumble it with my injured hand. After it clicks, our gazes lock, his face a breath away from mine. I squeak out the words that I've been dying to say. "Make my death quick, and please don't tie me up. I'm claustrophobic."

Now it's his turn to roll his eyes and disregard my request as preposterous, but he doesn't.

"Noted." He winks. A *very* conspiratorial, evil wink. "Paws in, Swarley," he says louder just before closing both doors.

CHAPTER FIVE

Day One
Destination: Chicago, Illinois

"Do you hate me?" I break the silence after thirty minutes into our road trip.

A tiny smile quirks the corner of Jake's mouth as he keeps his eyes on the road. "No. I don't hate you. I don't really know you."

"But I annoy you?"

"Your kind annoy me."

"My *kind*? You mean women?"

"No."

I wait for further explanation, but he doesn't give any.

"Are you going to stare at me the whole way?"

My head jerks forward. "How uncouth of you to call me out on it. I was just ..."

He makes a quick sidelong glance. "What? Scowling at me?"

"Wondering what girl pissed on your kale salad."

"Oh, we're back to this? You think I hate women. I like women just fine. Some more than others."

"Some *kinds* more than others?"

Another amused purse of his lips. "Yes. I suppose that would be accurate."

"I'm not stupid."

"Good for you."

His indifference and perfect skin irritate me.

"I was valedictorian in high school."

Jake drums his fingers on the top of the steering wheel a few times.

"I turned down a scholarship to the University of Illinois." Drawing in a slow breath, I wait for his response.

No response.

"Did you go to college?"

"Nope."

"Not even culinary school?"

"Nope."

"Probably a good thing. Speech is usually a freshman requirement for most degrees, and you clearly would have failed that class."

He takes the next exit and pulls off on the side of the road by a produce stand. "Let Swarley out, but be back in five or I'm leaving without you."

I frown.

He winks.

Stupid wink. I hate winkers.

"Jake Matthews!"

Shooing Swarley toward the grass, I roll my eyes at the lady's enthusiasm to see Mr. Anti-personality.

"Carley, you look younger every time I see you." He hugs her, lifting her off the ground.

My gaze flits between Swarley and the flex of Jake's

muscles. All muscles. No brains. That's what I tell myself to tame the itty-bitty part of me that physically reacts to him.

I'm done with men. Period.

"I just turned forty-five, but I feel better than I did at thirty-five. I like this." Carley ruffles Jake's thick, blond hair. "I bet all the girls like it." She winks.

Great. Another winker.

"Whatcha got today?" He follows her to her produce stand.

"All the berries—blue, black, strawberry, and raspberry. I also have asparagus and red leaf lettuce."

"Sold." He pulls out a wad of cash from his pocket, shooting me a quick glance, eyes squinted against the sun.

I jerk my attention back to Swarley. "Oh, Swarley. No, no, no."

He pooped. I suppose it's better now than passing his lethal gas in the truck. I grab a poop bag from the backseat of the truck.

As Swarley sniffs his way back to me, I cringe. He has a piece of poop hanging from his backside, suspended by a long hair—probably one of mine—that he ate. This dog hates me on every level, conscious and subconscious.

"Hi." I smile at Carley.

"Hi, darling." She gives Jake an inflated grin. "Who's your lady friend?"

Jake keeps his focus on bagging his produce. "Friend might be an overstatement. We just met. Hitchhiker would be more accurate. Carley, Avery. Avery, Carley."

Carley laughs. "You don't pick up hitchhikers." She holds out her hand to me. "So this stunning young lady must be someone really special."

"No. She's not," he deadpans.

I narrow my eyes at him while shaking Carley's hand.

"Nice to meet you, Carley. Jake offered me a ride to L.A. My car died. I can't fly because I have my sister's dog with me, and my dad's heart wouldn't handle me making the trip alone. And do you by chance have a napkin or paper towel?"

"Oh. I have a rag." She grabs a cloth towel from a crate beneath her table.

"No. I need something disposable."

"Time to go, Avery," Jake says my name with less contempt. Must be the Carley effect.

"I have a tissue in my purse. Will that work?"

I glance back at Swarley and his dangling turd. "Several tissues might work. Thank you."

Carley digs into her purse and pulls out a wadded-up tissue.

Just one.

One, one-ply tissue.

Possibly already been used.

Biting my lips together, I wrinkle my nose. "Is that all you've got?"

"I'm afraid so, darling." She leans closer and whispers, "Did you get your period? I have a sanitary napkin in the glove compartment of my truck."

I look back at the dangling turd one more time. It's the size of a large walnut. "Would you mind if I took what's in your glove compartment?"

"Not at all." She goes to her truck, and Jake gets in his driver's seat.

"Avery, let's go! Get your dog."

"Just a minute!"

Carley hands me the wadded sanitary napkin. Thankfully, it's simply old, not used. "Thank you. I really appreciate it."

"No problem. It was nice to meet you. You've got yourself quite the guy there."

I find my fake grin. "He's something all right. Bye, Carley." I press the pad together in my good hand like a puppet. It slips out, falling to the ground, so I pick it up and remove the paper strip. The adhesive isn't the best, but it should keep it from slipping from my hand while I nab the dangling turd.

"Avery? In the truck or you're getting left behind."

"I said, just a minute!" I whistle for Swarley. He comes right to me.

A miracle.

"Hold still." I rest my injured hand on his back to steady him while I move in for the kill. "Hold still!"

He wiggles, arching his body to sniff the pad in my hand.

I chase him in circles. "Swarley! Would you just stop and hold still?"

True to his evil nature, he wiggles more, whipping the turd every which way, making it impossible to nab it.

"What the hell are you doing?"

I glance back at Jake as I continue to chase the turd in a circle. "He has a chunk of poop dangling from his backside. Do you really want him getting in the back of your truck with it?"

He crosses his arms over his chest, widening his stance. "Hurry up."

"Hurry up?" I step away from the chase, squaring myself to Mr. Not Helpful.

He grins that perfect surfer grin, with his stupid, perfect hair all perfectly messed up, and that annoying twinkle in his blue eyes.

I hate him.

"Yes. Chop chop, Avery." He glances down at me with amusement gleaming across his face.

My teeth gnash together. "I have one good hand." I hold up my left hand and move my puppet pad in his face.

A single eyebrow lifts up his forehead. "Is that a period pad?"

"Hold Swarley." I shoot him a narrow-eyed challenge.

After a stare-off, I win. Jake brushes past me and hugs Swarley to his body. "You've got ten seconds before I leave you behind to work for Carley."

I lift Swarley's bobbed tail and grab the hair-bound turd. "Got it." I stand.

Swarley dashes off to the truck when Jake releases him.

I grin, feeling a mix of disgust at the turd in the folded pad and a twinge of triumph that I got it without getting any poop on my hands.

Plop.

The pad slips out of my hand, landing turd side down on the top of my sandaled foot. "Eww!" I jerk my foot, but the moist turd is stuck and so is the pad. "Eww eww eww ... get it off!"

"Clean up and get in the truck." Jake saunters off, leaving me jumping on one foot while trying to fling off the turd and pad with my other foot.

The growing crowd at Carley's produce stand watches in amusement. The burn of embarrassment crawls up my neck. I bend down and flick the pad off, leaving a smeared streak of shit on my foot and the toe strap to my sandal—my $300 Italian leather sandals.

I stomp back to the truck with a permanent cringe of disgust affixed to my face. Jake rubs a hand over his mouth. The bastard is laughing at me.

"Don't speak." I reach over the seat and grab his water canteen.

"That's not—"

"Shut it!" I snap, shooting daggers at him with one look.

I unscrew the lid and pour. "Shit!"

Jake clears his throat. "It's green juice."

"I see that. Where's my water?"

"You didn't bring any." He pops a blackberry into his mouth.

I hop on one foot, shaking the juice from my dirty foot. "I need water."

Jake pops another berry.

"Ugh! You are the worst." I glare at Jake.

Swarley whines.

"Both of you!" I slam the door and hobble to the produce stand. "Carley, do you have some—" My breath catches as I'm swooped up into Jake's arms.

"You are a pain in the ass, woman," he mumbles, carrying me to the truck. He opens the back and plops me down on the tailgate.

"I was going to ask Carley for some water."

Jake opens a plastic tub. "And I'm sure she would give you her drinking water for the day so you can clean your foot because she's nice like that. But it's going to be hot, so only an inconsiderate person would accept such an offer."

"I would not have taken her only water. I just thought ..." My jaw drops as he pulls out a gallon jug of water and a roll of paper towels.

"Bastard! You watched me chase a turd with a sanitary napkin. You let me pour juice on my $300 Italian leather sandals while a gallon of water and paper towels were in the back of your truck?"

He unfastens my sandal and washes my foot and sandal

without saying another word, without so much as a glance up at me.

"Italian leather doesn't like water." I frown at my shoe as he dries my foot and shoves it back into my sandal.

Jake glances up at me with a hard look. "Don't even get me started on things I don't like." With zero effort, he lifts me off the tailgate. "Let's go."

"Thanks for offering me some berries." As the skyline of Chicago comes into view, I break the silence again.

Jake turns down the country music. "What?"

"I said, thanks for offering me some berries." I stare at the four empty pint containers between the seats.

"If you wanted berries, why didn't you get some?"

"Because I had to deal with Swarley and the poop fiasco."

"Then why didn't you ask if you could have some of mine?" He shoots me a wide-eyed look with a tight smile.

"Because that's not how it works. You don't ask for something that's not yours. You wait until someone with *manners* offers it to you."

"You were going to ask Carley for her water."

"Okay, okay ... enough about the water. You act like I was going to take food from a starving child."

"What are you doing?"

"Snapchat."

"You just took a picture of me?"

"Yup." I caption the photo of Jake.

"Beware! Satan has good hair, but he's still a snake."

"You can't upload photos of me without a photo release."

"Well, I did. What are you going to do about it?"

Jake snatches my phone.

"Hey!"

He tucks it under his leg.

"Not cool. Give it back."

"No. Taking my picture without permission and posting it to Snapchat is what's *not cool*."

I cross my arms and stare out my window the rest of the way to Chicago.

"Where are we?"

"Grocery store. Go get what you need." He unlocks the door.

"What I need?"

"Food, Avery. It's a grocery store. Or do you have a personal shopper who gets your groceries?"

"No. My personal shopper—ex-personal shopper—mainly bought my clothes."

"Christ ..." He shakes his head.

"Aren't you getting anything? Where are we going for lunch? Chicago has some great restaurants. Did you call ahead for reservations? Am I just getting snacks here or what?"

"Whatever you need to survive for the next forty-eight hours. I have a blender, and I'll start a fire. You didn't bring a cooler, but I might let you rent some space in mine." He smiles. It's much sweeter than his words. Satan—totally Satan.

"We're in Chicago. Why would we camp in Chicago? There are hundreds of hotels."

"Skip along, Princess. I don't want to spend the whole day in this parking lot."

"My phone." I hold out my hand.

He slides it out from under his leg. I drop it in my purse, pausing to gather my emotions that have been all over the place.

"Avery Montgomery." I hold out my hand.

Jake stares at it then at me.

"Let's rewind and start over. I fear your first impression of me was inaccurate. I just came off a bad breakup. If my anti-male vibe rubbed you the wrong way and therefore caused you to act a little douchey toward me, I understand."

He nods slowly, taking my proffered hand. "Jake Matthews."

"Nice to meet you, Jake. Thank you for the ride. You are a lifesaver."

A tiny line creases along the bridge of his nose, a residual sign of his unease. His distrust. I don't let it phase me. This trip doesn't have to be miserable for either one of us. I'll show him every assumption he made about me is wrong.

"You're welcome."

I grin. It feels good to smile. It feels good to start again on the right foot. "I'll be quick. Are you sure I can't get you anything?"

"I'm good. Thank you."

Shedding the weight of the world, I inhale the summer air, toss my hair over my shoulders, and make my way into the store.

Fifteen minutes later, I push my cart into the checkout line. The cashier scans my necessities, and I swipe my card.

Declined.

My lips twist. I try the card again.

Declined.

"I'm from out of town. I should have informed my credit card company."

The cashier gives me a sympathetic smile.

I try another credit card.

Declined.

"What is going on?" I try every credit card. They are all declined. I try my debit card. I *know* I have enough money in my bank account to cover seventy dollars in groceries.

Nope. *Declined.*

The voices in my head give my emotions a pep talk.

Keep your shit together.

Don't cry.

Don't cry.

Don't cry.

"Do you have cash?" the cashier asks with pity in her hushed words.

I have thirty dollars in cash. When we stopped for gas, I was planning on getting more cash from the ATM.

"I'll just take the water." Food is overrated. I can live for days with just water. It's the perfect time for a cleanse. My skin will look almost as amazing as Jake's.

"Just the water?"

I nod, blinking back the tears.

She calls someone from customer service to void the transaction and rings through just the water. I stop outside of the entrance, out of sight from Jake's truck, and call Anthony.

"Avery," he answers in a cold tone.

"What the hell have you done? None of my credit cards work and neither does my debit card!"

"Funny ... I said those same words when I found my BMW trashed."

"You fucked the cook, you asshole! You're lucky I didn't

do to you what I did to your car. I have *nothing*. I'm traveling across the country with a complete stranger, my sister's dog, and thirty dollars in my purse."

Twenty and change after buying the water.

"How did you even get access to my account?"

"My brother is your banker. All I had to do was show him my car."

"I'm going to sue his ass, Anthony! And yours too."

"Baby, we can make this all go away. I want you back. You have a place in my life, all you have to do is say yes. I'll get a driver to bring you and the mutt home. We'll get all this silliness with your bank account straightened out. It will be like it never happened."

I stare at the water spots on my leather sandal and the chips in my manicured nails. I think of camping with a stranger and chasing dangling turds. But then I think of what I saw on Anthony's computer and his hidden love of chocolate, and I press *End*.

"Three bottles of water? You were in the store for that long and you got three bottles of water?"

I smile through the pain and my fading confidence. I smile through the humiliation. "I had other things, but then I got to the checkout and one of those magazines on the rack had a feature on cleansing, so I put everything but the water back. Sorry to keep you waiting."

He eyes me with suspicion as I fasten my seat belt. "Occasional cleansing is good."

I nod, unable to speak past the knot of emotion in my throat. Over the next hour to our destination, he continues to give me quick glances. I sense his confusion, a better feeling than pity, but I refuse to look at him.

"Whoa ..." My face presses to the window. "You're such

a tease, Jake Matthews. We're staying at a boutique hotel. It's ... incredible."

He chuckles. "It's a house. Not mine. We are camping on the property."

"You're joking."

"I'm not."

"Whose house?"

"A friend's."

I give him a scrunched-nose look. "I'm pretty sure friends let friends stay in the house, not offer them a ten-by-ten space for a pop-up tent. It's unfortunate I have to break the news to you, but this dude is not your friend."

He parks a few hundred yards from the house that sits atop a hill overlooking acres of rolling woods and a winding creek. "*She* is my friend. I choose to camp."

"Is she home? I'd love to meet her ... see the inside of the house ... check out the guest bedrooms ..."

"Not home." He hops out and I do the same, letting Swarley out to roam.

"But you have a key to the house, right?"

"Nope."

"What if there's a storm? A tornado?"

He smirks, opening the back of the truck. "We'll kiss each other's ass goodbye. Here."

I shake my head and hold up my hand as he attempts to pass a large bag my way. "I can only carry light stuff. Doctor's orders."

"I see." He frowns at my hand like it's my fault I'm injured.

"Then take your suitcases." He plops them on the ground.

"Dude! Those are Gucci. The wheels alone are probably five hundred dollars." I inspect the two suitcases.

He tosses a few other things out of the back and jumps down, nearly knocking me over.

"Oh shit! You scared me." I hold my hand over my chest.

"Don't be scared." He looks down on me like I'm dinner.

I never thought I'd say the words *thank god he's vegan*, but seriously ... thank god he's vegan.

"We agreed. I won't tie you up to kill you." Another stupid wink.

It's wrong for that shade of blue eyes to be wasted on a guy. I bet he can get any girl with just a wink. Good thing I've never been just any girl.

"We started from scratch. Remember? The handshake."

He nods slowly, his gaze making deliberate strokes along my entire body.

Violating bastard!

"Owning a suitcase with wheels that cost five hundred dollars each severed our newly formed friendship." He shrugs, turning back toward the bed of his truck to grab the cooler. "Did your preacher dad forget to tell you that there are starving people in the world?"

"Thanks for the biblical shaming. I didn't realize my driver is holier-than-thou." I drag my suitcases through the grass, cringing as the wheels *thunk* against the uneven terrain, jarring my injured hand.

"I'm not your driver, or bellhop, or lightning shield."

"Then what are you besides terribly unmannered?"

Jake plops the cooler down in a small clearing at the bottom of the hill, not too far from the creek.

"Well..." he turns, squinting against the setting sun "... since we agree I'm holier-than-thou, then I'd say I'm your savior. But don't worry..." he heads back toward the truck

"...I'm not expecting constant praise and worship. Silence is your best gift to me."

"If you get struck by lightning tonight, but leave your truck keys next to my purse, that would be the best gift for *me*."

He chuckles. "Noted."

CHAPTER SIX

Jake

Avery Montgomery is an interesting creature.

Flip-the-visor-down-every-twenty-minutes interesting.

Part-her-hair-a-hundred-different-ways-to-check-for-something interesting.

I'm not sure what she's checking for with the constant scalp inspections, but I have a good guess.

After I unload everything and set up the tent while she files her nails, frown pinned to her face, I get my dinner.

"Beans? That's it?" She swats at the swarm of bugs preying on her, thanks to her strong perfume.

"No." I point my spoon toward the bag of greens on my lap.

"Looks super yummy. Plain beans and greens with no dressing. Scat!" She slaps her arm, squashing a bug.

I return nothing more than a single peaked eyebrow.

"I'm just saying, you own a restaurant—two restaurants. I'd expect you to be more creative than beans and greens."

"I'm easy to please."

"No. You're not. I have yet to please you."

I return two raised eyebrows this time.

"Ouch!" She slaps her neck. "Don't give me that look. I'm not implying I'm going to suck your dick like these stupid bugs are sucking my blood."

Choking on my food, I lean forward and cough into my fist.

Avery sighs, inspecting the ends of her hair much the same way she does her scalp. "I'm just saying it would be nice if we could get along on this trip. You know? Let's get to know each other. I just don't want you to think I'm some materialistic person." She holds up her cell phone. "Gah! No cell service. How can that be? Do you think if I walk closer to the truck I can get internet from your friend's house?"

"Maybe." I wipe my mouth with the bottom of my shirt.

Her nose wrinkles. "Ever heard of a napkin?"

"T-shirts are great reusable napkins. Very eco-friendly. Now ... get going." I shoo her toward the truck. "Go find some Wi-Fi."

Lightning flashes, followed by a crack of thunder.

Avery jumps out of her seat. "There's metal in the chairs! Get up!"

I glance around, taking another bite of my beans. "Don't you mean, leave my truck keys by your purse?"

This earns me an evil scowl. "I was kidding. Whatever. I'm going to get some internet so I can message my dad and my sister to let them know I'm still alive."

"Okie dokie. Hope you don't get zapped by lightning since you're wearing so much metal. Maybe before you head toward the truck, you should leave your purse by my keys. I'll put the rest of the gas on your credit card if you die."

"Good luck with that," she mumbles, using her cell phone light to see her way back toward the truck. "Come, Swarley."

He lifts his head from his blanket by the tent, giving me the is-she-fucking-crazy look. I return the yes-she's-totally-fucking-crazy look, and we go back to what we were doing before she ruined my dinner by speaking.

"Swarley, now!"

"Why does he need to go with you?"

"To protect me."

"From what?"

"Raccoons. Badgers. Skunks. Snakes. I can go on all night."

"Please don't. Just simply *go*. I could use a few minutes of peace and quiet."

"It's going to rain. I won't be long."

"Thanks for the warning."

"About the rain?"

"About your imminent return."

"Ha ha. Not funny. Swarley, get over here now. You owe me for chasing that cat and ruining my hand."

The old dog lumbers to his feet. He must know she's the hand that feeds him, even if it's a gimpy hand.

"Sorry, buddy. Watch out for the bears." I pat his head as he walks past me."

"Bears?"

"Shh ..." I lean back in my chair, closing my eyes. "My peace and quiet starts now."

"Don't say bears then shush me. Are there bears around here? I'm from Illinois. I don't recall there being bears. I'm pretty sure the bear population around here ended in the late 1800's, but they anticipated a repopulation. Have there been sightings?"

I have no clue, but I now believe it's possible Avery may have told the truth about the scholarship she turned down. And just like that, she's become that much more interesting.

Likable?

No.

But definitely interesting.

"Go." I keep my eyes closed.

There is no sound more beautiful than her fading steps, leaving me with my thoughts. I reclaim my solitude as the humidity hits its breaking point, chasing the animals into hiding and leaving the tree leaves waiting idly for the storm.

I had so few moments of this kind of quietude when I was younger. Now I crave them like I used to crave fighting, fatiguing my body, proving my strength, and silencing the demons.

Several drops of rain hit my face, and before I can sit up straight, the clouds let loose.

"Dang! That was fast." I jump up, collapse the two chairs, slide them under the outer flap to the tent, and slip inside.

Avery.

I sigh. This is where I usually plop down on my sleeping bag and listen to the storm. Instead, I have to find *her.* Maybe Miss I Turned Down A Scholarship is smart enough to find her way back or take cover somewhere else until it lets up.

"Jake! Ahhh!"

Maybe not.

I unzip the tent. Rain surges inside. Why did I agree to this?

Thunder booms, branches screech under the gusts of wind, and a dog barks. It's hard to see my hand in front of my face, let alone the path uphill toward the truck.

"Jake! Hurry!"

I follow the sound of Avery's cries for help, my pace picking up as my mind starts to go in crazy directions. Fuck ... what if there are bears? What if a tree branch broke and landed on her. How will I explain this to her dad and Deedy? I should have gone with her. My need for a few minutes to myself overrode all other thoughts that might have involved going with her.

Swarley runs up to me, barking while circling me and leading me to the steep embankment. I squint, unable to see her.

Dammit! She fell over the edge.

"Avery?"

"Jake!"

I track her voice. It's coming from further up the hill. As I jog closer, her silhouette comes into view. She didn't fall over the edge.

"Hurry!" She points down the embankment.

I inspect her drenched body from head to toe, not seeing any injuries.

"My shoe!"

Glancing over the edge, I catch site of her sandal hooked on a broken root sticking out from the dirt.

"Get a rope before it blows off and lands in the creek."

"What? How did this happen?"

She turns, revealing mud and grass stuck to her ass and the backsides of her legs. "I slipped and lost my shoe over the edge."

"Tough break, Princess." I turn back toward the tent.

"Are you getting a rope?"

I chuckle as the rain starts to let up. "No."

"Why not?"

"Because I'm a chef and I can throw a few good punches, but a lassoing cowboy I am not."

"But what about my shoe?"

I stop and turn. "You have two suitcases. Surely someone who owns a tiara must travel with more than one pair of shoes."

"Did I mention they are custom made from Italian leather?" Her fight starts to dissipate into a drowned-rat defeat.

"Yes. Blessed by the Pope, Italian leather. Had you not had that poor cow killed to *custom* make your shoes, it could have dug its hooves into the ground to keep you from falling off the embankment."

"Don't be *that* person."

"You mean holier-than-thou?" I wink and keep walking.

"Jake?"

"What? For fuck's sake, woman. What do you want now?"

She lifts her shoulders. "I can't walk with one shoe. I could step on something that could cut my foot."

Do it for Deedy.

I smile, clenching my teeth as I stomp back up the hill.

Her nipples are happy to see me through her thin shirt and bra. She tugs the shirt away from her chest, cringing a bit.

"Chilly?" I scoop her up in my arms.

"Shut up."

"Careful. This taxi runs on gratitude. I'd hate to drop you. Your other sandal could fall to the same fate as its buddy."

"A gentleman would never embarrass a lady in distress."

"I've heard fairy tales about these mythical creatures

you refer to as gentlemen, but I'm not sure I've met any. Have you?"

"Yes." She sighs, glancing away even though our faces are just inches apart.

"Wherever did you find one?"

"In ... well ..." Her face wrinkles as her lips twist. "They exist. It's just all the good ones have already been taken."

"Let me know if you spot one on our trip." I set her on her shoed foot.

"Watch my hair." She gathers it gently in her hand as I release her.

I duck into the tent. "Yeah, about your hair. Let me grab some apple cider vinegar to rinse your hair before you get in the tent.

"Let me in so I can get out of the rain. I don't need a stupid vinegar rinse." She nudges my backside as I sift through one of my bags.

"It's barely a drizzle. Besides, we need to shed our clothes before we get everything wet."

"I'm not shedding anything for you."

"Then you're not getting in *my* tent." I slip back out, holding a bottle of apple cider vinegar.

"Just let me in so I can change into dry clothes, then I'll face the corner while you do the same."

"Sure. But not until we clean the mud and grass from your backside and rinse your hair with this." I shake the bottle.

"Dude! What's your deal with the apple cider vinegar? I hate the smell of it. There's no way you're putting that in my hair." She crosses her arms over her chest.

Too bad. The most pleasant part of her is her perky nipples. I like to pretend they're attached to a body that's not so fake.

"You've been obsessed with your hair, checking your scalp every time there's a mirror in front of you or with the camera to your phone. And you've been scratching it a lot."

She pats a gentle hand over her hair. Brows drawn tightly, eyes averted to the ground. "So? I just need a shower with softened water and a good conditioning treatment."

I shake my head, holding the bottle in her line of vision. "It's going to take more than softened water and conditioner to get rid of lice."

"Lice?" Her head snaps up.

"I don't want them. You've already been in close proximity to me. I'm going to do a rinse too just to make sure I don't get them too."

Her jaw falls open. "I do *not* have lice, you presumptuous, arrogant, insensitive jerk!"

"No?" I cock my head. "Bad psoriasis?"

"No! Oh my god! Why do you hate me so much?"

I start to list the reasons but stop myself before actual words escape.

"Can you show a little compassion instead of speaking every cruel word that comes to mind? Not all truths in life need a voice."

I frown. "I'm not trying to be mean. I'm simply trying to prevent the spread of lice."

Her light blue eyes meet my gaze, cheeks streaked in dark eye makeup, questionably infectious hair matted to her face. "I don't have lice. My *issue* isn't contagious, and if you have a single sympathetic bone in your body, then you'll not say anything else about my hair."

After inspecting her as if I don't trust her, because I don't, I set the bottle down and pick her back up.

"What are you doing?"

"Taking you down to the creek to get the mud and grass washed off."

For once, she says nothing until I ease her onto a large rock sticking out of the edge of the water. "Thank you," she whispers.

I nod once.

Avery slips off her single sandal, stares at it, up at me, and back at her sandal. "What's happened to my life?" she mumbles, pitching the sandal down the creek.

It's littering, but I don't mention it. This moment has a more significant purpose. Princess Avery Montgomery has been knocked down a few pegs because she caught a ride with a guy who doesn't bow to anyone, instead of the never-before-seen "gentleman" with expert lassoing skills.

"It's not your life. It's a moment in time. The only thing defining you at this moment is your decision to throw in the towel or come back fighting. You have an injured hand. It will heal. Some guy apparently did wrong by you, he was clearly not worth your time."

"You sound a bit hardened to life." She eases her body down into the water that only reaches a few inches above her knees. "Jeez, it's cold."

As she washes her legs, I splash water onto her back.

"Cold!" She straightens like a board.

I grin. "It's not that cold."

Avery smiles for a split second before her eyes narrow into revenge. "It's not that cold," she mimics while plowing her hands through the water to splash me. "It's cold, isn't it, Mr. Tough Guy?"

"Don't start something you can't handle, Princess."

"Enough with the princess!" She whips more water in my direction.

"Last warning." I take a step toward her.

Stumbling back, she continues to splash me. "Last warning," she mimics again.

A rush of adrenaline fills my veins. Avery, pampered princess, likes to play out of her league.

"Stop! Help!"

I flip her over my shoulder and haul her taunting ass a few yards down into deeper water, just above my waist. "No one can hear your pleas. Should have thought about that before you poked the bear."

"Jake!" She pounds my back.

I heave her into the water. She goes under for a few seconds while finding her feet.

"Not cool!" She gasps, wiping her eyes.

I cant my head. "Hmm ... not yet."

"Not yet, wha—no!" She cries to the wild as I sweep her up again and drop her into the water.

This is fun—a sentiment I never imagined having on this road trip.

"You're going to drown me, you big bully!"

I cant my head again. "Better."

"Don't—" She jerks back as I reach for her face. When she realizes I'm not going to pick her up, she pauses, letting me rub my thumbs under her eyes to remove the last few streaks of black eye makeup.

"Much better." I wink. "I'm not sure why you feel the need to put so much shit on this face of yours. It's ..."

Her hands rest on my wrists. "It's what?"

"It's a..." I weigh my words "...a decent face all on its own."

"Decent?" Her eyes widen.

"Decent." I grin. "Let's go."

"Jake, no!"

I flip her over my shoulder again. "Chill. I'm just

carrying you back to the tent." This day has been *something*. I'm not sure how to describe it. I've wanted to wrap my hands around her neck and strangle the diva out of her, but I can also say it's been awhile since I've smiled like I just did in the creek with her.

She steadies herself with my biceps as I set her on her feet.

"Strip before you go in the tent."

Those big eyes inspect me again. I turn around. "I'll give you ten seconds before I turn back around, so you'd better get out of those wet clothes and get your naked ass in the tent. One ..."

"Jeez, did you never learn to count past ten?"

"Two ..."

"I'm stripping, but it's not easy when I'm soaking wet."

"Three ..."

She dives into the tent by seven. I glance back at the pile of her clothes, including her pink panties and matching bra.

"Behave," I whisper to myself. "Can you dress as quickly as you strip? I don't mean to offend you, but you're good at stripping."

"Shut it. And don't you dare come in here yet. You have to let me decide what I'm going to wear before you count to ten like a big boy."

"You're playing with fire."

"Can you just pretend to have manners for a few minutes?"

"Sixty seconds is my manner limit."

"Done!" She peeks out of the tent wearing more pink—short shorts and a tank top—and a ridiculous grin.

I start to shrug off my wet shirt.

"Oh jeepers ..." She hides back inside the tent. "Things I don't need to see."

I smirk to myself.

"I'm ready when you are," she calls.

"Ready for what?"

"You to come inside."

I unzip the flap the rest of the way.

"I can't see you."

Just when I'm certain things can't get any crazier, they do. She's perched in the corner in lotus pose on her sleeping bag with a pink satin sleep mask over her eyes.

"Just tell me when you're dressed."

With my back to her, I pull up my gym shorts, sans underwear, halfway up my legs. "I'm basically there."

"Okay—oh! Oh, oh, oh! No! You are *not* dressed yet." She slaps her hands over her face, fumbling to get her mask back down over her eyes. "Why would you do that?"

I slide my shorts up the rest of the way and pull on a T-shirt before hunching down in front of her to peel her hands away from her face.

Avery exhales in relief until her gaze meets my T-shirt.

My heart has no room for you,
but the trunk of my car definitely does.

"Nice shirt. You know, a lesser woman would be offended by you wearing it in her presence."

"But you're definitely not a lesser woman, are you?"

"No." Her timid reply holds no conviction.

"Well, I'm calling it a night."

Her head jerks back. "It's not even nine."

I grab my toothbrush. "I'm an early riser."

"Ugh! Not me." She wrestles with her sleeping bag. "We need to stop and pick me up a blowup mattress.

There's no way in hell I'm sleeping on the ground from here to L.A."

"Noted." I brush my teeth and fall like a tree onto my sleeping bag while she fumbles with her shitload of stuff.

Somewhere between her bitching about the temperature in the tent and the lumpy ground, I fall asleep.

By six the next morning, she's snoring loud enough to wake every animal within a five-mile radius. Naturally, I take a video of it with my phone. At some point, I will have to bring her to heel, and I think this little piece of cinematography will do the trick.

"Rise and shine. It's time to hit the road."

She grumbles rolling to her side. "Oh my back ..." Peeking out from under her eye mask, she inspects me. "Did you shower?"

"Bathed in the creek after my jog."

"You've jogged already?"

"Yes. Get up. Let's go."

"I need a bathroom. A shower."

"The creek feels amazingly refreshing this morning."

Avery sits up, fiddling with her hair again. "I'm not bathing in the creek."

"Then you can grab a shower at the next stop. Campgrounds with facilities."

"Pee! I need to pee, Jake! Why do you make me spell everything out for you?"

"Oh ..." I hold up a finger and retrieve a gift for her from my plastic container.

"What the hell is this?" She frowns as I hand her the gift.

"It's a feminine urination device. You can use it to stand up and piss. Basically, it's a portable penis."

She pulls it out of the tube and looks at the directions. "Huh ... looks pretty simple."

I nod with pride.

She grabs her pink silk robe and slides her feet into heeled slippers with feathers on the top. In all fairness, when she packed for her trip to visit her dad, she probably never expected to be sleeping in a tent, but seriously ... heeled slippers?

Brushing by me, she sniffs. "You smell good, like soapy good."

"I used liquid Castile soap in the creek."

"I'm not bathing in that creek. There's no way to get clean in dirty water."

I shrug. "Well, you sure think I smell clean."

"Humph." Avery takes off to find a spot behind a tree to pee.

After a few expletives, she returns, flicking the funneled device at me. I let it fall to the ground since it's covered in urine, just like her inner thighs and silk robe.

"I've got pee all over myself and THERE'S NO SHOWER!"

I bite back my smile as she marches over to the creek. "Wanna use my soap?"

"Yes, get the fucking soap and throw that stupid practical joke in the trash. Clearly a cruel man invented that."

After she simmers off in the creek and dresses to the nines again for the second day of our trip, I load up the pickup while she pouts in the front seat, messing with her tangled and ratted hair.

"I need a shower so bad ..." she says for the hundredth time. "I'm disintegrating from the outside in."

"Taking off?"

I glance up and cringe as my friend, Addy, walks our way from the house.

"You forgot your razor." She holds up her hand with my razor.

"What the fuck?" Avery whispers, kicking open her door the rest of the way.

"Oh." Addy's gaze flits from me to Avery. "You have a guest?" She holds out her hand to Avery. "I'm Addy. Jake didn't mention you were with him. Did you need to shower inside too?"

My balls crawl up into my body for protection as Avery slowly turns toward me.

CHAPTER SEVEN

Avery plots my long, torturous death with one single look before returning her attention to Addy. "I'm Avery and I would love a shower. I would be forever in your debt for a shower. I'm certain I would sell my soul for a shower."

Addy laughs. "The shower is free. You can keep your soul and leave here debt free."

"Sorry." I offer both women a tight smile. "Where are my manners? Addy, Avery. Avery, Addy. Sounds like a rhyme."

Addy smiles. Avery does not.

Swarley whines. That's basically all he does. He spent most of the night under the outside cover to the tent, probably to avoid the warm fuzzies between Avery and me. He whined, Avery told him to get inside the tent. He refused.

I stayed out of it.

Not my dog. Not my problem.

"Have you eaten, Avery? Can I get you something?"

"Avery's on a water fast." I pull out her suitcases, not knowing which one has her bathing shit.

Avery lets Swarley out of the back of the truck since

we're clearly not leaving for awhile. "I *was* yesterday, but I'm breaking the fast this morning. If it wouldn't be too much trouble, I'd be happy with a banana or a handful of crackers. I'm starving."

Addy nods toward the house. "I think I can do better than a banana and a handful of crackers. I'm a little surprised Chef Matthews didn't offer you something from his stash."

I roll my eyes as Avery tugs her suitcases toward the house.

"Jake, *manners*. Don't make her lug those suitcases." Addy punches me in the arm.

"Avery's very independent."

Avery releases the suitcases and keeps walking without a glance back. "I'm really not. Swarley, go lie down." She points to a shady spot before the steps to the front door.

Addy snickers as I grab the suitcases, holding my breath to keep from grumbling.

"Top of the stairs to the left, Avery. Towels are in the warmer. Help yourself to soap, shampoo, absolutely anything. I'll start making breakfast."

"Thank you so much." Avery gives Addy a genuine, I-owe-you-my-life smile, but when her gaze lands on me nudging her toward the stairs, she narrows her eyes, jaw muscles working overtime.

I smirk. "I'm not claustrophobic. You can tie me up before you kill me. Have you ever tied a man up, Avery?"

In spite of her obvious hatred toward me at the moment, her lips fight what I know is a grin.

"Anything else?" I set her suitcases just outside of the bathroom door.

After making a slow inspection of the bathroom, she turns back to me. "Your friend has good taste in decor."

I lean against the doorframe. "She does."

"Except when it comes to friends." Avery crosses her arms over her chest. "You are a terrible person. The king of scumbags. I don't know how someone as nice as her ever befriended you."

I nod, biting my lips together. "I'll be downstairs. Take your time as long as it's less than twenty minutes."

"Asshole." She grabs the door.

"Princess." I step back just as she slams it in my face.

"Still here?"

I turn toward the familiar Latin accent. "Yes, Quinn, unfortunately I'm still here." I head down the stairs as Addy's husband follows me.

"Gentlemen." Addy eyes us both with her have-you-been-playing-nicely look as her hands stay busy preparing food in their gourmet kitchen.

"Beautiful." Quinn presses his chest to her back, kissing her neck and whispering something in her ear that makes her blush.

She nudges him with her elbow and clears her throat. "So, Jake, you've found a good match, huh?"

I pull out the barstool and slide onto it as Quinn pours a glass of juice. "Avery?" I chuckle. "Just met her. I'm giving her and the dog a ride to L.A. for a friend."

"Wow!" Addy's eyes shoot open wide. "That's how you treat someone you just met? You must really like her."

"What?" I jerk my head back.

"You're pretending that she irritates you, when what really irritates you is that she does in fact rub you the wrong way for whatever reason, yet you're *still* attracted to her."

I glance at Quinn. He eyes me over the rim of his juice glass.

"I hated Quinn ... seriously hated him." Addy twists her lips.

"Thanks a lot, baby." He sets his glass in the sink. "I'll be in my office. Let me know when the kiddos wake up."

She shakes her head. "It's summer. I don't think we'll see them for another hour or so."

"You're happy." I smile.

Addy matches my smile. "Deliriously. But you know this, so stop trying to change the subject."

"What subject?"

"You and Avery."

I lace my fingers behind my head. "There is no me and Avery. I've known her for two seconds. She's a diva. I prefer the dog to her, but I feel indebted to a friend, so I'm sacrificing my summer road trip to chauffeur them to L.A."

"She's pretty." Addy smirks.

"She's fake looking."

"Does she have a boyfriend?"

"No. Yes. I don't know. What does it matter?" Irritation strains my words.

Addy returns her attention to the plates she's assembling with fruit, avocado toast, tomatoes, and sprouts. "Oh man ... she's way up under your skin already. This is going to get really good. You should message me with updates."

"So remind me again why you're home?"

"Nice diversion, Jake. I told you, Elena didn't want to miss her friend's birthday party, so we agreed to wait another day."

"Oh, yeah, that's right. So, how are the kids?"

"Jake, you're such a guy. They're fine. We're fine. And don't think we're done talking about *you*." She slides a plate in front of me. "But first, I'm going to go check on Avery."

Avery

"AVERY?" Addy knocks on the door.

I open it, wrapped in a white robe that was folded like new next to the shower. "I hope you don't mind." I tug at the sash to the robe.

"That's what it's there for." She tucks her long, blond hair behind her ears. It looks a lot healthier than mine.

"Jake made me bathe in the creek. I can't tell you how amazing that shower felt." I ease the towel off my head.

"Jake's got a great personality. He's such a jokester."

"Jokester?" I glance at her reflection in the mirror as I work the comb through my hair with cautious strokes. "I'm not sure he's joking." Thinking back to last night in the creek, I mentally smile. That was fun, a kind of fun I hadn't had in years. "Does he joke with you like that? Would he make you bathe in a creek?"

Addy rubs her lips together. "I had a different relationship with Jake years ago, and yes, it was playful."

I pause the comb. "Different?"

"It was before I married my husband, Quinn. We broke up for awhile, and Jake, who worked for me at the time, was exactly what I needed at that point in my life. He made me feel young and carefree. We had so much fun together."

She's good with words, particularly saying everything and nothing at the same time. "So ... you were in a relationship with Jake?"

"Yes, a casual one."

I nod slowly, resuming my combing. "I just got out of a relationship. Anthony wanted to marry me."

"Oh, I'm sorry. What happened?"

"He lied to me. Said he didn't like chocolate."

Addy's forehead wrinkles. "Did you find his chocolate stash?"

"No. Caught him eating chocolate mousse ... in the kitchen ... off the naked body of his cook."

"Ohhh ... that's ..."

I shrug. "Pretty much the story of my life." Whether she wants to hear it or not, I back up the truck and dump my entire saga onto her. If my sister, Sydney, were here, she'd be my sounding board, therapist, and surgeon to put my life back together. By the time I finish doing my hair, makeup, and filing my nails, Addy has the whole story.

"I'm very sorry, Avery."

I draw in a deep breath, feeling so much better for finding a sympathetic ear—the shower and well-lit mirror to do my makeup helped too. "Thank you for listening. It's not the end of the world. I'm just in a rut."

"Come on, let's feed you. And don't let Jake ruffle your feathers. He has his own issues, but I thought when he gave up fighting, he let those go. Apparently, you've unintentionally brought a few to the surface again."

I follow her down the stairs. "Fighting?"

"Yes. He was an underground fighter, ultimate fighter ... something like that. I'm not an expert on it, but I watched him send a guy out on a stretcher. Not my thing, but it was kind of ..." She glances over her shoulder and winks. "Hot."

Well great. I'm traveling with someone who has no issue beating another human within inches of their life. If I didn't feel I could be that next human, I might share Addy's assessment of Jake's strength being kind of hot.

"Wait."

Addy stops at the bottom of the stairs. "Yeah?"

I glance around, seeing no sign of anyone else in

earshot. "So you had a fling with Jake, yet he comes here and camps on your property, uses your bathroom, and your husband is okay with it? Does he not know about your past with Jake?"

Her smile is a bit wicked. "Oh, Quinn knows everything. It took a few years before I could even say Jake's name without him losing his shit. But Jake took over my business, and I still make investments in it. Jake and I share a passion that's for a greater good—changing the way people look at food. And Quinn loves me, so he *deals* with my relationship with Jake. I think their relationship has finally hit lukewarm, but I'm guessing that's where it will peak."

"Mom?"

Addy looks up the stairs with a smile that I've seen a million times before on my sister's face. It's the mother smile. "Elena, good morning, sleepyhead."

A blond-haired girl with olive skin makes her way down the stairs, eyeing me the whole time.

"Elena, this is Avery, Jake's friend."

I'm not Jake's friend. Not by a long shot. Not in this lifetime. Not if he was the last man standing. Nope. Never ever. "Hi, Elena. Nice to meet you. I have a niece that's just about your size. She likes to surf. What do you like to do?"

"I sail on a boat with my mom." She hugs Addy.

"That sounds fun."

"It is." Addy kisses the top of her head. "Elena loves the water. Her twin, Ben, gets so seasick. Go figure."

"There's my girl." Jake grins, showing all those perfectly irritating teeth.

"Jake," Elena whispers, hiding behind Addy.

Oh my gosh. She's blushing.

Addy chuckles. "My darling daughter has a crush on Jake, much to her father's disapproval."

"We've got time to get your dad's blessing on our marriage in another decade."

Elena goes from pink to chili pepper red when Jake kisses her on the cheek.

"Eat up, Avery. We're leaving soon. I fed Swarley while you two ladies were upstairs talking about me." He gives me a pointed look while passing by to head up the stairs. "I'll grab your luggage. Don't forget to tip the bellboy."

"Yes, come eat." Addy motions to the kitchen. "I'm going to pack you some food to go as well."

"Oh, you don't have to do that." I start to inhale the food.

"I insist."

I don't argue. I'll need my strength to bring down a two-hundred-plus-pound fighter who thinks he can manipulate me with lies. Before I take my last bite, Satan stabs my happy bubble with his pointy trident.

"Ready?"

I ignore him. "Addy, is this quartz or granite?" I rub the white countertop.

"Avery, chop chop."

Addy grins as her gaze ping-pongs between us. I turn my last bite into five, like a mouse nibbling cheese.

"Quartz."

"My dad built my mom this house to get her back." Elena grins, picking sliced strawberries off her avocado toast.

"Is that so? Tell me more." I shift my stool toward Elena kneeled on the stool next to mine.

"No time for more. I'm leaving without you in five minutes."

Poke. Poke.

I'm going to stab that trident up his ass. He just doesn't know it yet.

"You have a lovely home, Addy. I can't thank you enough for your generosity. It's hard to find truly kind people these days."

Addy hands me a bag. "You are welcome anytime."

She won't think that when I murder her business buddy. "It was nice meeting you, Elena."

Elena ignores me because her dreamy Jake is in the room. Poor girl is headed down the road of heartbreak. She will cross a million Jakes in her life, and most of them will be dick cheese.

"Taking off?"

Hold. The. Phone.

God has appeared.

Dear Heavenly Father,

I had no idea you were Latino in your human form. Good choice! Are you here to save me from Satan?

"Yes." Jake gives Latino God a slight smile.

Addy married a god. I want to high-five her, but we haven't known each other long enough to celebrate snagging a really hot guy.

"Quinn, this is Jake's friend, Avery. Avery this is my husband, Quinn."

Jake grumbles something under his breath at the mention of our friendship. I'm right there with him, but I don't grumble because I'm too busy sighing a dreamy breath of envy.

"Nice to meet you, Avery." Quinn holds out his hand.

It takes me a moment to shake it since I'm in a daze from his sexy accent. I need a guy with an accent. Okay, I don't need any guy at the moment, but if I decide to entertain the idea of male companionship again, he will need to be Latino *and* upfront with his feelings about chocolate.

"Very nice seeing you—uh, I mean meeting you." I cringe behind my smile.

Super smooth.

He pulls his hand from mine because I don't let go. I like his hand and all that goes with it.

Very nice seeing you.

Geesh. It's as if we've met before. Nope. I meant it in the most literal sense. Seeing, staring, gawking at Quinn is very nice. Seriously, would it be too weird to high-five Addy? I want to give her a slow clap for a job well done.

"You for thank everything."

Addy chuckles.

I said that. Gah! I'm tongue-tied over a man while standing in front of his wife.

"Or ..." Jake grips my arm, pulling me out of the kitchen. "Thank you for everything."

"Yes ..." I nod, mildly grateful for my translator. The gratitude will wear off by the time we get in his truck.

We make it out the door without any further embarrassment, load up Swarley, and take off for our next destination. Dear God, please let it involve a room key, running water, and thick terry cloth robes. What are the chances my asshole driver knows other ridiculously rich people between here and L.A.?

"Just so you know, I'm *done* talking to you. What you did was unforgivable."

Keeping his eyes on the road, Jake nods. "I'm totally good with you being done talking to me, but I'd hardly call what happened this morning *unforgivable*." He turns up the music.

As minutes and miles pass, my bladder fills—mourning

each rest stop we pass. If Swarley would speak up with a simple whine, Jake might pull over for a pit stop.

Nope.

Swarley's asleep.

Bump. Bump. Bump.

After four hours, we hit a stretch of road that's in need of new pavement. I could ask him to pull over, but I made a vow of silence until he apologizes to me. If I urinate in his truck, will it expedite his apology without me saying more than "oops?"

When the St. Louis arch comes into sight, he pulls off the main road, takes a few dizzying lefts and rights before pulling into a gas station. My bladder cheers while my dignity wipes sweat from its brow.

I jump out, waddling into the building as quickly as I can without springing a leak.

"Don't worry. I'll let *your* dog out."

I don't have enough bladder control to acknowledge Jake. Maybe he can read my mind. *Yes, Jake, let Swarley out, and I won't piss all over your truck. Fair trade? I think so too.*

"Ladies' room?" I flash the cashier a tight smile.

"Unisex restroom. Just one. Side of the building."

Gah! Side of the building. We're in a major city. The restrooms should be inside the building. I make a U-turn.

"Ma'am, you'll need the key." He holds up a key attached to a chain—attached to an old steering wheel. It looks like something from a vintage car or maybe even a tractor. It's huge.

I grab the steering wheel and drive myself to the side of the building. Jake glances up from the grassy area by the street where Swarley sniffs for the perfect spot to mark. Jake rubs his hand over his mouth.

Go ahead, Jake the Jerk, laugh all you want. I don't care. Nothing in the world matters at this moment as much as the emptying of my bladder.

No toilet seat liner.

No place to hang my purse or the steering wheel.

Screw it.

I slide my purse strap around my neck, do the same with the steering wheel, shimmy out of my denim shorts, and plop down on the germ-infested toilet seat.

"Oh ... my .... god ..." I whisper, closing my eyes. This feels better than my last orgasm.

After peeing out an entire swimming pool, I reach for the toilet paper.

None. Why doesn't that surprise me?

I don't have a single tissue in my purse, so I'm forced to shake and go.

Wash my hands.

Shake them dry as well because ... yep, no paper towels or a hand dryer.

Opening the door with my shirt protecting my hand, I let it close behind me. Then I work the steering wheel back over my head to lock the door.

But ...

"Dammit!" It catches on my purse strap so I twist it free, trying not to damage the strap.

Left. Right. Up. Down.

I work it in every direction, tipping my chin up, tucking it down, working the steering wheel and my head every which way.

"Ugh!" I cringe as it pulls at my hair. Can't have that. It just slipped over my head. Why won't it come off?

"Don't lock it. I need to take a piss. Swarley's back in

the truck. You're welcome. And don't worry, I paid for the gas."

I roll my eyes at his agitating voice behind me. "It's all yours." Turning, I push back my shoulders, chin up, like I don't have my purse and a steering wheel hanging from my neck.

He lifts an eyebrow. "Nice bling."

My lips curl together.

"The cashier said you have the key. Give it to me so I can lock it back up when I'm done."

Dear Heavenly Father,

I'm sorry. The purity ring I wore in high school was a promise to you that I would keep my virginity. I shouldn't have used it as a revirginization ring. If I wasn't supposed to give my body to another until later in life, would it have killed you to delay the onset of puberty? Totally not putting all the blame on you, just thinking aloud. Anyway ... if you still love me. Hell—I mean heck—if you ever loved me, could you please let this steering wheel slip off my head as easily as it slipped on? In three ... two ... one.

Flashing Jake my most confident smile, I put all of my trust in God and ease the steering wheel over my head. Only, it catches on my chin, then my nose, then my ear, threatening to rip out my diamond stud earring.

My gaze lifts to the sky. *Unconditional love my ass!*

"Avery, the key. Let's go." Jake holds out his hand.

"Ugh!" I grip the steering wheel. "Son of a—mother fu—damn this life!"

Jake's gaze lands on the key dangling from the chain, dangling from my *bling*. "Do I even want to know?"

I deflate. "Stupid bathroom has no hooks, and I didn't want to set anything on the ground. And who puts a key on a flipping steering wheel—"

He silences me with a flat palm held up accompanied by a half dozen headshakes. "It wasn't a rhetorical question. I was seriously asking myself if I wanted to know. The answer is no. I don't want to know how you ended up with a steering wheel stuck around your neck."

I'm on a road trip with the Devil. How does this happen to a preacher's daughter?

"Don't give me that look like this is all my fault."

He squints, scratching his newly shaven chin. "Is it not your fault? Dog shit on your foot, a lost sandal, and a steering wheel stuck around your neck all within the span of twenty-four hours. Whose fault might this be?"

"Just ..." I frown. "Go do your thing. I'm going to talk to the guy inside."

Jake chuckles. "Good idea. I'm sure this happens all the time. I bet he'll abracadabra you right out of there. But would you mind waiting until I get done in here. I'd like to see how he fixes your situation. You know ... in case it happens again along the way."

Resting my hands on my hips, I huff out an exasperated breath. "Would it kill you to treat me with a little more compassion and humanity?"

He opens the bathroom door and looks back over his shoulder. "Ask me that when you don't have a steering wheel stuck around your neck." Holding up his phone, he takes a picture and his mouth twists into a stupid smirk just before he shuts the door.

"Did you seriously just take a picture of me!?"

"Yep." He hollers from the other side of the door. "I needed a good snap. Thinking of letting my friends caption it."

Bastard!

CHAPTER EIGHT

Turns out Avery is the first customer to get her head stuck in the steering wheel.

"Jake!"

The attendant coughs to hide his amusement as I work it over her head.

Her hands claw my arms. "My hair! Oh my god, my hair! My neck. My earrings. Stop!"

"Get in the truck." I point to the door after she stumbles backward, realizing her freedom. I hand the steering wheel to the cashier while pinning her with a firm look. "Don't touch anything. Don't step in anything. Straight to the truck. Can you handle that, Princess?"

Her hands ghost over her hair, surveying any possible damage. She nods. I think she's actually shaking a bit. Unexpected tussles with steering wheels will do that to you.

She inspects her hair all the way to the truck as the cashier scans my bottles of water.

"Just a sec ..." I sift through a cubby of T-shirts, looking for my size. "This too."

A minute later, I'm out the door, shrugging off one shirt

and pulling on my new one. Avery slaps the visor mirror shut when I open the door. Of course she was messing with her hair.

"What's that supposed to mean?" She eyes my new shirt.

"If I have to explain it, then it's clear why you've had relationship issues."

Karma is Like 69
You Get What You Give

"I'm not a fan of Karma at the moment."

I start the truck. "And 69?" Rolling my lips together, I hide my grin.

"It's ..." She shrugs, drumming her fingers on her legs, lips twisted. "Efficient."

Chuckling, I pull out of the parking lot. Most of the time I want to wrap my hands around her neck and shake, but there have been moments, like now, that I find myself intrigued, mildly entertained by her remarks.

"And if you ask me if I'm efficient, I will jump out of the truck. I don't like talking about that stuff."

"Are you efficient?"

She giggles, shaking her head while giving her focus to the window. It's a surprisingly pleasant sound. "Sorry. I'm still mad at you. We're not having this conversation."

"No conversation works for me." I turn up the radio.

She grabs a container that Addy sent with her. I give her a quick sidelong glance.

"I'm not sharing. You didn't share your berries with me yesterday."

I grin, returning my focus to the road.

"God ..." She hums. "This is the best chocolate zucchini bread I've ever had."

"It is."

Avery licks her fingers. "No Pilates. No calorie counting. I'm going to pay for this."

"How so?"

"Hello? Hips, ass, abs. All the places excess food likes to settle on my body."

At the stoplight, I give her the once-over. "Nothing seems to be settling on your hips, ass, and abs."

"Yet," she mumbles over a mouthful of bread.

"Happy, healthy, helpful."

Wrapping up the rest of the bread, she shoots me a questioning glance. "I'm not following."

"Instead of hips, ass, and abs, you should focus on happy, healthy, and helpful. Are you happy? Do you have your health? At the end of every day, can you say that you helped someone?"

"Helped someone?"

I nod. "It doesn't have to be grand, like donating a kidney. Something as simple as opening the door for a stranger. Did you make someone feel good? Did you put the needs of another above your own? Did you make a difference in the world?"

After a few seconds, she releases a long exhale, turning her attention back to her window. "Are *you* happy, healthy, and helpful?"

"Well ..." I shoot her a quick look. "There's a stranger in my passenger seat and her dog in my backseat. I'd say I'm quite helpful. I exercise every day and eat real food. Yes, I'd say I'm healthy."

I pull into an angled parking spot in the downtown.

"And happy? Are you happy?"

Turning off the ignition, I shrug. "I'm content."

"Cont—"

Shutting the door before she can respond, I glance up at the partly cloudy sky.

Happy? Two out of three ain't bad.

My phone vibrates.

Deedy: *Hey! Just wanted to thank you again for taking Avery and Swarley back to L.A. :) You are a kind human, Jake Matthews. Please never forget that.*

"Deedy ..." I mumble, walking around to the other side of my truck. "I'm enduring this for you—only you." Opening Avery's door, I hide my gritted teeth behind my tightlipped smile. "S'up, Princess?"

She rubs her lips together, focusing on her reflection in the visor mirror while capping her lip gloss. "Freshening up."

"For what?"

"For getting out. By the way, where are we going?" She uncaps a tube of mascara.

No. No, no, no ...

I grab it from her hands, shove it back in her makeup bag, and toss the makeup bag into her fancy purse. "We're grabbing lunch before setting up camp. Nobody here cares about the color of your lips or the length of your lashes. Get out."

Flipping the visor up, she turns toward me, still rubbing her lips together. Her gaze scans up and down my body, pausing an extra few seconds on my arms. "Funny ... you seem to feel the need to mark your skin—to express yourself outwardly to the world. Yet I'm a princess for wanting to fix my makeup?"

I grin—a real one. Why? Hell if I know. Lifting my arm

between us, I twist it to show her some of my *self-expression*.

"Why do you wear so much makeup?" I glance up at her as she inspects my arm.

"My lips are pale," Avery murmurs, tracing her finger over the script on my arm for a brief second before her hand balls into a fist as if I burned it. Vulnerable, blue eyes flit up to meet my gaze.

If she weren't such a pill, I would say beneath her ten thousand layers of vanity, Avery just might be pretty fucking beautiful.

If...

"My lashes are too thin. My skin tone is uneven."

"I get tattoos to remember where I've been, people I've loved, and what's important in life."

Her focus slips, eyes averting to the distance beyond my shoulder.

"I'm not hiding anything behind the ink on my skin. It doesn't cover any perceived imperfections."

Keeping her gaze over my shoulder, she twists her lips and grunts a laugh. "Well..." she shoves me out of the way and hops out of the truck "...lucky you. Come on, Swarley."

He jumps out, running straight to the light post to paint it with yellow graffiti.

"I'm not eating." She nearly stumbles over the curb, trying to reel Swarley back in on his leash with her good hand. "You're killing me, dog. What did I ever do to you?"

Swarley glances back at her, cocking his head. I think his expression says, "Are you talking to me, Princess?"

"Then I'll get my food to go so we can get to the campsite quicker."

The fake smile on her fake face pleases me. Why do I

find such pleasure in bringing out the jilted-woman side of her?

"Perfect." Her lack of sincerity doubles. "There's nothing I love more than watching you re-live your failed childhood. How old were you when they kicked you out of Boy Scouts for being the only kid roasting a piece of tofu on the campfire?"

And ... that's why I felt content letting her bathe in the creek this morning.

"Careful, Princess, snarky comments lower your metabolism. If you don't watch what you say, you won't be able to fasten your fancy Penelope shorts tomorrow."

"*Paige* shorts, you stupid grass grazer. And if you don't stop calling me princess, I'm going to bludgeon you in your sleep."

It's really hard to take all one hundred and twenty (at most) pounds of Avery Montgomery seriously when I know she would never lift a finger to hurt me because she might break a nail. But damn! I sure do find her feistiness oddly addictive. So of course, I can't resist ...

"Paige, Penelope, *Princess*. I can't keep them straight. Sorry." I wink, rolling my lips between my teeth.

"Sleep with one eye open." Her eyes narrow as she stabs me in the chest with her finger.

I chuckle. "Hang tight while I grab my lunch." Sidestepping her, I laugh some more. "Don't lose anything or step in anything ... and for the love of God ... don't stick your head into anything."

Avery bestows another round of the silent treatment upon me while we drive to the campground. It's not my usual stop, but after adjusting my travel dates to accommodate the princess and her steed, I had to scrounge for a new place to camp.

"I'm going for a hike." I hop onto my tailgate and change my shoes.

Avery remains silent, still sitting in the passenger's seat of the truck, flipping pages of her fashion magazine while Swarley overdoses on all the smells around our tent—the tent I put up by myself.

"I'd invite you, but the trails are not paved in gold or lined with red carpet."

The door to my truck clicks open.

I grin.

"For your information ..."

Give me all the information, Ave.

I inwardly smirk, shutting the tailgate.

She slams the door and arches her back, moving it from side to side. "I'm in excellent physical condition—except for my hand." She frowns, holding it to her chest. "I do Pilates, yoga, cardio, strength training—"

"Great." I nod toward the direction of the trailhead. "Grab your dog. Let's get in a few miles before we settle down for the pre-bludgeoning campfire."

My new favorite game is called Make Avery Smile because I find her tolerable—just—when she fights back a grin or laughter. Life is too short to take yourself so seriously.

"Come on, Swarley." She whistles.

"Shoes?" I stare at her rhinestone flip-flops.

"How long is the hike?" She tips her chin up.

"More than ten yards. Change your shoes. I'm not carrying you."

"Pfft ... I'm good. In spite of what you might think from

the past two days, I'm not a damsel in distress. I can walk for miles in these. They are actually more comfortable than they look."

I have a long list of thoughts and lingering first impressions of this woman, but something tells me taking her for a hike in flip-flops will not change a single one of them.

"I'm not carrying you."

"I'm not deaf. I heard you the first time. I won't need you to carry me. Sheesh ..." She attaches Swarley's leash, flipping and flopping her way to the start of the trail.

"This won't end well ..." I mumble, spending a little too much time staring at her sashaying ass. My dick gives me a stern warning.

"Jaaake?"

"Wait, buddy." I whistle and Swarley stops. After pouring him some water in the lid of my canteen, I retreat in the direction of the whiney voice calling my name.

Avery cringes, easing onto an old tree stump.

"What is it?" Planting my hands on my hips, I glare down at her, daring her to say one fucking word about her feet.

"We've been walking for miles. How much farther do we have to go?"

"Another mile or so. Why?" My eyebrows lift.

Say it, Princess. I dare you.

"I'm ..." Her lips curl between her teeth.

"You're what?"

"Hungry and thirsty. I didn't bring water with me."

Her feet are streaked in red marks from rocks and brush scratching them, and I'm certain the area between her first and second toes has to be raw. But ... she's hungry and thirsty.

I nod, pulling a granola bar from the side pocket of my shorts.

She turns her nose up. "Why is it wrapped like that?"

I stare at the bar wrapped in parchment paper inside a plastic bag. "Like what?"

"Like you didn't buy it from a store."

"Because I made it."

"Oh ..." She takes it from me as if it contains a grenade missing its pin.

"Come on. Eat while you walk so we can get back to the tent before it gets dark."

Giving me a tight grin, she stands. I don't miss the flash of a grimace as her step falters.

"You good?"

"Fine." Her shoulders pull backward. "Water?" She stares at the canteen in my right hand.

"Sure." I hand it to her.

Avery twists it in one direction then the other. "What side did you drink out of?"

"Really? You've probably eaten pig assholes in the form of a hot dog, yet you're worried about my germs?"

She glares at me.

I smirk. "Fine. I'll pour some in the lid."

Tiny, painful grunts sound behind me as I lead her down the hill toward Swarley.

"Wait! No. Dude ..." Her nose scrunches as I start to pour water into the canteen lid. "Did you let Swarley drink out of that?"

"Yes. I gave water to *your* dog since you didn't think to bring any. You're welcome. So if you are truly thirsty, then you will have to make the tough decision." I hold up the canteen in one hand and the water-filled lid in my other hand. "My germs or Swarley's?"

Her gaze flits between my two hands.

"You know ..." Extending out my hand with the lid, I withdraw one of her options. "I don't want your pig-asshole germs, and he's your dog, so if you want the water, you'll have to drink it from the lid." Tipping up the canteen, I take a long swig.

"I do not have pig-asshole germs!" She tries to snag the canteen from my hand, practically hugging my arm in the process. "Give me a drink."

I turn in a circle, keeping the coveted prize above her head as she chases my hand like a dog after its tail.

"Give me a drink! Stop being such a big jerk!"

I stop.

She stumbles over my feet.

With my free arm, I catch her, holding her to my chest.

She pants, eyes wild with adrenaline and maybe a little fear. "Don't hurt me," she whispers.

I flinch. Has someone hurt her? Physically hurt her?

Searching her eyes, I look for the answer. I don't see it.

"I might kill you, Avery. But I won't hurt you."

Her unblinking eyes widen.

I grin. "It will be quick and painless." Releasing her from my chest, I hold up my three middle fingers. "Scout's honor."

After several long seconds, she blinks. I offer her the canteen.

Slowly shaking her head, she clears her throat. "Is it true you had opponents leave on stretchers after fighting you?"

Do I want the upper hand? Do I need it?

"Yes." My toothy grin does nothing to bring color back

to her face—except her lips. Whatever the hell she put on her lips still shimmers red.

Keeping her gaze locked to mine, she wraps her hand around the canteen, just above mine, and pulls it to her mouth.

Gulp. Gulp. Gulp.

After draining the rest of it, she steps back, breathless, with a drop of water running down her chin. "Did you feel bad?"

"No. Well ... maybe in the beginning. But I learned to let those emotions go."

"Why?"

I shrug. "I didn't jump those men in an alley and beat the shit out of them. It's a sport. There are winners and losers. One of us was going to end up facedown. That's just how it works."

"Do you still do that?"

I shake my head while rubbing my thumb along her wet chin. Avery pulls back, rolling her lips together and feathering her fingers over the spot where my thumb touched her face.

"Can I be honest with you?" She bats her eyelashes.

Bats her eyelashes. What the ...

"No. Swarley, let's go." Turning, I let Swarley lead the way down the hill.

"You don't even know what I'm going to say." Avery chases after us.

"I do." I pick up my pace.

"Jake!"

"Nope."

"But Jake—"

"Not happening."

"My feet hurt!"

"Not happening."

Her shoes skid against the lose rock behind me.

Flip flop flip flop.

"I'll pay you!"

I stop, turning slowly. "How much?"

She hops on one foot while rubbing the other, then changes feet. "Twenty dollars."

I grunt a laugh. "Twenty dollars? To carry you a mile? I bet you spent at least fifty dollars on those stupid shoes."

She murmurs a quick response. I don't hear it clearly, but I'm fairly certain she said, "Two hundred."

"I'll carry you half the way for one hundred dollars."

Avery traps the corner of her lower lip between her teeth, nose wrinkled. "Twenty is my limit."

"Your limit, huh? Don't even get me started on my limits." With a quick whistle, I bring Swarley back onto the trail.

"At the end of the day, don't you want to be able to say that you helped someone?"

"Princess?" I keep walking. "Do you have a steering wheel stuck around your neck? No? Well, then I think I already did my helpful deed for the day. I will sleep *just fine* tonight."

"Until you wake up dead!"

I chuckle. "Aw, yes ... until that. There's nothing worse than waking up dead."

By the time we make it to the campsite, she's fuming. "You are *not* a gentleman!"

I stack wood and paper into the pit and start a fire. She plops into one of the camping chairs and slips off her flip-flops. Then she rants.

And rants.

And rants.

Squatting down in front of her, I rest my hands on her bare thighs. She jumps, holding her breath.

Mission accomplished.

"I need some peace and quiet now. Can you do that? Can you just not talk for a bit?"

She frowns, her rage simmering into something resembling defeat. "Why didn't you help me out? Why would my dad and Deedy let someone like you take me across the country?"

I squeeze her legs until her muscles flex beneath my touch. There's no denying she has spectacular legs, but flirting is not my intention. Still ...

Fucking spectacular legs.

"I did help you. I suggested you wear sensible hiking shoes. Why should I be an enabler to your lack of common sense, stubbornness, excessive vanity, or whatever weird, self-destructive, female fucked-upness you seem to have?"

Her chin dips, gaze focused on my hands. I expect to see her bottom lip start to quiver and tears fill her eyes.

"I'm not happy," she whispers.

No tears.

No quivering lip.

There's just this shell of a woman with emotionless words spoken in a numbing tone.

After a few moments of welcomed silence, I move my hands from her legs to her wrists on the arms of the chair. Easing my body back to standing, I lean over her, letting my face linger over the top of her head. For a few moments, I contemplate pressing my lips to her hair—a friendly kiss that says, "*Me neither.*"

But I don't. Instead, I press my forehead to the top of her head and give her wrists a slight squeeze. Avery sucks in a shaky breath. I close my eyes.

CHAPTER NINE

Avery

Day Three

"Psst …"

I nudge Jake. He groans.

"Psst!"

He rolls away from me.

"Jake! I need the truck keys," I whisper-yell.

Another groan.

My eyes flit between his bared torso turned away from me and his partially unzipped duffel bag at his feet. Jake has nice feet. I'm not sure I've ever thought this about a guy before. But—I move my phone's flashlight an inch closer—yes indeed, he has nice feet. Not a single nasty callous, and his toenails are perfect.

Not fair. What the heck, God? Why would you give a guy such perfect feet? Jackass Jake must use an expensive foot cream.

I roll my eyes at myself. What is this? The beginning of

a foot fetish? Therapy of some sort might be in my future. After one last inspection of his flawless feet, and maybe a nanosecond glance back up his bare torso—because why the hell not?—I inspect the contents of his bag.

It has five outer pockets, but I come up empty. No truck keys. Unzipping the main part feels a little too snoopy. Biting the corner of my lip, I sweep the beam of my phone's light across his still body. If I'm completely honest, his feet are attached to some other really nice body parts, but why start being honest now?

The light goes out. "Shit." I frown at the dead screen. What happened to my final three percent?

Key.

I need the key. I need to charge my phone.

"Jakey Jakey, wakey wakey," I whisper, knowing he's nothing more than a dead log on top of a sleeping bag. A dead log with sexy feet and a drool-worthy trunk I could climb—

Gah!

I must NEVER think of the Devil as sexy. Did I learn nothing about temptation from Eve and the complete debacle in Eden? A questionably flawed story if you ask me. Still—religion permanently haunts one's conscience, and I'm no exception.

Don't snoop.

Wait until he wakes up.

It's not like it's an emergency.

It's just my phone—my connection to the rest of the world, a way to see in the dark, keeper of time, contact list, social media notifications, my savior in an emergency ... MY LIFE!

Muzzling my conscience, I dive into the main compartment of Jake's duffle bag, the way a police officer would break open a door after a 9-1-1 call. It's filled with clothes, but within ten seconds I have all aforementioned clothes strewn all around me.

No keys.

A jingle startles me, and my head whips back, but it's just Swarley. "Don't!" I warn in my sternest whisper as he abandons his spot in the corner and plops down on my sleeping bag. "Get. Off!"

He shakes his head once. I realize how crazy that sounds, but it's true. Swarley is not your average dog, he's a demon—much like Jake—out to destroy me. He can do things like nod and shake his head as well as rip my poor hand apart when he sees something worth chasing, much like Anthony ripped my heart apart when he discovered that chocolate does in fact taste amazing.

Fucker.

Before my herbivorous travel buddy wakes up, I start shoving his clothes back into his bag, taking a deep inhale. What's that smell? It's good. Really good.

Herbaceous? Woodsy? Maybe piney, but we're not amidst that many pine trees here. Bringing one of Jake's shirts to my nose, I take a whiff.

Oh ... that's nice. Son of a bitch! Sexy—uh—I mean, soft feet *and* amazing detergent.

Eat the shiny red apple, Eve ...

I'm not going to eat his shirt, but I indulge in one more sniff before—

"Why are you smelling my underwear?"

"Shit!" I jump, tucking the shirt behind my back.

Jake jackknifes to sitting so his face is inches from mine, those deep blue eyes alight from the shard of moonlight filtering in from the tent's vent. They narrow a fraction as he inspects me kneeled next to his legs and his open duffle bag.

"My phone is dead." I breathe out past the booming of my racing heart.

"Your phone is dead?"

I nod slowly, staring at his mouth that's pulled into a firm line fighting something that resembles a smirk.

"And?"

I gulp down an ocean of saliva. "And I need to charge it."

I can't look away from his mouth. It's nice too.

For fuck's sake ...

Therapy. Lots of therapy.

"And?" He inches his head to the side a fraction.

"I was looking for the key to the truck."

"In my bag?"

I nod, ripping my focus from his lips to meet his gaze.

Jake surrenders to a cocky smile.

Asshole.

His gaze dips to my mouth, and it does very unwanted things to my body—specifically to parts of my body that are supposed to be on strike from giving a single shit about any man.

"But it's dark."

"Yes," I say with a ridiculous raspiness to my voice.

"So you're sniffing them out ... specifically in my underwear?"

"What?" I jerk my head back.

Playful eyes find mine, underscored by a gotcha grin.

"No, you sicko."

"Then what's behind your back."

"Nothing." My spine grows an inch. He's not going to make me squirm—anymore.

"Avery," he says my name a syllable at a time as he inches closer.

He's going to kiss me. Why is he going to kiss me? I hate him. And men. And tattoos. And vegans with freakishly soft feet.

My heart stops and the air in my lungs freezes as his cheek brushes past mine. Of course my stupid nipples boing out because they just don't know any better.

God ... *he* smells good. It's not just his clothes.

My lips part and my eyes leaden as his lips ghost next to my ear and his hand slides along my arm. Every inch of his naked torso radiates heat, and it's igniting mine.

"Give me my underwear," he whispers.

It takes my mushy mind several seconds to realize he's not going to kiss me or seduce me—NOT that I want him to do either.

I don't.

My nipples are just being rebels. I'll have a talk with them later.

After a pause, I jerk my arm away as he tries to take his shirt from me. "It's a shirt you big jerk, not your—"

The letters J-O-C on a wide waistband come into view as I dangle them between us.

My nose wrinkles. I drop them like they're on fire.

Jake, of course, grins. "The dirty ones are in the side pocket if that smell does it for you even more."

I die—not like a peaceful passing, more like a slow, torturous death where the murderer insists on embarrassing his victim before inching the tip of a knife into his victim's carotid artery.

"Nothing about you *does it* for me."

His eyebrows slide up his forehead as his gaze dips to inspect my chest. "You sure about that?"

Mother trucker ...

"I'm cold."

"You have sweat along your brow."

"It's a cold sweat."

"It's like eighty degrees in here."

"I have a sluggish thyroid."

His grin grows a fraction as his gaze dips to my mouth again for a brief second. "You should sprinkle kelp on your food."

"Where's the key to the truck?"

"What do my underwear smell like?"

I squint at him, desperate for a really good comeback. I *need* one. He's been one step ahead of me this entire trip. I NEED to get the upper hand, just once.

Vegan farts? No. That won't give me the upper hand.

Asscrack cologne? No. That's dumb.

Dick cheese? Maybe.

Putrid pubes? No. I'm not sure he has them. Maybe he's shaven in that region. I direct my gaze to just below his abs. It's too dark to say for sure, but I'm certain there's a teasing of a happy trail, surely that thing doesn't end in a barren convergence of skin, two low-hanging sacs, and a bobbing appendage.

Biting my lips together in contemplation, I glance back up at him. "Stop staring at my boobs."

"Stop staring at my junk."

"Oh my gosh!" I climb to my feet, finding the center of the tent where I can fully stand. "You are so full of yourself. I was not staring at your junk, I was just seeing if you had ..."

He lies back, propping his head up on a bent arm. It does nice things to his abs.

Avery ... you suck.

"If I had what? Junk?"

"Hair." There. I just said it.

He runs his other hand through his thick head of hair. My nipples are screwed.

"I used to have a shaved head, but I've had hair for several years."

My teeth work side to side. One chance. I just need one good chance to get the upper hand, but he snags it every time.

"But ... that's not the hair you were looking for. I'm guessing."

"The key, Jake."

He grins, scratching just below his navel at the start of his happy trail. "It goes all the way."

"The key, now."

"The sun's not up. I'm not letting you start my truck. There are other campers nearby. You don't need to make noise and fill the surrounding air with exhaust. Settle in with your dog and you can charge it in a few hours."

I glance back at Swarley, now sleeping in my spot. "I need to pee. I'll be back later." I shove my feet into my flip-flops. "Or not at all if I can find a kind soul to take me to the nearest airport. My sister will pay you a lot of money for returning Swarley to L.A."

Jake sits up, pulling on a tee and grabbing a flashlight. "Your sister can keep her money. If you find this kind soul, then I'm certain they will figure out a way to get your sister's dog back to her."

"Where are you going?" I ask as he stands close to me—too close.

"I'm taking you to the toilet up the hill."

"I know how to get there."

He moves past me and unzips the tent flap. "I'm sure you do."

"Then why are you taking me?" I follow him out of the tent and chase his long strides.

"Because there could be a few strangers in this camping area that are not *kind souls*."

I stumble on a rock and catch myself before landing on my face. "I took a self-defense class. I have skills."

Jake stops, letting me make it out in front of him, strutting all of my confidence.

"Ahhh!!!" My scream muffles in his large hand as he covers my mouth with it and restrains my arms to my sides with his other arm snaked around my body. I wriggle and scream, but I go nowhere, and my screams are muted to nothing more than a soft pulsing hum.

"Show me your skills, Avery," he whispers in my ear.

All of my attempts to twist free, headbutt him, elbow his ribs, basically *anything*, are thwarted by his solid body encasing me like a concrete tomb.

"What if a *kind soul* held you like this? What would you do? Let me tell you ..."

Unexpected tears sting my eyes.

"You would shit your fancy pants, ruin your manicured nails trying to unsuccessfully claw at Mr. Kind Soul's arm, then you would end up tied to something cold while he made you feel absolutely anything but sexy. You'd long for the days of *dick cheese* buying you expensive shit then using you for a good lay."

Before I blink out a single tear, he releases me, takes my hand, and pulls me up the hill to the toilet.

"False confidence is dangerous to your health, your self-esteem, and your entire soul. You need to be something a helluva lot more than a compilation of expensive labels." He lets go of my hand at the door to the shithole with four wood walls and no sink.

I swallow back the pain and the fear and push open the door. With my back to him, I shrug. "It was a free class. Two hours. I had a crush on the instructor. He told me I was a natural at self-defense. He said I had good moves."

Jake grunts a laugh. "I'm sure he did. Men tell women whatever it takes to get into their pants."

When the sting of the truth starts to hurt, I step into the nasty stall, hating that the walls don't go to the ground or block the sound of me peeing.

"I can't see anything."

He points the flashlight into the foot gap at the bottom of the wall.

"Thank you." I almost choke on the words, but he walked me up the hill and now he's holding a flashlight for me.

"What do you say?" I hold a squat to prevent from touching anything as I tinkle.

"You're welcome."

I roll my eyes. "I'm not talking about the flashlight. What do you say to women to get into their pants?"

Again, no toilet paper. How did I forget to grab a few tissues? I shake and pull up my panties and pink silk night shorts. I open the door, feeling all kinds of disgusting.

No toilet paper.

No sink.

Who lives like this? Aren't there laws that require a sink with a toilet? Maybe only flushable toilets.

Flushable toilets ... best invention ever.

Jake stands from his squatted position where he held the flashlight for me.

"What?"

He shakes his head.

"Don't shake your head. Why were you looking at me like that? Is it my hair?" I smooth both palms over my fragile locks. I need my hairdresser like a heart attack patient needs a heart surgeon.

Hairdresser STAT!

"What's up with your hair?" He inspects my head with the light like I had done to his perfect feet, only I don't think the grimace on his face has anything to do with my *perfect* hair. "Why are you messing with it all the time? Scratching your scalp all the damn time? If not lice, is it psoriasis? A yeast infection?"

"Jeez." I shove the light away. "I told you not to mention my hair. Don't talk about it, don't look at it, and whatever you do don't touch it."

He brings the light back up to my head.

"Stop!" I try to shove him away again.

"Fair is fair. You were inspecting my feet for a really long time."

I don't need a mirror to know that all the blood has drained from my face. How the hell does he know that? "What?" I whisper.

Taking one step closer, he aims the flashlight between us so his flip-flop clad feet are illuminated. "When you were searching for the keys, you stopped to stare at my feet, and..." he smiles "...the rest of me."

My jaw unhinges. "You are so full of yourself. I was not looking at any part of you, especially your ugly, stinky feet." I cross my arms over my chest. "But *if* I had been looking at your fungus-infected feet, how would you have known since you were sleeping?"

"It's hard to sleep when you keep telling me to wake up."

A gasp catches in my throat. "You bastard! If you were awake, why didn't you answer me?"

I hate his grin.

Stupid, stupid grin. I don't care how white his smile happens to be, it's a terrible grin.

I hate the way his eyes smile. Yep, smiling eyes. I bet it's an early sign of something like ... foot fungus or erectile dysfunction.

"As we speak, mosquitoes are buzzing around us, but I don't acknowledge them. I'm aware of their pesky little buzzing, but I'm not going to let them ruin my trip or keep me from sleeping."

"Oh ... my ... god ... Are you comparing me to a blood-sucking insect?"

"If the overpriced shoe fits ..." He's grinning like ...

Gah!

I don't really know what his grin resembles. It's mocking, flirty, devious, and incredibly infuriating because he only smiles like that when he's poking fun at me.

"You didn't answer my question." I plant my hands on my hips.

He shines the flashlight in my face. "What question was that?"

I flinch, backing away from him and the smell of the shithole behind us. "What do you say to a woman to get into her pants?"

His lips purse. "I ask them if they want to smell my underwear."

Before my mouth falls into yet another offended gasp, I grit my teeth and formulate ... something.

What? I'm not sure. I have skills. I just need to use them to my benefit. Sadly my guy-skills involve a lot of flirting and ... other bodily exchanges.

Forcing my jaw to relax, I plaster on my best smile—the one that gets me all kinds of things from men who have posed a bigger challenge than Mr. Kale Salad.

"I bet they do." I bite my bottom lip, closing the distance between us. Running my fingernail down his defined chest, I trace some of his ink before teasing the waistband to his boxer briefs peeking above his low riding shorts. His abs tighten even more. "I bet they want to smell every inch of you."

"Avery," he warns in a gritty voice.

I slip my fingernail just under the waistband, giving it a teasing tug while shifting my gaze to meet his hooded eyes.

Shit ... I swallow back the saliva pooling in my mouth. I'm falling apart in the middle of my one chance to take the lead—get the upper hand. I'm turning myself on as much as him. His cock is waking up, but dammit if I'm not feeling my own arousal tingling between my legs.

I was wet just from him saying my name in that unhinged voice. The timbre in it is almost too much to take.

Almost ... but the need for revenge trumps it.

I curl both hands into his shorts, clutching his briefs too.

"Ave ..." He shakes his head slowly, but when he swallows hard, I know I've got him. Jake is a lot of things, but he's still just a guy who would let the world end around him if it meant that a woman was going to get on her knees and take him in her mouth.

"You know what I'm craving, *Jake?*" I lace each word with as much seduction as I can, which isn't hard because ... I'm so damn aroused.

His lips part and I know he can't even speak. Yeah ... I've got this.

I give him a sexy, sly grin. "Revenge." Yanking as hard

as I can, I pull down his pants, snatch the flashlight, and run like chased prey to the tent.

"Oh my gosh. Oh shit. Oh, oh, oh!" Panic inflames my veins as I navigate the uneven terrain while thinking of what I just did, but more than that … what I just saw.

Holy Batman! I saw Jake's junk and it's not at all junky. It's almost as perfect and big as his feet. When it sprang free, it nearly poked my eye out. Skidding into the tent, completely breathless, I zip it shut and punch the air a hundred times in celebration before shoving Swarley off my sleeping bag and sliding into it until just my eyes peek out of the top.

I did it! I'm the queen, not a princess. Queen Don't Mess With Me Avery.

My lungs hold my breath hostage as twigs crack beneath the approaching footsteps. Not even the thick sleeping bag hides the visible shaking of my body. I'm nothing more than a bundle of adrenaline and hormones.

Horny.

I'm so horny I could hump an inanimate object like Swarley does.

Light flickers and Jake unzips the flap and picks up the flashlight that I accidentally dropped while hurrying to get inside here.

"How old are you?" He pins me to the ground with a stern glare.

I don't blink, but what he can't see is my grin, and it's every bit as big as his stupid, ridiculous, making-fun-of-Avery grins.

"Five? Are you five, Avery?" He shrugs off his tee.

I allow one blink to prevent my eyes from drying out. De-panting someone is not really a five-year-old prank. It's probably more of a thirteen-year-old prank, but I don't actually correct him because I've never pulled someone's pants down out of revenge. Had I done it before, then I surely would have known to keep my face at a safe distance from the springy appendage.

After I refuse to give him more than a blink, he eases onto his sleeping bag and shuts off the flashlight.

"Avery?"

I contemplate giving him any sort of response, but after a few seconds, I hum a questioning response. "Ahhh!" I gasp then yelp as he grips my sleeping bag and pulls the whole thing, with me trapped in it, onto his body so we're nose to nose, and the head of his still-erect cock nudges the apex of my legs. I swear cocks are natural pussy homing devices. "I'm claustrophobic," I say on a panicked whisper. My arms are trapped. I can't move.

Still, I'm desperate to widen my legs an inch for *very* shameful, once-a-hussy-always-a-hussy reasons.

Jake's nose brushes mine as his minty breath invades my personal space, or maybe it's his personal space. Things are a bit weird at the moment. I'm not sure whose space we're occupying. "When you least expect it, I'm going to pull down your pants and sniff your panties ... probably in public. You've been warned. Understood?"

Oh my god ...

With as much ease and at the same lightning speed that he snatched me from my spot, he returns me to the ground next to Swarley.

CHAPTER TEN

Day Four
Ozark National Forest

Jake buys a new T-shirt.

I used to be a people person, but you ruined that for me.

Day Five

Ozark National Forest with hard water, deteriorating hair, and seven out of ten fingernails chipped, ripped, and cringe-worthy.

Jake buys a new T-shirt.

Scratch N Sniff

Dumbass.

Day Six

Ozark National Park. Shitty cell phone signal. We don't leave the campsite. I contemplate slitting his throat or my wrists.

Day Seven

STILL in the freaking Ozarks! I have never been so disheveled from my witchy head to my calloused toes. We make a food run—thank god. I had to swing another fasting session because I ran out of Addy's snacks. In all fairness, Jake offered me some of his food, but with the looming threat of losing my pants in public, I couldn't risk getting anywhere near him or his food.

Jake winds us through the mountains to a small grocery store.

"Get your shit and I'll meet you at the checkout. I'll roll down the windows, but I have a feeling Swarley could go into a barking frenzy no matter what."

"Maybe." I shrug, patting a gentle hand over my hair.

"Fucking lice." Jake rolls his eyes.

"It's not lice, asshat. I told you that." I chase him into the store. He grabs a basket and sets off toward the produce. I grab a basket and make my way to end caps with sale items.

With fifteen dollars' worth of snacks in my basket, I make my way to the checkout.

"Well damn," I whisper when I come across a stand of T-shirts with funny sayings. But not just funny sayings—THE perfect shirt to wear for my travel companion.

Life is short and so is your penis.

But ... it's ten dollars. Food? Or revenge?

It's a no-brainer. I exchange my first choice of food

items for five ninety-nine cent pouches of Pasta O's with tomato sauce. The tax on the shirt leaves me with less than five dollars left to my name. I might have to pawn off something to make it back to L.A. without starving.

Maybe Swarley?

I inwardly giggle.

Jake frowns at my small bag when he loads his expensive produce onto the conveyor belt. I smile. Yeah, it's pretty shitty food, but *so* worth it.

"Did you get some tea tree oil for your lice?" He stares at my hair after paying for his groceries.

"Nope." I fish out my new shirt and hold out my bag for him to hold.

Of course he can't just take it. He has to scowl at me like holding it is the most inconvenient thing he has ever had to do. After he takes it, I head out the door and slip on my new shirt, whipping around to face him while walking backward as he walks forward, inspecting my shirt.

After he reads it, his gaze flits to meet mine. I try to keep my smugness to a minimum like, *Yeah, it's an awesome shirt because I'm awesome like that, no big deal.* Unfortunately, I suck at subtle.

Jake? He's a master at masking his emotions—the opposite of an open book. A closed book, with no cover and no blurb.

"I noticed those shorts of yours are a bit loose around the waist."

Taking quicker steps backward to keep him from trampling me, I glance down at my shorts. They're a bit loose, but that's not a surprise given my recent fasting.

"Yeah, so?" I glance up.

He pins me with a hard, expectant stare.

Shit.

"When's the last time you mooned someone, Avery?"

"Jake." I shake my head.

One side of his mouth curls a fraction as his pace picks up.

"No." I hold out my finger.

"Yes." He reaches for me.

"Jake, no!" I turn and run.

Where? Well, that's just it. I have nowhere to go but in circles around the parking lot. But he is *not* pulling down my shorts in the parking lot of a grocery store.

His steps gain on me.

"Help!"

"Shh ..." He laughs just behind me.

"Stop. Don't! I'm going to fall in these heels!"

"Shh ..." Jake's hand snags the back of my shorts.

My fingers clench the waist of them as he pulls me to a stop and drags me back to the truck, wedging them up my ass in the process.

"Jake—"

"Shh ... stop squealing like a damn pig. I'm not going to pull your pants down ... yet."

I wrap both of my hands around his wrist, tugging at his firm grip on the back of my shorts. He opens my door to the truck and tosses the bags in next to Swarley. After he shuts the door, he releases me. I jump into my seat and fasten the seat belt, hoping it aids in keeping my pants on me.

Resting his hand on the top of my door, he inspects me with that indiscernible look for a few moments as I start to mess with my hair then decide to just keep my hands idle on my lap to prevent him from making some stupid comment about lice.

"Can't say I've ever chased anyone around a parking lot before." He bites his lips together.

Screw him. I am not going to mirror that stupid grin he has on his mild-to-moderately handsome face. We are grownups. Playing chase is something ten-year-olds do. He's reduced me to an adolescent again.

"Shut the door, short dick." I grab for the handle, but he keeps a firm hold on the door. It's not going to shut until he's ready.

I huff a long breath, crossing my arms over my chest. Looking forward, I ignore the hole he's boring into the side of my head. He knows I saw his big dick. I'm not going to acknowledge it.

Nope. Never.

The door shuts. He gets in, rolls down the windows, and guns it out of the parking lot, tossing a disapproving frown in the direction of my high heels.

"They were for the grocery store."

"I'm sure the eighty-year-old woman at the checkout was very impressed with you."

"Shut up. I dress for myself sometimes, you know? Is there something wrong with wanting to feel good about myself? Lord knows the rest of me is in dire need of some maintenance."

He cocks an eyebrow at me.

I ignore his condescending look and try to put my window up as we pick up speed, but he's locked it from his side.

"Put my window up." I gather my hair and hold it back, but the wind keeps pulling at it. "Jake, put my window up. I can't have my hair blowing everywhere!"

"What?" He holds his hand up to his ear.

"My hair!"

"Still can't hear you." He shrugs. "Tell me when we get back to the campsite."

I scowl at him while Swarley pokes his nose up between the seat and the door to enjoy the wind as well. Traitor.

"My dad used to bring Sydney and me here for long weekends after our mom died. We rented a cabin that came with a fishing boat."

Jake shoots me a glance, which means he can hear me. After a few seconds, he rolls up the windows. I inwardly grin.

Winner, winner, chicken dinner.

"There are at least four species of venomous snakes in the Ozarks. They're most active midmorning and late afternoon. Maybe that's when you should take your hikes while Swarley and I stay in the truck. Please leave the keys, in case you don't make it back. Do you have family I can contact when you die?"

Jake responds with a twisted face. I return a toothy smile.

My gaze shifts to the gravel road that goes to our campsite. I inspect my nails. They are a disaster. *I* am a disaster. This torture needs to stop.

Jake

THERE ARE good Samaritans and there are saints.

I am a saint.

The god of patience. The greatest man who ever lived.

A couple weeks ago I would have settled for the simple hard-working, nice-guy label. A couple weeks ago Avery Montgomery, Diva Bitch, wasn't on my radar. Hell, she wasn't even in the same state.

"I think I'm getting jungle rot." She slips off her Barbie shoes and rubs her toes.

"Jungle rot?" I shoot her a quick glance, getting out of the truck and taking a deep inhale of mountain air as Swarley jumps out behind me.

Diva Bitch hasn't taken a single deep breath over the course of our journey. However, she hasn't missed one opportunity to whine about the scuff marks on her toe-mangling shoes or the damage to her hair from the hard water at the campgrounds and the wind.

"Haven't you watched G.I. Jane?" She frowns at my lack of engagement while opening her door.

I chuckle, fighting to keep my sense of humor. If I lose it —she's a *dead* diva bitch. I've been out of the ring for a few years, but I'm certain I could end the misery—my misery—with one quick move.

"Jake ..." She whines again. It's too much to handle.

"It's a fucking blister, you materialistic, chronically pessimistic, vain, grouchy, dog-hating, bit—" Okay, I may have already lost my sense of humor. My best guesstimate ... it scattered in the wind a few miles back when Avery threw her tantrum over me rolling down the windows, adding even more irreparable damage to her hair.

"Bitch? Were you about to call me a bitch?"

She's not stupid. I get it. Flaunting her looks instead of her intelligence has probably suited her needs over the years. Until now ...

Her mantra of all-men-are-lying-cheating-monkey-spanking dick cheese will not win her points in the male community, even if she is a walking wet dream. I can't even acknowledge her word choice. Dick cannot be an adjective to cheese. Nope. No fucking way.

"Bitter. I was going to say bitter woman." Bitch. Total bitch.

"Typical. Men love to break women down, use them for dick warmers, and cry bitch when we decide to stand up for ourselves."

I hold the flap open for her to get her bitchy ass in the tent. The quicker she goes to sleep, the quicker I can have some peace and quiet.

"Tomorrow we get a hotel." She huffs.

"The only luxury tomorrow may bestow upon you is me not killing you. My trip. My truck. My choice where we stay. I make this trip every year. And every year I stay at campsites along the way."

"It's been a week and we're not even halfway to L.A.! My sister is probably home and wanting her dog back, but I wouldn't know because my phone is dead half the time and we don't have a signal the other half."

I grit my teeth, fisting my hands to keep them from encircling her neck. "I said I take my time getting to the West Coast. You said 'I'm in no hurry.' You said 'I don't want to be an inconvenience. Just pretend I'm not here.'"

Avery grimaces while sliding her jungle rot feet back into her high heels. She pushes out her chest and tips her chin up. I bite back my grin as she hobbles like a broken princess to the tent.

"Come, Swarley," she says.

The elderly Weimaraner lumbers to all fours from his spot in the cool grass. I bet he'd rather sleep right there than share space with Avery. I'm sure he's tired of hearing her drone on about how he ruined her life.

I lock up the truck and enter the campground gates of Hell.

"Out!" Avery holds her wadded shirt up to her chest. "You're supposed to ask if it's okay to come in here."

I shrug, zipping the tent flaps behind me. "I'm taking your advice ... pretending you're not here."

"But I AM here."

I shoot her a barely detectable smile while moving to the center of the tent, the only part where I can stand straight. It's also where my hitchhiking leach happens to be. Her blue eyes widen as she stiffens a little more.

"Swarley, did you hear something?" I shrug off my shirt.

Avery's lips part.

I shrug. "Me neither." As if she's not gasping just inches from me, I unfasten my cargo shorts and let them fall to my feet. I didn't think her eyes could get any wider. I was wrong.

"I've seen it and ... I-I'm not impressed. Also, I don't like tattoos. Or ... or bulky muscles." She shakes her head, nose wrinkled. "Your hair is too short ... and blond. I like men with dark hair. And your eyes are the wrong shade of blue. And your ..."

Keeping my head bowed, I toe off my shoes, hiding my amusement behind twisted lips. "My what? My cock is too big?" I glance up as the horror intensifies, reddening her cheeks.

Her jaw unhinges. "Listen, *short dick,* I want nothing to do with your cock. Or any cock ever again."

"Thank god ... my cock threatened to hold its breath until it turns blue and falls clean off my body if I even think of sticking it in your battery-acid lined cu—" I stop myself, clinging to the tiny bit of control I have left.

Another gasp. Can she really be that shocked?

"Cu? Cunt? Was that the word tripping out of your mouth? You are the most vulgar man I have ever met."

Really? She's from L.A. I'm not vulgar. This infuriating woman just brings out the fighter in me. I need to let this go and take the high road.

"Sorry. Lady bits? Vajayjay? Hoo-haw? Quim?"

"Vagina! Vagina, vagina, vagina, vagina." She balls her fists.

I lift a single brow. "Okay." I bow. "Good night, Your Royal Vagina."

"You're such a dick," she mumbles as I turn, retrieving my toothbrush and toothpaste from my backpack.

"Penis. Penis, penis, penis, penis. If we're being anatomically correct, you think I'm such a penis." I shove my toothbrush into my mouth and wrap my lips around it to ward off my amusement.

"My boyfriend stuck his *penis* into another woman ... but I'm certain I hate you more."

I pause my brushing motion, jerking my head back. Damn! What a declaration. I'm not sure if I should be offended or honored. Honored. Definitely honored. I continue brushing.

Avery huffs and turns, keeping her back to me as she removes her bra and slips on a satin nightie. Yup ... I've been camping for the past week with a stranger hell-bent on torturing me in every possible way.

I unzip the tent's entrance and spit out my suds.

"Wait ..." she mumbles over her toothbrush, crawling toward the opening.

Before I can get the flap pushed completely open, she spits ... all over the inside of it.

"Nice, Ave ... real nice." I shake my head.

She wrinkles her nose, wiping her mouth with the back of her hand as her wide eyes flit between the mess and me. "Sorry."

"Yeah, I'm sure you are." I grab the first thing I can find and wipe off the nylon flap.

"Hey!" Avery grabs my wrist. "That's my shirt! That's an eighty-dollar shirt you're using like some bar rag."

I nudge her to keep her away, refusing to relinquish the overpriced white T-shirt until the inside of my tent is free from her spit-up mess.

"Stop! Give it!" She attacks my arm, pressing her satin-clad body to my bare back.

Swarley barks.

"Get off me. You're upsetting him, you crazy freak." But I still don't give her the shirt. I wad it up, throw it outside, and zip the flap.

"Bastard!" Her hand flies through the air toward my face.

I intercept it just before she connects with my cheek. The prissy princess with fake lashes, too much lip gloss, Barbie smooth hair, and miles of attitude drives me to the brink of murder. But ... this hot mess with windblown hair—albeit curiously flawed—and a face devoid of anything God didn't give her ... she's fucking beautiful.

Wild.

Lawless.

Lively.

So. Damn. Sexy.

"Get. My. Shirt. NOW!"

I nod to her taped fingers. "I think it would have hurt you more than me."

"Get my shirt!"

The grin on my face feels incredible. "Let it be."

Avery dives for the door. I stand on my knees and block her with my body, holding her to my chest with one arm around her waist.

She shoves my shoulders.

"Ave ..."

Breathless, with anger staining her cheeks crimson, she huffs out a long exhale just inches from my mouth.

"Let it be," I repeat.

"It's—"

My other hand fists the back of her hair, giving it a firm jerk until her neck begs for my mouth. "Let. It. Be."

CHAPTER ELEVEN

Avery

I LIKE OLDER men in suits who don't feel the need to express themselves by marring their skin. I like hotel suites. Sit-down dining. Air-conditioning. Daily showers with hot water. Luxury beds. Silk pillowcases. Expensive cars with leather seats.

My heart has been broken too many times to count. I'm not sure it's really a heart anymore—just a fleshy doormat.

Things make me feel good. Not everyone gets the same happily ever after. Maybe mine is an empty bed but a closet full of shoes and handbags. So what?

I grew up without my mother—she died. My father is a preacher. That fueled my rebellion from an early age. I hated boundaries, laws, and scriptures that made me feel guilty for the thoughts I couldn't control.

I'm a girly girl who likes all things feminine, sexy, flowery, and pink—NOT muscle-bound vegan chefs with pickup trucks and a shit ton of tattoos. Yet, in spite of his vulgarity and complete disrespect for my shirt, I can't keep my heart from hammering into my chest as he fists my hair.

"My hair," I whisper. He's going to damage my hair, and that should matter more than anything right now ... but it doesn't. His added tug on it confirms that he feels the same.

"A raccoon could steal my shirt."

He brushes his lips along my neck, not kissing, not tasting ... just feeling. I shiver.

"Do we really care?" he whispers in my ear.

Normally, yes. I would care very much. But at the moment, I can't stay focused on the shirt because there's a large hand sliding over my ass.

"Ouch!" I jump when he squeezes it—hard.

He chuckles, fisting my hair tighter.

Fuck! He's going to pull it out!

Double fuck! I don't even care.

His mouth opens against my bare shoulder. His teeth tease my skin for a few seconds before his hot tongue flicks out like a whip.

I swallow hard. "I ... I don't think this is a smart idea."

Jake lifts his head, blinking several times before cocking it to the side. "You have a better idea?"

Wetting my lips, I rub them together. I wasn't expecting that response. "Not ... necessarily."

He nods slowly, letting his gaze slide along my body. "Clearly you're a pain in any man's ass. But I'd say most men would overlook that. Unless ..." His eyes meet mine. A cocky grin teasing the corners of his mouth.

I squint. "Unless what?"

"Unless you're incredibly bad at sex."

"How dare you—"

He smashes his mouth to mine.

Wrong.

Stupid.

Impulsive.

His tongue taunts mine until I surrender. Dear sweet Jesus … he tastes better than champagne, perfectly ripe strawberries, the smoothest milk chocolate, and my favorite … everything.

He breaks the kiss. My lungs claw for air. His tongue makes a lazy stroke across his lower lip, ending with that damn grin. I'm a mess. What's he smiling about?

"I'm not bad at sex," I whisper between breaths.

"No?" He slides the spaghetti straps off my shoulders.

My nightie slips a few inches.

"No." I shake my head.

"Show me what you've got, Ave."

I *just* did that. I showed him my stuff. Well … my de-pants and run. Maybe that didn't count as sexy in his book. My smile twitches. "Why are you calling me Ave?"

"Figured you preferred it to Diva Bitch."

I scowl. "I still hate you."

He chuckles. "I wouldn't have it any other way."

Bastard. Sexy … delicious … irresistible … bastard.

Jake holds his hands out to his sides. "Let's see it, Ave. Do your worst."

What the hell? I wait, but he remains on his knees, statuesque. I slide off my nightie. His eyes follow with curiosity. Maybe … or is it disinterest? Gah! I don't know. Men have seriously messed with my head, chipping away at my confidence. What's left is artificial. A complete façade.

Resting my shaky hands flat on his chest, I lean in and press my lips to the corner of his mouth. He doesn't move. Ghosting more kisses over his jaw, I wait for him to respond … join in.

Nothing.

"Aren't you going to touch me?" I whisper, teasing my teeth across his earlobe.

"Do you want me to touch you?"

I freeze. What's going on? My body jerks back, but his expression gives away nothing.

"Is that the best you've got, Ave?"

I frown, shoulders deflating, but not as much as my ego. I survey his body. The prominent outline in his briefs gives me hope that I'm making progress. My hand slides down the front of them. His Adam's apple makes a quick dip. That's good. Right?

"Does that feel good?"

"Sure." He shrugs. HE. SHRUGS! "Does it feel good to you?"

"I'm doing it for you, not me." I can't entirely hide the frustration in my voice. I'm so damn turned on, but he's acting like someone stepping into a lukewarm bath.

"Well then ..." His hand clasps my wrist, pulling it from his briefs. "You're doing it all fucking wrong." Shoving both of my arms behind my back like I'm under arrest, he dips his head down and teases his tongue over the swell of my breast.

I feel chilled and ready to overheat at the same time. He dips lower. My back arches as he flirts with that invisible string that sends a thrumming pleasure right between my legs.

I seethe in a quick breath.

A soft groan rattles in his chest. That teases that invisible string too.

"You see..." he trails his lips along my chest, seeking my other breast "...the art of sex is all about selfish pleasure. You like what I'm doing..." he palms my breast, flicking his tongue over it until my legs pinch together to fight off the need to moan "...but I'm not doing it for you."

He lets go of my hands and hovers his lips over mine. "I'm doing it because I want to taste you ... because I want to hear you whimper ... because I want to feel you squirm. That gives *me* pleasure."

I nod slowly, but I can't find one word that's a suitable response.

He grabs my ass and lifts me, guiding my legs around his waist, my arms around his neck, so he can lay me down on his sleeping bag. Kissing me with an unhurried pace, he reaches behind him and unhooks my legs from his waist before tearing his mouth from mine. "And..." he sets my feet on the ground and slides off my panties "...when my tongue goes here..."

"Oh god ..." My hips jerk against the two fingers he shoves inside of me.

"...it's because I'm so fucking hungry." His tongue goes there, and he hums like I'm the best thing he's ever tasted. Gone ... I'm gone ... lost in the bliss of pleasure given by Satan himself. I curl my fingers into his coppery hair and hold him to me as I throw my head back, speaking to a god I'm certain wants nothing to do with my orgasm gratitude.

Jake

"Where are you going?" Avery lifts onto her elbows as I pull on my shorts. "We're not having sex?"

I grin, shaking my head. "I don't have a condom."

"It was YOUR idea! How can you not have a condom?"

I shrug. "It was a gamble, but I felt the odds were in my favor that I wouldn't need one."

Her mouth falls open. "Wh-what ... you thought I would fail? You felt certain that what? I'd be bad at sex?"

"I find that people who spend so much time trying to impress are usually the most unimpressive. Don't take it personally ... you have potential." I slip out the entrance and zip it closed.

"Bastard!"

I grin.

Nearly an hour later, the zipper sounds to my back. So much for hoping she fell asleep.

"You're just sitting out here?"

"Yep. Just sitting out here." I slip my bottled water into the drink holder of my camping chair.

"Why?"

I did some pushups, planks, dips, and crunches ... among other things that I'm not going to share with her. It's late. I'm tired of explaining everything.

"It's quiet."

"And I'm too loud?"

I grunt a laugh. "You're 'too' a lot of things."

"You're a jerk."

"Not usually."

"Oh, just with me?"

I glance over as she zips her pink hoodie over her short shorts, no shoes—shocking. She bends down and snags the expensive white tee off the ground, frowning at it as her hand smooths over it.

"Gah ... I didn't think I had that much spit. It's still really wet."

I rub my hand over my mouth and pinch my bottom lip

between my fingers. "Yeah ... you might want a squirt or two of hand sanitizer."

She shrugs, folding the shirt like it's fresh out of the dryer. "It's my spit."

"Yes. Some of it."

Her nose wrinkles, forehead drawn tightly in confusion as she holds the folded shirt with one hand and rubs together the fingers of her other hand. "Sticky toothpaste."

"It's not toothpaste." I scoot back in my chair, tipping my head back to admire the stars.

She stomps the ground, positioning herself right in front of my chair.

"Did you spill something and use my shirt?" She looks around. "You used it to clean your stupid windshield, didn't you?"

"Nope."

"Then what?" She brings the shirt to her nose.

I choke on my laugh. "No ... don't ... that's just ... wrong."

"Tell me!"

I lean forward, resting my elbows on my knees. "Come here."

Avery eyes me with caution for a few seconds before taking two steps forward. She jumps when I touch the pad of my finger to the inside of her knee. What can I say? I like torturing myself.

Sliding it up her leg, I whisper, "Are your panties still wet?"

Her lips part, releasing a ragged breath.

I don't wait for an answer before dipping my finger under the crotch of her shorts. Her breath catches as I rub my finger over her damp panties. "I'd say yes," I whisper.

Her teeth lay claim to her bottom lip.

"Why are they wet?"

Her forehead wrinkles a fraction.

"Did you clean my windshield with them?"

The wrinkles deepen for two seconds before realization ghosts along her face. "Oh my god!" She jumps back, dropping her T-shirt like it stung her. "You jerked off on my shirt? Who does that? What is wrong with you? Eww …" She jumps in a circle shaking out her hands. "Gross!"

Swarley barks from inside the tent.

Leaning back to enjoy the show, I untwist the cap from my water and take a long swig. As her energy wears off, she levels me with a death glare. An hour ago, I had condoms on my list of things to pick up in town tomorrow. I don't think I'll need them after all.

"Come here." I draw out the word come because she brings out the evil side of me.

"Fuck you."

I shake my bottled water.

Avery scowls. After the steam stops flowing from her nostrils, she holds out her hands. I pour some water onto them while she performs a surgical scrub.

"Some women swallow it."

"Water?"

I glance up at her, lifting an eyebrow. Okay, she's not as smart as I thought.

"Oh." She rolls her eyes, drying her hands on her sweatshirt. "Why are you so mean to me?"

"Mean? You think I'm mean?"

"I don't think chasing me in a grocery store parking lot, calling me a bitch, ruining my shirt, saying I'm bad at sex, and then teasing me about it is exactly what I'd call nice."

My lips twist to the side while I inspect this insecure

mess of a woman before me. "Maybe I'm just flirting with you."

"That's not flirting."

"No? Then what do you call flirting?"

She shoves her hands into the hoodie's pockets and shrugs. "Compliments. Flowers. Chocolates. Jewelry."

"Sounds like ass kissing to get into your pants."

Avery tips up her chin. "You could learn a few things from men who do that."

I laugh. "Avery, Avery, Avery ... I ruined your shirt, called you a bitch, and suggested you're shit at sex. Yet, in the next breath I had two fingers shoved in your ... *vagina*." I wink.

Heat crawls up her neck. I'm not a jerk. Really, I'm not. But Avery is one messed-up chick, and I feel like putting her in her place isn't a bad thing. She might not thank me now. In fact, I predict her hand making another shot for my face. But some day ... she might thank me when she finds a guy who doesn't treat her like a doormat, because she demands respect that can't be bought with elaborate gifts and her self-esteem reaches deeper than fake eyelashes and designer clothes.

"Don't touch me again. EVER!" She disappears into the tent.

"Good job, Ave. Stand the fuck up for yourself."

CHAPTER TWELVE

Avery

My life is a game of limbo—how low can I go? By four in the morning, I slip into jogging shorts, a tank top, and my most sensible shoes. If Jake's awake, listening to me get dressed, he doesn't let on. I slip out of the tent and climb to higher ground in search of a decent cell phone signal.

Satisfied with two bars, I call my sister.

"It's the middle of the night, Ave. What's the emergency? And why have you been ignoring my messages?" Sydney's groggy voice bleeds into my ear.

"My fucking phone won't work half the time. No damn signal."

"Whoa, sailor, what's with the language?"

"Don't start with me. I'm stuck in the Ozarks, and I fear I could be in Oklahoma or Texas by tonight. I can't do this. I thought I could, but I can't. It's unbearable."

"Is Swarley okay?"

I jerk my head back and hold the phone out as if I can't believe I'm talking to my sister—my flesh and blood. "Swarley? I'm calling you in the middle of the night confessing that I'm living under the most unbearable conditions, and you react with '*Is Swarley okay?*' What the hell, Syd?"

"Sorry. It's just that you can be ..."

"What?"

"Well, a bit dramatic."

"I'm not being dramatic. I have less than five dollars to my name; Anthony had all my accounts frozen. I'm physically, mentally, and emotionally a mess. And I'm roughing it with Satan and your dog that hates me."

"He doesn't hate you."

I bite my lips together. She doesn't know about my hand. I didn't want to ruin her trip with my grievances, but ... desperate times. "Before I left L.A., he chased a cat while I was walking him, and he ruined my hand. Major ligament damage. I may never work again."

Too much? Maybe.

"Oh, Ave—"

"No. I don't want you to feel bad or responsible. It was an unfortunate situation, but it's put me and your beloved dog on the outs of sorts. I'm just ... well, I've hit rock bottom. I thought I could make it to L.A. with Swarley and Satan, but I can't."

"Ave ... Lautner has a bad stomach bug. I think he caught something toward the end of our trip. Otherwise, I'd see if he could meet you somewhere, bring Swarley home, and let you fly back to L.A. But I can't leave the kids with him, and I don't want to pack them up for another long trip. If it's a true emergency, you should check with Dad and Deedy."

"Deedy?" I say slowly. "You know about the Deedy?"

Sydney chuckles. "All of us video chatted a few days ago. She's pretty great. I'm so happy for Dad. They're going to make a trip to California after they get married. We should plan a surprise party or reception type thing for them when they come to visit."

I glance around for the nearest tree to lean against so I don't fall down, even if everything else in my world is crumbling. "My life is shit," I say with a shaky voice as tears sting my eyes.

"Is it that Jake guy? Deedy told us he's incredibly kind and trustworthy. She and Dad feel confident that you couldn't be in better hands."

"He's a terrible person. I don't know what Deedy sees in him. Unless ..." I cover my mouth, swallowing a bit of bile.

"Unless what?"

"Oh ... my ... god ..."

"Jeez what? I'd like to get back to sleep, Ave."

"What if Deedy and Jake were ..." I retch again. "Intimate."

"You think Deedy was involved with the guy she suggested drive you back here?"

This horrible vision fills my head, replaying like a nightmare on a loop—Deedy naked with her head thrown back in ecstasy with Jake's head between her spread legs doing to her what he did to me, then in the next frame it's ... *my dad!*

I gag some more, spitting excess salvia onto the ground while coughing.

"Avery, what the heck is going on?" Sydney asks in a whisper-yell. She must still be in bed.

Jake tasted the Deedy, and my dad probably has too. It's like there's this unimaginable two degrees of separation between my dad's mouth and my ... Here they come, up my throat ... my Pasta O's from last night.

Dammit! I don't have calories to waste with so little money left in my wallet.

"Avery, answer me. You're scaring me."

"If it's true ... oh god ... if it's true ..." I wipe my mouth with the back of my hand.

"So what? I'm not trying to be insensitive, but you have very little room to talk about anyone else's number of sex partners."

"It's not the number! It's that he was with her and with me and dad's been with her and now—"

"Wait ... please tell me you didn't sleep with Jake."

"Of course I didn't sleep with Jake." I amaze myself with my quick response.

"Thank goodness."

"I let him go down on me, just once, and it will never happen again. He's the bane of my existence."

"Avery ..." Total defeat seeps through my phone. She's disappointed in me. A real shocker. *I'm* disappointed in me. "I'll send you some money. Just tell me how much. But I can't come get Swarley. If you're too stubborn to ask Dad and Deedy, then I don't know what to tell you. You shouldn't have left L.A. with Swarley until we got home."

"I had to leave. My life was falling apart. Anthony developed a craving for chocolate—one I couldn't satisfy—and I ..." I wipe the streams of tears from my cheeks. "I needed someone and you were gone, so I went to Dad."

"You're going to have to explain the *falling apart* and chocolate craving later, but I'm truly sorry you were in need of someone and I wasn't here for you."

I know it's not her intention, but she makes me sound so needy. Gah! Am I really that needy? Did she always feel like I needed her to fix shit in my life? I roll my eyes while drying my tears, clearly the middle-of-the-night phone call proves that theory correct.

"Ah, good ..."

My gaze flies over my shoulder. *He's* awake. Fabulous.

"You're up," Jake continues, stretching his arms over his head in one direction then the other, "and dressed for a quick hike. What a nice surprise. Let's do it so we can pack up and hit the road."

After I look for as many physical flaws in his body as I can find—too many tattoos is all I can find in this lighting—I point to my phone planted against my ear. "I'm on a call. Where's Swarley?"

"He marked the area and went back into the tent." Jake nods to my phone. "East Coast, I hope. If you're calling California, I bet whoever is on the other end of that call really hates you right now."

"Oh my gosh, he's adorable." Sydney laughs. "I don't hate you, Ave, but I don't hate him either. Sorry. And good to know someone's keeping track of my dog."

"Yeah, I agree, Sis, even his voice is obnoxiously annoying."

"Avery, stop! I didn't say—"

"Love you too, gotta go."

"The money, Avery. How much?"

"No worries for now. I'll let you know." I press *End*. "Were you awake when I was getting dressed?"

"Of course." He covers his yawn with his fist.

"You just like to play dead?"

"It's better than *being* dead."

"In your case, I disagree."

"Ouch." He presses a hand to his chest.

"Let's go." I start marching off.

"This way, Ave."

Huffing while coming to a stop, I pivot. He smirks.

"Fuck the hike. Let's take a jog. I have a lot of energy and anger to burn off."

"Now we're talking." He grins.

I roll my eyes at his cocky enthusiasm and start jogging in the right direction. Maybe I'm a princess in his eyes. Maybe not all of my shoes are camping-worthy. And maybe I try to give people more credit than slurping chocolate mousse from their employee's pussy or jerking off into someone else's T-shirt, but I'm not out of shape. It takes hard work to maintain my figure.

Jake, no doubt, can punch harder and lift more dead-weight than I can, but he's not going to outrun me. Not today. Not ever.

"Jesus Christ, woman! There's not a bear chasing us," he calls from a fair distance behind me after thirty minutes of fast-paced jogging on the somewhat level dirt trail.

Seeing the truck and tent up ahead, I slow to a walk, feeling so much better. Not a single step I just pounded changed my unfortunate situation, but my mental health feels completely recharged like I will survive another day.

"I bet you're too protein deficient to keep up with me. Maybe we should stop for hamburgers today. Your treat." I glance back and he shakes his head, chin tipped toward his feet as they scuff along the dirt. I bet those muscle-bound legs of his feel like two stumps of dead weight.

Off to my right are a few mushrooms that I recognize from my days of foraging mushrooms with my dad. I don't know the name of this species, but I do remember what happened to us when we mistook it for a morel. Giving Jake another quick glance, assuring his head is still bowed, I snatch one of the mushrooms.

"You making a smoothie today?" I ask.

He has a travel blender. I keep turning down his nasty-looking green concoctions, but it might be time for me to show a little interest.

"Yes."

"Why don't you show me what you put in it? I'll make it for you while you get a shower. I want to stretch a bit before showering."

Turning at the tent, I flash him my best smile while holding the mushroom behind my back. He narrows his eyes a tiny bit, giving me the once-over.

"You're hungry. You want me to share my smoothie today. Am I correct?"

Yes. I'm starving, but I'll again forego food to have an opportunity to take the lead. My conscience scolds me for being so immature in my thoughts. I blame it on too much time in the woods. Jake might think this is refreshing and a place to clear his head, but I'm *dying* for an eight-dollar cup of caffeine, shopping therapy, and a full day at a salon getting myself pieced back together.

"I am." I spread my legs for him last night. It's killing me to submit to him again, even if it's just a guise.

"A handful of spinach, a banana, two dates—pitted—coconut water, and a scoop of Cordyceps powder."

"Cordyceps?"

He shrugs off his tank top. I remind my eyes to keep my gaze above his neck.

"Mushrooms."

"Reeeally ..." I fail at keeping cool. Jake likes mushrooms in his smoothie. Well, isn't that just fate?

"Yes, really. You should try them." He slips into the tent. "Do you know where everything's at?"

"Yes, Jake. I've watched you flaunt your morning routine. It's predictable."

When he comes back out, I flash him a smile.

"You're in a good mood today. You forgive me for your shirt?"

Not ever, you monkey-spanking asshole.

"Mmm ..." I nod, biting my tongue.

"I'll be back in ten."

I continue nodding as he disappears around the trees toward the shower facilities.

In the back of the truck, I riffle through the cooler and plastic containers to get his smoothie shit out. He has three bananas left. I scarf down two. If a guy goes down on a girl, all food becomes communal. Cringing, I try to forget about what his tongue did to me because that same tongue probably did that same thing to Deedy.

Retch ...

I contemplate how much of my special mushroom to add to his smoothie, not wanting it to impart a noticeable taste. Half-sies feels about right. It's not like I want him dead—okay, maybe I do, but ...

Dear Heavenly Father,

Please don't let this kill Jake. Seriously, I mean it. My gut says it won't, but I need your magical powers as a backup in case things go wrong. I would never survive prison, but I'm sure you know this. Oh, and of course the guilt and remorse. I'm not suggesting prison is my number one concern, clearly human life trumps that—even Jake's. Once things between us feel a bit more even, I promise to act my age, and try to do what Jesus would do a little more often. Please forgive my moments of sin. I'm only human.

"The water is extra cold today."

My heart springs into my throat as I turn toward Jake's voice.

Be cool, Avery!

"Big surprise." I hand him his smoothie, once again reminding my gaze to ignore his bared chest, dripping hair, and those perfect flip-flop clad feed.

"Where's yours?"

"My what?" My eyes narrow.

"Your smoothie?"

"Already drank it."

"What did you think?"

"It was good. Hope you don't mind, but I used two bananas in mine."

He takes a sip of his smoothie. "Mmm ... you did good."

I hold my breath, waiting for him to keel over.

"Go shower. Let's hit the road as soon as possible."

"Good idea." I hustle to get my stuff and run to the shower. Of course I want to get on the road, but mostly I need to be close by if he dies. There will be a body to bury— I mean ... 9-1-1 to call.

CHAPTER THIRTEEN

Oklahoma. Just as I suspected.

We make it two hours down the road. I start to think I should have used the whole mushroom. The good news—if I can really look at it like that—is Jake's still alive.

"Fucker!"

Jake's body tenses with my outburst. Swarley whines, making his own adjustments in the backseat to hide behind Jake instead of me.

"I hate you! I. HATE. YOU!" I roll down my window and throw my phone out into the ditch.

"Av-er-y ..." Jake rolls up my window.

Clenching my teeth, I will away the tears. Anthony Fucking Asshole, chocolate-mousse liar, cheater, hateful man doesn't deserve my tears.

"Ave?" Jake rests his hand on my leg—*this* brings out the tears.

I don't want his kindness and sympathy.

"He had my cell phone disconnected," I whisper, swatting at my tears.

Jake squeezes my leg.

"Anthony wanted to marry me *and* he wanted to fuck his cook. Oh ... and he wanted me to be okay with it. I said no. Now he's ..." I shake my head. "It doesn't matter."

"Do you want me to kick his ass?"

My head snaps to the side, meeting his quick glance filled with concern and sincerity. "You'd beat a man up to defend my honor?"

"I'd do it as a favor."

"For me? Or ..." I wrinkle my nose as that stupid reel of Deedy in the throes of passion flashes in my head again. "How do you know Deedy?"

He shrugs. "What does it matter?"

"Oh ... it matters. It matters a whole helluva lot."

"Why?"

"Because she's marrying my dad."

"So?"

"Please ... please don't be this way. Don't make me spell it out for you."

"Sorry, Miss Valedictorian, but I must be the idiot who doesn't understand."

"Did you have sex with her?" My voice booms, but I'm not sure why. I blame it on Anthony and his uncouth way of handling a breakup that's his fault.

Jake waits a few seconds. It's a yes or no answer. There's no reason to wait, unless he's formulating a lie.

"I'm trying to figure out how my sexual history is relevant to you or your dad."

It's a yes. I cuff a hand around my neck as if I can manually keep the vomit from coming out. "If you did to her what you did to me ... and she's going to be my *stepmom,* and my dad has probably put his mouth where you put ..." I retch.

Jake pulls off the road. "Get out. Don't you dare vomit in my truck."

I jump out, bending over into the ditch. Nothing comes out, even after a few more gags that make my eyes water. This is payback, that bitch named Karma, for all the men I've slept with who have daughters close to my age—or younger. This is what I get. Life is cruel.

Gentle hands pull back my hair. I reach up to stop him.

"I know, be careful with your hair."

I nod, standing straight when I'm certain those two bananas are not coming up.

"I didn't have sex with Deedy," Jake whispers in my ear, sliding his arm around me just above my chest. He pulls my back against him and kisses my shoulder.

It's kind.

I didn't know he could be kind.

It's intimate.

I didn't think I wanted to feel intimacy with him or anyone.

"*We* didn't have sex, but you ..." I can't say it.

"I haven't been *physical* with Deedy. Is that what you want to know?" He kisses my shoulder again as his other hand slides around my waist over my exposed midsection below my crop top, but just above my high-waisted shorts.

I hate myself for wanting his touch. He hasn't earned the right to touch me like this, but at the same time, I feel like that's exactly what he's trying to do right now. If there were other cars passing by, they'd have to wonder what's going on, but Jake loves the roads less traveled, so I doubt anyone will drive by unless they are lost.

"Ave ..." His lips move to my neck. "I'm sorry."

I'm in who-knows-where Oklahoma, falling apart from the inside out, with a man who plays me emotionally and physically like no man before him. Buried beneath layers of self-loathing, resignation, and the total whiplash from my life hitting a brick wall, I let myself take the affection that's being offered.

"Jake ..." I swallow, weak in the knees and breathless. "Deedy said you're trustworthy and *kind*. I need that Jake. Can you show me that Jake for one day?"

"Yes." He turns me in his arms and kisses me. It's possessive, but not entitled. I feel wanted, but not guilted. I grab his shirt and hold him close to me.

He lifts me up and sets me back in the passenger's seat. We break apart, panting, eyes wild with need.

Swarley whines.

Jake opens the back door to let him out. Before I can worry about a leash or poop bags, those lips I hate to love crash against mine again. He kisses me like he's pissed at me yet desperate to get more. It's intoxicating and frightening. I know my demons, but his feel scarier than mine. He makes me feel like a war he must win.

"Spread your legs wider, Ave."

I obey. His hand inches up my inner thigh as his tongue makes slow strokes against mine.

I tug at his shorts, popping open the button.

He freezes, pulling away as his hands halt mine. "Stop."

I'm bad at sex. That's why he's stopping. Or he doesn't trust me to follow through. I'm a tease. He's too smart to let me fool him twice, but I'm not fooling him. I'm ready to throw off my clothes alongside the road in broad daylight and let him fuck me blind.

"Jake ..."

Sweat beads along his brow, accompanied by shallow breaths.

"Fuck ..." He turns and vomits—over and over.

I cover my mouth in horror and then ... in recognition. Oh my god, I poisoned him.

Oh my god! Oh my god! Oh my god!

What if he dies? He can't die. The *one* day he's not awful, I poison him. Me and my stupid need to get revenge.

I don't know what to say? Do I tell him why he's vomiting? He'll hate me. This morning I didn't care if he hated me, now I kind of don't want him to hate me—or die.

Easing out of the truck, I pat his back with a gentle hand. "Jake, are you okay?"

He expels one more round of smoothie—and my secret ingredient—before wiping his mouth. "No. I'm not okay." The pasty white sheen of his skin worries me. It's like his body has settled into the color it will be in his casket.

"Here." I grab his water bottle from the truck.

"Thank you." He takes it.

"No need to thank me."

Awkward.

Jake rinses and spits, before drinking several long swigs. "Did the spinach feel slimy to you?"

Biting my lips together while cringing, I shake my head.

"It feels like food poisoning. What the hell did I eat that was bad?"

My eyebrows lift. "I-I don't know."

I poisoned you. I'm so incredibly sorry.

How do I fail at something as simple as revenge? He blew his disgusting wad onto my expensive T-shirt. He called me a princess, diva, and bitch. The list of reasons why he deserves to come close to dying is so long, I can't even see the end of it with binoculars, but ... when I'm not hating Jake, I kinda like him.

"We have to go. Get Swarley."

"Go?"

"Just do it!" He walks around the truck, hunchbacked.

I get Swarley in the truck, and Jake fishtails back onto the main road.

"You're um ... going a bit fast."

Eighty.

Eighty-five.

Ninety.

Holy shit! We're burning down the road at ninety.

"Jake, I think you should slow down."

With a permanent grimace, he shakes his head. Within minutes, we pull into a gas station. I'm not sure it's even open or still in business. Jake nearly falls out as he opens the door then hightails it around the side of the building, buckled over and waddling like he has something stuck up his ass.

Swarley whines.

"Shh! I know. It was wrong." I bite my chipped thumbnail, nose wrinkled. "Please don't die," I whisper.

Fifteen minutes later, Jake emerges from the side of the building, looking like a corpse.

"I'll drive." I hop out and hold open the door.

"I'll drive," he mumbles with a weak voice.

"No way. You can barely keep your eyes open. Food poisoning can be very serious. We can't have you vomiting while driving, and we don't really know that it's poisoning ... uh food poisoning, that is."

On a shallow sigh, he nods and climbs into the passenger's side.

"Let's find the nearest hotel," he says as I buckle into the driver's seat.

Who knew all I had to do was poison him to get linens and an actual shower?

Terrible thoughts. Who celebrates poisoning someone?

"Okay." I restrain my slight enthusiasm.

Jake falls asleep while I pass up the nearest hotel that I'm certain is the kind that only rents by the hour. When I find a chain name that I recognize, I park the truck and tap his arm. "We're here."

Peeling his eyes open, he grumbles. "Get a room. Any room."

"Okay." I wait, holding my purse. This isn't how I wanted to confess my predicament, but given my phoneless status and credit-less situation, I have no choice. "I have less than five dollars to my name. Anthony's brother is a banker and he's managed to freeze all of my lines of credit, including my checking account and all credit cards."

Jake doesn't even respond with a look. Keeping his eyes closed, he tosses me his wallet.

"Oh ..." I cringe. "I realize you're more of a camper, but hotels require a photo I.D. and a credit card. My I.D. won't match your credit card, and your credit card won't match my I.D., so ..."

He grumbles, pawing for the door handle. I jump out and run around the truck, opening the door for him. Draping his big arm around my shoulders, I help him into the lobby. After securing a room, I take him straight up to it and help him into bed. Before I can get his shoes off, he dashes to the bathroom.

"I'll just ... get Swarley and our bags. Okay?"

A disgusting noise sounds from behind the bathroom door. I'm not sure which end is releasing the toxins, and I don't want to know.

Jake spends the rest of the day in the bathroom, refusing to let me in except to hand him water, a toothbrush and toothpaste, and a bag that has activated charcoal. He's such a Boy Scout, always prepared to be poisoned with mushrooms.

Gulp!

"Hey." I jump out of bed, muting the TV. "Are you feeling better? What can I get you? I ordered room service." I point to a tray of food. Most of it's gone because ... two bananas.

Taking a deep breath, he shakes his head. "No food." Collapsing onto the other bed, he rests his arm over his forehead. "I'm empty. Nothing else can come out of this body."

"You're going to live, right?"

"I think so."

Thank god!

"What can I do? You need to hydrate. Coconut water?"

"I'm not thirsty." His voice is weak like the rest of him. He's this pile of muscle and tattooed skin, but I'm certain I'm stronger than him right now.

"You *have* to hydrate. I'm going to get you something. Stay put." I grab my purse.

"You have no money," he murmurs.

I don't. No money. No phone.

"My wallet."

I nod even though he can't see me. After taking a twenty from his wallet, I brush my fingers over the top of his bare foot. It twitches beneath my touch. "I'm really sorry."

Like *really* sorry.

"It's not your fault." His red-streaked eyes peek out from under his arm.

I brought the mean giant to his knees. There should be a victory party. There should be gloating. There should be this grand sense of revenge and accomplishment—but there's not.

Faking the tiniest of smiles, I slide the money into my purse, whistle for Swarley to follow, and leave before guilt cracks me and my confession pours out of my pathetic conscience.

After a quick trip to a small store and an even quicker walk to let Swarley work out his own bowel issues and eat his dinner, I carry the bag of electrolyte water and coconut water to the hotel room on the third floor.

"Go lie down," I whisper to Swarley upon seeing Jake curled onto his side, sleeping.

Setting a water on the nightstand, I sit on the edge of his bed. Jake shifts a fraction without opening his eyes. My hand moves to his face, my palm hovering over his cheek for a few seconds—giving me a chance to admire his soft skin, marred with only a few pearly scars. When I let it rest on his cheek, he opens his eyes.

"Hey."

I smile past the gnawing guilt of being such an awful person. "Hey," I whisper.

"I think the charcoal did its job." He drags in a slow breath and releases it in one quick *whoosh* through his nose.

"Does that mean you're feeling better?"

Stretching out, he nods. "What time is it?"

"Ten-fifteen. Since you're feeling better, I'm going to jump in the shower." I jab my head toward the coconut water. "Hydrate."

"Yes, Dr. Montgomery." Something resembling a grin plays along his lips.

I try to mirror his kind sentiment, but I can't because I poisoned him.

Gah!

"Don't wait up for me. I'm not getting out of the shower

until I've drained all the hot water." Grabbing my clothes, I give him a don't-give-me-shit-about-it look.

"Do I want to know what you do in the shower?" He scoots up to a forty-five-degree angle and laces his hands behind his head. It does good things to his abs—really good things.

"Probably." I wink.

Why? Why did I wink? Why did I say *probably* in my most seductive voice? I can either want him for sex or want him dead, but I need to pick one before the next orgasm or *accidental* poisoning.

A hotel shower has never felt so good. Jake's asleep again by the time I emerge from the steamy bathroom. After re-taping my two fingers, I sit on the edge of my bed, watching Jake as I try to comb through my wet hair. Swarley lumbers onto my bed.

"No." I try to shoo him off. He ignores me. The second I snuggle into my spot, I smell dog breath and feel it warm and moist against the back of my head.

"Not cool, Swarley." Throwing off the covers, I sit up. There's room in Jake's bed. Maybe he's out of it enough that I could catch a few hours of good sleep and crawl back in the flea bed before Jake wakes up.

Making the stealth transition from my bed to Jake's, I manage to get positioned next to him without him stirring. Sleep takes me quickly, and I don't move an inch until morning.

Jake

NAKED LOVE

SHE'S ALL OVER ME! A leg over both of mine. Her head's using my chest as a pillow—and she's *drooling* on me. But her right hand? It's on my junk, and ... yeah, my junk is pretty damn hard because of it. However, that's not the most disturbing part. There are *chunks* of blond hair on my chest and neck, and they are not attached to her head.

"Ave?"

She readjusts, which involves her right hand clenching around me over my briefs like a bike handle. At this point, I'd be fine with her riding me, or even a good hand job. But my fear is she's going to wake up and somehow blame this on me.

"Avery?"

"Hmm?" Her hum doesn't convince me that she's really awake. "Oh my god!" She leaps from the bed, making Swarley jump out of her bed, whining.

Okay. She's awake now.

Rolling my lips between my teeth, I lift my eyebrows. Avery stares at my erection, rubbing her fingers together. I didn't come on her hand, but it was headed in that direction. When her gaze slides up my body, the horror that my dick just gave her is dwarfed by the ugly mask of total Armageddon destruction morphing her face.

Yes, Avery ... your hair is falling out. Why? I don't know.

"Oh my god ..." Her hands inch toward her head like she's afraid to touch a single lock.

Something tells me God's not listening to her. Maybe the line's busy. I imagine he has more pressing matters like starving children, genocide, and global warming. Avery's hair is really nothing when looking at the bigger picture. I don't think she's seeing the bigger picture at the moment.

Snatching the clumps of hair from my chest, like frantically grasping for scattered money on a sidewalk, Avery hugs it and runs to the bathroom.

"Avery ..."

The door slams shut followed by more pleas to God and indecipherable mumbling, possibly even a few sobs. I'm not sure where my faith stands right now. My youth was pretty shitty, so I'm not too close to God anymore. However, I get the impression Avery and God have been on the outs for a while.

"Why?" she cries. "I'm sorry."

I sit up in bed, smirking. She's apologizing. Her naughty list must be long. Downing the bottle of water she left by my bed, I choke on the last ounce as she continues to repent.

"I shouldn't have poisoned him."

What the actual fuck!?

Tossing the empty bottle aside, I take three long strides to the bathroom and slam my shoulder against the door while simultaneously trying to open it.

"Unlock the door! What did you just say? Poison? Did you POISON ME?"

Avery sobs more.

"Open the fucking door before I break it down!"

"Don't kill me. Please ... I'm sorry ... my hair ... it's ... my life ... it's ... why does God hate me?"

"I'm not going to—" I can't finish that thought. Truth? The door is going to open one way or another, and when it does, I'm going to kill her. "He hates you because you're a vain, self-centered bitch ... and a goddamn attempted murderer!"

"I didn't want you to die!" Her grief shifts from total despair to anger. "I just wanted you to stop being so mean to me."

"Well, killing me would accomplish that, wouldn't it?"

Avery rips the door open, eyes red and swollen, cheeks drowning in tears, but fire flaring from her nostrils. "If I wanted you dead, you'd be dead!" She shoves my chest.

I grab her wrist and twist her arm around her back, bringing us chest to chest. "What did you give me?"

"Nothing—STOP!"

I fist her hair, possibly pulling out more of it.

"Let go of my hair! Let go of my hair! Please. PLEASE!"

I anticipate a cop knocking at our hotel room door before too long.

"*Nothing* doesn't make me vomit and shit until everything inside of me feels raw."

"Mushroom. Part of one," she whispers like it's her last breath while her free hand tugs at mine tangled in her cluster-fuck of hair.

"You picked a random mushroom and put it in my smoothie?"

It's barely detectable but she nods.

"You have no moral limits."

She blinks, releasing another tear. I want to tie her up and let her completely fall apart, draining all the evil and vanity from her materialistic soul. Instead, I release her. She melts down the door to the ground, pressing her hands to her head as more sobs fill the air.

"Pull yourself together. We're leaving."

I pack my stuff and hers while she sits on the bathroom floor in the same spot at the bottom of the door. She hasn't moved, but her crying stopped five minutes ago. You'd think someone died and all hope is gone. My loyalty to Deedy starts to wane as I realize I'm going to have to take our stuff out to the truck, along with her dog, then carry her pathetic ass out as well.

But ... I do it.

Good thing I didn't die. Who the hell would take care of her?

A shaky breath rattles her body as I scoop her up and set her on the bed.

"I'm not going to wrangle shorts onto your limp body, so I found this dress in your bag." I hold up the black sundress.

She stares blankly at it. I remove her nightie, her hands cover her breasts.

Really?

I know what her most intimate part looks and tastes like, yet *now* she's showing some modesty? If only she could be a little more modest with her emotions. She cringes when the dress catches on her hair or nest or whatever we're calling that *situation* on her head.

"Am I carrying you or can the broken princess walk?"

She stands, staring at her feet, wiggling her toes in her flip-flops. I didn't take the time to find matching flip-flops. If that matters, then she'd better snap the hell out of this.

"This ends today." I grab her hand and pull her out to the truck.

Forty-five minutes later, with a refueled truck, we pull into a strip mall. Avery hasn't said a word. I should do flips over it, but her constant sniffling is worse than her bitching.

"Cheer up, buttercup." I lift her out of the truck.

She stares at her feet, shoulders curled inward.

"You're going to look like a million bucks—or according to the sign in the window, $14.99—by the time we leave."

Her head eases up as I pull her by her hand into the building.

"No." She tries to pull away.

"Yes." I tighten my grip.

"What can I do ya for?" The perky purple-haired girl asks.

"Her hair is falling out. I need you to make it stop."

"No!" Avery's fight comes back.

I still don't let go of her hand.

"I'm not doing this." She looks around, using her whole weight to try to pull away from my hold. "What is this place?" Her head shakes continuously.

"Savvy Savings Salon." Purple Hair smiles.

"No. Hell no! I can't let you touch my hair."

I grit my teeth behind my smile, getting in my fucking annoying little princess's face. "Here's the deal. You get a haircut right here, right now, and I take you all the way to California. You have another ridiculous meltdown and I leave you here. No ride. No money. No phone. What's it going to be?"

Another sob escapes Avery. I'm so numb to it at this point.

Purple Hair sticks out her lower lip. "Oh, no ... it's okay. I'll get you fixed up. I promise."

I drag Avery toward the chair. She shuffles her feet like the death row walk, eases into the chair while hiccupping on another sob, jerking her hand away from me while Purple Hair puts a cape around her.

"Looks like someone hasn't been taking care of her hair extensions." Purple Hair sticks her lower lip out again, giving Avery puppy dog eyes.

"It-it's h-his fault." Avery shoots me a scowl. "We've b-been camping."

"It's okay. I'm going to fix you right up."

"Great. You do that. I have a dog to feed and walk." The bell at the top of the door jingles when I push my way out of the cloud of estrogen and sheer male hatred.

An hour later, the door jingles again. I look around for Avery. No Avery.

"She's in the bathroom ... with my nail polish remover." Purple Hair grimaces. "She's been in there awhile. I had to take quite a bit off. I told her short hair is in. I think she looks really cute."

Avery's locked herself in the bathroom again. Just great.

I drop $40 on the counter.

"I'll get you change."

I shake my head, walking to the ladies' room. "Keep it. I'm sure you deserve it at this point."

"Avery?" I knock on the door.

"All ... most ..." Her voice sounds strained. "... done." The door swings open.

No more tears.

No more fire breathing.

Just Avery with layered, chin-length hair. No makeup. No polish on her fingernails or toenails.

Just. Avery.

She stares at my chest, but I'm not wearing a special shirt for her. What is she staring at?

"Much better." I smile, but she doesn't look up at me. "Let's go."

She follows me, still scuffing her mismatched flip-flop clad feet along the ground. I open her door for her.

She doesn't look at me.

I get in.

Nothing.

I don't sense she's mad at me like she was when I left her to get her haircut. This Avery is just ... sad.

Insecure?

I don't know.

She angles her body away from me, one foot covering the other with her toes curled and both of her hands fisted and locked between her legs.

"Lunch. My treat. Any place you want to go."

"I'm not hungry," Avery murmurs barely above a whisper.

She grabs her purse and digs through it. After a few seconds, she closes her eyes and deflates.

Her phone.

I think she just remembered she doesn't have one. Her hand slides along her hair, stopping at the end by her chin. She swallows hard, returning her attention to her window again and sliding her hands back between her legs like she's hiding them.

I turn up the radio, searching for a station she might like, then I just drive.

Welcome to Texas

Drive Friendly – The Texas Way

We pull into a campground about fifteen miles out of Amarillo. Avery doesn't sigh. She usually sighs when we pull into the campgrounds.

"Come, Swarley," she says, sliding out of the truck.

I don't recognize her voice. It's timid and lacking any sort of confidence, sass, or that signature princess snoot. Again, I should be jumping for joy that she's not being her annoying self, that she's not trying to poison me again.

But ... I'm not.

After erecting the tent and starting a fire, I make us both dinner, a can of veggie chili.

"I'm sharing my dinner tonight."

Still ... she doesn't look at me. Her attention remains on the fire. Her posture in the camping chair mimics how she sat in the truck—her whole body folded in on itself. I set the bowl of chili beside her and sit across the fire from her, eating my dinner and trying to figure her out. But more than that ... I'm trying to figure out why I feel the need to understand her.

I know why she drives me insane.

I know why I want to see her knocked down a few pegs.

I know why my dick betrays me around her.

But ... hell if I know why I feel this need to fix her.

When the fire dies to small glowing embers, I whistle for Swarley to get in the tent. Avery doesn't move. I set the bucket of water next to her chair instead of extinguishing the rest of the fire. She doesn't resist me when I lift her from the chair and sit my butt down with her cradled on my lap, her cheek resting on my chest.

I press a hand to the side of her head and kiss her soft hair. "My favorite songs are acoustic. Just a piano or a guitar and a voice. Sometimes I don't even realize how much I like a song until it's stripped down. The words mean more. The emotions are magnified. It's like the stars ... During the day we don't see them, but at night when the world around us feels stripped and bare, they shine so brightly."

I rest my cheek on the top of her head. "I'm not sure I've ever seen anything as beautiful as you are in this very moment."

And oh so slowly ... she looks up at me.

CHAPTER FOURTEEN

Avery

I LET my hand touch his face, let my fingertips ghost along his jaw. Jake doesn't move. When a man says something like that, it's hard to not want to give him everything. Tears fill my eyes, because I want to give him something I've never really given to a man.

The truth.

"My mom died when I was eight. I look just like she did." A bittersweet smile pulls at my lips as my hand slides down to rest on Jake's chest. I lay my head next to my hand and stare at the orange and red embers. "She was too pretty to be a preacher's wife. Beautiful curves hidden behind conservative clothes. My dad used to tell me physical beauty should be a gift given to your husband on your wedding night. A man should fall in love with your heart.

"But sometimes when my dad traveled on mission trips and Sydney would spend the night at a friend's house, my mom dug black satin and silk slips from her dresser drawer and we'd wear them like sexy dresses.

She curled our hair and pinned it up with little ringlets hanging down. She applied her makeup, extra heavy, and put some blue eyeshadow, pink blush, and red lipstick on me. Then we slipped on high heels from her closet, which weren't very high, and we tied scarves around our necks and danced in her bedroom to Donna Summer's 'Hot Stuff,' using hairbrushes as microphones."

Jake's chest vibrates with a soft chuckle.

"I had no idea what the lyrics meant. And I didn't feel sexy, because I didn't know what that meant either. All I knew was my mom looked really pretty, and she was deliriously happy. I don't know ... we probably did this a dozen or so times before she died. But they are some of my most cherished memories. When you feel pretty, you smile bigger, and it's fun to feel pretty."

I sigh. "She used to braid my hair. I love it when people braid my hair. But I dated a man who thought long hair wasn't sophisticated. So I cut it, about this length. I didn't cry that time, but I wanted to. I no longer saw my mom's reflection when I looked in the mirror." Grunting a painful laugh, I shake my head. "The asshole guy told me, after it was too late, that I didn't have the face for short hair. He said it accentuated my big ears and my big eyes. Then he left me two days later for someone younger with smaller eyes and ears."

Jake presses his lips to the top of my head again, it brings more emotions to my eyes. It makes my heart hurt for so many reasons. It's tender, not sexual. It's such a foreign feeling to me.

"Is that why you got fake hair?"

I laugh. "Extensions."

"Same thing."

"No." I giggle some more. "The extensions were real hair. Just not *my* hair."

"And that's not a little creepy to you? Wearing someone else's hair?"

"I have leather and fur clothing. I'm sure that offends you, but I clearly don't have issues with any of it."

"The length of your hair doesn't define you."

"Neither does the size of your muscles or the ink on your skin ... yet you have both. Did you know there have been comprehensive studies on narcissism, and the results show men are far more narcissistic than women? The stereotypical link between vanity and femininity is just that ... a stereotype. Look, he's strong, powerful, and in shape. He's stylish and sexy. S*he,* on the other hand, is self-absorbed, vain, materialistic, and fake."

"Hmm ..."

I wait for him to give me more than a contemplative hum. Nope. That's it.

"Long day. I'm tired." He eases me out of his lap.

I straighten my hoodie and reach for my hair to smooth it, stopping just shy of actually touching the short ends. Old habits. Jake doesn't miss it. He mirrors my weak smile.

"Do your thing." He nods toward the tent. "I'll put out the fire and lock up the truck."

"Okay," I say with crippled confidence—fully clothed yet completely naked.

THE NEXT MORNING I wake up first after a restless night of sleep. I can't help it that I like beds, air-conditioning, and guys who are transparent. Seriously, I'm traveling with a walking unsolved mystery. Does he hate me? Love me? Lust me? Want to kill me? Want to fuck me? I have absolutely no clue. He had me in tears yesterday for so many reasons.

I'm emotionally ripped into a million pieces at this point. If I had a mirror, I'm certain I wouldn't recognize the reflection in it.

Needing to burn off some energy, I slip into some exercise clothes that are in desperate need of laundering and take off on a morning hike, sans Swarley because he refuses to move from his spot.

"Lovely." I frown as I head up the small hill, attempting to pull my hair back into a ponytail. It's maybe a half-inch ponytail.

My eyes and ears must look huge. I inwardly laugh at the thought. Yes, I care about my appearance. I like girly things. Nice things. *Things* in general. But I like people too. My family means the world to me. Do I have to be grounded and selfless to the point of never looking in a mirror or wearing a paper sack around, so—god forbid—no one thinks I care about myself more than is considered acceptable?

Screw the ponytail. I slip the band around my wrist since the pounding of my feet against the trail causes my short hair to fall out of it. I don't even remember where we are. The past two days have been emotionally challenging. Time of day and day of the week don't register with me, let alone our location in the sticks.

Oklahoma?

Texas?

Hell if I know.

I jog the trail until my incessant thoughts evaporate, until my only focus is the way my body feels, not how it looks. I jog until I'm physically exhausted ... too exhausted for anything, short of a shower, to matter.

NAKED LOVE

"Mommy!"

I slow to a stop and look around for the high-pitched voice. Tiny sobs and hiccups whisper just beyond the trail.

"Mommy!"

"Hello?" I follow the young cries.

"M-mommy ..."

A little girl, maybe five or six, with ratty, light brown hair, and tear stained cheeks, peeks around a tree. A stuffed, gray rabbit hangs from her hand as her lower lip trembles.

"Hi. Are you lost?"

She nods, hazel eyes wide and unblinking. A ways back, I turned around to head back to the campsite, so I'm guessing we're a quarter mile from it. Scanning the area, I don't see or hear anyone else around.

"Did you camp last night?"

She nods, hugging her ragged stuffed bunny to her chest.

"My name is Avery. I'm going back to the camping area. I bet your mom is there. Do you want me to help you find her?" This is a tough thing to navigate. If her mom is like my sister, Sydney, then she's drilled stranger danger into her little head. But this girl is clearly lost, and there doesn't seem to be anyone looking for her around here.

The little girl nods, wipes her runny nose with her hand, and holds out the same hand for me to take. I stare at it for a few seconds. She could be my niece. She could also be the next Amber Alert if I don't help her find her family. I take her hand, snot and all, and walk with her back to the campsite.

"Where the fuck have you been?" A large, bearded man in jeans, a white tee, and a leather vest tosses his cigarette aside and grabs the girl by her arm, yanking her away from me without giving me so much as a second of eye contact.

"Mommy ..." she cries.

"It's not your *mommy's* fucking weekend to have you. So stop your whining and get your ass in the truck. It's time to go." He opens the door to the black pickup truck and practically throws her into the passenger seat as she whimpers, "Ouch, Daddy!" After slamming the door shut, he walks behind the travel trailer as if I don't exist.

"Excuse me, I found your daughter crying in the woods nearly a quarter mile away. I think you need to blame yourself instead of her. She's not a dog on a leash. She's your responsibility."

He lights up another cigarette. "Who the fuck are you?"

Planting my hands on my hips, I narrow my eyes. "I'm the person you should be thanking for finding your daughter before someone kidnapped her."

His disgusting gaze makes a skin-crawling inspection of me as he blows smoke in my face.

I cough.

"I could stick my dick in your ass for a few minutes. Then we'll call it even. How does that sound, Ms. Good Samaritan?"

Hot rage creeps up my neck. This man is a father. Good people try and fail to have children, and *this* asshole is a father. "Sorry, but your whole body won't fit in my ass. That's what you're implying, right? Because clearly you are nothing but a big, grimy, yellow-toothed, putrid-breathed, pocked-faced DICK!"

He grins before pinching his lips around his disgusting little habit. On another exhale in my face, he flicks the cigarette aside. "That answers that." He tugs at his belt, unfastening it. "My cock's going down your throat, just to shut you up, you stupid cunt."

I take a step back, heart slamming into my ribs.

"Wait in line, buddy. You can have a go at her when I'm done."

I squint at his ugly face. What is he talking about? Retreating another step, I jump with a tiny gasp.

A familiar hand slides around my waist, pressing flat to my exposed abs below my sports bra. He pulls my back flush to his chest. "Call 9-1-1, Ave," Jake says in an eerily calm tone while handing me his phone. "Tell them this man just tried to rape you."

An iciness slithers along my spine.

"Fuck you, asshole." The disgusting guy narrows his eyes at Jake.

"Ave," Jake whispers in my ear, his lips brushing against it. "Take the phone. Go to the front of the truck. Call 9-1-1. And stay there until I come get you. Understood?"

My head inches up and down as I take the phone, swallowing hard. Jake's hold on me vanishes, and I give the awful father one last look. He refastens his belt then tries to stand straight while pumping his fists at his sides.

One step.

Two steps.

I keep my focus on the door to the truck where the little girl waits to be reunited with her mommy.

Thwack!

Oomph!

The distinct sounds of flesh and bones colliding beckons me to look back, but I don't. Instead, I call 9-1-1 and report the attempted rape, then I get in the truck with the little girl and wait. Still ... I don't look back.

Ten minutes later, a police car arrives.

"Is Daddy going to jail again?" she whispers from my lap.

Again.

That breaks my heart.

My head whips right when the door squeaks open.

"They'll need a quick statement from you," Jake stares at me with a blank look, like he doesn't have blood on his hands, when he literally has blood on his knuckles but not a scratch on the rest of his body.

"Wait right here," I say to Carly. That's her name. She's five and just learned to ride her bike without training wheels. Her mom cries every time her dad has her for the weekend. And Carly is allergic to walnuts.

She nods, hugging Elsa, her bunny, to her chest.

Jake shuts the door behind me. I make a quick inspection of him, and he does the same to me as an ambulance pulls up next to the police car.

"Carly ..."

Jake shakes his head. "They'll deal with her. Find her family."

"Her mom."

Jake nods several times. "Yes. She'll be fine."

I don't know why, but a sudden wave of emotion hits me and tears pool in my eyes.

Jake keeps his blood-covered hands at his sides and leans down, putting us at eye level. "You're fine. Okay. Just tell them exactly what happened."

"Okay." I nod once.

The police officer asks me a few questions. There's some back and forth between Jake and the moaning asshole on the gurney. Sure, he's the one leaving on his back, but he threatened to rape me, and he threw the first punch at Jake—which apparently, he didn't land. By the time we're done and everyone has agreed that no charges will be filed, the ambulance leaves. There's another vehicle here with a lady helping Carly into the backseat. She gives me a shy wave with a smile.

Wow!

Her dad was just hauled off in an ambulance, and she's smiling. That proves how truly awful he is.

Jake leaves me staring at the departing car. "Let's go, Ave. Beating a man up because you felt the need to run off on your own is not exactly how I wanted to start my day."

"What? Are you serious?" I jog to catch up to him. "I went for a run. I didn't run off. The little girl was lost in the woods, so I helped her back to the campsite. It's not my fault her dad happened to be a total asshat. And you didn't have to beat him up so badly."

Jake grabs soap and paper towels out of the back of his truck and marches over to the spigot outside of the primitive facilities. He scrubs the blood off his hands.

"Seriously? You're mad at me?"

"You're my responsibility, Av-er-y. I don't want to deal with you getting raped or murdered. That's not the call I want to make to Deedy and your father."

"Av-er-y? Why are you saying my name like that? And for the record, I was dealing with that prick."

He scrubs his hands harder. "You were watching him get his dick out."

"He was a hundred pounds overweight. I could have outrun him."

Jake shuts off the spigot, shrugs off his gray T-shirt to dry his hands, and pins me with a narrow-eyed scowl. "He could have had five other buddies just around the corner ready to gang rape you."

I cross my arms over my chest. "His daughter was in the front seat of his truck."

"Too late, Ave. You've already proven you're too smart

to act this fucking naïve." He makes his way back to our tent.

"I'm a grown woman. Stop making me feel like an errant child."

"You're my responsibility." He opens the tent. Swarley ambles out to sniff around and find all the areas he needs to mark.

"Maybe you didn't hear me. Maybe you think I'm a child. Maybe you don't understand that being a smart woman means I know what I'm doing." I follow him into the tent, crowding the middle where we can fully stand while he grabs another shirt from his bag. "Maybe you—"

"*Maybe* you should find something better to do with your mouth than nip at my ankles and yip yap at my back." He turns around, invading my personal space—not that we really have any personal space. Tents are pretty much the anti of personal space.

His gaze drops to my mouth a split second before he kisses me.

"No!" I pull back. "I haven't brushed my teeth. And my lips are dry." My hand cups my mouth.

Jake's eyes widen a fraction. A smile creeps up his face as he drops his chin to his chest and shakes his head. "This ... this is why you're bad at sex, Ave."

My hand falls from my mouth. "I am *not* bad at sex. I'm just a little self-conscious and considerate. Don't you want to kiss someone who has fresh breath and doesn't smell like they just jogged five miles?"

His lips twist.

I want to kiss those lips. I really do. But my breath probably smells worse than Swarley's. My skin has to taste like a salt lick. With no makeup on, he'll be forced to stare at the bags under my eyes because I'm sleep deprived.

"You're one designer handbag short of most every woman alive."

I frown.

His head cocks to the side. "You're also one spontaneous act short of perfection."

"That's ..." I clear my throat.

Quite possibly the most heart-stopping words anyone has ever said to me.

"I'm going to go for a hike since you didn't wait for me." He slips one arm in his T-shirt.

I grab the shirt to stop him. His gaze homes in on my hand.

Everything feels so jumbled in my body.

So vulnerable.

So naked.

Yet so alive. "I don't need another handbag."

Jake lets his gaze slide up my body to meet my eyes. He's unreadable for the longest few seconds. "What do you need?"

I drag my teeth over the corner of my bottom lip, narrowing my eyes into a tiny grimace. "I need you to turn around for ten seconds while I wrestle out of this sports bra. It's the least sexy thing you'll ever see in your life. So ... let's spare you of that."

Jake's white teeth peek out from his swelling grin as he drops his T-shirt to our feet. "Lift your arms."

I shake my head.

He raises an expectant eyebrow.

I sigh and lift my arms, angling them toward the very center of the tent. Jake ghosts his fingers over my ribs, making me shiver. He smirks, sliding his fingers under the tight elastic and pushing it up over my breasts. My breath catches, and I hold it as his gaze makes a slow inspection of me before meeting mine again. He doesn't look away until the bra is almost to my elbows, covering my face.

"Jake ..." I seethe in a sharp breath when his warm mouth claims my left nipple. It shoots an immediate need right between my legs.

Even though I can't see past my bra, I pinch my eyes shut, dizzy from the desire he's ignited inside of me and equally horrified that he's tasting the salty, dried sweat on my breasts just inches from my smelly armpits.

Jake Matthews strips me from the inside out, magnifying every self-perpetuating belief that I've ever had about my flawed body. I want to shrink. Vanish from his touch.

I want to cry, but I did that yesterday. Jake *still* called me beautiful.

"Jake ..." My voice trembles along with the rest of my body as he sucks and drags his tongue over my other breast.

"Yes, Ave?"

I'm not going to cry today. I don't need another handbag. Today, I need to be his perfection.

Folding my arms inward, I grab my bra and tear it the rest of the way off. The insecure part of me wants to stand here and wait for his approval, wait for him to tell me what he wants me to do next.

I don't.

My mouth crashes to his. I don't taste him. I devour him. My hands claw at his back and shoulders, even my injured fingers bend into his skin, feeling no pain.

"Is that the best you've got, Ave?"

He taunts my thoughts.

My tongue battles his. This is my kiss. This is *me* kissing him.

"You see ... the art of sex is all about selfish pleasure."

I don't want him to want me. I just simply *want* him.

"You like what I'm doing ... but I'm not doing it for you. I'm doing it because I want to taste you ... because I want to hear you whimper ... because I want to feel you squirm. That gives *me* pleasure.*"*

Breaking our connection, I kiss my way down his neck as my fingers curl into his chest before I take his hand and guide it into the front of my exercise shorts. My fingers press over his, using him to give myself selfish pleasure.

"Fuck, Ave ..." he rasps with a weakness that is not a Jake I've experienced before.

My other hand works the prominent muscles of his back, massaging him. *This* I know I can do as well as anyone else. I knead each muscle all the way to the inside of his shorts, where he's not wearing anything underneath. My fingers find all the firm lines of his perfect ass, eliciting a deep groan from him.

My lips pull into another grin along his pec muscles for a brief moment before my teeth sink into them. This sets off a chain reaction. He rocks his erection into my stomach and slides his middle finger inside of me. I clench my hand over his, biting him harder on a soft moan.

"That's my girl." He bends his finger inside of me as I lift onto my toes to claim his mouth again because I crave him the way he craved me.

We kiss until neither one of us can stay standing for one more second. He slides his hand out of my pants and holds onto my head, keeping our mouths connected as we sink to the ground. It's desperate but perfectly slow at the same time. We just kiss—him hovering above me, me rolled on top of him, and us intertwined on our sides.

Naked from the waist up, with his chest pressed to mine and our mouths insatiable, we make out. I have never—ever —just kissed a guy for this long, like we're having sex with only our lips and our tongues. It's sensual, erotic, and passionate.

Passion. At least that's the word that comes to mind. I've never experienced anything like this before, but I have to believe this is passion—a completely uncontrollable emotion. The moment when mind and body collide into something indescribable.

Our heads tilt in every direction, my palms pressed to his stubbly face, his tangled in my hair. For the first time in the past twenty-four hours, I don't miss my hair. Jake doesn't just say I'm beautiful, he makes me *feel* beautiful with his whole body.

When passion explodes into undeniable need, I move my hands down his chest, letting my lips follow. Our lust-drunk gazes meet as I slide off his shorts, tasting him like he tasted me.

"Ave ..." he tugs on my hair like he's in pain. I glance up as I release him from my mouth.

Standing, I slide out of my jogging shorts and panties. Jake sits up and grabs my hips to bring my center to his mouth, making me weak in the knees as my eyelids grow heavy.

"Jake Matthews..." I say through my stolen breaths "...I love your mouth."

He closes his eyes and palms my ass like he's never enjoyed anything more in his life. When I'm ready to convulse and collapse onto him, he brings his hands back to my hips and kisses his way up my body while guiding me down onto his lap. It's almost everything—almost perfection —but not quite. I pull away from his mouth and lift onto my knees.

Without a second of hesitation, a moment of doubt, or a breath of uncertainty, he fists his cock and positions it between my legs. I slide my fingers through his hair and kiss him as he pulls me completely onto him.

We share soft moans.

We share tender touches.

We share the best. Sex. Of. My. Life.

CHAPTER FIFTEEN

Jake

AVERY MONTGOMERY IS my new favorite acoustic song. The sounds she makes when she's completely out of her skin with desire and out of her mind with need ... it's fucking incredible.

"I'm sleeping with the enemy," she mumbles into my neck, her naked body covering mine.

Did I mention she's my new favorite blanket too?

"I'm the enemy?"

"Yes." She lifts her head and hands me a pathetic frown. "You're the school bully who calls me names, pulls my hair, snaps my bra, then gives me chocolate. And I'm the gullible girl who lets said school bully feel me up because I like chocolate." Avery twists her lips. "Well, I don't like chocolate anymore, but I used to."

I chuckle. "Now I'm the school bully and you're the girl who lets a guy feel her up for chocolate? Avery, Avery, Avery ... God, I hope it was more than just a bag of candy from a vending machine."

"I'm just kidding." She rests her cheek on my chest. Her fingers trace my tattoos.

"Liar." I pinch her sides.

She jumps and giggles, rolling off me.

"Who was he? Choir boy? Quarterback? Math geek?"

Avery rolls to the other side of the tent to get away from me, giggling the whole way.

I crawl toward her.

"No!" She grabs my pillow and hugs it to her chest like it can protect her, but her back is pressed to the side of the tent. She has nowhere to go.

Swarley barks outside of the tent. I hold up my finger to my lips. "Shh ... you're upsetting him with your schoolgirl squealing."

"Then stop prowling toward me like that." Avery pulls the pillow up so just her blue eyes are peering over the top of it.

"Like what?" I snatch the pillow away from her.

"Eek!"

Swarley barks.

"Shh ..." I hook her waist and drag her to me.

She grins as I hover above her. It makes that thing in my chest hurt because I think I fucked up. In my effort to strip her down to just Avery, I may have gone too far—gave her too much of myself.

Avery widens her legs, positioning my newly aroused dick right at her entrance. When she pulls her knees back, I feel her wet and warm against me.

"Again," she says on a breathy whisper.

My conscience screams to get out of here. Buy her a plane ticket to L.A. and deliver the dog at a later date.

Right now, that screaming conscience falls on deaf ears.

"Again." I push into her as our mouths collide.

Welcome to New Mexico
The Land of Enchantment

"Hi, Daddy," Avery slips off her sandals and plants her sexy feet onto my dash. The windows are down. The breeze is warm.

Not a diva in sight.

Holding my phone to her ear, she glances over at me and winks. Yeah, she's going to ruin me.

"We're in New Mexico. No ... my phone battery isn't dead. The whole thing died. There was an incident, but I don't need it. How's Deedy?"

She says Deedy's name like she's sucking on a piece of hard, bitter candy. I have a feeling it's a mix of her being a daddy's girl and Deedy being close to her age.

"Jake's ... fine. I guess."

I give her a sidelong glance with a raised eyebrow. Avery smirks, keeping her gaze pointed at the road ahead.

"Oh ... she's going to wear an actual wedding dress? That's ... interesting." Her smirk drops into a solid frown. "Even though it's just the two of you and witnesses?" She picks at the frayed hem of her jean shorts.

After a few more uh huh's, okay's, and I supposes's, she says "I love you" in a very honest way and ends the call.

"Just to be really, really clear ... you've *never* been intimate, sexual, flirty, or anything like that with Deedy?" Avery glances over at me. "Have your lips ever touched any part of her body?"

"You really want to have this conversation?"

"JAKE! You lied to me! Eww ..." An exaggerated shake shimmies her whole body. "It's cross contamination. You can't do what you've done to me *and* have a history with my dad's fiancée. It's all kinds of wrong."

I laugh. "You realize you've done a few things to me too."

"But I didn't screw your mom's boyfriend." She wrinkles her nose. "That's my bad. Your parents are probably happily married. I'm not seriously suggesting she has a boyfriend. And I certainly haven't slept with him. Oh god ... at least I hope not."

"My mom is not alive."

Avery covers her mouth with her hand and shakes her head, closing her eyes. "Shit ... I'm sorry. I just shouldn't ... speak. I should stop talking indefinitely."

"It's fine."

She doesn't respond for several miles. I must not have sold the *fine* so well.

"Can I ask how she died?"

I clear my throat, keeping my eyes on the carless road in front of us. "She was sick."

"Oh. I'm sorry. Cancer? That's how my mom died."

I shake my head. "Not cancer."

"Oh ... um ..."

I hate that this is so fucking hard. I always thought it would get easier. It hasn't. Years of physically fighting away the demons, and I'm still filled with anger when I think about it too long. "She battled depression."

Avery nods slowly, not saying a word for several miles. Finally, she breaks the silence. "How long ago did your mom die?"

"I was fourteen."

"What do you remember about her?"

"If I don't want to talk about this, does that make me an asshole? I know you shared about your mom, but—"

"No. Doesn't make you an asshole." Avery's reassurance sounds anything but reassuring as I hand over five dollars for parking.

I bite my tongue from making up a million reasons for why I don't want to talk about my mom, since the real reason isn't ready to come out. By the time we reach Santa Rosa, Avery seems to be fine. I think. She's hard to read when she's so quiet.

"Are we good?" I reach over and squeeze her leg after I shut off the truck.

"Yeah. Everything is fine." She returns a tight smile.

I scratch the start of a beard growing along my jaw. Her *fine* sounds like anything but fine.

Avery unfastens her seat belt and tosses me a smile. It borders on a cringe, clearly a forced smile. "So, what are we doing here? What is Blue Hole?"

"It was once known as Blue Lake. It's just a blue gem in the middle of the desert. Great place for scuba diving, but we're just going to cool off for a bit since it's insanely hot."

She nods slowly. "I don't have a swimsuit."

"I'll grab your sports bra and shorts from this morning. They'll work. You let Swarley out."

Avery nods slowly again, face tense with apprehension. Bringing her out of her comfort zone is my new high.

After Swarley does his thing, we do a quick change into swimming attire, grab towels, and put him in the truck with all the windows down and his travel bowl of water on the floor.

"It's blue. Really blue." Avery's eyes widen as we approach the rock cliffs around the swimming hole.

"Together?" I give her hand a squeeze.

"What? Wait ..." She tries to pull away. "I'm an ease-it-in sort of girl."

"Yeah, I know." I smirk.

She rolls her eyes.

"But this is not an ease-it-in kind of lake. It's a heart-stopping-take-the-plunge kind of lake."

Her head shakes. "Nope. I like my heart beating."

"Ave ..." I don't release her hand, no matter how hard she tries to wriggle out of my grasp.

"No."

"Yes."

"Nooooo!" she shrieks when I toss her into the lake and quickly follow her.

"Oh my god! Oh my god! COLD! COLD! COLD!" She slaps at the water, making her way to the edge.

Not gonna lie. It's cold as fuck. A crisp sixty-five degrees. I grab her waist and pull her back out.

"Jake!"

"Shh ..." I laugh. "Lie back and float."

"C-c-cold." Her teeth chatter.

"Thirty seconds." I relax my body and float on my back.

She does the same thing.

I close my eyes and just breathe. This ... this is the good stuff in life. My hand brushes hers, and I latch a finger to hers so we drift as one. Thirty seconds pass ... then several minutes pass. She'll never admit it, but she knows it too ... this is the good stuff.

"T-times ... u-up." She swims to the edge and we get out. "B-b-brrr..." Avery hugs herself as I grab our towels, wrapping her up first.

"Your lips are blue like the water." I fist the towel by her chin, keeping it wrapped tightly around her.

"E-evil. Y-you're p-pure e-evil."

I envelop her in my arms and kiss the cold from her lips,

sucking on them until they're warm again. "I'll warm you up."

"H-hypothermia ..."

"Nah." I squat down and slip her flip-flops on her feet.

When I stand again, her eyes shoot to mine, a bit wide.

"Were you checking me out?" I cock my head to the side.

She shakes her head.

"I think you were. You've seen me naked."

"I w-wasn't. And e-even if I w-was ... s-so what."

I think she has an actual smile on her face, but it might just be a residual grimace.

"Let's go dry out in the sun. I'll grab something to make for lunch. We can eat over at the park."

I clasp my index finger with hers and guide her to the truck just as another vehicle pulls in next to us. As the couple gets out, I stop, tugging on Avery to stop too. She glances back at me with confusion wrinkling her brow.

"Let's go over to the shop," I mumble, turning back the other way.

"What? No. I-I'm cold."

"Jake?" A gratingly familiar voice says my name.

I stop and close my eyes, releasing a long sigh. How the fuck did this happen?

"Son?"

I turn slowly. "Call me that again and it will be the last word you speak in this lifetime."

He shuts the door to his black SUV, slipping a baseball cap on over his black and gray hair. Pulling the toothpick from his mouth, he lets his gaze sweep over Avery, a slight grin tugging his lips. I want to kill him.

"Ave, get in the truck, please."

"Ave is it? Is that short for something?" he asks, his fucking smirk doubling.

Avery's wide-eyed gaze bounces between us. "Um, Avery."

"Jake, nice to see you."

Grinding my teeth, I ignore the woman rounding the vehicle.

"It's been too long," the sperm donor says.

"Funny ..." I take my towel and wrap it around Avery's waist because I'm not going to stand here and watch this man stare at her. "I was just thinking it hasn't been long enough."

"You still baking?" He enjoys this, mocking my profession. "How does one go from a fighter to a baker?"

"He's a chef."

"Ave ..." I grab her hand and tug it toward the truck. "Don't correct him. He's too fucking stupid to remember anything."

"I'm Francine ... Frannie." She holds out her hand to Avery. I still don't look at her. "Are you Jake's wife?"

I let go of Avery's hand and grab her bag out of the back of the truck to get her dry clothes.

"No." Avery doesn't elaborate.

"What do you want out of here?" I ask in a clipped voice.

"I'll get it." Avery takes the bag.

"Nice Louis Vuitton. I have the same one in black." Francine's voice claws at my nerves.

I slide on a T-shirt.

"Thanks. I love it. Just got it a few months ago." Avery seems quite pleased that someone noticed her overpriced bag.

Clearly her need for that shit is hardwired.

"Nice watch." Avery points to the chunky gold thing on Francine's wrist.

"Thanks. Howie gave it to me for my birthday."

Howie smirks at me. He's trying to lose all of his teeth with one fucking grin. I clench my fists.

"Looks like we have the same taste in women, Jake."

That's it. I grab his shirt and shove him up against his SUV.

"Jake!" Francine and Avery yell at the same time.

"I hate you and I hate your fucking materialistic whore. So don't you ever think we have one goddamn thing in common." I release him with a sudden jerk and step back.

Francine shuffles in her heels to his aid.

"Jake ..." Avery starts to grab my arm.

I pull away. "For the last time, Avery ... get in the fucking truck."

CHAPTER SIXTEEN

Avery

"I'M NOT GOING to jump just because you tell me to jump." I tighten the towel he tied around my waist.

The muscles in Jake's jaw pulse several times.

"Good for you," Frannie says as she and Howie squeeze behind Jake to open the back of their vehicle.

Jake gives them a quick glance over his shoulder. I'm sure he's scowling even harder at them as they get their wetsuits out of the back. His dad scuba dives. I find that very cool.

"Good seeing you, Jake. Look me up when you want to make amends. We're just outside of Albuquerque. Good luck, Avery. You're going to need it."

I expect Jake to attack Howie again, but he doesn't. When his dad and Frannie are out of earshot, he returns his attention to me. "This is a hard limit for me." He hands me his phone. "Call your sister or your dad. I'll get Swarley to L.A. for you. I'm sorry if you don't like the way I need to protect you. I'm sorry if it's not delicate and polite enough for you. But it is in fact for *you*." He pushes his phone into my hand, punctuating his point like a fist punched into my heart.

"You wanted me to stand up for myself, and now that I'm doing just that, you want me to submit to you?" I take his phone.

"I'm not the enemy." Jake walks around the truck and grabs his wallet from the bag behind the seat. He retrieves some cash from it.

I shake my head. "I don't want your money."

He tries to shove it toward me. "You're not going to get very far without it."

I stare at it. "Please," I whisper.

"Please what?" He exhales a sharp breath.

I look up, feeling on the verge of either laughing hysterically or crying. "*Please* get in the truck, Avery," I say, settling on a simple, defeated shrug. "That's it. One tiny word." Turning, I toss his phone on the driver's seat and grab my clothes from the bag I unzipped a few minutes ago. After slipping on a sundress, I worm my way out of my impossibly tight and wet sports bra and bottoms, then I slip on my panties.

Before I can turn back toward him, his hands slide around my waist, hugging my back to his chest as his lips brush along my ear. "*Please* forgive me."

Blinking back the pain, I drag in a shaky breath. "Francine ... I remind you of her. That's why you hate me."

"You're not her."

I turn in his arms, leaning back to get a clear look at his face. "No. I'm not. But do you really believe that, or do you have to talk yourself into seeing past the part of me that *is* like her?"

His gaze falls to the small space between us.

Sometimes silence feels like the coward's truth.

"It's fine, Jake. You fucked me good today. Hope that helped you work out some of your issues. I know *I* figured some shit out today. My days of trusting men are over. At least my fancy bags and expensive shoes make me look good. Men are so much worse than anything materialistic. You say the right things for the wrong reasons. You lie to get what you want. You make me look bad. You make me *feel* bad. There's nothing wrong with my taste in fashion. It's my taste in men that's fucked-up." I push his hands off my waist and climb into the truck.

Swarley rests his snout on the console like he's trying to show me some sympathy. How ironic that my K9 nemesis has become my source of comfort. I run my hand over his head, and he sighs.

I don't care that Jake's still standing at my open door. There's no way I'm looking at him. After a few moments, he shuts the door.

Anthony and I were together so much longer than I've known Jake. We discussed marriage. He said he loved me. Yet, this hurts more than the chocolate incident because I allowed Jake to see me emotionally stripped. It's embarrassing. It's degrading. It's just ... fucking painful.

When he gets in the truck, I angle my body away from him, keeping my gaze affixed to the road outside my window.

"Do you want to stop for lunch?" he asks after several hours on the road.

I don't acknowledge him.

We stop for Swarley. I get out, not giving Jake a single glance. Not a single word.

We drive until after dark, making one more stop for Swarley to get out of the truck and do his business. When we do stop for the night, it's a small motel in Sedona, Arizona instead of a campsite.

Still, I don't give him a glance or a word. Even my hunger wanes under the shadows of my anger. Swarley and I sleep in one bed. Jake sleeps in the other bed.

The next morning, I wake early, slip back on my sundress, and catch a pretty spectacular sunrise from the wood bench outside our door while Swarley sniffs the surrounding area. When the sun hits its halfway point on the horizon, the motel room door opens. I lift my knees onto the bench and hug them to my chest, trying hard to ignore Jake in his jeans and naked inked chest. I try to ignore his sexy, messy morning hair and his scruffy and equally sexy face.

He stands directly in front of me, blocking my view and replacing it with his well-defined abs and low-hanging jeans.

Blink.

Blink.

I'm not going to look at his face. Nope. He can block my sunshine in every sense, but I'm not going to acknowledge his existence.

He squats in front of me, resting his hands on my bare feet, sans toenail polish. As soon as I get back to L.A., I'm going to get a mani and pedi. I'm going to get hair extensions. And I'm going to sell some jewelry to buy new clothes because I like that stuff. Screw Jake and his bullshit. I don't want to be his perfection. It's an impossible role. I'll take the designer handbag.

I just …. I just wish his touch stopped at my feet. It would make it easier to step on it—to walk away. Why do I have to feel the ache of his touch behind my ribs?

"Please …" he whispers.

My eyes betray me. They meet his gaze. It's so sad, just like the slope of his lips.

"Please what?"

His forehead rests against my bent legs. "Please everything. Just … please …"

"This is messed-up, Jake," I say slowly … with little fight left in me. "I remind you of a woman you obviously despise." My fingers find their way to his hair. When I run them through his thick, blond strands, he lets out a soft sigh.

He's in pain, but I can't fix him when I'm still scattered in so many pieces. And as much as he might like to put me together to fit the mold he desires, I can't bend that way anymore.

"*Good job, Ave. Stand the fuck up for yourself.* You said that to me. So this is me, standing up for myself. I have no job, no money, no car, and I probably won't have a home by the time we get to L.A. But … I'm going to stand up, even if the only thing covering my naked body is an itty-bitty piece of self-worth."

Jake lifts his head. I hold my breath as he gives me an unreadable expression. Bravery isn't a trait, it's a few moments of time where we pretend that we're not vulnerable. My chin tilts up a fraction. If he doesn't say something soon, my bravery will slip, and once again I'll be nothing more than a hot mess.

"You don't want to go home."

I narrow my eyes. "I hate camping."

"But that doesn't mean you want to go home. You could be home by the end of the day. I could hang out with

Swarley and enjoy the peaceful camping I'm used to every summer. Your dad would expedite your trip home if you just asked. So would Deedy. So would your sister. Yet here you are ... with me."

My gaze drifts over his shoulder to the unquestioning sunrise. It just does its thing. It doesn't ask why we need it. Why can't Jake just do his thing and take me home? Why can't he be the unquestioning sun—guiding me home?

I shrug. "You could have driven me to any airport along the way and put me on a plane to L.A. with the promise of delivering Swarley. Yet here you are ... with me." Letting my focus return to him, I swallow hard.

I'm not sure either one of us really has a damn thing to give the other one. Yet here we are, on this road trip—marking time, delaying the inevitable.

Jake's sad face finds a hint of a smile. "Here I am ... with you." He pulls my feet off the bench, scooting me closer to him so his torso wedges between my legs, our faces just inches apart.

"We have nowhere to go," I whisper past the lump of fear in my throat.

His gaze finds my mouth, and it sends a tingly feeling to the rest of my body. "We have lots of places to go, Ave ... just nowhere we need to be."

Nowhere we need to be ...

That's liberating and sad at the same time. When did my existence become so inconsequential?

"Why me?" I don't completely fall apart into an I'm-everything-you-despise mess. It's not that I don't understand why some men have wanted me, but I have no idea why Jake wants me.

"I don't know." Lines crease his forehead.

"I need more than that. Anything really. It can be the

sex—which, since I'm obviously so bad at it, I don't know why it would be that."

He smirks.

"Are you bored? Am I a frivolous challenge? Is this a lesson you're trying to teach me? Revenge?"

Jake's head inches side to side.

"Then what?" I push at his chest until he stands and steps back. Running my fingers through my hair, I sidestep him enough to put him behind me because I don't know what to do with this pull I have toward him. It feels dangerous to my heart. "You're not the guy who needs a date to take to fundraisers. You're not old and desperately searching for something—someone—to make you feel young again. I'm not a tree-hugging girl who works part-time at an animal sanctuary. You're this sexy guy who could have that girl." I turn back to him, letting my arms fall limp to my sides. "You could have someone who shares your dreams. You could probably have *any* girl you want. So ... it makes no sense for you to want me."

He rubs his lips together, nodding slowly. "True."

I wait.

Nothing.

That's it? Really? I cough a laugh and shake my head. "A toy. I'm just a toy to you." Retrieving my room key from my pocket, I open the door. Swarley follows me inside. I grab his bowl out of his bag and fill it with a cup of food. Then I get him water from the bathroom faucet. Jake observes me from the door to the room, his back leaned against it, hands resting in his jeans' pockets.

"I don't know, Ave."

I laugh again. "Yes, Jake, I got that loud and clear." Rifling through my bag, I look for something clean. I have *nothing* that's clean. Perfect.

"I like that I don't know."

My eyes close, feeling the warmth of his bare chest pressed to my back, his hands sliding around me possessively like they did yesterday.

"What if we can't explain it?" He continues. "Maybe the attraction *is* that nothing about it makes sense. Who chases the familiar? Who stays up all night solving mysteries that have already been solved?"

"Have you lost sleep over trying to solve this attraction?"

"So much," he whispers in my ear. "Your incessant fidgeting with your hair, your nails, your clothes, your lipstick ... it drives me fucking crazy."

I stiffen in defense, and he squeezes me harder as if his arms are saying "wait."

"But ... for a mysterious reason, I find myself equally mesmerized by it." He kisses my neck. "Three is your number. You comb your hair in the same spot three times before moving on to another section of hair. Three times powdering your nose. Three swipes with the wand to your lip gloss. When you put on a pair of shorts or pants, you brush your hands down the front and the back of them three times each."

Emotion thickens in my throat and burns my eyes. I'm not sure I've ever been with a guy who knew the color of my eyes without looking directly into them, or my favorite fragrance, or anything other than my name and maybe my favorite flower.

Three.

My mom used to hug me and count to three with me when I would get angry or frustrated. A three-second hug made the monsters in my closet disappear. And the last time she kissed me, she did so once on each cheek and once to the middle of my forehead—three kisses goodbye.

I didn't know that I did these things three times. Jake Matthews just knocked on the window to my soul and whispered, "I see *you*." Not the million imperfections I see in the mirror.

Holding my breath for *three* seconds, I close my eyes. Then ... I fall. It feels like an out of body experience, and I realize that I've never truly fallen before. "Take me with you," I whisper.

"Where?"

My teary eyes open as I turn in his arms. "Everywhere ... nowhere." I grin. "Just take me."

White teeth peek through his lips. I want those lips. And that smile.

Everything.

I want everything, and none of it costs a dime, comes with a label, or will ever go out of style.

Jake lifts my sundress over my head and steals the kiss of all kisses. My fingers work the button and zipper to his jeans. We lose the rest of our clothes in the *three* steps it takes to get to the bed.

"Jesus ..." he says on a tight, labored breath when he sinks into me. "It's hard to breathe when I'm inside of you." He kisses along my neck. "Another anomaly I'll spend countless hours trying to figure out."

I curl my fingers into his hair and smile as my hips lift to feel him as deep as possible.

Yeah ... right there. Take everything, Jake ...

CHAPTER SEVENTEEN

Jake

"Never thought I'd be so happy to see a laundromat." Avery twists her lips and sighs, staring at the building as I grab our bags of dirty clothes out of the back of the truck.

"Never thought I'd have to carry so many clothes into a laundromat."

In spite of the grin that steals her mouth, she manages to feign irritation with an eye roll. "You're my hero." She holds open the door.

"Actions speak louder than words, Ave." I give her a look.

"I'll polish your saber later. Deal?"

I chuckle. "I think that's what you did in exchange for me letting you shower first." I drop the bags on the floor by the last row of washing machines.

"No, pumpkin, *that* wasn't for letting me shower first. That was for the forty dollars I borrowed from your wallet while you were in the shower."

"Forty-dollar blow job? That's a little steep considering

I'm driving your fine ass to California. Can I ask what you're doing with my forty dollars?"

Avery starts sorting clothes into several washing machines. She has domestic skills. Why does that surprise me? I keep my shock to myself.

"I'm going to pay you back. The blow job was just the interest."

An older lady an aisle over gives us wide eyes.

"Still doesn't answer my question." I slip money into the slots.

"It's a surprise." She makes a separate pile with just her bras and panties.

I resist the urge to slide it onto the floor and roll around in it. Instead, I play to our audience of one. Bringing a pair of Avery's satin and lace panties to my nose, I take a long, slow inhale.

There they go ... the old lady's eyes roll onto the floor as she gasps, clutching her invisible pearls.

"Jake!" Avery rips the pink panties from my grasp and shoots the lady a tight, apologetic smile.

I chuckle and lift my hand, giving the unsuspecting woman a no-hard-feelings wave. She hides behind her book to cover her face.

"You're an animal." Avery puts her undergarments into another washer on delicate cycle.

I add money to the machine. "The forty dollars. What's the surprise?"

"Not telling. Let's go." She nods toward the door. "There's a deli across the street. Let's grab lunch."

"Are you paying with my forty dollars?"

Avery turns, walking backward while giving me a flirty grin. The wind catches her hair and blows the now-shorter strands across her face—her makeup-less face. Her wrinkled dress hugs her curves. I know every pair of panties she brought with her is in that washing machine, along with her bras. She's naked under that dress.

I stop just before stepping off the sidewalk, feeling like the wind has been knocked out of me.

Her smile fades. "What's wrong?"

"You're beautiful."

Avery gives me a nervous smile then shakes her head, averting her gaze. "Whatever ... not all blow jobs will involve a forty-dollar loan."

I don't react to her insecurity, no matter how much I hate it. Instead, I wait for her to really look at me. I wait for her to see the absolute truth in my words.

"Don't." Her head inches side to side.

"Why?"

Her wavering self-esteem fills her eyes with unshed tears. It's tragic.

"Because I don't see it. Not now. Not when I'm such a mess." Her hands wring together as her shoulders fold inward like a wilting flower in need of water and a day of sunshine.

"It's not your hair or your dress. It's the way you rub your lips together to hide your smile—and the way your teeth break through because you *have* to smile. It's the little lines that form at the corners of your eyes when you do smile. It's not that your eyes are blue like the sky, it's that when you look at me like you are right now ... it's a truly beautiful day. And it's pretty fucking incredible to be the recipient of that look, that glimmer in your eyes."

Her lower lip quivers just before she turns her back to me. I give her a minute because I'm not done stripping her down. But ... that's good for today.

"I don't care what you say," she says after clearing her

throat. "I'm getting a sandwich with tons of meat and cheese, no veggies, extra mayo, and a bag of cheesy ranch and bacon flavored chips."

Stepping off the curb, I wrap an arm around her shoulders, pulling her back to my chest and kissing the top of her head while she takes another moment to wipe the emotion from her eyes. "Okay, Ave." I chuckle.

"Okay." She draws in a shaky breath, pushing some confidence into her spine. "I'm glad we got that straight."

"Me too." I take her hand and guide her toward the restaurant.

We grab lunch and perch on the truck's tailgate to eat it in the scorching sun. Terrible idea. Swarley stretches his legs before begging to get back in the shade of the backseat.

"My dad cheated on my mom." I stare at the busy road beyond the parking lot, legs swinging from the tailgate while eating my hummus wrap. "He asked for forgiveness. She gave it to him. He did it again—told her it was because she'd let herself go. She got pregnant when I was eight and lost the baby before it was born. I just remember her being sad all the time. She fed her grief with food. He fed his with other women. The things he said to her ... the way he made her feel ... I hated him. Now there's not a word strong enough to describe how much I despise him."

Avery stills her swaying legs and drops the last third of her sandwich into the paper bag. "I should have just gotten into the truck," she whispers.

"No." I blow a quick breath out of my nose. "That's not why I'm telling you this. I was angry. I think I'll always be angry. But can you fucking believe it? I grew up outside of Los Angeles. My dad left four years before my mom died. Just ... left. As a ten-year-old, I didn't really know what that meant. She said he was angry, and when he cooled off he'd be home. He came home four years later. With fucking Francine." I laugh. It still hurts. God ... I think it will always hurt.

"He brought his whore to my mother's funeral. It was the day I found out that I could land a punch ... that I could break someone's face. That I *wanted* to break someone like that. And after all these years, having no idea where he lives, we run into him at a fucking swimming hole in New Mexico. What are the chances?"

Avery rests her hand on my leg. "Did you have to live with your dad after your mom died?"

"No." I grunt a breath of sarcasm. "I lived with my uncle—my dad's brother. He was more like a cousin to me because we were only eight years apart in age. He'd just gotten an apartment in L.A. after being abroad for two years.

"After the incident at the funeral, everyone knew there was no way I was going to live with my dad and Francine. She was twenty. *Six* years older than me. Skinny ... big boobs ... and she had it all on display at the funeral. My mother killed herself because she'd gained over one hundred pounds, was morbidly obese, and diagnosed with diabetes. My father never missed a chance to make her feel ugly and worthless. Kids at school made fun of my mom before she died. I hated them. I hated my dad. I hated every person who reminded me of the women he slept with while my mom ordered takeout and cried herself to sleep."

Avery starts to slide her hand off my lap, but I grab it.

"Don't." My gaze remains fixed on the busy road. "You're not her. You're not them. You're not my revenge."

"I think you're saying that because I'm here, out of my element. But you didn't feel that way the day I walked into your cafe. Had we not been forced to be together for this long, you wouldn't have asked me out on a date. You wouldn't have given me a second look because, upon that first look, all you saw was another Francine."

"And all you saw was another guy who would break your heart—*monkey-spanking dick cheese*. Had I asked for your phone number, you would have taken one look at me, made a shitload of assumptions, and walked out without a single glance back."

She pulls harder, freeing her hand from mine, and hops off the tailgate. "We don't make sense together."

I slide off the tailgate and close it. "Probably not."

Avery turns toward me. "Eventually, we have to go home. And there will be questions to answer."

"What questions?"

"Questions like, *what are we doing?*"

"We'll answer them later."

She shakes her head. "You're delaying the inevitable."

I take the sack from her and walk toward the door to the laundromat. "I'm not."

Avery follows me. I hold the door open for her as she gives me a narrow-eyed glare while walking into the building. "You are. You're using me for sex on your summer road trip."

"I'm *having* sex with you on my summer road trip. And it's surprisingly good sex. The questions ... well, maybe by the time we get to L.A., we'll have the answers."

I don't really believe that at all. I don't have a fucking clue what I'm doing. But it doesn't serve a purpose to let her know that right now.

"Surprisingly good sex? Wow ..." She opens the first washer and piles clothes into the rolling basket. "That statement sounds like the preamble to the rest of our trip—*no sex.*"

I help change the loads to the dryers, keeping my gaze on her and a smirk firmly planted to my face while she tries to ignore me.

"So what do you do in L.A.?"

Avery shuts the dryer door and stops, giving me two raised eyebrows. "I'm a massage therapist. *Was* a massage therapist."

I shake my head. "When you're not working or shopping or going to get your hair and nails done ... what do you do?"

She blinks several times. Damn! That's *all* she does. I swallow the reality in small doses so I don't choke on it. Avery *is* a diva.

"Never mind. I didn't mean to put you on the spot." I shoulder past her to put money into the dryers.

"That's not it," she murmurs. "You didn't put me on the spot. It's just ..."

"It's fine, Ave. That's a lot, and there's only twenty-four hours in a day." I continue to change clothes from the washers to the dryers, moving twice as fast as Avery.

"Don't be a dick."

I feed coins into the last dryer and turn around. Avery eases onto a clothes-folding table. Her wrinkled brow cast down with her gaze as her feet dangle in the air.

"I'm being a dick?"

She answers with silence.

"I'm just trying to get to know you."

More silence.

I rub my forehead and blow out a slow breath. "I cook. It's not just my profession, it's my passion. When a shipment of fresh, local produce arrives, it gives me a ridiculous high. I can't wait to create something pleasing to both the palate and the eye. When I'm not cooking, I'm reading food blogs. When I'm not doing that, I'm on my Harley or walking dogs from the animal shelter because I did it with Addy, and..." I shrug "...it's just something I've continued to do."

Avery lifts her head.

Without taking a breath, I continue. "I like space, the infinity I see through my telescope. It makes my troubles feel insignificant. I like old sayings, but not as much as I like new ideas."

"What are your troubles?" Avery whispers. Worry shrouds her sunny blue eyes, turning them blue-gray like an impending storm.

"Memories."

Her teeth brush her lower lip several times as the lines on her forehead intensify. "I like baseball and peanuts. I *love* peanuts. The saltier, the better. I mean ... I want to tell you that I love to travel, watch Broadway shows, spend warm afternoons at vineyards sipping wine and eating bruschetta ... but those are things I've done with men. Wealthy men. I'm not wealthy. In fact ..." Avery frowns. "I'm dirt poor at the moment. I can usually snag tickets from friends at work to see a baseball game. Peanuts are in my budget. And when I'm by myself—alone—I like ..."

I wait.

She stares at her feet swinging from the table in a slow rhythm.

"You like ..."

Avery's nose wrinkles. "These videos."

"Videos?"

"Never mind. Forget it. It's dumb." Her cheeks flush as she glances around the laundromat, looking everywhere but directly at me.

"Ave, are you into porn?" I push off the wall of dryers and wedge my body between her dangling legs.

Giving me a quick headshake, she presses her lips into a firm line and continues to survey our surroundings.

My hands squeeze her legs, forcing her mouth into a tiny smile. "If you don't tell me, I'll be forced to think your favorite past time is watching porn."

"What if that's it?" She halts her wandering gaze, focused on mine. "What if *all* I enjoy is shopping and long afternoons at the salon? What if I've never stuck a dime in the red kettle at Christmastime or paid it forward? What if my favorite foreplay is watching other people have sex? Does that deflate your tree-loving heart? Does it take a little more effort to get an erection for me?"

I grin.

Her eyes narrow. "This isn't funny. You need to find a sliver of goodness in me to justify what's happening between us. And the truth is, you're just like every other guy I've dated—you want my body, but *you,* Jake Matthews, have this nagging conscience. You have a reputation for being a nice guy who does the right thing. And nice guys doing the right thing don't settle for someone like me."

I can strip her down, take her apart. We can sort through the pieces. But *she* needs to decide how to put things back together where they belong and what she no longer needs. I can't be part of what makes her whole again. People don't fill voids, even if they create them.

Leaning forward, I ghost my mouth along her jaw to her ear. "Tell me about the videos. I know they're not porn." I kiss her earlobe. "I think it's something *very* unsexy. Yet..." I kiss her neck "...something tells me it's going to make my whole damn day."

She shivers as her shaky hands lay claim to my arms. "Jake ..." My name falls breathlessly from her lips.

My hands ascend another inch up her legs as my lips remain idle against her soft flesh. "Tell me, Ave ..."

Her fingers curl into my biceps. "Documentaries. I like watching documentaries. Especially the *True Facts* series by Ze Frank. He shares crazy but mostly true facts about various animals in a Morgan Freeman-like narration. It's hilarious and completely inappropriate because he often fixates on genital facts, but I laugh myself into a giggle-fit every time."

And *this* is why I'm on the road to nowhere with this woman—and with no incentive to rush a single moment. I get to see something I'm sure no human before me has ever truly seen. It's pretty fucking incredible.

"Real sexy, huh?" Insecurity. I hate the insecurity in her voice.

Wrapping my arms around her waist, I lift her from the counter.

"Jake—"

I silence her with a hard look two seconds before kissing her. With no knowledge of what's in the back of the laundromat, I walk us toward two vending machines down a small hallway ending in a "staff only" door.

It's a little dark and a lot cramped, but I don't need any light or much space to make my point.

Her sundress.

Her sans-panties body.

It's almost wrong to not do this right here, right now.

I wedge us into the four-foot space between the two machines, pin her back to one of them, and free myself from my jeans. Messy, disheveled, giggles-at-animal-genitalia-jokes Avery has me very hard at the moment. And completely out of my mind.

"Jake, not ... here ..." Her protest evaporates into the musty air between us as I fill her with every inch of my cock.

We kiss, tongues making desperate jabs into each other's mouths as her hands ball into tight fists filled with my hair.

I growl.

She tightens her grip.

I slide my hands to hold her bare ass as I fuck her harder, rattling the vending machine, attempting to infuse some sense into her. She's worthy of whatever the hell she wants in life.

We all are.

Her legs tighten around my waist as I pick up the pace. What is she doing to me? When did my despise morph into such an uncontrollable need? I feel like a horny teenager possessed with the need to get off all day long.

The front door creaks open.

"Jake—"

"Shh ..." I kiss her harder, fuck her faster.

Two vending machines hide us in a dim hallway. Eighties music stutters out of old speakers to block our noise. We've got this. And even if someone heads toward us, I can't stop.

It's not just me. Avery rocks her pelvis in a clawing rhythm to get off before time runs out.

That's all it takes for me to release. "God ... damn ..." I bite her neck to muffle my pleasure.

"No ..." Avery yanks my hair again, hips grinding frantically as I still.

"Let it go." I chuckle, thrusting into her several more times as my right thumb finds her clit.

"Yes ... yes ... yesss ..." she whispers out of breath.

With my final thrust to get her off, something clinks and thunks into the bottom opening of the vending machine at Avery's back.

Avery lifts her head, flushed from neck to forehead. She grins, realizing we just rattled out a snack. "Dibs."

She can have dibs on the candy bar. I want dibs on her.

CHAPTER EIGHTEEN

Avery

"Swarley won't eat his chew stick." Twisted in my seat, I frown at a drowsy Swarley as we make our way to the Grand Canyon.

"It's hot. He's probably just tired." Jake gives me a quick sidelong glance.

"It's buffalo and honey, his favorite. He always scarfs it down. I'm worried something is wrong with him."

"Well, I can call a friend of mine. She's a vet, moved from L.A. to Flagstaff two years ago."

She.

Why am I tripping over that? I don't want to be that girl. Not with Jake. Yet ... I'm that girl. *Gah!*

"That would be great. I can't kill Swarley. My sister will never forgive me."

Jake chuckles. "Killing someone's dog *is* pretty unforgivable. So is poisoning them."

"So is depriving someone of a proper shower."

"Poisoning and shower deprivation. Yeah, those are on the same level."

"Don't be bitter." I slide off my sandals and prop my feet up on the dash for two seconds before my gnarly, unmanicured feet frighten me into dropping them back to the floor.

"Don't be self-conscious." He hands me another quick look with a knowing smirk.

I want to go home, and yet I don't. Everything will change when we get to L.A. How can it not? I live there. Jake lives in Milwaukee. That's a lot of miles to solve.

"Your mom. Is she why you eat the way you do? Is she why you take such good care of your body?" I grunt a laugh. "That's actually odd if the answer is yes because you were a fighter. You let people beat the shit out of you. That's the opposite of taking care of your body. Right?"

"I was the guy beating the shit out of other fighters. But thanks, Ave, for assuming I suck." He grabs my knee and squeezes it until I jump.

Why does Jake the fighter turn me on? I'm not a violent person nor have I ever been into watching any sort of fighting. I don't even care for action movies. Yet the idea of Jake winning fights makes me squirm in my seat, well, that and the memories of the laundromat.

"Why? Was it for the money?" I grab his hand on my knee and bring it to my lips, kissing his knuckles one at a time.

"The money was good. But no, that's not why I started fighting. My uncle was a fighter. When he saw me spiraling out of control after my mom died, he trained me, put me in the ring, and told me to fight the demons. I did. I fought my father, the memories of my mother losing herself, the kids who made fun of her right in front of me. Everything ... I just kept knocking everything down. I was never going to use food the way my mom did. I was never going to take another snide remark from my father. I wanted—I needed—total control of my life."

"And vegans are in control?"

He laughs. "Sure. And that explains why you're such a hot mess. You consume too many angry animals' spirits. They're pissed off about being slaughtered and having their udders pumped to the point of bleeding."

"Ew ... too far."

Jake laughs more. "Sorry. Probably a tad too far."

"Can you love me even if I eat said slaughtered animals?" I slap my hand over my mouth.

Oh my god.

"That was ..." I shake my head, mumbling through my cupped hand. "Not what I meant to say."

"Your life, Ave. Not mine. Your journey. Your conscience. Your beliefs. Not mine."

He fails to acknowledge the L-word I just flung in his direction. I don't know if I should feel relieved or terrified.

I twist around when Swarley makes a noise. "Oh my gosh!"

He vomits on the seat.

"Jake! He's sick." I unfasten my seat belt and wedge my body behind the console to flip up his blanket so the vomit doesn't run down behind the seats.

"Okay. Calm down. I'm pulling over." Jake veers onto the shoulder. Thankfully, we're not on a main road with heavy traffic. He hops out and opens the back door.

Swarley struggles to get out, so Jake helps him.

"Oh no!" I cover my mouth as Swarley retches again, but very little comes out.

"He probably got into something that's upset his stomach." Jake squats next to him and strokes his back.

"Call your friend. Call her now." My stomach clenches like an angry fist as panic sends my heart sprinting to keep up with the fear that something is not right. Swarley is not a young dog anymore.

"Grab my phone." He stays next to Swarley.

I get it and push the voice command button.

"Call Megan," Jake says as I hold it close to his mouth.

Megan. I now have a name for the irrational jealousy that's on my horizon. It rings on speaker three times before she picks up.

"Hey, sexy!"

Yeah. I hate her. After she fixes Swarley, I will kill her to eliminate my competition. Friend ... Addy is his friend. He had sex with Addy. Doesn't he have any male friends? Look at him ... of course all his friends are women who willingly sleep with him. And they stay friends. Will we be friends when whatever this is ends in L.A.?

"Hey, Meg. Are you home today?"

"Depends. Are you coming to visit me?"

"As a matter of fact, I'm thirty minutes away. But I need a favor."

"Is it sexual?"

I raise my brows, returning a tight smile as Jake tosses me a grimace.

"Uh ... funny. No."

"Am I laughing? Come on, throw me a bone or boner." Now she laughs.

It's a terrible laugh, and I'm not being catty or biased. Really.

"Totally kidding, Jake. But single life sucks. I never

should have gotten married. The asshole just sucked all the good years out of me, and now I'm used goods."

"I don't have time to feed your ego, Meg. I need a favor."

"You sound serious."

Swarley retches again, but nothing comes out except tons of drool dangling from his lips.

"I'm traveling with someone. She has her sister's dog with her, and she's worried he might be sick or something. He's vomiting and drooling excessively. He probably ate something he should not have. Would you be willing to check him out?"

"Of course. What breed of dog?"

"Weimaraner."

"I'll text you my clinic address and meet you there. I'm at home right now."

"Thanks, Meg. You're the best. See you soon." He ends the call.

"Wow ..." I shake my head while removing the soiled blanket from the backseat, retching a few times myself because it smells so bad. "I get to meet two of your friends slash past lovers on this trip. Yay me."

Jake grabs a few towels from the back of the truck and lays them across the backseats. "Meg and I are friends. That's it. We met at a fight years ago. Her husband made a lot of money betting on me. They both followed me to countless fights. We all became friends ... until he cheated on her. They've been divorced now for two years. That's when she moved to Flagstaff. Meg and I just stayed in touch. No big deal."

I frown while he helps Swarley into the truck. "He has to be okay. Sydney will kill me if anything happens to him."

"He'll be fine. Dogs get sick just like humans." Jake

shuts the back door and turns to me, pulling me into his broad chest. "Okay?"

This space he makes for me feels like it's mine—his arms, the crook of his neck, the bold, woodsy soap scent clinging to his skin. This is my spot. I don't want to lose my spot.

As soon as we pull out onto the road, I flip down the visor and check my hair and naked face.

"You're beautiful."

"You've had your dick in me three times today. I'm worried you're not really seeing me clearly through your post-coital goggles." I frown at my reflection. "Ten bucks says she's wearing makeup and has at least one hair product in her hair."

"We stayed at a motel last night. You had a mirror and light this morning. Why didn't you put on makeup?"

I shrug.

"Well?"

"You guilt me into ignoring my appearance. If I even check for an eyelash in my eye, you give me a look like I'm obsessing over my appearance."

"Why do you care what I think?"

I start to speak but snap my mouth shut. Jake baits me into knee-jerk reactions. He pushes me. Sometimes he challenges me in ways I need to be challenged. But right now, I'm out of my comfort zone with a man I've known all of two seconds, and my sister's beloved dog is sick on my watch. This isn't the right time to speak my mind.

OUR SILENCE BREAKS as Jake parks outside a tiny, dark wood building. "Oh Jesus ..." I gasp at the excessive drool coming from Swarley's mouth, and I think something is oozing from his nose too.

Jake shuts off the engine and opens the back door. "Come on, buddy."

Swarley lifts his head an inch then rests it back on the seat.

"Hey, Jake."

I turn to the long-haired brunette in skinny jeans and a fitted gray tee. Yep. She's wearing makeup and her hair is not naturally this perfect. No way.

It's so wrong of me to envy her hair when Swarley is in bad shape, but it's a natural reaction. Maybe I am a terrible person.

Jake hugs her. It knocks the wind out of me for a few seconds. She's in my spot.

"Good to see you, Meg." He kisses her cheek.

Those are my lips. Why did he kiss her with lips that are supposed to be just for me? Why am I feeling so overcome with jealousy while my hands shake with panic because Swarley can barely lift his head?

"This is Avery. Avery, this is my friend, Megan."

I offer her my shaky hand. She takes it and covers it with her other hand as well, giving me a gentle squeeze. "Nice to meet you. Don't worry, I'm going to take good care of your dog. What's his name?"

"Swarley." Her kindness sends instant tears to my eyes.

It's official. I'm an awful person for letting unwarranted jealousy get to me.

"Jake, let's get Swarley inside."

Jake and Megan carry him inside while I hold open the doors. "You can come back if you'd like, or you can wait out here while I examine him."

"I'll wait out here." I return a shaky smile as I hug my arms to my torso.

"I'll be right back." Jake gives me a reassuring nod, but I don't feel reassured of anything because Swarley looks so lifeless.

"Don't die. Don't die. Don't you dare die on me," I chant to myself while pacing the waiting room. "You owe me for injuring my fingers." I curl the fingers of my injured hand and pump them into a fist several times. The pain is gone, but I can't completely bend them all the way. They are stiff. I took off to my dad's house instead of staying home and going to physical therapy. It's all Anthony's fault—and Swarley's fault. But I can't blame him for anything right now because I just need him to not die.

As for Anthony, he can choke and die on a chocolate-covered pussy for all I care.

"Is he going to be okay?" I run into Jake's arms when he opens the door to the waiting room.

"Meg called her nurse. She should be here soon. She thinks it could be GDV, basically a twisted stomach. He's probably going to need surgery."

"Oh my god ..." Tears escape my burning eyes. I cry for my nemesis.

I cry because I have to call Sydney and tell her I failed her.

I cry because Swarley was the only one there for me right after Anthony cheated on me.

I cry because he's old and I'm really, really scared.

"Shh ..." Jake frames my face with his strong hands and kisses the tears from my cheeks. "Meg is going to fix him. Okay?" His lips brush mine, and I nod before kissing him.

And that's what Megan does. She performs surgery to

untwist Swarley's stomach while I make the phone call I don't want to make.

"Hello?" Sydney answers.

"It's me." I bite my lips together and take a slow inhale to keep from falling apart.

"Avery, where are you? Would it kill you to check in a little more often? I get that you lost your phone, but clearly you *can* call." She's in mom mode. Worried. And angry because I made her worry.

"I'm sorry."

"Are you okay? Where are you?"

"I'm fine." I walk to the opposite corner of the waiting room to distance myself from Jake. I don't want him to see more of my insecurities and shame. "We're in Flagstaff."

"Wow ... that's not exactly on the route to L.A. Listen, I don't mind you spending your summer vacation camping with Jake, but we'd like our Swarley back. Ocean keeps asking about him."

"That's what I'm calling about. He ..." I fist my hand at my mouth and swallow hard. "He ended up with a twisted stomach."

"GVD? Avery, he has GVD? Where are you? Tell me he's okay. Tell me—"

"He's in surgery." I wipe a tear that escapes as I stare out the window. "Jake's friend is a vet. He's in good hands."

"Text me the address. We'll get there as soon as we can. Don't let him die, Ave." Her voice breaks.

I choke on a sob and nod, but I can't speak. So I end the call. Jake's arms wait for me. What would I do without him?

Hours pass and we shift in a hundred different directions, fighting the stiff waiting room chairs. On a long sigh, I turn toward Jake with his head resting in his hands, hunched over with his elbows planted on his knees.

"I'm sorry," he says with complete defeat. "I should have taken you and Swarley straight home."

Straight home.

Would that have meant a few long days of driving in awkward silence and a semi-amicable goodbye. Probably a good riddance on his part. Straight home wouldn't have given us a chance to ... what? Fall in love?

I inwardly laugh. Are we in love?

I know my answer, but I don't trust it because I don't trust myself. My life has been filled with terrible choices, chronic grief, and debilitating envy that everyone around me has found happiness, a meaningful life, and someone to share it with them.

Is Swarley suffering because I only thought about myself?

Yes.

"It's not your fault. It's mine." My fingers caress his hair.

He looks up with craters of pain lining his forehead.

"It's nobody's fault." We turn toward Megan's voice. She unties her surgical gown. "GVD is not fully understood. There are precautions you can take to lessen the chances of it happening, but some dogs have it happen despite all cautionary measures. Don't blame yourselves. The surgery went well, but we'll need to monitor him closely for a couple days. If he makes it through the night, that's a good sign."

More emotions burn my nose and eyes. *If he makes it through the night.*

"Thank you." Jake stands and hugs Megan.

I remain idle, suffocating under so much guilt. Maybe ... just maybe it's not really anyone's fault. But it happened on my watch, and I'm not sure Sydney will see it as simply an unfortunate, unpreventable happenstance.

"Thank you." I manage to choke out two words and offer Megan another handshake where, once again, my hand shakes on its own.

"You're welcome. There's really nothing to do here right now. Why don't the two of you go back to my house? Grab a shower, make yourselves at home. I'm going to stay here tonight with Swarley."

"I can't leave him. My sister is on her way."

"Is she driving?" Jake asks.

"I ... I assume so. They'll have to take him home, so ..."

He slides his arm around my waist. "Then it's going to be hours before they arrive. Let's go back to Meg's. We'll come back before they get here. And you'll call if anything changes?"

Megan nods and returns a sad smile. Why is her smile so sad? Is there something she's not telling us?

"Can I see him before we leave?"

"Sure." She gestures with her head to follow her. "He's not awake yet, and he's hooked up to a monitor, and we're giving him oxygen, so don't be alarmed. It's all normal."

I see him through a glass window before we get to the door. My feet halt in this quicksand of shock that wants to pull me into the ground and drown me in a reality I'm not ready to accept. "Swarley ..." I whisper. "He looks ..." I can't say it.

"Alive. He's alive." Megan rests her hand on my shoulder.

He's not mine. He drives me crazy. He's made me cry.

I don't even think he likes me.

Yet ...

I'm certain I love him. The idea of losing him makes it hard to breathe.

I turn.

"Ave ..." Jake slides his hand along my neck and cups the back of my head, bringing me to my spot. The warmth of his cheek resting on the top of my head hurts so much because ... I love them. I love the two males who have been there for me over the past few weeks. And I don't want to lose either one of them.

"Let him rest. Come with me."

JAKE DRIVES me to Megan's house. The truck feels so empty without Swarley in the backseat. Sydney blows up Jake's phone with a million messages. I reply to every one of them, doing my best to reassure her that Swarley will be fine.

I have no idea if he will be fine. Everyone told me my mom would be fine. She wasn't fine.

"Ave?"

I glance over at Jake holding my door open. When did we get here? My thoughts are sluggish. I just need things to slow down, except Sydney getting here. I need her right now, but I don't want her to hurry since I found out she's driving alone.

Jake unbuckles my seat belt and scoops me up in his arms.

"I can walk."

"And I can carry you."

Two of the sturdiest dogs I have ever seen rush to greet us.

"Hey, pups." Jake hunches down and gives them some love.

"Pups? They don't look like pups."

He chuckles. "Odin and Jord are South African Boerboels."

I squat next to Jake and let them lick my face. Jake raises a single brow.

"I'm not a diva."

I'm sometimes a diva.

We give them a few seconds of attention before they run off again. I follow Jake to Megan's kitchen. She has a cozy house with an open-floor plan. It's painted in shades of white and gray with soft green and gold accents and dog toys are scattered on the tile floor.

"I'll make us something to eat, and we can take dinner to Megan since she'll be there all night." He hands me his vibrating phone. "Your sister."

Any change?

I type back.

No. Sorry :(

"I get to watch you cook in a kitchen, not just over a campfire. Exciting."

He glances over his shoulder at me as he inspects the contents of Megan's refrigerator. "I aim to please."

"Yes, I know." My skin heats from memories of all the ways Jake has pleased me.

He pulls out produce bags of various veggies, beans and cashews from the pantry, and a slew of spices.

"Where do you stay in L.A.?" I say this instead of "I've never had a guy cook for me." Jake is the epitome of everything that's missing in my life. In other words ... a life.

"I have an apartment above my restaurant, similar to my apartment above the location in Milwaukee."

"I've been to Sage Leaf in L.A. I asked someone who worked there what was above the cafe, and they said 'nothing.'"

"As they should."

"How long do you stay there?"

He shrugs with his back to me as he chops onions like a ninja. "Maybe five or six weeks out of the year."

"You ever think of making L.A. your permanent home and spending five or six weeks in Milwaukee instead?" I miss subtle by the full length of an ocean.

"Too many fires and not enough snow."

This is when we talk about *us*. Right? I'm giving him every opportunity, but nope. Is this it? Are we just two bodies keeping each other warm on cool nights in a tent? I can't do this. Jake has seen me naked in every possible way. I have to stop here. No begging for more.

Stand the fuck up for yourself.

He finishes dinner while I play with Jord and Odin and keep my panicking sister at ease with "no news is good news" messages. We eat—it's amazing. Then I do dishes, earning me another disbelieving brow raise.

"Meg just messaged me."

I turn, holding my breath while drying my hands. Jake stands from his spot on the sofa with the two mammoth dogs.

"She asked us to feed Jord and Odin before going back to the clinic. And Swarley is awake and still stable."

I exhale as my whole posture melts in relief.

"I'm sorry. Really." He slides his hands in his jeans' front pockets, pushing his shoulders up toward his ears. It makes him look vulnerable. "Deedy expected me to get you and Swarley safely home. I just should have..." he shakes his head "...taken you straight home. I could have stayed for a week or two and made my trip back to Milwaukee the one where I stopped to camp. I was just ..."

I fiddle with the towel, twisting and tugging it, but it

does little to settle my nerves. "Pissed off that you had to bring us along."

He nods once, regret creasing his brow.

"And now things have changed."

Another nod.

"And you don't know what to do with me because we're going to run out of places to go, and eventually we will need to be somewhere."

His lips twist as he lets his gaze fall to his feet with one last tiny nod.

"Well ..." A nervous laugh stumbles from my mouth. "Maybe you're right. Maybe you should have taken us to L.A. as quickly as possible. Maybe we should have kept things less ... messy."

I'm scared.

I'm scared to say I don't regret any of it. I'm scared to ask him if he's ready for it to be over. I'm scared because I have nothing to offer.

My nonexistent life awaits my return. Still ... this hurts. I like Jake for Jake.

His smile when he's being playful.

His brooding need to protect me.

His sexy voice when he says "Ave."

Every tattoo.

Every touch.

Every word that strips me to my very soul, that makes me question who I am and where I'm going in my life.

He holds out his phone. "Sydney's calling."

I take it and swipe the screen. "I hate that you keep calling and texting when you're driving alone."

"It's the life of a doctor's wife. I feel like he's always on call. And the time he took off from being sick doesn't help. Luckily our neighbor was willing to come over and watch the kids. Ocean wanted to come so badly, but I ..." She clears her throat, and I can feel the emotion she's suppressing.

"You didn't want her to see him if he's not the Swarley she's used to seeing."

"Yeah," she whispers.

Jake feeds the dogs then crawls around on the floor with them, giving them more love. I smile even though he's not looking at me.

"Are you almost to the clinic?"

"Forty-five minutes out."

"We'll head that way too. Jake just heard from the vet, Megan. She said he's awake and stable."

"K."

K ... she's so choked with emotion. I want to crawl through the phone and wrap my arms around her. I want to apologize to her with as much sincerity and regret as Jake just did to me.

"Drive safely." I disconnect.

Jake glances up, sitting back on his heels. He's so handsome in those faded jeans and old tee, tattoos all down his arms. I want to ease onto his lap and taste his mouth, die in his hunger for me, let the world around us fade into another life.

"We should go. Sydney will be there soon."

His gaze slips from mine. It's like we're a sinking ship, but there's no hole or crack to fix. We just carry too much baggage to stay afloat—or maybe it's just that we have nowhere to go but down.

Jake finds a bag for Megan's dinner, and we make our way to the truck in silence, drive to the clinic in silence, *sink* in silence.

I climb out and stare at the dim light coming from the

front window of the clinic. Jake steps in front of me and sets the paper bag on the ground by our feet. My gaze sticks to the bag because I can't look into his blue eyes. I can't watch the night's shadows dance across his handsome face. I just can't …

His fingertips feather along the inside of my palms, touching me deeper than should be possible. "What if I can't let go?"

CHAPTER NINETEEN

Jake

"Jake ..." Avery bites her quivering lower lip.

Instant regret hammers my chest. Why did I say that? Before I say more or attempt to erase the words I just said, an SUV pulls into the parking spot next to my truck.

"My sister..." Avery jogs away, hugging the brunette that gets out of the vehicle.

They embrace as if they haven't seen each other in years. I feel like the idiot stranger waiting for an introduction. *Hi, I'm Jake. I'm the reason you're here instead of home with your family and healthy dog.*

"I'm so sorry." Avery chokes on her words. "I shouldn't have left L.A. with him."

Sydney pulls back, pressing her palms to Avery's cheeks. "Stop. This isn't your fault."

Avery releases a tiny sob.

"Let's go inside."

Avery nods. "Oh ... um ... this is Jake."

I hold out my hand.

Sydney takes my hand, offering a forced smile shackled with worry. "Nice to meet you."

I nod toward the door. "You too. Let's see how he's doing."

Avery loops her arm around Sydney's arm. I'm not sure who's supporting whom. I hold open the door, and Avery gives me a sad smile.

Megan shuffles into the waiting room with a cup of coffee in her hand. We make quick introductions, and I wait here while Sydney and Avery go back to see Swarley. A few minutes later, Megan reappears.

I hand her the bag of food. "Is he going to be fine? Don't sugarcoat it with me. There's no need. We've been through too much together."

Megan eases into a chair. "I don't know yet. It's hard to say. The surgery went well, but he's an older dog. Too many uncontrollable things could still happen."

I sit next to her, blowing out a slow breath.

"Quite the sigh. Is it about Swarley or Avery?" She opens the container and gives me a wry smile.

"Hell if I know." I run my hands though my hair and bend forward, resting my elbows on my knees.

"Sounds complicated."

"It wasn't supposed to be. It was a favor for Deedy. An inconvenience. Avery was a nightmare. High maintenance. Whiny …"

"You're in love." Megan taps the fork on her lower lip.

"You're crazy."

"I saw you with her earlier. The tender side of Jake Matthews. The way you looked at her. Really, the way you couldn't *stop* looking at her. Steve used to look at me like that."

"She's …" I rest my forehead in my palms.

"Beautiful? Sexy? Blond? Just like you?" She nudges her arm into mine.

"She's nothing like me. She's nothing I thought I'd ever like. Avery's ..." I blow out another sigh, shaking my head. "She's stereotypical and completely blindsiding at the same time. It's messing with my head. She's Francine one minute and my mom the next minute. I don't know if I should embrace her vulnerability or run from her vanity."

Megan grunts. "Jake Matthews, that's your problem. You see her in this black and white ... two-dimensional way, and that's not fair to her. You don't need to embrace her vulnerability, you need to feed her spirit. And don't run from her vanity, simply admire her beauty in all its perfect *and* flawed states. Love her as a whole, not just the parts you find worthy of love."

"The hell, Meg ... what happened to my bitter friend who threatened to cut off her cheating husband's junk? When did you channel your inner Gandhi?"

She chuckles. "I had my sink-or-swim moment. Drown under the weight of my anger and hatred or let it go to save myself—to free myself. I let it go."

I nod several times as her words hang in the air. "I saw my father—very unexpectedly—at a stop in New Mexico. Francine too. I'm not sure I would know how to coexist with him in a world where I don't hate him."

"Why?"

I shrug, massaging my temples. "It's just always been my way of coping with my mom's death."

Megan rests her hand on my leg. I wait for more of her voice of reason, but she remains silent. Sometimes no words are the best words.

Avery

"He's been with me through the most defining moments of my adult life," Sydney speaks after fifteen minutes of nothing but tears and soft whimpers while stroking Swarley's head.

I continue to give her space, hanging back a few feet so she and Swarley can have their bubble of privacy. Her whispered confession draws a new round of tears from my swollen eyes.

Words of comfort and reassurance congest in my throat. *He'll be fine.* But will he? *He's had a long and wonderful life.* So what? We'll still miss him every day. *I'm sorry I took Swarley with me.* But then I wouldn't have made this trip with Jake.

Why can't the blade of regret be smooth, quick, and painless? Why must it be jagged and messy? Why must it rip and tear with such unforgiving pain?

"Hey," Megan's soft voice draws our attention away from Swarley. She observes the monitor and gives Sydney a tiny smile. "I'm staying all night. You can stay too or you can go back to my place with Avery and Jake. I'll need to keep him here for a couple more days. I suggest you consider getting sleep while you can so you're well-rested when it's time to take him home."

Sydney's forehead wrinkles as she gazes at Swarley.

"I'll call you if there's any change."

Swallowing hard, Sydney clears her throat. "What if something happens and I can't get here in time?"

Megan rests her hand on Sydney's hand, stilling it on Swarley's head. "Do you have other children?"

Other children. Megan's good. She doesn't dismiss the obvious—Swarley *is* one of my sister's children.

"Yes," Avery whispers.

"Then you know that you can't be everywhere. And every goodbye should mean everything."

Sydney's lower lip quivers as she nods once.

"Do you need another minute?" Megan asks.

Sydney nods again before lowering her head closer to Swarley's ear. Megan slides past me to exit the room. I can't bring myself to move out of her way, or say a word, or make my lungs take another breath. Until ... I see Sydney's lips move, whispering something to Swarley and it. Breaks. My. Heart.

"Excuse me." I brush by Megan and her nurse standing just outside of the room then hurry to the waiting room.

"Ave—" Jake stands.

My body crashes into his. I squeeze him, burying my face into his neck. "Don't let me go." A sob breaks, rattling my ribs. "Don't wh-whisper something in ... m-my ear and let m-me go."

Not like Sydney is doing to Swarley.

Not like my dad did to my mom.

Not like every man who has claimed to love me.

Love me, Jake. Not for now—love me forever.

He cradles the back of my head with his hand. My body slides into the hard, *familiar* curves of his torso. And when my heart knocks on my chest, reaching for his heart, I lose myself.

Dreams blur.

The familiar becomes the unknown.

Life feels suffocated by death.

"We can go."

Jake releases me as I turn toward Sydney, wiping my eyes only for them to refill with tears when I see my own sadness multiplied in the tears on her cheeks.

"It's out of our control. His fate is in God's hands."

I swallow the lump of reality lingering in my throat and step away from Jake to hug my sister. She's so much stronger than I will ever be.

"That's what Dad said about Mom," I whisper.

Sydney nods.

"I'll call if there's any change." Megan's gaze sweeps around the waiting room.

It's hard to walk away, so I wait for Sydney to take the lead. She does, and Jake rests his hand on the small of my back to usher me out the door behind my sister.

"Towels and bedding are in the hall closet."

"Thanks, Meg," Jake replies.

"I'm going to drive Sydney." I turn to Jake as we reach his truck.

"Good idea." He nods, taking my hand to give it a quick squeeze.

"I'm never getting a dog," I whisper as Sydney distances herself, bringing her phone to her ear. Probably checking in at home.

Jake's lips curl into a doleful smile.

"They're terrible creatures. They ..." I shake my head. "They're impulsive and needy. They piss all over stuff. They lick their butts and beg for food. They whine and bark. And then they ..." I pinch the bridge of my nose to push away the emotions burning my eyes. "They give you this look. Stupid, puppy dog eyes that they never grow out of. They rest their snout on your leg and just look at you. Always reminding you that when everything else in life fails, they will be there for you. They listen and never interrupt. They come when you call. They're always loyal ... to the very end."

"He's not dead."

I return a tiny nod. "But he's old. And ..." I fight past this stupid ball of pain choking me. "He looks tired. My mom looked tired."

Sydney says "I love you" to someone on the phone.

I clear my throat. "See you at Megan's?"

Jake nods as he bends forward to kiss my cheek. It's incredibly intimate, like a whispered promise that doesn't require a single word. Like Swarley gave me when I needed it the most.

Inside, I smile. Is Jake my Swarley? Can he hurt me but still love me? Can he be loyal? That would be a first for me.

I take the key fob from Sydney and nod for her to get in on the passenger's side.

"I'm so incredibly sorry," I say as we follow Jake's truck out of the parking lot.

"You have no reason to apologize for this." Sydney exhales, staring out her window.

"But if he doesn't make it—"

"Then he doesn't make it." She sniffles.

JAKE OPENS Sydney's door for her when we pull into Megan's driveway. He shows her to the guest bedroom, gets her clean towels, and offers to make her something to eat.

I watch the man I've fallen in love with treat my sister like family, like he's known her forever. Jake's compassionate side blinds me, wraps itself around my heart, and infiltrates my soul.

"I'm not hungry, but thank you, Jake." Sydney's smile falters. "I'm going to try to get a little sleep in case Megan calls about Swarley before morning."

"Night." She gives me one more hug before disappearing into the guest bedroom.

We play with Megan's dogs for a few minutes before taking turns using the shower. I tell him to go first because I need a longer shower, the kind that washes away these desperate emotions—the fear of what's to come. By the time I emerge from the steamy bathroom, wearing Jakes shirt—

My heart has no room for you,
but the trunk of my car definitely does.

—he's changed the sheets on Megan's bed. Perched on the side with his tattooed back to me, his thumbs ghost across his phone screen.

"Megan?"

Jake looks over his shoulder as I crawl onto the bed behind him. "Nice shirt." He smirks.

"You should see what's underneath it." I match his grin.

"Are you texting Megan?"

He shakes his head and sets his phone on the nightstand. "Deedy. But I think she was in the middle of doing something. She seemed a little short and frustrated in her replies. Said she needed fifteen, maybe twenty minutes to finish up."

I hug his back and kiss his shoulder. "What do you think she was doing?"

"Your dad."

"What? Ew ..." I push away and fall onto my back, covering my head with a pillow. "No. Yuck! That's so wrong. Why would you say that?"

Laughter rumbles from his chest as he tugs the pillow away from me. I cover my eyes with the heels of my hands as he covers my body with his, nestling his narrow hips between my legs.

A satisfied grin slides up his face when I uncover my eyes. "You have *nothing* on under my shirt." Restrained by his boxer briefs, his erection nudges me like an arrow pointing due north.

"Just ..." My breath evaporates from my chest. He does that. Jake is a thief who takes breaths, slays words before they fall from my lips, and steals hearts.

Yeah, he's stolen my heart.

"Just what, Ave?" He pushes my shirt—his shirt—up, eyeing my exposed breasts and wetting his lips. Raw masculinity delivers his words. Even on a whisper, his deep voice reverberates along my skin.

Commanding.

Arresting.

Seductive.

I shiver with anticipation seconds before everything burns with need. Jake doesn't just reside in my head and my heart. He lives in every cell of my body.

"I'm not bad at sex."

He grins. It's arrogant for two seconds before his eyes shine with something that feels like adoration—maybe even love.

"No? Would you like to back that statement up with proof?"

My head eases side to side. "I want to give you a massage."

"A massage?" His thick eyebrows lift up on his forehead a bit.

"Yes. I'm good at it. I want you to know I'm good at *something*."

"Your fingers are injured."

I hold up my hand, bending and flexing my fingers several times without pain, but a stiffness remains. They may never be the same, since I left town instead of visiting a physical therapist. "But I'm fine."

After several slow blinks, his grin returns.

"Jake ..." I close my eyes on a weak protest as he plants open-mouth kisses along my neck, rocking his pelvis an inch —an inch that draws a sharp breath from my chest. "I'm serious."

He takes his time dragging his skillful mouth up my neck, along my jaw, halting at the corner of my mouth.

The Jake Effect feels like what I've always imagined resurrection to feel like—minus the throbbing need between my legs.

Dear Heavenly Father,

Please forgive me for thinking of you and an orgasm in the same thought. But if we're not meant to have this kind of pleasure—a lot—then why give women a clitoris with over 8,000 nerve endings? DOUBLE what you gave the penis! Sometimes I feel like we just walk around trying to act normal—human—when all we really want to do is have an orgasm because it's the BEST feeling. Why make it so amazing? And if it's only meant for reproduction, then why does it feel good all the time? Why not make it feel good only when the body is primed to reproduce? Did you mess up? I mean ... you created the world. THE WORLD! Surely you could have put this pleasure mechanism on a timer. Why leave cookies in a cookie jar if we're not supposed to eat cookies all the time?

On that note ... my research has led me to discover that a lot of the animal kingdom masturbates, so what's up with that? I thought humans and their insatiable sexual needs possibly stemmed from the fiasco in the Garden of Eden, but that doesn't explain the animals. Any who ... just things that will need to be explained when I see you someday.

"Ave?"

"Hmm?"

"Where were you?" Jake whispers, feathering his lips over mine.

"Just ... talking to God."

His eyebrows knit together. "About Swarley?"

"Um ... yes."

I'm going to Hell. But that's not a newsflash.

On a sympathetic sigh, he rolls to the side, pulling me into his body for a hug. "I feel like an ass for trying to seduce you while your mind is clearly on Swarley ... where it should be tonight."

Rubbing my lips together, I leave my focus on my hands pressed flat to his chest. If I look at him, he'll know. He'll see my lies, my perversion. My sins.

"Do you pray for him to live or do you pray for him to find peace as well as your sister and her family?"

I'm a terrible person.

I pray that God will provide him with a soft blanket to hump in his afterlife.

"I'm going to Hell," I whisper.

"No. Why would you say that?" He slides a leg between mine, bringing us even closer.

I push away. "Naked and on your stomach."

His lips twist into a restrained but sexy grin.

"One sec." I fetch a towel from the bathroom and toss it to him. "Cover your goods with this." I turn my back and retrieve lotion from my bag.

He chuckles. It's playful, and I could listen to it forever like a song that speaks to the heart, making it overflow with bliss. "My ass? Is that what you're calling my goods? And is there a reason you have your back to me?"

Squeezing my legs together, I clear my throat and cross my arms over my chest. "I'm trying to be professional."

"Professional Avery. I like where this is going."

"Just ..." I roll my eyes. "Are you ready?"

"Yes, ma'am."

I turn. Damn ... he's six feet, two hundred plus pounds of raw sex appeal on his stomach with his to-die-for ass mostly covered with a much-too-tiny hand towel. Coincidence? I think not. "What kind of pressure do you like?" Kneeling beside him on the bed, I draw in a slow *professional* breath and squirt lotion onto my hand.

He rests his head on the opposite cheek, peering back at me. "You know I like it hard, Ave. Just like you."

Harnessing my poker face, I nod. "Firm pressure. Noted."

He smirks, but I cling to my stoic expression, even if I'm drowning in my own arousal in *other* areas.

My hands, forearms, and elbows go to work on his back. He moans, eyelids drifting shut. My knees pull inward to stave off the desire that's out of my control. After twenty minutes of working on his back, I wipe the sweat from my brow.

This might have been a bad idea. I'm a good massage therapist. Clients pile up on waiting lists to see me, but Jake might not see my amazingness shine through because I'm a bitch in heat.

Rules of massage: focus all your thoughts on your client, let go of extraneous thoughts.

Done.

I'm *all* about Jake right now.

Powerful messages—palpable sensations—can be transferred from my fingers and palms to my client.

Done.

By now Jake should know I want to touch him everywhere with every part of my body. I want to give pleasure and take some of my own as well.

Moving on to his legs, I scoot off the bed and stand at the end, working my thumbs deep into his muscles.

"Ave ... you're so ... fucking ... incredible," he mumbles like a drunk.

"I know." I grin, but if I'm honest, Jake's approval of my skills makes fireworks explode inside of me. His moaned words trump every glowing review I've ever received.

After another thirty minutes, I'm not sure he's awake. Stilling my hands on his calves, I give his legs a gentle shake. "Roll onto your back." I turn, flexing and bending my fingers, rubbing them to relieve the stiffness.

"Ready," he says.

"Oh!" I cover my mouth, eyes wide.

Jake grins without opening his eyes.

I was wrong. He's far from being lulled to sleep. He's very much awake. I toss a pillow over his midsection because the towel lost the battle with his stiff cock.

After I work my way back up his body, I kneel just above his head, massaging his scalp. His eyes blink open. He just ... stares at me with an unreadable expression. I lose the stare-off and look away while my fingers continue to make tiny circles.

"Come closer," he whispers.

I pause, meeting his gaze again.

No smiles. No telling expressions.

My head descends a few inches.

"Closer."

I don't know what it is, but it's like something just shifted between us, and it happened in a single blink. And now ... I'm scared and vulnerable and just ... naked to my bones.

Moving closer, the tips of my damp hair brush his face, our lips a whisper away.

"I love you."

Sucking in a shaky breath, tears race to fill my eyes, blurring his beautiful face.

"I live in L.A." Panic rides in on its giant horse, drawing its sword to slay my dreams before disappointment takes me hostage.

"I love you." He doesn't give my reply the tiniest of flinches.

"I love shopping and cheese," I whisper as his hand cups the back of my head.

"I love *you*." He brings our lips to meet in a patient kiss, a slow dance. An unbreakable promise.

Fear and lack of worth bleed from my eyes in big tears. He pulls my body around to face his, losing the towel and pillow seconds before sliding his shirt from my body.

Yeah, something has shifted. The earth tips the other way on its axis and starts spinning in the opposite direction, obliterating my sense of being. Gravity no longer exists in my world.

My back arches, eyelids heavy, body surrenders as he pushes into me. When he stills, stealing my breath on a heavy moan, I force my eyes open.

Intense blues greet me.

My fingers find his hair when he dips his head, leaving a trail of kisses along my jaw as he moves inside of me. It's familiar. Our bodies connected is familiar and easy and ... *perfect*.

"Oh god ... this is it," I whisper.

He stops. "This is what?"

Our gazes lock. "This is what it feels like to be in love—deeply ... uncontrollably ... eternally in love."

Jake's brow tenses for a moment before the lines vanish and his lips ghost over mine. "Yes."

CHAPTER TWENTY

Jake

AVERY KISSES ME, curling her fingers in my hair, sliding her tongue against mine. Her long legs wrap around my waist for several minutes while we move together. Then she pushes me onto my back without breaking our connection. Her body moves along mine with uninhibited desire. Taking what she wants with a confidence that's so beyond sexy, I think I could die. She pleases herself.

Craving me.

Tasting me.

Taking what she wants—what she needs.

Pleasuring herself with my body.

And pleasuring me with her fucking incredible confidence.

This ... this is the naked, breathtaking, ineffable woman I saw long before she knew it existed within her.

"Touch me ..." She pushes my hand where she wants it.

I grin, obliging her.

"Harder ..." Her nails indent my skin.

I give it to her harder, mesmerized by this perfect moment.

"Kiss me ..." She opens her lust-leaden eyes, gazing down at me.

Per—fection.

I have to keep myself from begging her to marry me. I have to scold myself for trying to imagine what she might look like nine months pregnant with my baby. No woman has ever made me this delirious, and I still have no logical explanation as to what exactly it is about Avery that's clawed its way into my heart and taken up permanent residence.

"Dammit, Jake ... kiss me." Her impatience sends an extra jolt to my dick.

I sit up, bringing us face to face, and lean in to kiss her.

"Lower ..." she rocks her pelvis against mine.

I kiss her neck.

"Lower ..." she whispers, guiding my hand to where we are joined. "Kiss me here."

My gaze flits up to meet hers.

Before I can grin, and believe me, this makes me happier than I've ever been in my whole damn life, Avery crashes her mouth to mine. Her hungry *mmm* brings me to the brink of orgasm, but she pulls away, mumbling against my lips. "What are you waiting for, Matthews?"

Dead.

She just buried me.

Game over.

Avery Montgomery is officially out of my league.

I fold, throwing down a pretty good hand. She just played a royal flush.

My dick will have to wait on standby because I love this woman, and she's earned this from me.

"Attagirl, Ave." I grab her waist and lower her back to the mattress.

Her breaths quicken even more when I mark the inside of her thighs with my whiskered jaw as I make my way to fulfill her request. "If you just ask…" her hips jerk "…there's nothing I wouldn't give you."

"You …" Her head falls to the side, fingers in my hair, voice strained with emotion. "I just want you …"

Four in the morning.

My phone rings. Avery jumps. I kiss her head and reach for my phone.

"Hey, Meg."

"Hey, Jake." She doesn't need to say another word. The tone of her voice says it all. "Swarley passed away. We did everything we could to revive him. I'm so sorry."

I sit up with my legs dangling off the bed, my back to Avery. "Okay." It's hard to speak. My throat feels so fucking tight with the words I'm not sure I can relay to Avery and Sydney.

"There's no need to come now, unless they feel the need to be here. Either way, I'll be here when they're ready to come for him."

"No …" Avery chokes on a sob before I disconnect.

Bad news is a feeling that arrives like an executioner in your chest before the words are ever spoken. It's a look. A sad smile. It's an invisible poison. And no words can soften the blow after that first wordless hit.

"Thanks, Meg." I set my phone down.

"No …" Avery's forehead and palms press to my back.

"Don't say it ... please don't say it." Another sob breaks from her chest.

I twist my torso, and she falls into my lap with her hands covering her face.

"I'm sorry, Ave."

"No, no, no ..." Her body shakes as I pull her closer, a ball of brokenness on my lap.

The door to the room creaks. I glance up. The dim light from the hall behind Sydney makes it hard to see her face, but I don't miss her hand covering her mouth. No words are needed.

Unlike Avery, Sydney breaks slowly ... silently ... until she's hunched down like she might vomit.

I remember this moment with my mom. It's when this space in your heart feels most raw, hollowed, yet heavy—like grief rushes in to fill the void. And there is a void, no matter what anyone says. We don't remember them in our heart, we remember them in our mind. All the heart can do is feel, and when someone dies, the only thing left to feel is pain.

"I'm sorry ..." It's all I can say. It's all that anyone can say.

When Avery realizes my words are not just meant for her, she glances up and flies off my lap. "Syd ..." Avery envelopes her sister, and they collapse the rest of the way to the floor.

An audible cry escapes from Sydney.

I pinch the bridge of my nose, resisting the urge to fix the unfixable.

Avery has my shirt on, but I'm naked beneath the sheet, so I wrap it around my waist and grab my shorts, slipping into them. Squatting next to them, I rest my hand on

Avery's back. "I'll be in the living room. Take the bed. Let me know what you need from me."

She doesn't respond. They cling to each other—sobbing and shaking.

"He-he's gone ..."

I cringe, rubbing the back of my neck as Sydney's words bleed behind me.

Easing onto the sofa, I bring up Deedy's number and hit the green button.

"Jake?" Deedy answers on the first ring. She's in a different time zone and an early riser. "Oh my gosh, I forgot to call you back. Was it important? It's early there—what's wrong? Something must be wrong. Please tell me nothing has happened to Avery."

"Swarley died."

A few seconds of silence steal the line.

"What?" It's barely a whisper.

"It's ..." I blow out a long breath, running a frustrated hand over my face. "It's messed-up. I don't understand how this happened so quickly. And I have no fucking clue what I should do about it. Sydney and Ave are on the floor in the hall, crying. I don't know what to do or what to say. I don't know Sydney's husband's number, or if it's even my place to call him. I just ..."

"Jake, just take a breath."

I do. I take a breath.

"Just be patient. Be there for them when they need you. I'll wake Tommy and we'll deal with the rest. Okay?"

I hum my acknowledgement.

"I'm sure this is nobody's fault. It's life. You know about life. So just know that you've done your part—more than your part. I can't tell you how much Tommy and I appreciate all you've done for his family."

Yeah, I tortured his daughter, stripped her down to tears, then fell in love with her. Oh ... and his grand-dog died on my watch. I'm sure Tom Montgomery will be so grateful.

"Thanks, Deedy."

I end the call and toss my phone onto the sofa next to me.

"Fuck ..." I lean my head back and close my eyes.

Avery

"I NEED TO C-CALL H-HOME." Sydney wipes her nose with her arm as we lean against the wall, still on the floor after what feels like an eternity of crying.

The pain has settled into a miserable numbness.

"How do I tell my kids?"

Swarley owned my niece's heart, possibly more than her parents did. She dressed him up like a unicorn and he let her. He's been there for every step of her life. He's been her best friend and loyal protector.

"It's going to feel like he's dying all over again when I get home."

I nod. "I know. Ocean will be ..." My words crack under the gravity of what's happened and what will happen when Sydney arrives home with Swarley. "Crushed beyond words."

"Yes," Sydney whispers, hiccupping on another sob.

I squeeze her hand as we stare at our outstretched legs.

"Oh my god ... I haven't seen you without toenail polish since you were ... six months old."

I wipe a few stray tears and laugh. "My fingers are naked too." I hold out my hands.

"What happened to you?"

I welcome the new topic, even if it's about the demise of my appearance, knowing the second we leave here to get Swarley, the emotions will return. "Jake happened."

"Is that like shit happens?" She sniffles and I sense she, too, needs a new topic.

"He's awful. Just ... the worst. He's crude, and he calls me names. He doesn't understand my need to have nice things and look pretty. And he's a vegan. Gah! How does one eat a keto diet and be a vegan? I can't do it. He likes tents. I like hotel suites. He has tattoos, and I don't like tattoos. And he likes just ... staring at the sky like the stars are the most fascinating thing he has ever seen. I honestly think he was deprived of fireworks as a child."

"You're sleeping with him."

I shrug. "He knows his way around ... *things*."

Sydney chuckles, but it's not her jovial cackle. It's tarnished with grief because not even our self-made bubble can shelter us from reality.

"You're in deep, huh?" Her hand finds mine, and now she's the one giving me a squeeze of understanding.

Drawing in a shaky breath, I nod. "So deep it hurts. So deep it scares me. So deep I'm certain I won't survive whatever this is if he changes his mind. And he's going to change his mind. They always do."

"I married the man who looked at me the way Jake looks at you."

"I'm not you. Had Jake met single Sydney, he would have chosen you without a second thought. I fear we've been out of touch with reality—out in the woods—for so long, he thinks he has feelings for me. What if we get to L.A., and I'm no longer the best choice?"

"What if you are?" *His* voice sounds.

We jump as Jake steps around the corner, pinning me with a look that makes me squirm. He looks offended. Maybe even angry? I can't tell.

Sydney stands, wiping her eyes. "Hey, I'm going to take a shower before we go. And I need to call home." Reality seeps back into the moment.

Jake nods and shares a sympathetic smile with her. When she squeezes past him, he returns his attention to me and holds out his hand.

I take it, and he pulls me to my feet, peering down at me like he can reduce me to ashes with his evil stare.

He wins. My gaze slips to his bare chest.

"I'm going to pretend that this lack of confidence you have this morning is just a side effect of grief."

I shake my head. "It's just the side effect of being human. Sorry to disappoint you."

Jake lifts my chin with his finger. I wait for the lecture. I wait for that look that says I've let him down. I wait for the flinch of regret.

Nothing.

Instead, he lowers his mouth to mine and kisses me. It's soft and patient. It's a reminder of the words that were exchanged last night. Tears find their way down my face.

He pulls away and wipes them with his thumbs. "Swarley?"

I shake my head. "Jake."

He smiles and it's real. *It's ... real.*

"You going to shower?"

I shake my head again. "Showers are overrated. Besides, I like how you smell on me."

Jake brushes his lips along my cheek, stopping at my ear, eliciting visible chills along my skin. "Me too," he whispers.

I hug him. He lifts me up and carries me to the bed. Jake's physical strength is quite possibly the sexiest thing I've ever experienced with a man. I've felt financial security, a strong social standing, showered in gifts, but never just raw, strong, all-man sex appeal. Jake is just ...

Sigh ...

He sits on the end of the bed. "Are you going to drive back home with your sister? I think you should."

Biting my lips together, I nod several times. "You're probably right. She's going to have Swarley. I don't want her making the drive alone."

"I'll follow you."

"Yeah?" I can't hide my spark of excitement.

"Ave ..." He shakes his head like my questioning him is somehow ridiculous.

I can't help it. Wanting something this much is not just scary, it's impossible to breathe when you're so close to having everything. Jake's a world I never knew existed. He's my favorite surprise. My guiltiest pleasure. The dream that finds a place in reality.

Just as I open my mouth to ask Jake for some reassurance that we will find a way to really be together, a photo on the far wall of Megan's bedroom catches my attention. "What's that?" I climb off his lap and take slow steps to the gray-framed photo.

"It's Ranger. Megan's husky. She and her ex-husband rescued him from an abusive home. Ranger died a week after their divorce." Jake presses his chest to my back and wraps his arms around my waist, resting his chin on my shoulder.

My dad was wrong. Sometimes God does give you more than you can handle.

"What happened to his eye?" It's hard to speak without the ability to breathe, but I manage to get five words past my airless lungs.

"Previous owner shot him with a BB gun."

My hand moves to my mouth.

"Unimaginable, huh?"

I nod. It's *all* unimaginable. But nothing is quite as unimaginable as the expensive gold engraved tag hanging from the dog's collar that *I* gave him.

"You said Meg's husband cheated on her?"

"Yep."

No air. Where's the air? Why can't I breathe?

"Did she catch him?" I whisper, gaze affixed to the photo.

"No, Steve confessed at the worst possible time."

S*teve.*

His mom had cancer.

I close my eyes.

"Megan was pregnant, and she..." Jake clears his throat like he's choking on some residual emotion "...miscarried the day after he told her about the affair."

My eyes snap open. "W-what?"

He wasn't married. No, no, no ... He didn't have a pregnant wife.

"Fucking asshole cheated on her when she was pregnant. I wanted to kill him. I wanted to kill him *and* his home-wrecking whore."

I blink, releasing big, heartbreaking, regretful, angry, God-hates-me tears.

"Anyway ... Ranger was a good dog." Jake gives me a

squeeze and kisses my wet cheek. "Ave?" He turns me toward him.

This time I don't hide from him. My teary gaze stays on his contorted face.

"I'm sorry. I said too much. Swarley was a good dog too."

If I lie, we will never be real. And I don't want the lies. I want love. Real. Honest. Soul-consuming. Naked love.

"His mom had cancer. *Cancer.*" I shake my head and back away.

Jake's brows pull together as he cocks his head. "Who? What are you talking about?"

"He had to move away to take care of *his mother*. He told me not to wait. He said sometimes life just happens."

"Ave ... I'm not following. *Who* said that?"

The tears won't stop, but I don't look away. God ... maybe he'll see how blindsided I was by this. He'll see the truth.

"Ranger was a stray dog he found at the park. Ranger lived with Steve's mom most of the time. A therapy dog." I continue to shake my head as I repeat the lies I was told. "He wasn't married. He had *never* been married."

Realization softens Jake's brow as disbelief—shock—ghosts along his face, dulling the life in his eyes.

Home-wrecking whore.

"Avery ..." His tone loses all kindness, all the love. It's cold. The kind of cold that feels like a knife against my skin.

"He said he loved me. He said one day he wanted to marry me." I continue to shake my head, pressing my hand against my chest.

"He wanted in your fucking pants! That's why he said that to you!"

I choke on a sob as I gasp at his words.

Jake clenches his teeth, a hint of regret flashes in his eyes, but it fades in seconds, squashed by his anger.

"I'm not a whore." I shove as much confidence as I can into that statement.

Jake grunts. "Tell that to Megan."

Megan. Megan who lost her baby and her dog. Megan who was cheated on by her lying husband. Megan who tried to save Swarley. Megan who welcomed us into her home. Megan—Jake's friend.

"You." He shakes his head like he can wake himself up, like it's not real. "You. Jesus ... it was you? This can't be happening." He continues to shake his head. "He told her the other woman—*you*—meant nothing. Do you like that, Ave? Have you just never cared whether or not you truly mean something to a man? As long as they buy you *things,* then you carelessly turn a blind eye to minor details like *wives*? Do you know what that makes you?"

"Is everything okay?" Sydney peeks into the room, her dark, wet hair tied back into a ponytail.

She eyes me with concern. Then she shoots Jake a questioning look, but he keeps his back to her.

I wipe away my tears, no longer able to tolerate the disdain on Jake's face. "It's fine. Are you ready?"

Sydney nods slowly, concern still marring her face.

"Give me five minutes to get dressed." I bend down and riffle through my bag for clothes.

"I'll be in the kitchen," Sydney says.

"Okay." I keep my head down, my complete devastation hidden from my grieving sister and the man who clearly hates me. The man who wanted me dead when I was an unknown *whore* to him.

This defensive little voice in my head wants to jump out and spew off all the reasons Jake has no right to be upset with me. It wasn't my fault. I didn't know. Steve lied and he was good at it. I didn't ruin Megan's marriage. Steve did. But I can't say any of these words because Swarley died, and Megan doesn't need her past dug up and hashed out all over again.

"This isn't the time or place to discuss this." I stand, braving a glance up at Jake.

His shoulders are slumped, his jaw still cemented into a disapproving scowl. He looks angry and disappointed and ... hurt. He shakes his head. "There's nothing to discuss. I think you filled in the missing pieces."

I step into my shorts and slip off Jake's shirt. He turns away from me.

This ... *this* hurts. Last night I was the woman he loved. This morning I'm the whore not worthy of his eyes on my bared flesh. I turn my back to him too as I put on my bra.

Tears burn.

Pride suffocates.

Hearts break.

Words fail.

And I ... well, I focus on Sydney and her family who will be devastated when we bring Swarley home in a body bag. As for Jake, I regret nothing. He taught me a lot about myself.

Attagirl, Ave.

Stand the fuck up for yourself.

Show me whatcha got.

He tore me down and made me put myself back together. I'm so much stronger than I was when I left L.A. But *this* is still going to destroy my heart—a heart that's been jerked around, kicked, punched, and dismissed so many times, I'm not sure it even remembers how to beat.

I close my bag and hike my purse onto my shoulder.

Jake turns. My entire body tingles with pain. He reaches for my bag, but I pull it just out of his reach.

"Don't ..." My throat constricts, strangling my words. Maybe it's my body's way of saving face, if that's even still possible. Maybe we've come full circle. He hated me when we left Milwaukee. I've gone from a bitch to a whore.

Funny, I just wanted to be the smile on his face. The object of his affection. I wanted to be the part of his life that felt utterly undefinable yet completely impossible to live without.

We don't always get what we want.

"Avery?" Sydney's voice from the other room brings me out of this suspended moment.

I angle my body to squeeze by Jake without touching him.

CHAPTER TWENTY-ONE

"Ave—" Sydney gives me a tiny frown.

I stop her with a sharp headshake. We can't talk about Jake just like we can't talk about Swarley or all the other painful moments we've survived.

Her frown deepens. It's been her job to put her little sister back together. That's the motherly role she took on after our mom died. I don't want her to feel bad for me. I don't want her to fix me when she's broken.

I just ... I just want to go home.

I take *three* slow breaths, and I follow her out the door, into her vehicle, and we make our way to the clinic under a cloud of unspoken words.

"Tell me." Sydney puts the vehicle into park and shuts off the engine in the clinic parking lot. "When I get home, my kids are going to need me. And you're hurting right now, and I know it's more than Swarley. I don't want you to feel alone when I'm pulled in another direction. So ... before I do one of the hardest thing I've ever had to do, just tell me. Let me be here for you even if it's just for the next few minutes until we walk into the clinic."

My face contorts into a silent ugly cry, and I hold my breath until I just can't hold it anymore.

"Ave ... oh, Avery ..." Sydney unfastens her seat belt and leans over the console to hug me.

I weep so hard my ribs feel like they're cracked, poking into my heart, making each breath feel like it's tearing me apart. Love is jagged and gritty. It's Hell. It's suffocating. It demands to be felt even when there's nothing left to feel but this painful emptiness.

"Is it over?"

I keep a tight hold on her and nod.

"Are you sure?"

My lips tremble with each stuttered sob as I nod again.

"You'll tell me why, right?"

"S-someday ... b-but n-not now."

"Alright. But I need to know that you're going to be okay."

I'm the furthest thing from okay, but I'll get there. I always do. "Yes."

She releases me, holding my face by my cheeks. "You're going to find *the one* someday, and he's going to love you with his whole heart. His eyes will only magnify the good. His heart will be blind to any imperfections. And you'll feel safe with him. You'll know he's there to pick you up. He'll be there when you need him the most because he'll just ... know. He'll just ..." Sydney glances over my shoulder and tears fill her eyes. "Know ..."

I turn to the familiar vehicle parked next to us.

Lautner.

He gets out and slides his sunglasses onto his head. Sydney sobs as he walks around the front of the vehicle. She knows all about "the one." She married him. And I've silently envied their love for years.

"Baby ..." he says in a reverent tone as he opens her door.

"You're here." She falls into his arms, and I tear up, sharing their loss, mourning my own loss, aching for a man to love me like that.

"Your dad called, but I was already on my way," he says.

"You're here." She wraps her arms around him, and he holds her like she's his world, all the stars, the oceans and mountains, the air he breathes.

"Of course I'm here."

"The kids—"

"Home with my dad. Your dad and Deedy are on their way now."

After he calms her down, his attention shifts to me. "Ave."

"Pool guy." I find a small smile for him.

"You okay?"

I nod.

"She's not." Sydney pulls away, wiping her eyes.

"I am." I shrug. "I will be."

Jake's truck pulls in two spaces to the left of us. He gets out of the truck and introduces himself to Lautner like nothing has happened between us.

I get out of Sydney's Lexus and head to his truck, using this opportunity to get the rest of my stuff out of it while he's distracted with Lautner.

Unfortunately, the distraction doesn't last.

"I'll get it." Jake eases the tailgate down just before I can release it.

I step away. I look away. I wish I could just fly away.

He sets my other bags down on the ground and gets Swarley's stuff out of the backseat. Without saying a word, I open the back of Sydney's SUV and start loading the stuff with Jake's help.

He shuts the back when we're done. Sydney and Lautner already went inside. I assume they'll ride together with Swarley in Lautner's vehicle while I follow them in Sydney's Lexus.

"I'm not going to tell Megan." Jake slides his fingers into the front pockets of his jeans. "Nothing good can come from it."

I blink several times as I process his words, but really it's his tone that says the most. He's genuinely angry with me. And maybe part of his anger is the letdown of thinking he loved me, of thinking that he *could* love me. "I don't care if you tell her or not. If you want me to tell her, I will tell her. If you want me to leave without a word, I will do that."

Again, I stop before I go into full defensive mode. I want to scream at him. *I didn't know he was married!* But maybe I should have known. Right now I can't think past the grief and pain, so I question my memory. I wonder if I missed some clues along the way. Did I see Steve how I wanted to see him, instead of how he really was? Did I miss the tan line from a wedding band? Secret texts? Should I have questioned the traveling he did for "business," or his mother's supposed cancer diagnosis? The dog? The apartment he rented instead of owning a house? Did I blindly let our relationship be what I wanted it to be instead of what it really was?

"I won't say anything. And I'm sorry. I—"

"Don't." He shakes his head. "She lost a child. Do you get that? How can you be with someone and not make actual connections to their life? Did you meet his 'sick' mother? Did you meet his best friend? An uncle? A coworker? The only reason you should have agreed to let me give you a ride was because of my relationship to Deedy. There was a connection. That meant you knew I didn't have a hidden life. For the love of God, Avery ... know *something* about a man before you crawl into his bed!"

"Don't!" I shove his chest. "You don't get to lecture me." I shove him again, but he doesn't budge. "You weren't in my shoes. *You* fell in love with me. So it shouldn't be some fucking surprise that maybe someone else did too. It's not my fault. I didn't know he was married. Do you have any idea how many men travel to L.A. for business and even own apartments there? YOU own one there!

"I asked about his family. He said his dad died and his mom had cancer. He said he was an only child. *I* don't have that many close friends, so I didn't question him not introducing me to his BFF. And I'm sorry Megan miscarried, but maybe it was somehow meant to be since Steve was cheating on her. She can find someone else and start a family and just ..." I press my palms to the side of my head and close my eyes on a long exhale. "Just forget about him."

When I open my eyes, Jake clenches his fists and his jaw. There's not forgiveness in his eyes. It *wasn't* my fault. Why can't he see past this?

"She was twenty-two weeks pregnant. He told her about the affair and then he left. She asked him to leave, but still ... he fucking left her. Need I say where I suspect he went? The next day, she started bleeding. Over the next twenty-four hours, *I* was by her side when she lost her child, twelve units of blood, and her uterus when they had to perform a hysterectomy. Then I held her hand while she was in the ICU on life support. I said I was her husband because Steve wasn't ... fucking ... there!"

My eyes release one round of tears after another as I remain idle, rooted to the ground, and numb to my bones. I remember the call in the middle of the night. Steve flew out of bed, frantic because his mom had been taken to the hospital and was in the ICU. His *mom*.

Fuck you, Steve.

I want to say something—anything. This isn't me. I don't sleep with married men. I'm probably too materialistic sometimes, and I should spend more time cultivating friendships than looking for the perfect handbag and the perfect man. But I'm not a home-wrecker. I would never knowingly be with a married man. I'm a lot of things, not all of them good, but I am. Not. That. Woman.

I'm not Francine.

"Ave, ready?"

I turn toward Lautner's voice as he carries ...

Oh god ...

Swarley's in a black bag in Lautner's arms. Sydney silently weeps as she opens the back door to his vehicle. Megan steps outside and wraps her arms around her body. She looks tired and mournful—kind and innocent.

I turn back toward Jake. Before this trip, I would have been a slave to my ego and coddled my wounded pride. I would have bit my tongue and hopped in the vehicle, content with no goodbye. Jaded by yet another failed relationship.

Jake changed things. I'm not that Avery anymore.

The car door behind me closes, and I hear the heart-ripping sob of Sydney.

"We'll survive this, baby," Lautner says to her as he gets in on his side.

I don't have to see them to know that he's holding her, loving her, and being *the one* for which all other men should strive to be. He forgave her of so many things. His love never wavered. They were stronger than bad days, bad decisions, and bad timing.

I want a love like that.

Clenching Jake's shirt in my fists, I lift onto my toes and kiss the angle of his jaw next to his ear. "Thank you."

He swallows hard, hands limp at his sides. I step back, seeing something resembling true emotion—painful emotion—in his reddening eyes.

I turn and make the five steps to Megan. "Thank you." I offer my hand to her.

She pulls me in for a hug, squeezing out several tears. "I'm so sorry I couldn't do more."

My reply can't wedge its way past the aching heart lodged in my throat, so I just nod and hope she knows I appreciate all she did. I embrace her tighter, praying she'll remember this moment if Jake ever tells her the truth.

I'm so incredibly sorry.

"I hope we get to spend more time together under better circumstances next time."

I release her and find a tiny smile. There won't be a next time. This isn't a love story. It's a tragedy of the heart.

Rolling my lips together to muzzle the pain that's screaming to be heard, I wipe my tears and nod.

Lautner starts his car. I tap on his window, and he rolls it down.

"I don't have a phone," I whisper because anything more than this will involve me vomiting my heart.

He hands me Sydney's phone. "The code is 870100."

I swat away more tears and take the phone, giving a quick glance to the black bag in their backseat.

Swarley ...

Jake stands on the edge of the curb as I get into the driver's seat of Sydney's Lexus. I slip on my sunglasses, fasten my seat belt, and start the engine—but I don't look his way.

As soon as I back out of this parking spot, I can let go of these emotions. I can try to breathe, even if it hurts. I just need to hold it together for ten more seconds.

Ten.
Nine.
Eight.
Seven.

I start to back out.

Bang!

I brake.

Jake's hand is pressed to the window. He closes his eyes and curls it into a fist, his chest expanding like he's taking all the oxygen from the air. His hand slides to the door handle and he waits, blinking open his eyes and giving me an expectant look.

I put the car in *park* and unlock the door.

He opens it and emotion fills his eyes. "Why did it have to be you?" His hand cups the back of my head and he kisses me.

Five four three two one.

I release a muffled sob as he kisses me.

Just as quickly as his lips crashed to mine, he peels them away. "Bye, Ave."

CHAPTER TWENTY-TWO

SYDNEY AND LAUTNER send me home when we get to L.A., leaving me with a temporary phone and Sydney's Lexus. They want time alone with the kids to break the news about Swarley. I don't argue. I'm nothing more than an empty vessel with a pulse. Watching Ocean react to Swarley's death would end me completely.

"Your stuff is gone."

I glance back at my neighbor, Dave, as he steps out of his apartment across the hall and locks his door.

"What?" I turn my key and open the door to my *empty* apartment. A sigh escapes my mouth, a slowly deflating tire. This should cue the tears, but I don't have any more tears. I gave them to Swarley and Jake. Then I drained the last few drops of salty grief on my way home.

Home.

Where the hell is that?

"Three days ago. That fancy-suited guy of yours arrived with a small moving crew. Everything was gone in just under two hours. Honestly, I was afraid to ask, but I thought maybe something had happened to you. I even checked the obituaries yesterday. Glad you're not dead."

"Well, that makes one of us," I murmur.

"I overheard the manager out here yesterday. They're changing the locks tomorrow. There goes your deposit."

I nod, entranced by the emptiness of my apartment.

And my heart.

My life.

It's numbing. But numb is good at the moment.

"Do you have a place to stay?"

The Lexus. I'm going to sleep in a vehicle, then I'll stay with Sydney tomorrow, but I'm not going to their house tonight.

Leather seats.

No bugs.

It will be a huge upgrade for me.

"Avery, if you need a place to stay for a few nights, Randy is out of town until next week. You can crash in his room."

Everything. Anthony took *everything*.

Jake ... well, *he* took all the intangibles.

"Avery?" Dave dangles a key in front of my face. "Yes? No? You look like a zombie. Listen, it's up to you, but I have to get to the hospital for a soul-draining twenty-four-hour shift."

Leather seats versus neighbor's likely old mattress and a shower.

"Shower," I whisper.

"What?"

I shake my head, trying to bring it above the surface to keep from drowning in my ugly reality. "Um, yes. Thank you. I'd be so grateful if you'd let me stay tonight. I'll go to my sister's tomorrow."

"Cool." He hands me the key. "Make yourself at home."

I muster the closest thing to a smile that my lips can form. "Thank you." Taking his key with my left hand, I drop my apartment key from my right hand. It clinks on the hard floor.

Dave glances at my discarded key for a few seconds before giving me a sad smile. "Chin up, buttercup. I'll see you later."

"Later," I whisper as he takes the stairs to the main level. Grabbing the one suitcase I brought up with me, I wheel it into Dave's apartment, shut and lock the door, and collapse onto the sofa. I don't need a bed or even a shower at the moment. I just need to sleep to escape the pain for a few hours.

THE NEXT DAY, we say a final goodbye to Swarley with a proper burial, a tree planted next to him, and lots of tears. Dad and the Deedy arrived last night and stayed at a nearby hotel to give Sydney's family the privacy they needed to break the news to the kids. They planned on getting married before making the trip to California, but life tends to laugh at plans.

It's presumptuous of humans to think we have one bit of control over what happens in life. I may be a little angry at the moment.

"We are going to the beach. Lautner took a personal day. Thought it would be a good idea to spend the day with the kids. Take some pictures. I haven't had my camera out in a long time. Dad and Deedy are staying here, but you should come with us." Sydney puts the brunch leftovers in the fridge while I wash the dishes, staring out the window at the Deedy standing next to Ocean by Swarley's grave just beyond the fenced-in pool.

Ocean hugs Deedy, wiping her teary face on Deedy's sundress. They've bonded quickly. Good for Ocean; she's more mature than her Aunt Avery. I bet she's never thought about Deedy and Papa naked, doing things that could cause Papa to have another heart attack. Her innocence is enviable at the moment.

"I need to find a job."

"Lautner said you need to see a physical therapist about your hand."

"Those cost money."

"We'll loan you money until you find a job and get some health benefits."

I shake my head as Sydney retrieves a towel from the drawer next to me and dries the dishes. "I'm not looking for charity. Well ... I could use a place to stay until I get something figured out."

"Stay? What do you mean? Where did you stay last night?"

"On my neighbor's sofa. Actually ..." My lips twist. "I suppose ex-neighbor since I no longer live there."

"Ave ..."

"Gone." I draw in a shaky breath, keeping my focus on the sudsy serving tray in my hands. "All of my stuff was gone. Anthony took everything."

"What? He can't do that. There's no way everything in your apartment was purchased by him. You need an attorney, Ave. You can't just let him get away with this."

"Yeah, well ... attorneys cost money too."

"We'll pay for—"

"No, Syd. I don't want you fighting this battle for me.

Hell, I don't even want the battle. Whatever ... it's just stuff."

Sydney takes the serving tray from me and rinses it. "Um ... who are you? *It's just stuff?*"

"Yeah, I don't want it. I don't need it. I don't need ..." I close my eyes, rolling my lips between my teeth.

"Dad said we're going to the beach." Ocean and Deedy come in the back door.

"Yes, sweetie pie. We are." Sydney drops the towel on the counter and hugs her daughter.

"Is Aunt Avery coming?"

I pin a stiff smile onto my face and turn around. "Actually, I'm going to stay here with Papa and the De—" I clear my throat. "Deedy. I'll take you to the beach next week. Just the two of us for girl time. Does that sound okay?"

Ocean rubs her red eyes and nods. "Okay. I guess ..."

"Let's go get changed." Sydney runs a loving hand through Ocean's long, dark hair and guides her toward the stairs.

"I'm going to have a cup of tea. Can I get you one?" Deedy asks, filling the electric tea kettle.

I shake my head and return to the sink filled with dishes. "Where's my dad?"

"He said he had a quick errand to run, but he had this mischievous look in his eyes, so I'm not sure what he has up his sleeve." She takes over Sydney's job and dries the dishes while waiting for her water to heat up. "I talked to Jake last night."

"That's nice."

"He seemed really distressed."

The Deedy doesn't understand that "that's nice" is code for I don't want to talk about Jake.

"I'd gathered something might be going on between you two ... Sydney leaked that much to your dad and me. But after talking with Jake, I now realize it was something quite serious. I'm sorry, Avery. You must be emotionally exhausted. If you want to talk about it."

"What's there to talk about? Jake makes everyone think he's amazing, while I'm just the whore he screwed on a road trip. Does that about sum it up?" I scrub the shit out of the glass pitcher.

"You're going to etch the surface." Deedy takes the abrasive scrubber and the pitcher from my hands. Then she rinses it off. "Coffee more your taste?" She holds up the half-full coffee pot.

Resting my hands on the edge of the sink, I close my eyes and nod once.

"Cream? Sugar?"

"No."

"Please, have a seat ... just for a few minutes. The dishes can wait."

On a defeated sigh, I surrender, taking a seat at the kitchen table. Deedy sets a red mug of coffee in front of me and sits across from me with her hot tea.

"I met Gavin in college."

I sip my coffee and glance over at her when she doesn't elaborate. "Gavin?"

She shakes her head, staring at the tea bag as she bobs it in the hot water. "Jake didn't share much about himself. Did he?"

My shoulders lift a fraction as my lips twist. I hate that Deedy knows things about Jake that I don't know. It makes me feel like a fool who spread her legs for him. I fell in love with a man I don't really know. And he fell in love with the version of me he created. Now our bubble no longer exists, and we are nothing.

"He's a vegan chef who owns two restaurants. He was a fighter or boxer ... or something. I met his dad and Francine. She's basically me—in his mind. That led to a fight and a confession. His mother committed suicide after losing a battle with depression. She lost a baby, so he's an only child." I glance up from my coffee mug. "But I don't know about anyone named Gavin. And I don't even know how you two met."

Deedy removes her tea bag, squeezing the excess water out before setting it on a napkin. "Gavin was my husband."

I nod slowly.

"And Jake's uncle."

My eyes widen, lips parted, words muted as my brain pieces things together. Jake's uncle. That means Deedy is Jake's aunt. She's going to marry my dad. That will make me ... Jake's cousin? No, that's not right. But it feels like there's a family tie that makes what we've done even more wrong.

"You have a disgusted look on your face. Is it the coffee?"

"No. It's just that makes Jake ..."

"Gavin was his father's younger brother—a lot younger and nothing like his father. Jake and Gavin were more like cousins or brothers than uncle and nephew. After Jake's mom died, he lived with Gavin because—"

"He didn't want to live with his father. He told me that."

"Yes. Gavin is the one who helped channel Jake's anger into a better outlet. Fighting. He trained him. Jake was like another brother to me. I never thought of him as a nephew after Gavin and I got married." She shrugs and gives me a soft smile. "Jake's my family. He always will be family."

"Well, clearly he thinks a lot of you because I can't tell you how many times his mumbled mantra 'do it for Deedy' kept him from literally killing me on our trip."

Deedy grunts a laugh. "Jake feels indebted to me. He feels guilty ... responsible for Gavin's death."

"Why?" My head cocks to the side a bit.

Deedy takes a slow breath. Then she bites her bottom lip, eyes focused on the blank table space between us.

"They went to a fight to watch a mutual friend. I stayed home to pack for a mission trip we were supposed to take the following day." Her gaze meets mine. Time hasn't erased the pain. It's red in her eyes, very much still alive.

"After the fight, there was a dispute. Some guy who Jake fought years earlier wasn't happy to see him again. He was one of Jake's opponents who left on a stretcher." Deedy blows out another breath and returns her gaze to the table and three years earlier.

"Gavin started to argue with the guy. Jake tried to keep things from getting out of hand, so he pushed Gavin back to put himself between them. Gavin tripped on something and fell backward. He hit his head on a concrete ledge of the next level of seating."

Deedy shakes her head slowly. "No cut. No bump. He didn't lose consciousness. Got up on his own and dusted himself off like it was no big deal. Seemingly unscathed. Jake suggested he get checked out by a doctor, but Gavin said he'd taken much harder hits to his head when he was a fighter."

She's The Deedy. Stealer of my father. Haunter of my Jake fantasies. Yet, I can't keep my hand from reaching for hers, giving it a gentle squeeze.

Deedy smiles at our hands. "He came home. Showered. I looked at his head, but it looked fine. He was fine. Fine ..." Her face contorts into a grimace. "Until he wasn't. He got this severe headache and felt dizzy. His words were confusing. I called Jake and told him I was going to take Gavin to the hospital. He told me to call 9-1-1." Her words come out shaky. She clears her throat. "He died later that night. It was an epidural hematoma caused by blunt impact."

I don't speak or even move. What's there to say?

"So..." Deedy pulls her hand from mine and wraps it around her cup of tea "...there you have it. Jake's endured a wide array of trauma in his life. He carries guilt like an inoperable tumor attached to his conscience. Working with food. Caring for the environment. These things have helped him deal with his suppressed emotions. But he's not without triggers."

I laugh through the pain. "I'm clearly a trigger for more than one of his traumatic moments in life. But ... that's over. Doesn't matter now. However, I'm truly sorry for your loss."

"Gavin was my first love. I believe Tommy is my last love."

Tommy. I grin, but I fear it might look like a cringe.

"Sorry. Your dad. Tom? Thomas? What works for you? I don't like it when you're uncomfortable with our relationship. I want us to be friends, not just family by marriage."

The Deedy and I forging a friendship? I'm not sure about this, but it feels like the odds are in her favor now that I know for sure there was nothing sexual between her and Jake.

"He's going to be your husband." I smile. "Call him whatever you want to call him. I've just never heard anyone call him Tommy before, but maybe that makes it even more fitting for you to call him that. I think had my mom called him that, it would feel wrong in a bad way, not just in an unfamiliar way. Does that make sense?"

"Perfect sense."

This is awkward. I had my mind set on hating Deedy for no particular reason. Immature? Sure. But I've got my own baggage. "So ..." I stand before the silence gets too weird. "Tell me about the wedding." I busy myself with the dishes again.

"We're out of here. Sure you don't want to come?" Sydney peeks her head into the kitchen.

"I'm good, but thank you."

Deedy gives Sydney a wave just before my sister and her family head out the door. "Well, I assume we'll have the ceremony as soon as we return to Milwaukee. Everyone is invited; we just didn't want to make a big deal out of it or have anyone feel like they had to make the trip, so that's why we said we'd get married then come out here for a family reception of sorts."

"Well, it's kind of a big deal if you bought a wedding dress." Okay, our friendship is a work in progress. It's none of my business what Deedy wears for her second wedding. Maybe she eloped with Gavin and never had a chance to wear the white gown. No judgment here.

Dammit!

Maybe a little judgment. Old habits ...

"Wedding dress?" Deedy chuckles. "Your dad is something else. I heard him telling you about my *wedding dress*. I love him, but he's still such a guy. I bought a dress. It's white. I'd wear it to church or someone else's wedding. There's no train. It hits just below my knees. No rhinestones. No lace. Just a simple white dress."

With my back to her, I grin. Fucking hell anyway ...

Sorry, Heavenly Father.

Darn it anyway ... I think I like Deedy. How did this happen?

"It sounds perfect."

"Yeah, it's still a church wedding, but small. Mainly our church family. But I'm excited. And for what it's worth, I'm just as excited to walk down the aisle to marry your dad as I was when I married Gavin."

I nod, keeping my gaze firmly planted to the sink. No way. Friends or not. Deedy is not going to make me cry. I've hit my yearly limit of tears in the course of a month.

"You know ..." Deedy resumes her dish-drying job. "Jake told me about your relationship with Megan's ex-husband."

Relationship. "Huh ... that's interesting. Last I checked, being someone's whore is not really a relationship."

"Avery, don't say that. Please ... that is not true at all."

"Yeah, well, tell Jake that."

"I did. What happened to Megan when she lost her baby, that really affected Jake because he was the one there for her, even when they weren't sure if she'd live. His anger was sharp and unforgiving."

"I know. I felt that sharp and unforgiving anger." I can't help the anger in my words.

"Whatever he said to you, it was not Jake. It was anger over what happened to his friend and fear of his feelings for you. Give him time. He'll come around."

I laugh and it grows into something bordering hysterical. "That's ..." I catch my breath and calm my painful amusement. "That's just it ... I don't care if he comes around." Drying my hands, I pace the kitchen to expend some of this energy before it explodes, sending me into a ranting lunatic.

"Don't get me wrong, being the object of Jake's affection

is incredible. His brooding attitude—his need to protect—it's like nothing I have ever experienced in my life. And when he's kind and loving, well ... it's so intense I could die and not regret a single moment of my life. But when he's not nice, when he's degrading, when he's as you say *not Jake*, I feel stupid. And I'm not stupid. I have to stop being a disposable girlfriend."

"I can assure you, he doesn't think you're a disposable girlfriend."

"He does. The girlfriends you keep? The ones you marry? You don't let them walk away. You. Keep. Them. And you don't have sex with your cook and develop a sudden affinity to chocolate all while claiming to love your girlfriend!"

So much for averting the ranting lunatic.

"Whoa ... wait. Jake had sex with his cook? An employee at his restaurant? When?"

"No. Not Jake. Anthony. Just ... never mind. My point is, Jake treating me like every girl he's ever hated makes him like every asshole I've had the displeasure of dating. I'm not going to train him to be worthy of me. That's bullshit. I'm worthy of a good man. A *good,* honest, loving man. A man who really sees me, even if I don't see myself, even if it's not always a beautiful sight ... he loves me. And I thought that was Jake, but it wasn't. Jake didn't see me. He saw what he wanted to see to justify his attraction to me. I will never live up to his expectations of me. It's too exhausting. It's ... too much."

Deedy leans against the counter as I pick up my pacing speed, preparing for her to jump to Jake's defense.

I wait.

And I wait.

"Good for you. You absolutely deserve that kind of man. Don't ever think otherwise."

I stop, mouth agape.

More waiting.

"And?"

Deedy shrugs. "And nothing."

"You're not going to sing Jake's praises and convince me to forgive him *if* he comes around and wants my forgiveness?"

"Nope. Honestly, while Jake is family in my heart, I try to let him make his own decisions. I try to let him distance himself from the past where I was married to Gavin. I haven't even told your dad everything about Jake and his relationship with Gavin. I want Jake to share those details if and when he's ready."

My clenched hands relax along with my tense shoulders and stiff jaw. "Okay then. Just ..." I blow out my pent-up anger. "Know that I do love him. I just need to love myself more—in an emotional, self-preservation way. And thank you for not telling my dad every detail. Even now, I don't want him worrying about me."

"I'll eventually tell him because I don't want to have secrets between us."

I nod slowly.

"But Avery ... going back to what you just said ...you don't have to love yourself before you love someone else, but it sure is a gift to them if you do. And you owe me no explanation for whatever you decide about Jake."

Ouch. Did I expect Jake to love me enough for both of us?

"I think I need time," I whisper.

"Time is good." She walks toward me.

We are not hugging it out.

Crap.

She wraps her arms around me. I stiffen. She hugs me tighter. I hold my ground.

Hold it.

Hold tightly.

Hold my breath.

Double dammit, Deedy! Here come the tears.

CHAPTER TWENTY-THREE

"Where's my stuff?"

"Hey, baby. You back in town? We should have dinner and discuss your dilemma." Anthony's once honey-smooth voice feels like a nasty case of road rash on my nerves.

Dilemma? My knee will show his shriveled nuts a dilemma, right after I knock out his stupid capped teeth so *all* he can do is lick chocolate mousse from Kim's loose lower lips.

"My stuff, asshole. I had a place to live filled with furnishings before I met you."

"I got you a bigger apartment."

"I didn't ask you to do that. So you can hand it all back over to me or my attorney will make sure you pay out the ass for all the emotional stress you put me through over the past month."

"I let Kim go."

"I don't care."

"I miss you."

"I despise you."

"Sounds like a recipe for angry, make-up sex.

Remember that, baby? Remember how you used to get all pissed off at me for something and we'd fuck like rabid animals."

"Don't flatter your geriatric ego. I'd hardly call doggy style *fucking like rabid animals*. I'm not sure you ever actually finished that way. You'd get a cramp in your leg, and I'd have to ride it out on top and finish you with a hand job because you forgot your ED medication. Now, if we're done pretending you're young, sexy, or even a remotely decent human, can you just tell me where *my* stuff is, so I can never talk to you again?"

"One meal. Dinner. If you still want us to be over after dinner, I'll have all of your stuff delivered wherever you're living now. Deal?"

"YOU HAVE MY STUFF! WE'RE NOT PLAYING LET'S MAKE A DEAL. I'VE BEEN FUCKING ANOTHER MAN WITH A MUCH BIGGER COCK FOR WEEKS. WE. ARE. OVER!"

Someone clears their throat. I turn from my hiding spot on the side of the pool house. I thought I was the only one out here.

"Uh ... Syd was looking for her phone," Lautner says with *my dad* standing next to him.

Dear Heavenly Father,

I'll make this one question quick. Why? Just ... why?

"Gimme a sec. Okay?" I whisper, returning a tight smile. Just lovely. My brother-in-law—Mr. Perfect—and my minister father now know about my extracurricular activities on my road trip—and the approximate size of Jake's cock.

Lautner nods. Dad scowls. I roll my eyes and turn my back to them.

"Baby—"

"Nope. Not your baby. Not having dinner with you. Just going to call my attorney as soon as I hang up which is right..." I glance over my shoulder to make sure the eavesdroppers have scattered "...*fucking* now." I press end.

Three nights with my sister and her perfect family is too much. I need a place of my own. I need out. I need space. I need quietude and freedom from constant, sympathetic glances.

My loving family goes silent when I walk in the house, all eyes on me.

"Sorry. Here's your phone." I set Sydney's phone on the end of the kitchen counter.

"No big deal. I just need a phone number out of my contacts. Is ... everything okay?"

I frown at my dad and Lautner. They divert their gazes. Cowards. Tattletales.

Homeless. Phoneless. Carless. Yep, I'm great.

"Everything's great. So ... what's the plan for dinner?"

"We're going out. Lautner made reservations. It's sort of a ... rehearsal dinner." Sydney smiles, giving our dad and Deedy a warm expression.

"Rehearsal dinner?"

Deedy opens the top of a shipping box that's on the kitchen table. "Tommy arranged to have my dress shipped here." She holds up the white dress. It's pretty, but she's right; it's not a wedding gown.

Dad rests his hand on Deedy's lower back. "We're getting married tomorrow. I arranged everything. It's at a small church near Lautner's hospital. An old pastor friend of mine, it's his church. He's agreed to marry us."

Everyone watches me like I'm the final say in this plan. I'm not. I don't have anything at the moment. Are these people really going to entrust me with blessing a wedding?

"Alrighty then." I smile.

A collective sigh spreads across the room. Geesh ... am I really that bad? Everyone scatters like there are a million things to do to beat the clock.

"Grab your purse. We're going for manis and pedis in ten minutes," Sydney says just before leaving the kitchen.

"I can't afford it."

"My treat."

"I don't want it!" I cringe as Deedy and my dad look at me, and the scattering bodies freeze. Clearing my throat, I paste on an apologetic smile. "I just mean, I'm giving my nails a break from polish. They haven't seen freedom in years."

Sydney nods slowly. "Just a mani and pedi. You can do that without getting them polished."

"Um ..." I feel so stupid and lost and ... out of my mind because Jake messed me up. "Sure. That would be great. Thank you."

Dad kisses Deedy on the cheek then me on the head before leaving the room.

"There's one other thing," Deedy says like she's getting ready to end my already fragile existence. "Gosh, this is hard." She rests her hands on her hips and stares at her feet.

"What is it? Just say it. As long as you're not planning on leaving my dad at the altar, then we're good."

"My father passed away the year before Gavin died. And my mom lives in Florida, but she's afraid to fly. My brother died, and my sister lives in Germany."

"Oh Deedy..." I smile "...of course I'll be your maid of honor."

"Oh ..." She returns a stiff smile. "Um ... actually I asked Sydney, but only because Ocean is the flower girl and Lautner is standing up with Tommy. I just ... I mean ..."

"No. Totally fine." I flick my wrist at her and make some stupid sound like I'm blowing a raspberry on my nephew's cheek. "Silly of me to assume it."

Now it's just awkward. I've made her feel bad.

"It's not silly. In fact, you should absolutely stand up with me too. There's no rule saying bridesmaids and groomsmen have to be equal in number."

"I'm fine, Deedy. Really. So, what were you going to say before I interrupted you with my assumptions?"

"Oh, yeah ... I uh ... asked Jake to walk me down the aisle."

I don't react at all. It's like that moment you step in gum or dog poop and you just freeze, too afraid to assess the damage.

"I'm not trying to put you in an awkward situation. I worried about asking your dad about it too. He didn't know the whole story with Jake and Gavin, but I told him everything last night, and he's good with it. So ..."

"Nope." I manage to squeeze out one word without blinking or even moving my jaw. "It's fine." Yay me! Three, stiff, constipated words.

"Are you sure? It's just that he's here in L.A., and he's the closest thing that I have to family around here."

Slowly, I reach around and pull the stick out of my ass. Once my body relaxes, acclimating to reality, I reach for Deedy's hand. "It's your day. Despite what my family may believe or even what you've witnessed since we've met, I have self-control. I can be in the same vicinity as Jake and not make a scene. I can be amicable."

Controlled. Medicated. Partially drunk. Whatever it takes.

"Oh, thank you, Avery." Deedy attacks me with a suffocating hug. "Thank you. Thank you. Thank you. And ..."

She releases me. "It's actually one day and one night. He'll be at the rehearsal and rehearsal dinner tonight. It's his birthday today too."

I smile and swallow past the lump in my throat. I know it's his birthday. After snooping through his wallet to find out his age, I discovered his birth date. And I stole/borrowed forty dollars to buy him something nice. *That* was the forty dollars. I still have it. Never got around to finding that something nice. "Good. Fine." I grit my teeth. Stupid emotions.

"You're sure?"

I nod. "Sure."

"Great. Let's go to the salon. Oh ... and we're going to stop by Dress Barn. Tommy and I want to buy you girls new dresses for tomorrow."

Dress Barn ...

How is it possible to feel completely broken and yet stronger than ever at the same time? That's the war battling inside of me at this very moment as I can't make myself get out of the car to walk into the church.

"Come on, Avery." Ocean waves me out of the car as she holds open the door.

I return a nervous smile.

"Sweetie, go inside with your dad and brother. Avery and I will be inside in a few minutes." Sydney kisses Ocean on the head then slides into the backseat next to me. "Do we hate Jake?"

My eyes narrow at her.

She rests her hand on mine. "You never told me exactly what happened between you two. So ... he's here as Deedy's family. I won't knee him in the nuts or anything, but I just need to know if we hate him? I'm Team Avery, with or without an explanation."

"Damn you ..." I glance away, fighting back the tears. "Not today. Today I just need you to tell me to pull up my big girl panties, plaster on a fake smile, and be on my best behavior for the good of the family."

"Fine, don't cry. I don't want your mascara running."

I grunt a laugh. "I'm not wearing mascara. Or lash extensions. Or foundation. Or ... fuck ... I'm wearing a tiny bit of eye shadow and lip gloss."

"Oh, well, you look amazing."

I turn back to her.

She shrugs. "You were the lucky one who inherited Mom's natural beauty. If Jake's the one who helped you see that, then maybe we don't hate him."

No. Way.

I'm not giving that asshat credit for anything. "We hate him. That's the law today. Got it?" I grab my purse and fish out my makeup bag.

"Um ..."

"Sydney..." I pin her with a firm look "...we hate him. You asked. I've confirmed it. Now go inside and get the hate vibe going. I'll be in as soon as I fix my face."

Her eyebrows shoot up her forehead. "O ... K ..." She mouths while easing out of the vehicle.

I unzip my makeup bag and get to work. By the time Ocean knocks on the window, a good twenty minutes later, I'm satisfied with my transformation.

"Hey, girly girl. Did they start without me?" I hop out, making sure I don't rub up against the vehicle in my white pants and black, sleeveless blouse.

"Not yet, but everyone is waiting for you."

I follow her into the church, blinking my right eye several times and pressing my extensions back into place. I think the adhesive went to shit on the trip. Probably too many days in the hot truck. They're not my favorite fake lashes, but they work in a pinch. Just barely ...

"Hey." Sydney smiles, waiting for me just outside of the sanctuary. "I see you did a little more than fix your makeup."

I smile through my dark red lips.

"It's on your teeth." Sydney's nose wrinkles.

I rub my finger over my teeth. "Better?"

"Sure. You uh ... went extra smoky with your eyes. Interesting choice for a wedding rehearsal at a church." She loops her arm around mine and guides me into the church.

"It's past five. Evening makeup is always darker."

"Well, you definitely nailed it."

I pinch her arm. She chuckles as the rest of the family gathered in the front pews turns toward us.

My eyes keep laser focus on Asher, my nephew, because he's not Jake, and he's the only family member who's not giving me the WTF-did-you-do-to-your-face look. It's not that I look bad. I followed proper makeup application rules. I just went a little heavier—a little darker. It's the look I'd wear with a black teddy, garters, thigh-high hose, and stilettos while touching myself at the foot of a four-poster bed. OR ... an evening wedding rehearsal for my father and his younger bride-to-be. It really is a versatile look.

"Good, everyone is here. Let's get started," the minister says.

Sydney and I sit in the front row next to Ocean. Through my peripheral vision, I caught a blurry glimpse of Jake before I sat down, so I know he's right behind us. I know he's got some sort of product making his hair look fuckable—Pot. Kettle. Black.

I know he's wearing a sharp blue button-down with the sleeves rolled up to show off his ink. It's possible I stole more than just a glimpse, but I definitely didn't make eye contact with him.

The minister chats it up a bit about how he knows my dad. Then he gives a brief summary of the ceremony before we do an actual test run.

One groomsman.

Two bridesmaids.

I'm such a third wheel.

Luckily, my uncooperative eyelashes make it easy to keep my gaze at my feet the whole time as I dab my watery eye and keep pushing the lashes back into place. I manage to survive the forty-five minutes without making eye contact with Jake—or anyone else for that matter.

"Avery." Lautner smirks, holding open my door as we load up to head to the rehearsal dinner.

"Shut it." I scowl.

He chuckles.

On the way to dinner, I replace my bad extension with a new one and fix my smeared eye makeup.

When we arrive, I chat with anyone who is not near Jake as we wait a few minutes for our reserved table to be ready.

"Avery, sit next to me!" Ocean calls as everyone files into the private dining room.

I smile at her until I notice my dad has already taken the seat to her left, which means if I sit by her, it will be on her right—in the chair next to Jake.

"Avery, take my seat." My dad starts to stand. But if he moves, he won't be sitting next to Deedy. And the fact that he's offering must mean Deedy or Sydney gave him the whole scoop on Jake.

"No. You stay." I smile and take the seat next to Ocean, scooting my chair as close to hers as possible.

"Before we eat, I'd like to pray." Dad holds out his hands. Deedy takes one, and Ocean takes his other hand as everyone else joins hands.

"Hold his hand." Ocean nudges me, peeking open one eye.

Jake opens his hand, palm up on the table. I move my hand above his in a hover mode, jerking it back a fraction when one of our fingertips actually touch.

"Avery ..." Ocean grits my name through her teeth. "Hold it."

Freaking hand-holding police.

Before I can make up some excuse to leave the table during prayer, Jake grabs my hand, holding it hard like he's pissed off about something. While my dad gives thanks for the food, his family, Deedy, and the many years we had Swarley in our lives, I completely chew Jake's ass up one side and down the other—in my head.

Don't hold my hand so damn hard. YOU have nothing to be upset about. I was your sex toy. Your experiment. Your punching bag. I gave you everything I had to give. I bared everything right down to my soul and my ugliest secrets. You ... you stupid asshole! You gave me nothing! NOTHING! So stop holding my hand so fucking tight!

"In your name we pray, amen."

I open my eyes and rip my hand away from Jake. He has the audacity to give me a questioning look like he has no idea why I'm acting like he has the plague.

"Hi," he says in a soft voice, followed by a kind smile.

No. NO! NO! NO! He doesn't get to say hi to me like

some stranger. He doesn't get to be kind with his smile. Awful words were said. Hurtful assumptions were made.

Hearts broken.

Dreams shattered.

Jake holds my attention without saying another word. I hate that he has that effect on me and the way everything and everyone else in the room disappears. The moments we shared replay in my head. We had good moments—the best moments.

"Why did it have to be you?" I whisper.

Jake's smile fades.

The muted voices come to life.

And it's no longer just the two of us in the room.

The moment ... is over.

We are over.

"Have you arranged to get your stuff back?" Sydney asks.

I bite my lips together, laying my napkin across my lap. "Not yet. He refuses to budge on any of it until I agree to have dinner with him."

"Dinner?" Lautner looks up from across the table. "Tell him to make reservations for four. Sydney and I will go with you."

Chuckling, I glance over the menu. "Hmm ... is this brotherly love or your way of getting me out of your house?"

"Definitely brotherly love." He smirks. "What's not to like about a live-in babysitter?"

Everyone laughs as I shoot him a teasing scowl. Well, I don't think Jake's laughing.

"No need to worry about furniture until you have a place to put it, which requires a job, which usually requires transportation. We need to tackle one obstacle at a time."

My dad leans forward past Ocean and shoots me a reassuring smile.

Parents have a way of bitch-slapping their kids with a heavy dose of reality under the guise of love. Yep. I definitely don't need furniture at the moment.

"She needs a job to afford a car, and she won't take money from us, so ..." Sydney eyes me over the top of her menu.

Nope. There's nothing degrading and completely embarrassing about this conversation. I should be angry with my family for discussing *my situation* in front of Jake, but he's seen me naked in every sense of the word. None of this should be a surprise to him.

"I don't want your money, Sis. I just want your Lexus. I'm certain I could live out of it until I save up for an apartment."

"You know ..." Deedy sets her menu down and rests her hand on my dad's leg. "You should borrow my car. We're leaving for another mission trip in six weeks. When I am home, I ride my bike and walk most places. We have Tommy's car for longer trips and bad weather."

"Or you could take public transportation," Lautner murmurs, hiding his grin behind his glass of water. "Have you ever taken public transportation?"

I scratch my chin with my middle finger. "That's like a limo, right? Yeah, I've taken public transportation a lot."

Sydney shoves her elbow into the ribs of her snarky husband. "Play nice, you two."

"So, Jake ..." My dad clears his throat. "I really do appreciate all you did for Avery."

Whoa!

Okay, so my dad must not know *everything*. He missed

the newsflash—we hate Jake. He did nothing but break me down. No appreciation needed for that.

Jake takes a long sip of his water, probably sorting out the best response to my dad's misplaced gratitude.

"You're welcome."

I stare at my index finger tapping the end of my fork.

And I wait ...

Nothing.

Really? You're welcome? No elaboration. No "It was my pleasure." No "Anything for Deedy." Or "We had a good time."

"She can be a bit of a handful sometimes." Dad laughs.

Sydney and Lautner stifle their reactions.

Jake rubs the back of his neck. "A bit."

I ram the heel of my shoe into his shin.

He grunts, bending forward slightly and fisting his hand at his mouth as if to mask his reaction as a cough.

"Can I get everyone's drink order?" the waiter asks.

We order drinks and food. The conversation shifts to the wedding, Dad's and Deedy's upcoming trip, my niece and nephew, and Jake's restaurants. I fall off the grid of conversation, which ends in everyone (except me) singing Happy Birthday to Jake.

CHAPTER TWENTY-FOUR

Jake

I NEED to talk to her.

Of course, I have no idea what I can say to undo the things I have done. To say I'm ashamed of the things I said to Avery and the way I said them would be a monumental understatement. It's like I broke a vase and all I can do is stare at the shattered pieces with no fucking clue how to fix it.

I follow Avery and her family to the restaurant parking lot. A million words sit idle on my tongue. If I don't say them the right way, it will make things worse. If I don't say them at all, I will choke on them and die.

"I'm sorry." I lean down by her ear and whisper as she waits for her niece to wedge her way out of the restaurant's entrance.

Avery coughs on a laugh and shakes her head, keeping her back to me as she follows Ocean.

"Please let me drive you home so we can talk."

Avery stops in the middle of the parking lot, letting her

family continue toward their vehicle. "Home?" She turns around. "I don't have a home. Or a car. Or a job. I don't have furniture, a majority of my clothes, pots and pans, forks, knives, spoons. I don't have a fucking flyswatter! But..." she takes a step toward me and holds up her thumb and index finger a fraction of an inch apart "...I have nothing but a teeny tiny shred of dignity. And I'll step in front of a speeding train before I let you take it from me."

"Avery? You coming?" Sydney yells.

"Twenty minutes. Give me twenty minutes." I can't mask the desperation in my voice. Hell, I don't *want* to mask it.

Avery shakes her head and laughs, the kind that borders on insanity. "Anthony wants dinner. You want twenty minutes. You know what I want?" Her eyebrows inch up her forehead.

I shake my head slowly, afraid to make any sudden movement around her.

"No?" Her head cocks to the side. "Then you don't deserve twenty minutes." Avery pivots and clicks her heels to the vehicle.

"Good job, Ave. Way to stand the fuck up for yourself," I whisper just before blowing out a long, defeated breath.

I pull my phone out of my pocket and text Deedy.

I need a favor.

Avery

"You're up early." Sydney sits across from me at the kitchen table. "And you already went for coffee." She nods to the to-go cup fisted in my hand.

I frown, take a sip, and slide the half-empty cup to her. "Not exactly."

She reads the writing on the side of the cup.

Good morning, my sexy wife. Had to check on a patient, see you at the church. Xo

Sydney tosses me a scowl and peels the lid off. "You drank half of *my* chai tea latte from *my* husband? Have you no shame?"

On a big yawn, I stretch my arms above my head. "You're loud. Embarrassingly loud. Seriously, our father is in the house."

Sydney snorts and covers her mouth as her face reddens. "Oh god ... it was the wine I had with dinner. Wine makes me ..."

"Loud. It makes you loud yet oddly distinct—well enunciated in your demands."

"Ugh!" She covers her face.

"I mean ... every woman has a *there*. What's yours? Because you were pretty elated when he got *there*. Do your kids wonder why Mommy screams, 'Yes! There! Right there! Don't stop!'?"

"Shh ... stop!" She drops her hand-covered face to the table next to the latte that's a bit too sweet for my taste.

"What does Lautner do when he sees Dad? Like ... a high-five for thoroughly nailing his daughter? Dad has some health issues, but I don't think impaired hearing is one of them."

Sydney lifts her head to speak then clamps her jaw shut as Deedy walks into the kitchen, tying her robe.

"Good morning."

We smile at Deedy and return pleasantries.

She pours a cup of coffee and joins us at the table.

"Someone had a good night." Deedy takes a sip of coffee but not before smirking.

"Oh god!" Sydney covers her face again.

"Don't be embarrassed. I have a feeling Tommy will make me sing later too."

"NO!" Sydney and I yell at the same time.

I shake my head. "Sorry. You can call him Tommy, Dicky, or Harry, but he's still our dad. And in our naïve, little world, our Daddy doesn't ever go *there* like Lautner or —" My posture deflates.

Deedy and Sydney stare at me, sympathy pouring from their tiny frowns.

"Jake ..." I say his name on a slow sigh. "He was good at going *there*. Really, really good."

"And by *there* you mean—" Deedy bites her lower lip.

"Wherever your there might be." I cut her off.

Deedy nods slowly. "Oh ... my there is—"

"Nope." I hold up my index finger and wave it side to side. "It was a statement, not a question."

Sydney snorts, and Deedy grins while nodding. "Fair."

There's a knock at the front door. Sydney slides the cup back to me as she stands. "I don't want your backwash." She answers the door and returns with an envelope. "Special courier delivery."

I take the envelope with my name on it and open it.

"Who's it from?" Sydney asks while taking a seat again at the table.

I shake my head, reading his message. "Anthony," I mumble as a key drops onto the table. "It's the address for a storage facility where he's keeping my stuff."

"You have a month to empty out your stuff, a grand in your checking account, and a new phone will be delivered

tomorrow to your sister's house. Don't ever contact me again."

"Wh—are you serious?" Sydney picks up the key and inspects it. "Did you message him or call him after dinner last night?"

"No." I set down the letter and stare at it, rereading his words. "Don't ever contact me again. Sounds like he's mad. How did he go from begging for dinner to this?"

Sydney slides the key back to me. "Who cares? We'll get that storage unit emptied tomorrow. You need to take that grand and open an account at a different bank and make sure the phone is brand-new and with a different provider. You need to completely cut him out of your life."

"Amen." Deedy holds up her mug of coffee like a toast.

Me? I read the letter a third time. It makes no sense. Anthony thrives on winning. This isn't him winning. It's him surrendering.

"Deedy, I'll get Ocean up and have Dad watch Asher. We are going to get our hair done because it's your wedding day!" Sydney's so much better at Team Deedy than I am, but I'll get there.

I stare at my fingernails. They are neat and trimmed, but I should've gotten them painted. Men are *done* ruling my life, toying with my emotions, and trampling my self-esteem. "Do we have time to stop someplace so I can get a couple coats of polish on my nails?"

Sydney grins. "Absolutely."

"Fuck me ..." I whisper.

"Shh!" Sydney nudges my elbow. "We're in church,"

she grits through her fake smile as Jake walks Deedy down the aisle.

Jake Matthews in a suit. My ovaries just exploded, sending a volcano of heat down to disintegrate my panties. I didn't think I could possibly hate him more, but I do. He gets an extra dose of hate from me today because of how fuckable he looks in that black suit and mustard and white tie that matches the color of our strapless Dress Barn dresses.

I think it's that Jake looks completely out of place in a suit, which makes him look vulnerable despite everything else about him that screams confidence.

Peeling my gaze off Jake, I watch my dad. He often looked at my mom that way. I don't remember all the looks he gave her, I was young, but I remember this one. It's bittersweet because I'm happy for him, but I miss my mom. It's bittersweet because I caught a few glimpses of Jake looking at me like that on our trip. But that's all they were —glimpses.

I deserve a man who looks at me like that, even on my worst day. And the most bittersweet reality of all is that I might not have ever realized my true self-worth had I not met Jake Matthews.

A tear releases from one eye. I quickly wipe it off my cheek.

The minister starts to speak of second-chance love.

Another unavoidable tear.

My dad mouths "I love you" to Deedy, and ten more tears insist on breaking free.

Lautner winks at Sydney.

More stupid tears.

Jake, from the front pew next to Asher, hands Ocean a handkerchief to give me, and … I die.

"Pull it together," Sydney whispers.

I blow out a slow, shaky breath and think of something ... anything to dam the emotions. Focusing on Deedy and my father, I think about tonight—their wedding night—and how she's going to ask him to go *there*. And then I imagine where there might be and what he might do to her when he gets there.

Yep, that dries up all the tears. Now, I need to deal with the bile crawling up my throat.

"I pronounce you husband and wife."

Our tiny gathering cheers as my dad kisses Deedy. It's soft and fairly quick. PG for the grandkids. He takes her hand and leads her out of the sanctuary. Lautner follows them with his wife and two beautiful children.

The minister waits, but after a few moments of me staying rooted to the same spot and Jake unmoving from his seat on the pew, he exits the sanctuary as well.

And then there were two ...

I can't not look at him. Just his presence manages to demand my attention.

"I know what you want." He leans forward, resting his elbows on his knees.

I tighten my grip on my small bouquet, tighten my jaw, tighten the chains around my heart.

"Acceptance. You want me to accept you for who you are. The good, the bad, and everything in between."

Acceptance.

I play with that word in my mind, applying it to the things that I've done, the person I am, the dreams I have, and the fears that haunt me.

"No." I take three steps to walk toward the back of the sanctuary.

Jake grabs my wrist. "Ave ..." Like his grip on me, his voice leaks desperation.

I jerk my arm from his grasp. "I don't want you to accept me. I don't *accept* how you've treated me. I don't *accept* Anthony cheating on me. But here's the thing with acceptance ... it's not really a choice. Not accepting something doesn't change the fact that it happened or that something just is. Acceptance is this illusion that we're in control. I unknowingly had a relationship with a married man. It. Happened. You choosing to accept it doesn't change a single thing. So if your acceptance is simply your brain finally wrapping itself around reality, then yay for you. Good job, Jake. Whatever helps you sleep at night." My feet move on their own, spurred by the self-preservation signal from my brain.

Just as I reach the back doors to the sanctuary, Jake's defeated voice stops me. "So, that's it? We're over? There's nothing I can say to make things right between us? Not a million sorry's for what I said to you? Not begging you to forgive me for letting my past and all my resentment toward my past tear us apart? Nothing?"

I chuckle, but it's the kind that hurts, the kind that steps up to take the pain when you're just too cried out. "The English language has hundreds of thousands of words. There's always ... *something* to say."

CHAPTER TWENTY-FIVE

A WEEK AGO, we said goodbye to Dad and Deedy as they headed off on an impromptu honeymoon in a rental car pointed toward wine country. Today, I had a job interview.

"I got the job," I interrupt Lautner as he drones on about some object he pulled out of a kid's nose today.

Sydney hands me another slice of pizza as everyone at the table gives me their attention. Lautner doesn't look bothered by my interruption. He holds a hopeful gleam in his blue eyes.

"It's just part-time, so I'm not quite ready to move out." I give him a tiny cringe of apology.

"No one said you have to move out." He grins.

Why does he have to be so perfect? And why did he fall in love with Sydney before I had the chance to take him for myself?

"That's great, Ave. And you think your hand is good? You'll be able to massage people?" Sydney nods to the kids when Ocean asks if they can be excused from the table.

I want a table with kids who ask to be excused, and a husband who lovingly welcomes the homeless and jobless.

One step at a time.

"It's barefoot bar. I'll be fine. But I need to find something else to supplement that income. Also, I've been contacting some friends, looking for a roommate. I'm pretty sure it's going to be awhile before I can rent on my own." I take a bite of pizza.

Sydney and Lautner stare at me, eerily still and expressionless. On second thought, they look utterly shocked. Yeah, that's the vibe I'm getting.

"What?" I shrug.

"Who are you?" Sydney chuckles, a nervous kind of laugh. "What happened to you between Milwaukee and here?"

I sigh, wiping my mouth. "The past month has bestowed several heavy doses of reality upon me. Love. Heartbreak. Loss. Humiliation. Maybe I found God again. Wouldn't that make Dad proud?"

Sydney nods in micro increments, eyes slightly narrowed. "Give us a minute, babe."

Lautner pauses the pizza at his mouth.

"Take the rest." She shoves the box in his direction, tossing him a wicked smile.

I love their story. Their looks. The exchanges that say so much about how hard they worked to get to this point in their life. Will I ever share that same smile? The same kind of love?

He stands, bending over to bite her neck. She jumps and giggles. Her smile settles into something more somber and sympathetic when he saunters off with the rest of the pizza. Her attention returns to me.

"If Jake said he's sorry, and you love him, what's holding you back?" Sydney sets her napkin on the table and leans back in her chair, arms folded across her chest.

"Why did you wait so long to tell Lautner about Ocean?"

She frowns.

I shake my head on a slow sigh. "It's not a real question. I know the answer. I know you were crippled by fear, the idea of rejection, and the need to protect your heart. Well ..." I lean forward, resting my arms on the table. "I'm doing the same thing. I'd say it's a Montgomery trait, but I think it's a human trait. If Jake were emotionally stable, free of a troubled past, if he simply had this knee-jerk reaction to my confession ... I think it would be easier to ..."

"Forgive him?"

I shake my head. "I forgive him. I just don't trust him. He has too many demons, and I'm a trigger for all of them."

"So you love him. You forgive him. But you don't think you can trust him?"

"Bingo."

Sydney's lips twist to the side. "Deedy thinks he's quite the catch. Kind. Loyal. Protective. I don't sense she feels he's not trustworthy. But ... I'm Team Avery. So, if he's not trustworthy for you, then I support your decision. I never imagined you'd be the calm in the storm these past few weeks, but other than the makeup incident at the rehearsal dinner, you've been helpful with the kids—"

"I love Ocean and Asher. That's nothing new. And what do you mean by *makeup incident*?"

"Really?" She curls a few strands of hair around her finger. "So you didn't panic at the thought of seeing Jake? You didn't want to prove to him that you're your own person?"

"Pfft ... I didn't panic. I had an epiphany. Two totally different things."

Laughter bubbles from Sydney's chest. "An epiphany?"

"Yes. I realized that I let him in my head to the point that I didn't know if my thoughts were mine or his." I shrug. "The fact is ... I like makeup and clothes. I like it when my hair looks nice and my nails are painted. If I don't use these things to measure my self-worth, then I don't see why it's a problem."

She stands, gathering the dirty plates. "Maybe you did find God." A smirk tugs at her lips. "You do you, Ave. Just make sure you're not letting your ego and pride steal something that has great potential."

I help her clear the table, opening my mouth several times before clamping it shut. Sydney gives me several knowing glances, taunting me to react, to say more.

"He's a good kisser." I break the silence.

"Yeah?" Sydney gives me a raised eyebrow.

Biting back my grin, I nod. "If he could love me the way he kisses me ... you'd be the jealous sister for once." I wink at her.

Jake

Two weeks later.
Sage Leaf Cafe, Los Angeles

"Yo, Jake! A group of women out front are asking for you. Hot ones." Seth wipes his hands on a white bar towel and grins at me before pushing his way back through the swinging door to the front of the restaurant.

I finish entering a few sales figures into my accounting program and shut my laptop.

"You didn't think I was going to leave without saying

goodbye, did you?" Deedy saunters around the counter and gives me a big hug and kisses me on the cheek.

My gaze falls over her shoulder to Sydney, Ocean, and Avery, and my chest tightens. "How was wine country?" I force confidence and enthusiasm into my words. Avery makes me nervous and anxious—and awkward. It's not easy being friendly but not overbearing. Confident, even when I want to beg her to just tell me how to make things right.

"Beautiful. We stayed at three different B&B's. I don't want to go home, but duty calls. The honeymoon is over." She grabs my hand and pulls me around the counter. "I wanted to have lunch with you and my new favorite girls before leaving. Know a good place to eat?"

Sydney chuckles when I smile, and Avery's lips turn up just a fraction. Her airy white top accentuates her tan. Her denim miniskirt is probably designer, like her bag and shoes, but her hair is messy, perfectly windblown, and her face bears very little makeup.

However, that gaze of hers ... it ping-pongs around the room like it's too much to look at me for more than a few seconds. This intensifies the pain in my chest. Deedy gave me Avery's new phone number. My thumb has hovered over the call button a hundred times. I've driven past Sydney's house at least another hundred times.

Words.

So many damn words.

I can't find the right ones. When I think I've figure it out, this little voice in my head convinces me to find new ones, better ones. But right now, I can't find a single one.

"Or ... do you not have time for us?"

"What?" I shake out of my Avery daze and refocus on Deedy. "Real funny. Yeah, I do happen to know a place.

Hey, Seth. We'll be upstairs. Can you please bring up an assortment from the menu?"

"You got it."

"Upstairs? Did you finish repainting?" Deedy asks.

"Yep, last week. Follow me."

I lead them up the backstairs to my apartment. At the top of the stairs, I hold open the door for everyone. Avery is last in line. She risks a quick glance at me while bending down to slip off her platform sandals. I give her my best smile. Maybe it will help me channel the best words.

"This table is amazing!" Sydney runs her hand along my irregular-shaped table made from several old tree stumps.

"Thanks. It was custom made from an eco-friendly furniture store up in San Francisco."

"And your view. Ocean, come look at the surfers." Sydney waves Ocean toward the wall of windows.

Avery takes slow steps around my studio apartment with her fingers dipped into the front, shallow pockets of her miniskirt. She says nothing but seems to give everything a thorough inspection.

"Can we walk down to the beach?" Ocean asks.

"Maybe after lunch."

"You guys surf?" I get everyone glasses of fresh citrus water.

"Ocean and Lautner surf. I take pictures." Sydney sits at the table, running her hand over the glassy-smooth surface again.

"Ave, do you surf?" I ask like she's a recent acquaintance, not like having her here, in my space, has my heart hammering against my chest because all I want to do is go back in time and change how I reacted to her confession.

She cocks her head at a black and white photo of me

from my very last fight. I was more ripped then, my head shaven, one eye swollen shut. Unrecognizable to anyone who didn't know me then, except for my tattoos. It's not a glamour shot. But ... I won.

"Sometimes," she mumbles, cocking her head to the other side.

"Rarely." Sydney rolls her eyes.

"More than you." Avery's tone remains even, like she's answering on autopilot, not at all bothered by her sister challenging her.

My lungs trap my breath as Avery's finger brushes along the photo over my swollen eye and the trail of blood down my cheek.

Blood, sweat, and tears.

That's what Gavin told me it would take to beat my undefeated opponent. I'm pretty sure that it's going to take so much more than that to make things right with the woman I love.

After three quick knocks, I open the door and take the trays of food from Seth. "Thanks, buddy."

I serve the food, giving Deedy a wink when she leaves the chair next to Avery for me.

Avery pulls her phone out of her purse and glances at something on the screen for a few seconds before sliding the phone back into her purse.

"New phone?" I hand everyone napkins.

"Yes." She inspects my face like she's still trying to connect it to the one in the photo.

"New phone. And she got all of her stuff back from Anthony without a fight or meeting him for dinner. Dad gave his 'God works in mysterious ways' speech. And Lautner's friend owns a car dealership, and he's loaned Ave a used car to 'test drive' until she gets a full-time job." Sydney, taps her fork on her lower lip. "Which really another part-time job would work. Right, Ave?"

Avery lifts the top of the bun to her chickpea sandwich, probably looking for bacon. "Maybe."

"Avery's back to giving massages, mostly barefoot bar." Deedy adds. "But it's only part-time."

Avery has a true fan club today. That's good. She deserves it.

I take a bite of my sandwich and wait for Avery to look at me, but she doesn't. "I know the owner of the cafe downstairs. He has a part-time opening if you can run a blender and a juicer."

This gets her attention. Eyes wide. Lips parted.

I shrug. "No guarantee. I'm just saying I could put in a good word for you."

"Sounds perfect." Sydney grins.

Avery whips her head toward her sister, shooting her a traitorous scowl.

"What? It does. It's a job. Not a career. It will help give you back some independence until you can regroup and figure out where you want to be long term."

Avery takes a bite of her food and doesn't say another word or look at anyone for the rest of lunch.

"Can we go to the beach now?" Ocean tugs on Sydney's arm.

"Yes, sweetie. You two coming?"

"Absolutely." Deedy sets the rest of the dishes by the kitchen sink and gives me a sideways glance while lowering her voice. "Her family wants to know what you did to her. They say she's not the same person she was before the trip."

I lift a questioning brow at Deedy for a few seconds then glance back at Avery and Sydney, who aren't paying attention to us. "I ... I don't know." My gaze returns to Deedy.

"Why'd you hurt her?"

"I didn't mean to. I just didn't know how to deal with ... things."

"And by things you mean you didn't think before you lashed out about something that wasn't her fault?"

Rubbing my hand over my face, I mumble my frustration with a low groan and take another quick glance over my shoulder. "Yes. It's just that in the moment, when she told me about the affair, it took me back to everything Meg went through, and it felt like Avery was partly to blame."

"She told you about the affair?"

I nod.

Deedy leans closer, keeping her voice low. "She *voluntarily* told you about it, and you acted that way?"

Another nod.

"You fucked up."

My head jerks back. Missionary Deedy dropping the F-bomb is a new experience for me.

"Well ..." She smirks, picking invisible lint from the sleeve of my T-shirt. "There's really no other good way to say it. Avery is my family now, but you are too. So, figure out a way to make things amicable."

I shrug. "They are. We just ate lunch together. We did fine at the wedding."

"No. She's being fake friendly for my benefit. She's secretly hating you because she loves you, and you changed her. Now she doesn't know what the hell to do with herself. You fucked *her* up. Fix it."

"Ocean used the restroom. Let's go, ladies." Sydney interrupts our hushed conversation. "Ave?" Sydney tugs on the hem of Avery's shirt to get her attention.

Avery looks up over her shoulder, standing close to the window by my bed. "No." She glances at me. "I need to have a few *words* with Jake."

Sydney nods, jerking her head toward the door to the stairs. Ocean and Deedy follow her.

"We'll be back in an hour or so. Sound good?" Deedy lifts an eyebrow at Avery.

She nods.

Then Deedy scowls at me with a stern warning in her eyes, just before the door clicks shut behind them.

Avery walks to the middle of the room again, rubbing her hands down the front of her skirt *three times*. I ease into my recliner and wait for her to set the tone for whatever is supposed to be said.

"Deedy told me about Gavin's death."

I try to clench my jaw and hold still to hide my reaction. The day will never come that his name alone doesn't cause every muscle in my body to tighten with regret. It was an accident. I know it, but it doesn't change the consequences. Bad things happen all the time as a result of an accident. Gavin died. He was a good person. My mom died. She was a good person. Megan's baby died. He was perfect and completely innocent. But my father—the opposite of good and innocent—still walks the earth.

So. Fucking. Unfair.

"I'm sorry. And I'm sorry I unknowingly slept with a married man. I'm sorry I tried to poison you. I'm sorry you got roped into taking Swarley and me on your special road trip. I'm sorry for every second of inconvenience, for the oxygen I stole from your sacred little bubble."

"I never asked for an apology."

"I'm not apologizing *for* you. I'm apologizing *to* you."

She turns her back to me, once again, staring at the black and white photo.

I just want to hold her and make things right.

After a minute or two of silence, her posture deflates. "Part of me wishes I would have known you when this photo was taken. I would have loved to have been the girl waiting in your corner. I would have loved to have known that Jake ... the fearless one who didn't hold onto his anger. This ..." She steps closer to the photo.

"This was the stripped-down version of you. This was your acoustic song. I know this because when I left Megan's house, I felt like how you look in this photo—battered. Nearly broken. Exhausted. Unrecognizable. But..." she turns back toward me with tears in her eyes "...also victorious. Stronger. Changed. You did that. You gave me a fight when I needed it. You taught me to take a punch and get back up. You showed me that what we see on the outside can be very deceiving. A scar doesn't mean you were weak. A scar means you survived. A scar is a badge of strength."

When she blinks, several tears slide down her cheeks, but she doesn't move to wipe them away. "You left scars, but now I'm stronger. So ... thank you."

"I love you, Avery." The words tumble out. I hate how empty they probably sound to her, but it's all that's in my head and my heart.

She nods, slowly brushing away the tears and sniffling. "I know you do. But it won't last because it was built on something weak—your expectations of me. And I can't stand on those forever. I will stumble and fall. I will crash and crumble. And eventually, I won't be recognizable to you because you'll always remember me at my best, when loving me was easy."

"That's not true." I lean forward, resting my elbows on my knees.

"Isn't it? I think you see your mom in my fragility. You definitely see Francine in the *things* I like. And I think when I told you about my relationship with Megan's husband, you saw your father in me. I'm this all-encompassing demon you're determined to slay. If you can love me in spite of all the things you hate about me, then you win."

"You're running. That's what this is. You're running, and you're blaming it on me."

She chuckles, shaking her head and slipping her fingers into her front pockets again. "I'm here. I'm not going anywhere. You're the runner. You're the one who will be leaving for Milwaukee. And that's okay. *I'm* okay, Jake. But not in spite of you. I'm okay because of you."

There's a clawing need just under my skin, a need that makes my heart race. I don't want us to end, but I don't know what to say.

The words. The fucking words.

If I could just hand her my heart, wouldn't that be enough? Would it have to be served with some grand explanation?

Here, Ave. Take it. It's yours.

If it's not *I'm sorry* or *I love you*, then what is it?

How can she look so beautiful, so resigned to what's happened yet so confident at the same time when this is unraveling every fiber of my heart?

She smiles. It's stunning and real. "I'm going to find them at the beach."

"I leave in two weeks. Maybe we could ..." Desperation twists and crashes around in my head like a tornado. "Have dinner or something before I leave." I stand, slipping my hands into my pockets, mirroring her. These hands itch to touch her, but I don't think she's mine to touch anymore.

Rolling her lips together, she nods a half dozen times. "Maybe breakfast or lunch downstairs? We can discuss my part-time employment at your cafe. I need another job for awhile." She shrugs. "I'm willing to swallow my pride and admit it."

"The job is yours."

"No." She holds up a hand. "You interview me. Hire me only if you find my qualifications acceptable. I don't want any coworkers thinking I got the job out of pity or because I slept with the boss."

"It's running a juicer and blender. Seth makes all the other food. I'm sure you're plenty qualified."

Her lips twist. I want to kiss them. I want to drop to my knees and beg for time to rewind.

"But..." I step closer, leaving a few inches between her bare feet and mine "...I'll train you before I head back home."

"Home," she whispers, staring at our feet.

"Ave ..." I take the final step and cup the side of her face.

She leans into my touch, closing her eyes, face wrinkled like it pains her.

"I miss you so fucking much. And I know it's somehow not enough, but I am *truly* sorry for what I said to you, for how I treated you. If I could take it back, I would."

Her hand covers mine as she draws in a shaky breath. "I miss your touch."

Inching closer, I feather my lips across her opposite check. "Then let me touch you."

"Jake ..."

My mouth covers hers, swallowing her weak plea. Her

hands press to my chest and curl into fists, bringing me closer, deepening our kiss.

Please don't stop ... Please let me show you what you mean to me.

Her tongue slides into my mouth.

My hands slide into her hair.

We moan in unison.

How could I forget how much I love kissing this woman? She tastes like the orange and lime slices in the water. Her hair has a soft floral scent. And her skin ... it's all my hands ever want to touch. She's just ... all I ever want.

"St—stop." She pulls away breathless, pressing the pads of her fingers to her lips, wide blue eyes unblinking. "I'm not her." Her head inches side to side. "I'm not the girl you can manipulate with a kiss or empty promises. Not anymore."

"Ave ..." I run my fingers through my hair. "I'm not manipulating you."

"You are. You're distracting me. And you're good at it, but ... it's all wrong. You can't throw out temporary apologies and half-ass I love you's just to get into my panties."

"I ..." My jaw falls open and stays there. How can she honestly believe that?

Because that's all she's ever known.

"I don't want into your panties. I want into your heart, into your *life*."

"I'm supposed to believe that you don't want into my panties?" She crosses her arms over her chest, flipping her hip out to the side.

My eyes roll to the ceiling while I rest my hands on my hips, blowing out a slow breath. "I *like* what's in your panties—a lot. But ..." I return my attention to meet her expectant gaze. "I want *you* and all that that encompasses."

"Don't." She shakes her head, more emotion pooling in her eyes. "When I told you about Steve, you didn't grumble and clench your fists like I scratched the side of your truck. You basically called me a whore, a home-wrecker, a baby killer."

"No, Ave ..."

"Yes. Yes, Jake. That's how much you *love* me. I was honest with you, and you punished me for it. You just ... gave up on us."

"I'm not giving up on us." I step forward.

Avery steps back. "You did. And now that I'm put back together, you can't just waltz into my life and decide you want me again. And you have no one to blame for it but yourself. You told me to stand the fuck up for myself. Well ... this is me. And I'm not letting *any* man treat me like a whore ever again." She slips on her sandals and grabs the door handle. Then ... she freezes.

It takes me a few seconds to figure out what's captured her attention. Releasing the handle, she picks up a ripped piece of paper from the entry table next to the door.

"Oh my god ..." she whispers.

I close my eyes and sigh.

"You ... you did this."

My eyes open as she slowly turns toward me, holding up the paper with Anthony Bianchi's address on it.

"You're the reason he gave me back my stuff. The money ... the phone ... it was you."

I don't respond. Not even a flinch.

"How ..." She shakes her head, brow wrinkled. "How did you get this address? Sydney?"

Deedy got it from Sydney, but I don't say that.

"What did you do? Did you threaten him? Beat him up?"

I paid him a visit. There were subtle threats. He cooperated, so I didn't have to beat him up. I would have. I would kill for her. But I don't say that either.

"Why?" she whispers.

"You know why."

Her gaze slips. She lets the piece of paper fall from her hand. And then she leaves.

CHAPTER TWENTY-SIX

Avery

A week later, I stare at the string of texts from Jake. It was so nice of Deedy to give him my new number.

Jake: *The job is yours.*
Jake: *We can have an interview if you feel better about it. Noon tomorrow? Bring a resume.*
Jake: *Are you getting these messages?*
Jake: *I tried calling you. The voice mailbox isn't set up.*
Jake: *Fine, Ave. It's been a week with no response. I get the message. Hope you found another job. I'm heading back to Milwaukee this weekend. I'm sincerely sorry. I wish you only the best.*

This weekend. That's three days away.

"Taking off?" Heather, my friend who hired me to do barefoot bar massages, looks up as I slide my purse strap onto my shoulder.

"Yeah. If anything comes up, let me know. I can definitely fill in if one of the other girls calls in sick."

"Will do. Thanks, Avery."

I resist the urge to take my tiny paycheck and shop for a new handbag ... it's still hard to live on a budget. Old habits. Instead, I drive to Sydney's house and hope to catch lunch with my sister and my favorite little people.

"Hello?" I slip off my sandals and shut the back door.

"Mom's sick. I want to swim. Will you watch us?" Ocean shuffles into the kitchen, still in her pink nightshirt.

I cringe. "Well, I don't want to get sick, and you two squirts don't need to get sick, so yeah ... let's hang out by the pool today. Have you had lunch?"

She shakes her head.

"Okay. I'll make some snacks. We'll eat outside."

Ocean runs off. "Asher, put on your swimsuit!"

I peek into Sydney's room. "Hey."

"Hey," she mumbles, not opening her eyes or even moving from her fetal position.

"Did you call Dr. Lautner?"

"No. He has a conference today. I'm sick, not dying."

"Anything I can get you?"

"No. The kids want to swim."

"I'm on it. Text me if you need anything."

"A bowl. I need a bowl. In case I don't make it to the toilet."

"Eww ... Okay." I get her a bowl, surgically scrub my hands after leaving her room, and change into my bikini.

I perch myself in the shade, on lifeguard duty. As the kids play, I stare at Jake's texts again. "Why did it have to be you?" I whisper.

Me: *Can we do the interview tomorrow?*

I stare at my screen for a good five minutes, waiting for a response that's not coming. As soon as I slip my sunglasses back on, my phone chimes.

Jake: *I hired someone this morning. Sorry.*

Did I do this to myself? Is this my pride and ego? How do I know where that line is if I can't see it? And I can't ... I can't see the line. Everything in my life is blurry.

Grunting a laugh, I shake my head. I honestly thought he was making up the job opening—for me. Because he loves me. Because he'd do anything to keep us connected, even if it's in a small way like making me his employee halfway across the country. Another epic fail on my part. More bad judgment and inaccurate assumptions.

Me: *Glad you found someone.*
Jake: *Thank you.*
Me: *You're welcome.*

"Nice, Avery ..." I close my eyes and pinch the bridge of my nose. Really? I just had to say *you're welcome*. Why? Clearly because I can't let go.

Jake's on this infinitely long string, and no matter how far he goes, I will always feel that string connected to my heart, tugging and pulling. Reminding me that what we had was real.

"What we had was real." My hand presses to my chest.

My phone chimes again.

Jake: *If you need your own space, or if you get evicted from* *your sister's house, you can stay in my loft while I'm in Milwaukee.*

I grin. There's no way I'm staying in his loft, but the fact that he's offering it—that he feels the pull of that string—it makes everything inside of me come to life.

Why did it have to be Jake? The meanie. The bully. The crass-mouthed, over-tatted *vegan*. Why did my heart choose to take up residency in his lethal hands?

Me: *Thank you for the offer. I'll be fine.*
Jake: *I have no doubt that you'll be fine.*

Ouch. Letting go of Jake, in spite of all the terrible words that have been exchanged, feels like ripping off a Band-Aid one tiny millimeter at a time. Is this a mistake? Will my pride win at the expense of my happiness?

Me: *But ...*

I draw in a slow breath of courage as the midday sun shifts just enough to steal my shade.

Me: *On the off chance that I'm not fine. Knowing where you hide a key would be nice.*
Me: *If you're okay with that.*
Jake: *No key. It's a code. You can enter from the back of the building.*
Jake: *91169#*

I giggle.

Me: *Emergency 69?*
Jake: *Get your mind out of the gutter.*

I giggle more.
"Daddy to the rescue."
I turn. "What are you doing home?"
Lautner rolls his eyes as a drenched Asher hugs his leg, saturating his dress pants with pool water.
"My dear daughter messaged me."
Ocean smirks, beached out on a floating recliner.
"Your mom is not going to be happy that you messaged your dad. I'm here."
"It's fine. Family first." Lautner picks up Asher, not caring that he's so wet.
"Always Mr. Perfect."
"You know it." He grins at me. "Let's go check on Mommy." He kisses Asher's wet head of blond hair.

Me: *Need help?*

I erase it, having second thoughts. Third thoughts. Four hundred thoughts. I have so many thoughts warring in my head that I can't make sense of my life at the moment. Jake's leaving. That's good. Distance is good. I'll move on. He'll move on. We will simply go down in history as a close-but-not-quite relationship.

Me: *Need help packing?*

Gah! My stupid hands do their own thing. My body has never cooperated with my common sense when it comes to Jake.

Jake: *I'm basically packed. Just a few things to throw in my bag at the last minute.*

His next text is a facepalm emoji, not something I'd expect from him. It makes me giggle. He's on his game with me today.

Jake: *Yes. Of course I need help packing. Please!*
Me: *I'll iron your jeans while you make me dinner?*
Jake: *Who irons jeans?*

"What am I doing?" My teeth dig into my lower lip, suppressing the grin wanting to crawl up my face. He's leaving. I'm staying. We are toxic together. Nothing good can come from going to his place. Ironing his jeans. Sharing a meal. We can't be in the same room without wanting to kill each other or rip each other's clothes off.

Jake: *I'm here. If you want to iron my jeans ... I'm here until Saturday.*

FOUR HOURS LATER, I stare at the backstairs to his loft. He has a motorcycle parked next to his truck. I fidget with the long cuffs to my white boyfriend shirt. Then I tuck in just the front before smoothing my hands over my worn denim capris. Still ... all these weeks later, I attempt to run my fingers through my hair running down my shoulders onto my chest, but it stops just below my chin. It's like I've lost a limb, and I'm feeling the weight of phantom hair draped down my chest and back.

My feet wobble in my black heels as I take the stairs in slow motion. Why am I so nervous about seeing a man I spent weeks with in a tent and traveled miles with him in his pickup truck? My shaky fist knocks twice on the metal door.

"Hey!" He opens the door, grinning while attempting to tug on a T-shirt over his wet head.

Freshly showered Jake with a naked chest, ripped jeans, and bare feet. This was a really bad idea.

"Nice shirt." I roll my eyes.

Jake looks down like he has no idea what it says. There's a hand flipping a coin.

Heads I get tail. Tails I get head.

"It's just a shirt, not an agenda."

I nod once, eyeing him with caution as I step inside and slip off my impractical yet highly stylish heels. He shuts the door.

"Something smells good." I wring my hands together. *Gah!* I'm so nervous.

"It's a curry dish. I think it's actually the rice cooking that you smell. I love the smell of rice cooking."

I smile and nod. Bobbing my head is all I can do since my voice wants to shake as much as the rest of my body. We stand nearly toe to toe. I think it's out of habit. When you spend weeks with someone in such close quarters, the boundaries of personal space get skewed. It also happens when your favorite place to be with that person is as close as your bodies can get, touching at all points.

"Can I get you something to drink before you start ironing?"

I laugh. "Do you even own an iron?"

Jake smirks as his hands work a large knife, chopping

red bell peppers. "No. There's a dry cleaner across the street. If I need something pressed, I let Saul do it."

"So you lured me here under false pretenses?" My resolve weakens with every second I spend near Jake.

Time is magical. It doesn't erase things, but it gives a different perspective. There's a shift in magnification. The negative blurs over time, and the good moments—the important ones—they linger and intensify. They become the drug. You want more of those moments, and the risk that held little worth gains value with each passing day.

Has Jake become worth the risk? Is that why I'm here?

He pauses, glancing up at me as I lean my hip against the adjacent edge to the counter, hands tucked into the back pockets of my denim capris. His gaze slides over me as a slight wrinkle forms along his brow. "Maybe." The tension in his expression vanishes as he returns his focus to the chopping board. "But I thought you could look around the place and see if you have any questions. In case you decide to take me up on my offer to stay here for a while."

I glance around at the large space with exposed beams, a bed in the far corner, an open door into the bathroom.

"Clearly you can find everything. But I'll show you how the remotes work for the lighting, the shades to the windows, and I'll make sure you understand the security, including the cameras around the building." He pauses again, this time keeping his chin down. "I'm sure you've stayed or lived in places with fancy lighting and security."

My ego jumps to its feet, fists up. Instead of letting it throw the first punch, I focus on his words and the tone in his voice. He made a simple assumption. The assumption was correct. No underlying tones of accusation or disgust.

"I have, but you should show me anyway. It's probably a

little different than what I've encountered." I give myself a mental high-five. Look at me being a mature adult.

He slides the sliced peppers off the cutting board into a hot sauté pan where they sizzle and crackle.

"Are you taking your time driving back to Milwaukee? Camping along the way?"

Jake stirs vegetables, keeping his back to me. "I'll camp two nights. I need to get back and start working on the fall menu. Also, I have ... *friends* visiting next Friday. They're staying with me for a week or so."

"You have friends?"

He shoots me an evil look over his shoulder.

"Hey, I had to ask."

He traps his lip between his teeth, eyes narrowed. Gah! I wish I could read his mind.

"Jace and Mo visit this time every year." He clears his throat. It's odd. Something feels off.

"Jace was a fighter too. That's how we met. Mo is his ... uh ... sister, and she was his agent. Now they recruit MMA talent together. He trains, she does all the rest."

"Mo? Bethanne said you took Mo on your summer road trip two years ago. Is this the same Mo?"

"Yep."

"So ... you and Mo were a thing?"

He shrugs, dumping coconut milk into the pan along with a ton of different measured out spices. "Jace had surgery on his shoulder that summer, and Mo had a fighter in L.A. she wanted to check out. It was last minute. We just decided to drive out here together."

I return an easy nod and fake smile when he glances over at me. "That uh ... didn't exactly answer my question."

"Were we a *thing*?" He shrugs again.

I officially hate shrugs.

"I guess you'd say friends with benefits when it served a mutual … need."

I feel nauseous, probably from a bad case of delusion. In spite of one incident after another, I felt pretty damn special on our trip, like I was the first woman Jake had taken on his sacred summer trip. I thought Mo was a guy. Stupid, stupid me.

"Maureen?"

He nods. "She hates her name."

"And Jace is okay with you using his sister for these *mutual needs*?"

"We're adults. I'm not jerking her around, making lifetime promises. It's sex. He's not exactly a saint either."

It's sex. It *is* sex. Not *was* sex.

"So … when they come visit … do you uh …"

Jake turns the gas burner to simmer and covers the pan. "Do I what?" He wipes his hands and tosses the dishtowel over his shoulder.

I roll my eyes. Why does he have to be such a dick about this? He knows damn well what I'm implying. "Meet needs, Jake. Does she sleep in your bed and suck your dick?" Pressing the heels of my hands to my forehead, I sigh. "I shouldn't be here."

"Why?"

Letting my hands flop to my sides, I give him a wide-eyed look. "Why? WHY?" Heat burns my cheeks as rage crawls up my chest, constricting my throat. "Because we are terrible together! Because you say terrible things to me. Because you're leaving. Because I can't stop thinking about you, but I *need* to stop thinking about you! Because you can't figure out the three fucking words that you need to say to me. And because next Friday you'll be in Milwaukee with Mo in your bed!"

Jake's head inches back as his eyes widen like saucers.

Son ... of a bitch. I have done so well with this. After the "makeup incident" at the rehearsal, I put myself together. Stood up for myself. I slipped a bit when I let him kiss me here last week, but I quickly righted that wrong.

I've fallen headfirst off the wagon.

"Why are you here, Ave? It's not to iron my jeans or help me pack." He steps closer.

I step back. We cannot be close. Our brains shut down when we get too close.

"Are you here to tell me what I need to say to make things right between us? Are you ready to stop playing this stupid guessing game with me? I love you. I am sorry. What three words? Those are good words. I'm an idiot. How do you like those three words? I need you. I want you. Are those the right words?" He takes another step and grabs my wrist to prevent me from distancing myself from him.

When I try to pull away, he tugs me closer, hugging my arms to his chest. His gaze slips to my hand. "Nice nail polish. Those are three words. Are they the ones you're looking for?"

"*That's* exactly what I'm talking about, you big jerk!" All attempts to tear myself away from his hold are futile. "You're judging me because I have nail polish on my nails. I bet you were judging me when I walked in here with those five-hundred-dollar shoes. And my handbag that's made of dead cowhide. And my makeup that's covering up the bags under my eyes from lack of sleep. You can't love me unless I'm the person *you* created in your head."

"That's not—"

I bring my other hand to my mouth and my cheeks puff out. Oh god ... I'm going to be sick. Sydney will pay for this.

She's always grabbing the wrong water glass off the counter. Could there possibly be worse timing?

"Ave?" Jake loosens his grip on me.

I shake my head and pull away, keeping my mouth covered as I dart in the direction of the bathroom. Before I can shut the door behind me, I drop to my knees and expel the contents of my stomach as sweat beads along my brow.

"Go ..." I hold out a flat hand as Jake hands me a cup of water and a wet washcloth. "I don't want you to see this."

"Too late." He presses the washcloth to my forehead and shoves the glass of water into my hands as I sit back on my heels, wiping my mouth with a wad of toilet paper.

"Stay back. You don't want this. Sydney's sick. It's contagious. Just ..." I take the water, rinse my mouth, and flush the toilet.

He helps me to my feet.

"Yuck." I frown at the few splatters of vomit on the floor by his toilet. "I'm sorry."

I swish some water again and spit in the sink.

"I forgive you," he whispers. Barely even a whisper, but I hear it.

I glance up at his reflection in the mirror. He leans his shoulder against the doorframe, crossing his colorful arms over his chest.

Coughing on a bit of sarcasm, I shake my head. "Gee, thanks. It's good to know that vomiting on your floor isn't unforgivable in your high standards."

"I don't give a fuck about my floor."

I set the glass on the vanity and turn toward him, peeling a few strands of hair from my face. Why does he look so tortured with his lined forehead and downturned mouth?

"I'm saying it for me, *and* I'm saying it for you. I'm

saying it for us. Those are the words, aren't they? The three words. I. Forgive. You."

Tears burn my already red eyes. I don't want his acceptance. I want *this*. His love feels incomplete without ... his forgiveness. *All* I've wanted to hear are those three words. Maybe it's being raised in a church, or maybe it's because I've made a lot of mistakes, but for whatever reason, forgiveness is the pinnacle of love. It's unconditional. It's a baptism of the soul.

"You think love isn't the answer. You think I can't truly love you unless I forgive you for Steve, for Megan's baby, for poisoning me, for absolutely anything and everything about you that can be perceived as an imperfection. You're so wrong."

The tears fight their way to my cheeks.

Jake steps toward me.

"I'm sick." I hold up my hand.

"So what?" He palms the back of my head and brings me into his chest. I nuzzle his neck and let more tears find their way to my cheeks and his shirt.

"Ave, I forgive you *because* I love you. You think love is not enough, but it's everything. It's all encompassing. It's overpriced shoes and dead animals used to make bags. It's bright red nail polish and dark eyeshadow. It's jeans named after women and eyelashes that fall off. It's dog shit on shoes and untimely cases of head lice."

I laugh through my tears. "I didn't have head lice."

"You did. They ate through your hair extensions."

"Shut up." I cringe, pressing my hand to my nauseated stomach.

Thank you, Sydney. Thank you very much.

"Here." He releases me, riffles through the bottom vanity drawer, and pulls out a new toothbrush.

"Do I want to know why you have a supply of new toothbrushes?" I take the toothbrush after he puts a dab of toothpaste on it.

He nods to the electric toothbrush by the sink. "Because I use that one most of the time, but the dentist gives me a new one every six months. Over time, you get a collection."

I stare at him in the mirror, using the toothbrush in my mouth to hide my grin. After a quick brush, I shuffle my bare feet toward the kitchen where he's shutting off the stove.

"Sorry about dinner. I'm not hungry now. I just want to go home."

"I'll drive you." He grabs his keys off the counter.

"No. My car is here. I'm feeling a bit better, you know … that slight reprieve after you vomit?"

He nods once. Of course he knows. I poisoned him.

"But I'd better get going before a new wave hits."

"I'll get your car to you tomorrow. So, either you stay here tonight, or *I* drive you home."

At the same time I say, "Home," he says, "Stay."

"You leave in three days. You don't need to get sick."

"I'm leaving in three days. It's why you should stay."

I frown. He's so stubborn.

"I'll sleep on the sofa," I concede.

Jake sets his keys back on the counter. "You'll sleep in the bed. I'll sleep on the sofa. I'll wash my hands and take extra vitamins."

The frown won't wipe off my face. It's no longer his stubbornness, it's me. I feel like crap. I hate being sick. I'm the worst at being sick. He doesn't want to see this. At least at home, I have access to a doctor who's used to whiney patients.

"I need to lie down. I need a bowl. I need a blanket." I

hug my stomach and walk toward the bed. "I need water, not too warm, not too cold. And my phone. It's in my purse." I melt onto the bed, curling my body into itself on my side.

"I'll get you everything you need." Jake covers me up with his blankets. I close my eyes and pray for this bug to be quick. I'm a wuss. Wusses can't stay sick too long. It's just a law of nature.

"Perfect temperature water. Your phone. A bowl. And some ginger candy." He lines up everything on the nightstand. "Anything else?" The bed dips as he sits on the edge, stroking my hair and my back.

"Don't get sick and don't stay."

"Where am I going to go?" He chuckles.

I crack open my eyes. "I mean Saturday. You go home. I don't want you to stay here for me. You're not an L.A. person. You said it yourself. And I need to get my life back in order before I can be truly ... lovable. I need time. I need to go slow."

This elicits more laughter. "I'm leaving Saturday. I have a business to run and guests coming next week. You'll have all the time you need to do your thing."

Guests ... this makes me more nauseous.

"But, Ave ..." Jake kisses the side of my head. "I'll return." He goes into the bathroom.

I grab my phone, cringing with every little move.

Me: *You suck. I hope you feel better, but you suck.*
Sydney: *Where are you? And why do I suck?*
Me: *I'm visiting a friend and now I'm staying here because I'M VOMITING! Would it kill you to not use my water glass? Ugh! Thanks for sharing your virus.*

Sydney: *Do you want Lautner to come get you?*
Me: *No. I don't want to move. I just want to make you feel bad for getting me sick.*
Sydney: *Sorry you're sick. But it's not my fault.*
Me: *BS*
Sydney: *I don't have a virus. I'm pregnant.*

I stare at the screen. She's pregnant. I'm going to get another little niece or nephew. Not even the painful urge to retch can keep me from smiling.

Me: *OMGGGGGGG!!!!!!*
Sydney: *We've told no one. So you know nothing. Got it?*
Me: *OMGGGGGGG!!!!!!*
Sydney: *Love you too. Feel better. Call if you need us.*

"Is that a smile?" Jake shrugs off his shirt as he comes out of the bathroom.

I stare for a few seconds. His jeans are unfastened as well, just barely hanging onto his hips.

"Ave?"

"Huh?" I glance up.

He grins. "Were you just smiling?"

"Yeah. Sydney is ... well, I can't tell you. But I didn't get this virus from her because what she has is not contagious."

He studies me with a narrowed gaze for a few seconds. "So she's pregnant?"

"I did not say that."

"Got it." He winks.

I refocus on his abs and a bit lower. It distracts me from my nausea.

"I'm going to eat. Will that bother you?"

My gaze snaps back up to meet his knowing eyes. He smirks.

"No."

"I'm going to get you some coconut water. I want you to drink it before you go to sleep."

He's my Lautner. Why does this bring tears to my eyes? Because he's leaving on Saturday. Because Mo will be with him next week. Because ... I love him. "Okay," I whisper around the swell of emotion in my throat as I roll to my side again, putting my back to him.

A few seconds later, there's a pounding noise. I glance over my shoulder. He's pounding a hole into a young coconut. He's giving me coconut water from an actual coconut.

He might be better than Lautner.

"Thank you." I dab the corners of my eyes and ease to sitting. "Glass straw. Fancy."

He hands me the coconut.

"Only the best for you." He smiles.

I frown. "I brought you coconut water in a can when you were ... not well."

"When you poisoned me." He lifts an eyebrow.

"Yeah, when that happened." My lips wrap around the glass straw. "Go eat," I mumble.

He leans forward, kissing me on the forehead. "Get some rest. Feel better."

I fall asleep. By the time I wake up, Jake's asleep on the sofa. The dim lighting under the kitchen cabinets gives me just enough light to make it to the bathroom where I vomit the coconut water.

As I reach to flush the toilet, a cold damp cloth gets pressed to my forehead.

"I'm so sorry you're not feeling well," Jake whispers in

my ear, sliding his other hand around my waist to help me stand.

Closing my eyes, I rest the back of my head against his shoulder.

"Water?" He holds out a glass of water.

I lift my head and take a drink, swishing and spitting in the sink. I should brush my teeth again, but I'm just too tired. It must be the middle of the night.

When Jake scoops me up in his arms, I don't protest.

When he lays me on the bed next to him, I murmur a thank you.

When he molds his body to the back of mine, his face in my hair, his arms around my waist, I hold my breath and cry silently. I want *this* Jake.

Every.

Single.

Day.

CHAPTER TWENTY-SEVEN

I wake up alone.

Then I see the sprig of lavender on the pillow next to mine and a short note.

Three simple words: You are beautiful.

Below the pillow is a small bowl of granola and berries with what I assume are edible flowers garnishing the top. I scoot myself up to sitting, glancing around the room. No Jake.

Taking a slow breath, I check in on my body. I feel better. No nausea. Dr. Matthews cured me. Take that, Dr. Lautner Sullivan.

I eat the granola and fruit, passing on the flowers. They are too pretty to eat. And what if they're not edible? What if they're payback for the mushroom incident? Pulling my hair back into a ponytail, I rinse off in the shower, brush my teeth, and put back on my blouse and capris. It's not the first time I've worn dirty clothes.

His truck and motorcycle are out back, so Jake must be down at the cafe. I make my way down the stairs, my heels clicking on each wooden step.

"Good morning." Seth smiles, rushing past me with plates full of food. "Jake's out front," he calls just before pushing through the swinging door.

I follow him. A giggly girl bats her eyelashes at Jake as he shows her how to use the juicer. Must be the girl who got my job. She has long, blond hair. Long like mine used to be, only I think hers is all her own. And she's definitely younger than me.

Her smile loses a touch of momentum when she spies me.

Jake turns. "Morning, Ave." His smile beats hers by miles. "Feeling better? You look better."

I nod, trying to ignore the girl who got my job and the way she's eye-fucking Jake. My memory jumps back to him without his shirt, coming out of the bathroom, and that glorious V cut below his abs, and those faded unfastened jeans.

"Coffee?" Jake asks, wiping his hands.

"Juice?" I have this sadistic need to watch him show new girl how to run the juicer. Who knew my jealous side had such an appetite?

"Ginger, apple, lemon, cucumber," he fires off to new girl while taking the order of the next person in line.

A minute later, new girl hands me my juice, giving me the once-over and a catty smile. He should fire her. She's bad Karma. I can feel it.

"Jake's girlfriend?" she asks.

I take the juice. "Uh ..."

"Avery. Aspen. Aspen. Avery," Jake introduces us just before disappearing to the kitchen. Was that his way of avoiding Aspen's question? Preventing me from answering her?

"If not..." she leans in and whispers "...I call dibs."

Dibs? Did she really just call dibs on Jake?

Aspen, Mo ... stiff competition.

Before I sharpen my claws on her perfect skin, I turn and retreat to the kitchen.

Seth gives me a friendly nod as he and Jake assemble plates and bowls of food.

"Juice okay?" Jake asks as he perfectly garnishes a plate of some kind of hash and gravy with mushrooms.

I nod, sidling up to him. Lifting onto my toes, I press my lips against his ear. "Three words ... I need you."

His hands still as he pulls away from me just enough to see my face. If he can't read my come-hither expression, then he needs a thick pair of glasses. "Ave, I'm in the middle of the breakfast rush."

Seth takes the plate from Jake and runs it out front.

Rejection sucks. Would he reject Mo ... or perky little Aspen?

And the only thing that sucks worse than rejection is jealousy.

"K." I smile like it's no big deal. Like I'm not embarrassed for suggesting it. Then I pivot and make my way up the stairs to get my purse and get the hell out of here before I say or do anything else that's impulsive and stupid.

As I grab my purse, the door slams behind me. I turn. Before I can take a single breath, Jake's hands frame my face and his mouth crashes against mine.

It's all consuming.

It burns through my skin as we stumble to the bed, clawing and tearing at each other's clothes.

I moan as his tongue circles my nipple. My impatient hands tug down his jeans and boxer briefs. He attacks my mouth again, easing us to the bed.

It's slow and methodic, yet every stroke is deliberate and

perfectly timed. Guiding my knees to my chest, he pushes into me.

Thoughts vanish.

Toes curl.

My torso twists and jerks.

There. He's the best at finding my "there."

He's the best at bending me to his will.

He's the best at prolonging this feeling—finding the edge and keeping me there.

It's torture. God ... I love his kind of torture.

"I love you, Ave," he whispers in my ear as he pulls my hair gently, reentering me from behind while my body trembles on all fours.

Within seconds, I'm *there*. Mystical, magical *there*. I've fallen off the edge. I've arrived. Collapsing onto the bed, my face buried into the pillow, Jake grips my hips and slams into me *three* more times, my name a guttural moan from his lips.

His sweaty body falls onto mine, his chest to my back, his labored breaths warm against my ear.

"Sorry for disrupting your breakfast rush," I mumble into the pillow while turning my head to the side. My lungs can't find oxygen with his dead weight blanketing me.

"No, you're not." He rolls off me and smacks my ass.

I giggle as he pulls me to his chest, our legs scissoring together. "I'm really not. Thank you for the note and the lavender." Tipping my chin up, I smile at him. My fingers trace the lines of his chest and the ink that covers it.

He stares at me with a serious look for several moments before submitting to a tiny smile. "Was this your idea of going slow? Felt fast to me. We could try it again ... only slower."

This pang in my heart keeps me from fully appreciating

his humor. What are we doing? Really ... we couldn't be more opposite. "Do you think what we have is what two people on a stranded island feel? Do you think we ended up in bed together for a lack of a better choice? And now that we've rejoined reality, do you think regret will set in?"

"I'm no longer your first choice?" He messes with a few strands of my hair, focusing on them instead of holding my gaze.

"I'm not talking about me. I just said 'we' so you wouldn't feel like I was specifically talking about you. But now that you're questioning me, I'll admit ... I'm talking about you."

"You don't think you're my first choice?" His eyes meet my gaze again.

"I think you know I'm not as bad at sex as what you originally *assumed*."

We grin.

"But I also think Deedy marrying my dad connects us, and maybe that connection feels hard for you to break. What if your loyalty to Deedy is what's really keeping you tied to me?"

His lips twist as he scratches his head, tugging a bit at his messy, blond hair. "That would be tragic."

"You're making fun. Not nice." I push away.

He grabs my waist just as my feet touch the floor at the side of the bed. "It was a road trip." He kisses my neck. "The truck didn't break down. We weren't stranded. We weren't even away from what I assume you're referring to as 'reality' for very long. I wasn't sex starved and desperate. You weren't an impulse. What I feel for you right now—with a world of other choices—is real. I want you."

My next breath holds back the tears. I want to be strong —not for Jake. I want to be strong for me. "I like to shop.

And I like impractical shoes and manicured hands and feet."

"I know." He chuckles, kissing my neck again.

"And I have a past. A past dotted with moments and decisions I'm not proud of. But ... it's made me the person I am right now. So if you want me, then you have to—"

"Love you as a whole. Not the parts I find most attractive. I have to love you—*all* of you."

"Yes," I whisper. "I think you going back to Milwaukee is good timing. I need to get a better job and a place of my own to live. You need to spend time with your friends. Maybe when you have Mo at your place and I'm halfway across the country, you'll have a better perspective of your feelings for me."

His grip around my waist stiffens. His whole body pressed to my back goes rigid.

I twist around to look at him. Jake releases me and sits back against the wood headboard, covering his midsection with a pillow.

"What?" I pull the sheet to my chest ... since we're apparently covering up now. "Why do you have that look—that constipated look?"

"About Mo ..."

I tighten my grip on the sheet held to my chest, feeling extra vulnerable.

"I may have fictionalized her a bit ... to gauge where we stood. I wanted to know if you'd be jealous ... if you still cared. If you still wanted us."

My eyes widen, lips part. "Wh-what? You made her up?" My head jerks back.

He tips his head up, tightening the cords in his neck as he scratches his chin. "Mo is Jace's dog. Golden Retriever.

She's beautiful. And I took her camping with me two years ago while Jace scouted a fighter."

My shock transforms into a full scowl. "You. Ass!" I toss the sheet aside and collect my clothes from the floor like I'm mad at them more than him.

No. I love my clothes ... Yep, I love them more than the liar in the bed. If I didn't love these black Jimmy Choo's so much, I'd jab the heel into Jake's eye.

"Ave ..." He grabs his jeans at a much slower pace.

Before he gets them fastened, I have my bag on my shoulder, frantically fishing my keys out of it. "Bye, Jake. Don't get eaten by a bear on your trip home ... or do."

"Avery ..." He chases me down the backstairs to my loaner car.

"I don't like liars. One minute you're declaring your love and the next minute you're eating chocolate mousse from the pussy of another woman."

He grabs my door before I can shut it. "Stop." He leans into my car, no shirt, no shoes, jeans still unfastened. "I lied because I wanted you. I just needed to know if we stood a chance. I didn't lie because I am cheating on you."

"Doesn't matter." I try to pull the door shut, in spite of his body blocking it.

He laughs. *LAUGHS!*

"Fine, Ave. I love this stubborn side of you too. I'm leaving Saturday. I will be back. In the meantime, get a better job ... or don't. Find another place to live ... or don't. I don't care. I'll want you, love you, and need you no matter what. I'll wait as long as it takes for you to get that."

"Move. Now." I start the car.

"Fasten in, baby." He stretches the seat belt across my body and locks it.

I grit my teeth and stare straight ahead, hands death-gripping the steering wheel.

Why?

Why?

Why does he have to be terrible and amazing all the time at the same time?

"If you forgive me before Saturday, call me. If you don't, I'll call you from my first stop."

I won't answer your call.

"Drive safely. I love you." He kisses me.

I don't pull away, but I don't move my lips.

You're a jerk. And I've never loved anyone the way I love you.

Jake claimed every beating cell of my heart in under a month. But for now ... I need to be pissed off at him. Also, I'm not feeling so awesome at the moment.

He shuts the door and waits for me to back out before he retreats up the stairs.

"Hey." Sydney smiles, slathering sunscreen on the kids in the kitchen.

I swallow the rising bile and run to the bathroom. So much for the juice Aspen pressed for me. I flush the toilet, rinse my mouth, and splash cold water on my face. Lucky Jake; he's going to be sick. We swapped *all* the germs this morning. I feel marginally bad about his impending illness.

"That bad?" Sydney asks from the doorway.

I shake my head, drying my face with a hand towel. "I was better. Felt fine this morning. Then boom ... the second I left Jake's, I started feeling nauseous again."

"Jake's?"

I cringe.

"That's the *friend* you were visiting? You spent the night there?"

"I went to make amends of sorts. You know ... since he's close to Deedy, and now Deedy is family, so ..."

Sydney smirks. "For Deedy, huh? How mature of you."

"Move." I brush past her to get to my bed before I pass out or vomit again. "Don't give me that stupid smirk."

"Have you told him?"

Collapsing onto the bed, I curl into a ball. "Told who what?"

"Told Jake that you're pregnant."

I squint. "I thought we discussed this last night. What you have is not contagious. Which ... I'm so happy for you. And as soon as I don't want to die, I'll give you a big hug. But you don't want to get sick, so let's keep our distance for now."

She sits on the edge of the bed.

"I said to keep your distance." I cover my mouth to hide my germs.

A smile slides up her face. "I'm already pregnant. You can't infect me with your pregnancy."

"Sydney ... you know that's not it." I frown. Anthony thought I was going to marry him someday and have children with him. I wanted him to believe it. Hell, *I* wanted to believe it, but I've always known my children would be the kind you adopt.

"You were told there's a slim chance of getting pregnant. That's not zero percent."

"I'm on the pill anyway."

"You take it when you're supposed to take it? Never missing? Not one single time? Did you use condoms?"

I try to roll my eyes, but I'm too weak, too nauseous.

Condoms? No. We didn't have condoms. We were so fucking irresponsible, I can't even come up with a good reason. It just didn't feel real. The whole trip was just ... not real.

It's feeling mighty real right now.

"Because I kinda sorta took my pills, and as a result, I have two kids and a third one on the way."

"You don't have endometriosis," I grumble.

"When was your last period?"

"I'm irregular, so that doesn't mean anything." I close my eyes like our conversation is over, but really I'm thinking.

Thinking hard.

The more I think, the more nauseous I feel. It was ... before the chocolate incident. I think. No after. Gah! I don't remember. They only last a few days. I was a mess. I'm *still* a mess. But it's been after Anthony.

"Do we know who the daddy is?"

"What?" I open my eyes again.

"Is it Jake or Anthony?"

I shake my head, rubbing my temples. "I'm not pregnant."

"Well, there's only one way to find out." She stands. "Be right back." Sydney leaves the room, yells down to Ocean to turn on a movie until she's done helping Aunt Avery with her tummy.

I'm not pregnant. No. It's a virus. Or cancer. Or some awful parasite I picked up from bathing in unclean water.

Not. Pregnant.

"Come tinkle on this." Sydney holds up a pregnancy test. "I have two left. They're both yours."

"I'm not pregnant."

"Then the test should be negative."

"He's leaving for Milwaukee on Saturday. And he's a liar. And ..."

Sydney grins. "He's your baby daddy."

I roll over, putting Sydney at my back so she doesn't see my tears. But my body shakes with emotion.

"Ave ... no ..." The bed dips again as she crawls in next to me and hugs my back. "A baby, Ave. You could be having the one thing you didn't think you'd have. And I know you want this. I've seen you with Ocean and Asher. You are *so* good with them. You have so much love to give."

The nausea. The fear. The feeling of complete failure.

"I'm not married ... and I don't even have my own place to live. And I don't h-have a g-good job ... The timing is all w-wrong."

"No. Nope. No way ... You cannot talk to me about bad timing. Hello? You're talking to the queen of bad timing. But, in case you haven't noticed, my life is perfection. All the bad timing, all the pain, all the missed opportunities ... they led me to here."

I stare at the gray-blue wall while my sister hugs me.

A baby.

"Give me those sticks."

CHAPTER TWENTY-EIGHT

Jake

SHE DOESN'T CALL or text. Part of me feels like I should try harder to make things right with her, but a bigger part of me feels like she needs space. It's what brought her to my place the other night. I have to believe it will bring her to me again.

Maybe not today.

Maybe not even in a few weeks.

But ... eventually.

I will wait. I'll wait forever.

"When should we expect you again?" Seth asks as I close the tailgate to my truck, relishing the last day of balmy salt air as the sun stretches over the horizon.

"Hard to say. Couple weeks? Couple months?"

He chuckles. "What's that supposed to mean? Why would you be back in just weeks? To check up on Aspen. She's definitely worth checking up on." He winks.

I give him a lifted brow. "Behave."

He salutes me. "Would your indecisiveness have

anything to do with her?" He nods to something over my shoulder.

It's Avery pulling in next to my truck.

"Safe trip, man." Seth pats me on the shoulder before heading back around to the cafe.

She came to say goodbye. That's something. I think ...

Slipping my hands in my front pockets to keep them from grabbing her and kissing her into submission, I make my way to her car as she gets out. Of course she looks amazing in her fancy jeans, silver flats, and pink zipped hoodie. No makeup, maybe just some gloss on her lips.

I'm dying. How the hell do I leave her?

"Hi." I smile.

She shuts the door and shoves her hands into the pockets of her hoodie, shoulders high, chin tipped down. "Hi."

"I was just getting ready to pull out. Good timing. I'm surprised you're out of bed."

She glances up at me, wearing something between a smile and a cringe. This isn't good. I don't like that look. It's the nice-knowing-ya look.

"I figured you'd leave early, and I didn't want to miss you because ..." She draws in a slow breath.

My chest aches. She's telling me goodbye, but not a for-now goodbye. A forever goodbye.

"There are *words* to be said before you go."

"Words ..." I echo her, trying to mask my defeat, trying to pretend that I don't know exactly what she's going to say. I shouldn't have lied about Mo. It was impulsive and risky. I just needed to know if I mattered to her anymore. I needed to see if there was even a twitch of jealousy.

"Just your words? Do my words no longer matter?"

Tension bleeds into my voice. I can't help it. I can't hide my desperation.

"Nope." She shakes her head, staring at her feet. "Your words don't matter. My words are the only words that matter. They are the final words. And you can choose to *accept* them or not, but it changes nothing."

"Jesus, Ave ..." I step closer, unable to stop my hands from grabbing her face, forcing her to look at me as I rest my forehead on hers. "Don't do this."

"I have to," she whispers, reaching for the zipper to her hoodie, pulling it down slowly.

What is she doing?

I pull away just enough to see her better.

Fuck me ...

She keeps her gaze down as I read her white T-shirt with black lettering.

Congratulations, you knocked me up.

Baby feet are stamped on the belly of the shirt.

Teary blue eyes glance up at me. "I'm sorry." Her bottom lip quivers. "I know what you're going to say. We should have—"

"Shut up."

She swallows hard, blinking once to release the tears. I hate the fear in her eyes.

"This ..." Emotions strangle my words. "This day. This. Very. Moment ..." I thread my fingers through her hair, forcing her to look at me with her tear-drenched face. "It's the greatest moment of my life."

"I'm scared," she whispers.

I kiss the tears from her cheeks. I kiss her forehead. Then I kiss her lips. "I'm not, Ave. I'm not scared. I'm relieved. I'm tired of running from the demons. I'm tired of chasing something I can't see. For the first time in so *many* years ... I can breathe."

Her arms slide around my neck, and her body melts into mine, her face in my neck. I lift her off the ground, her legs wrap around my waist.

"I love you," she says on a long sigh.

Yeah, definitely the greatest moment of my life. She's never said those exact words to me. I don't think she probably realizes it. I've felt her love in a touch, an innocent smile, a tiny glance, but not until this moment has she said the actual words.

Avery Montgomery has finally given herself permission to love me. All of me. All of *us*.

"What are you doing?" She looks up as I open the passenger door to the truck.

"Getting you fastened in." I set her in the seat.

"Where are we going?"

I latch her seat belt and bend down. Pulling up the front of her shirt, I press my lips to her flat belly. "Milwaukee."

"What? No. I can't go with you. I have a job. I live here. My sister is here. I need to—"

"Shh ..." I grin, keeping my lips pressed to her stomach. "We'll return later."

"You'll return. I need to stay here." The panic in her voice escalates.

Lifting my head, I rest my hand on her leg, giving it a light squeeze as I nuzzle into her neck.

Her fingers slide into my hair. "Jake ..."

"Ave ... do you know what I need?"

"What?" she whispers with slight resignation in her reply.

"You. That's it. So can you do me a tiny favor?" I kiss her neck one last time and lift my head to capture her gaze.

"Can you just need me? Can you trust me to be everything you need?"

She blinks several times. "I don't have anything packed."

"We'll stop along the way and shop." I grin.

Avery tries to hide her delight by biting her lips together.

"Pregnant women shouldn't sleep on the ground in tents."

I chuckle. "We'll stay at the finest hotels."

"I don't have that much money."

"You should have the forty dollars you stole from me. But let's let that go." I wink at her. "I'll cover our lodging."

"I have nothing, Jake …"

"You have me." I press my forehead to hers and whisper, "Am I enough, Ave? Because you sure as hell are my everything."

She smiles, eyes filling with more tears. "Okay."

EPILOGUE

I ONLY NEEDED Jake and our simple life, but he gave me more.

A big wedding.
A closetful of clothes.
Spa days.
Flowers.
Date nights.
Passion.
Adoration.
Love.
And babies.

If getting pregnant once was a miracle, then we've had three miracles in five years—a boy then two girls.

"Is it wrong of me to love the lines on your stomach and the new shape of your belly button even more than I loved the pre-mom version of it?" Jake stands behind me as I stare at my reflection in the full-length mirror.

I'm sure many women judge me when they see me wearing a bikini with my stomach stretched out and distorted from three babies, two of them just over nine pounds. I know this because, at one point in my life, I was that person judging others. I'm not anymore.

Jake snakes his hands around me, palms pressed to my not-so-perfectly-flat stomach just above my bikini bottoms. He kisses my shoulder.

I cover his hands with mine and smile at his reflection—at my reflection. "I love my body." I don't just say the words. I mean them to the depths of my soul. "It's given us Tyler, Kylie, and Rylen. It's taken me many places. It's fed babies and held them. It's given my husband pleasure." I smirk.

Jake bites his bottom lip, but it doesn't hide his grin or that look. I love that look. It usually ends with me being pregnant, but I love it just the same.

"There are a dozen or more packages at the door, Miss Blogger." His right hand slips below the waist of my bikini. "I carried them inside, unpacked them, broke down the boxes, rinsed the sand and ocean off the kids, and packed their bags. Your dad and Deedy should be here soon to get them."

"Packages." I grin as my eyes grow heavy from his touch.

"Mommy? Grandpa and Grandma are here!" Tyler calls.

My eyes snap open.

Jake removes his hand from the inside of my bikini bottoms. "Go tell our kids goodbye. I'll be in the shower. Join me when you get them out the door."

I turn, sliding my arms around his neck. "A full week. We get a full week to ourselves. We haven't had a road trip to ourselves since I was pregnant with Tyler. Whatever will we do, Mr. Matthews?" My eyebrows waggle at him.

"No computer, Mrs. Matthews. No *The Princess and Her Peas* blog. All those items I just unpacked will have to wait a week to be tested and reviewed. Because..." he grabs my ass and brings me as close as possible to his firm body "... we have a week without kids. A week in the RV. A week I will spend inside of you, beneath you, on top of you, all the fuck over you. Okay, *Princess*?"

I grin. "Mkay. I like all of those scenarios, specifically the one where I'll be joining you in the shower soon. But count to five hundred before you turn on the water because I'm going to get the kids off first with Dad and Deedy. Then I'm going to look at my new stuff."

Old habits don't necessarily die hard. Some habits just never die. And my love of fashion is one of them. However, I changed my ways. My love for fashion shifted to eco-friendly fashion. I started a very successful blog about it, and companies send me *all the things* to test, try, and review on my blog—handbags, clothes, shoes, accessories, makeup. I make money doing my favorite thing.

We spend most of the year traveling in the RV with the kids to check up on Jake's restaurants. He and Addy now own eleven Sage Leaf Cafe locations in the U.S., and they have plans to open one in London next spring.

Me, London, and fashion? Yes, please!

Jake closes his eyes, rubbing me against him with a little more intensity. "Four hundred and ninety-nine, four hundred and ninety-eight."

I giggle, pressing a quick kiss to his lips before running out to the living room of our conservative house along the beach, a few miles from the cafe in L.A. Deedy and my dad took over the loft two years ago to be closer to family as we ran out of space when Rylen was born.

"Where's Trip's stuff?" Dad asks as Deedy scoops up Rylen and takes Kylie's hand.

"The mutt's coming with us." I wink.

"You're taking a five-hundred-pound dog with you on a romantic getaway?"

I chuckle, giving kisses to each one of my beautiful children, all blond-haired, blue-eyed babes. "Trip is not five-hundred pounds."

"Close enough." Dad smirks.

We found Trip three years ago at a campsite. No one else was there. He had no collar, no chip and he was a nice, medium-sized dog. A mix of some sort. We took him home. I obsessed over his rapid growth the following months, so I ordered a DNA test for him. Yeah, Trip is mostly a Mastiff, aka a small horse.

"Jake and I fell in love on a road trip with a dog. After three kids, we want to reconnect on a road trip, and we want to take Trip with us. I already called Sydney and told her you wouldn't be dropping Trip off on your way to Disney with the kiddos."

"Well ..." Dad gives Trip a twisted grin. "He does love to camp."

Trip cocks his head to the side.

I hear the water turn on in the master bathroom.

"Okay then. Did you already put their bags in the car?" I do my best to funnel everyone toward the door because ... Jake ... shower ... alone time.

"Tommy put them all in the back." Deedy smiles.

"Love you, babies." They all get one more round of hugs and kisses from me. "Thank you, both."

Dad and Deedy nod.

"Where's Jake?" Deedy asks.

"Um ... the shower. I think."

"Bye, guys. Thanks!" Jake peeks his head around the corner, wearing nothing but a white towel barely holding on to his waist.

Deedy waves at him then shoots me a sly grin.

I turn ten shades of red, returning a tightlipped smile.

Yeah, Deedy, as soon as you leave with our kids, I'm all over that.

Five years without one night of uninterrupted sleep.

Five years of sprinting through sex before someone calls Mommy or Daddy.

Five years of a child in the middle at some point, every single night.

Five years of dirty diapers, spit up, and leaky boobs.

I'm going to ride the Jake train for a solid week.

And if Trip enjoys time alone with his humping pillow, without one of the kids trying to take it from him ... well, that's just a bonus.

The door closes behind them.

I restrain myself from sprinting to the bathroom. When I pull open the glass door, Jake slicks back his wet, now longer, hair as rivulets of water venture down his perfectly inked body.

"Ave ..." He grins.

I step inside, closing the door behind me, trapping the steam in with us.

"Tell me how you love me." I press my lips to his chest as my hand slides lower, forcing his breath to catch.

His eyes drift shut for a few seconds before he kisses the top of my head. "I love you like an acoustic song. The words mean more. The emotions are magnified. It's like the stars ... during the day we don't see them, but at night when the world around us feels stripped and bare, they shine so brightly." He ghosts his hands up my hips and brushes his lips over my cheek to my mouth. "I've never seen anything as beautiful as you are in this very moment. Our love is … flawed but perfect." His tongue drags along my top lip. "It's honest and open. It's naked, Ave … our love is a naked love."

The End

ALSO BY JEWEL E. ANN

One

Idle Bloom

Undeniably You

Naked Love

Only Trick

Perfectly Adequate

Look The Part

When Life Happened

A Place Without You

Jersey Six

Scarlet Stone

Jack & Jill Series

End of Day

Middle of Knight

Dawn of Forever

Out of Love (*standalone*)

Holding You Series

Holding You

Releasing Me

Transcend Series

Transcend

Epoch

Fortuity

The Life Series

The Life That Mattered

The Life You Stole

Receive a FREE book and stay informed of new releases, sales, and exclusive stories:

Mailing List

https://www.jeweleann.com/free-booksubscribe

ACKNOWLEDGMENTS

Since I decided to publish this a month early—just for shits and giggles—these acknowledgments will be quick and dirty.

Thank you to my newsletter subscribers who followed along with this story while I wrote it and dished it out to you in small pieces over a year. It was fun sharing the creative journey with you.

The usual suspects deserve a huge thanks as well: Jennifer Beach, Leslie Skinner, Kambra Wylie, Maxann Dobson, Monique Tarver, Sian Lewis, Social Butterfly PR, and anyone else that I'm forgetting. If you're gasping at my lack of remembering your role in all of this, then give yourself a pat on the back. Job well done! Thank you, mystery forgotten ones. It sucks getting old. Yes, I'm playing the age card.

Tim, Logan, Carter, Asher ... I may write a million book boyfriends, but you will forever be my favorite guys. Love you!

ABOUT THE AUTHOR

Jewel is a free-spirited romance junkie with a quirky sense of humor.

With 10 years of flossing lectures under her belt, she took early retirement from her dental hygiene career to stay home with her three awesome boys and manage the family business.

After her best friend of nearly 30 years suggested a few books from the Contemporary Romance genre, Jewel was hooked. Devouring two and three books a week but still craving more, she decided to practice sustainable reading, AKA writing.

When she's not donning her cape and saving the planet one tree at a time, she enjoys yoga with friends, good food with family, rock climbing with her kids, watching How I Met Your Mother reruns, and of course...heart-wrenching, tear-jerking, panty-scorching novels.

www.jeweleann.com

Printed in the USA
CPSIA information can be obtained
at www.ICGtesting.com
LVHW011925080823
754680LV00003B/81